This Book Belongs To:

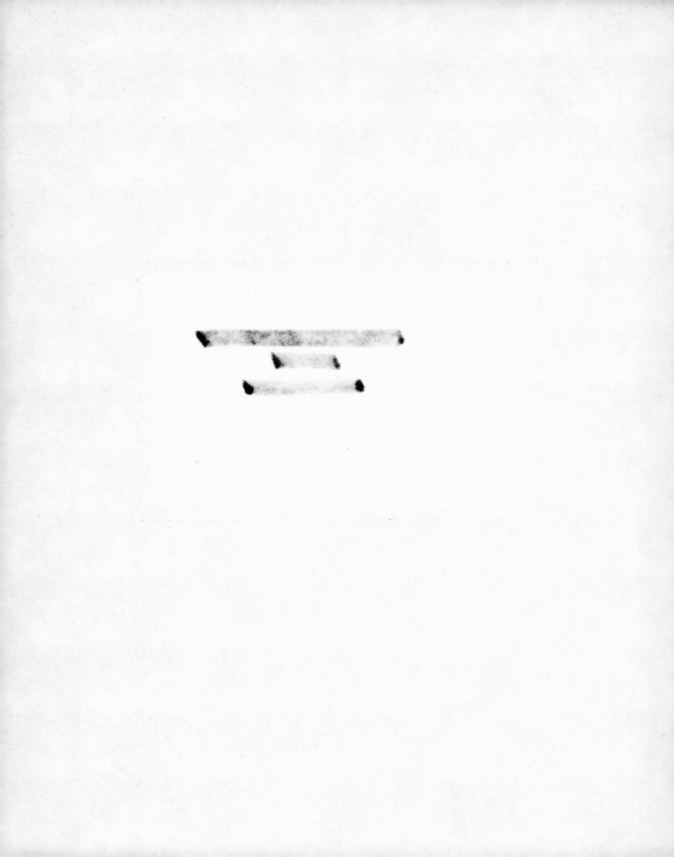

TALES
FROM
SHAKESPEARE

CHILDREN'S CLASSICS

This unique series of Children's Classics™ features accessible and highly readable texts paired with the work of talented and brilliant illustrators of bygone days to create fine editions for today's parents and children to rediscover and treasure. Besides being a handsome addition to any home library, this series features genuine bonded-leather spines stamped in gold, full-color illustrations, and high-quality acid-free paper that will enable these books to be passed from one generation to the next.

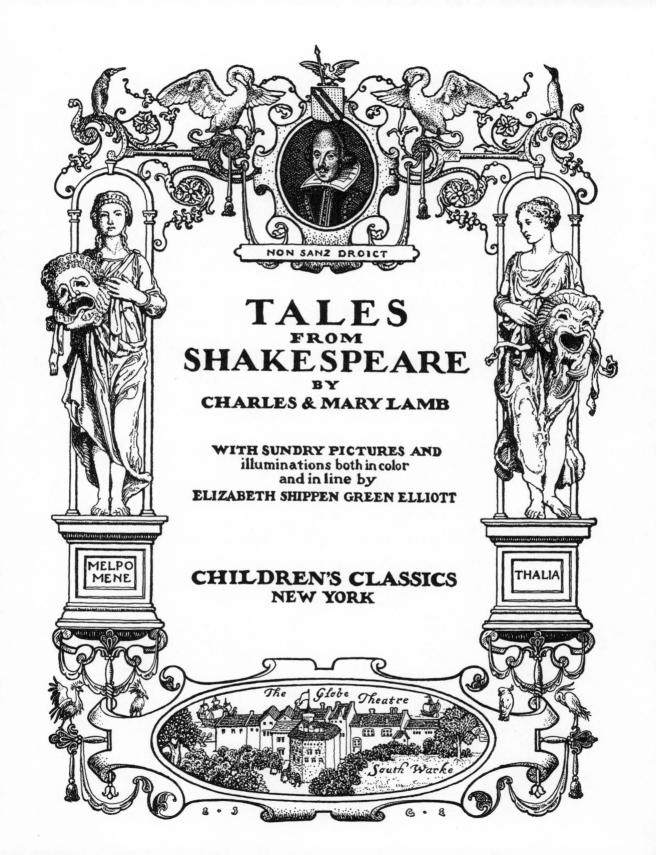

NON SANZ DROICT

TALES
FROM
SHAKESPEARE
BY
CHARLES & MARY LAMB

WITH SUNDRY PICTURES AND
illuminations both in color
and in line by
ELIZABETH SHIPPEN GREEN ELLIOTT

MELPO MENE

THALIA

CHILDREN'S CLASSICS
NEW YORK

The Globe Theatre

South Warke

This 1986 edition is published by Children's Classics,
a division of dilithium Press, Ltd., distributed by
Crown Publishers, Inc., 225 Park Avenue South,
New York, New York 10003.

CHILDREN'S CLASSICS is a trademark of
dilithium Press, Ltd.

Printed and Bound in the United States of America

Library of Congress Cataloging-in-Publication Data

Lamb, Charles, 1775–1834.
Tales from Shakespeare.

Summary: Shakespeare's fourteen comedies and six
tragedies retold in prose.
1. Shakespeare, William, 1564–1616—Adaptations.
[1. Shakespeare, William, 1564–1616—Adaptations]
I. Lamb, Mary, 1764–1847. II. Elliott, Elizabeth
Shippen Green, ill. III. Title.
PR2877.L3 1986   823′.7   86–13663
ISBN 0-517-62156-8

h g f e d c b a

Table of Contents

Foreword

IN order to fully appreciate and comprehend what Charles and Mary Lamb accomplished in their *Tales from Shakespeare*, one would have to be thoroughly familiar with each play in its original form: fortunately, such formidable knowledge is not necessary to enjoy this sparkling collection. The motivating force behind this colossal enterprise was a desire to enhance the children's literature of the early 1800s with vital and intricate stories that were at once appetizing and substantial. To turn to Shakespeare as a source was an obvious choice. That they would be aided by the artistry of Elizabeth Shippen Green Elliott whose illustrations were done more than a century later was hardly obvious but certainly providential.

In the twenty tales told in this book, the Lambs succeeded in paraphrasing the language of truly adult literature in children's terms. Let us not underestimate young readers: they love a complex story with many and varied characters, twists of plot, and turns of fate as much as anyone—in fact, more so—but they draw the line at reading in unfamiliar language. While the

Lambs cut the Shakespeare plays to the bare bones, they also managed to leave enough meat on those bones to provide a real feast of plain fare, and flavored it with as many tasty tidbits of Shakespearean language as they felt the young reader could easily digest. As a result, a young person has the satisfaction of reading the intrinsically appealing stories and, at the same time, can take pride in the knowledge that he or she has enough maturity and intelligence to truly enjoy Shakespeare.

Each tale has at least a paragraph or several lines from the original carefully selected for the greatest possible appeal to a youthful audience. In "A Midsummer Night's Dream," the Lambs focus on the conversations between the fairies and also quote the marvelous song the fairies sing to lull Titania, their queen, to sleep.

> You spotted snakes with double tongue,
> Thorny hedgehogs, be not seen,
> Newts and blind-worms do no wrong.
> Come not near our Fairy Queen.

In "The Merchant of Venice," much of the courtroom dialogue between Portia and Shylock is included; in "King Lear," a bit of the Fool's poetry; in "The Taming of the Shrew," some of the best repartee between Petruchio and Kate; and in "Hamlet," the bedchamber scene between Hamlet and his mother. In each tale, where dialogue is included, it is slipped deftly in and out of the narrative, so that the reader is almost unaware that the language patterns have changed.

Elizabeth Shippen Green Elliott's illustrations which accompany this edition are a visual banquet in themselves. The use of shadows and rich velvety tones remind one of the theatre, and of the effects that magnificent lighting can create when coupled with rich textures in costumes, scenery, and set pieces. They are the perfect companion to the *Tales*, in that they act as a constant reminder of the original medium of the material.

That these tales would survive almost two centuries and still be read and enjoyed today by young readers as an introduction to Shakespeare is surely more than the authors could have hoped for. Yet it is often the case that selfless devotion to improving existing conditions results in works of art for centuries to come. Charles and Mary Lamb's passion is our prized possession.

PATRICIA BARRETT PERKINS

Baltimore, Maryland
1986

TALES
FROM
SHAKESPEARE

The Tempest

THERE was a certain island in the sea, the only inhabitants of which were an old man, whose name was Prospero, and his daughter Miranda, a very beautiful young lady. She came to this island so young, that she had no memory of having seen any other human face than her father's.

They lived in a cave or cell, made out of a rock: it was divided into several apartments, one of which Prospero called his study; there he kept his books, which chiefly treated of magic, a study at that time much affected by all learned men: and the knowledge of this art he found very useful to him: for being thrown by a strange chance upon this island, which had been enchanted by a witch called Sycorax, who died there a short time before his arrival, Prospero, by virtue of his art, released many good spirits that Sycorax had imprisoned in the bodies of large trees, because they had refused to execute her wicked commands. These gentle spirits were ever after obedient to the will of Prospero. Of these Ariel was the chief.

The lively little sprite Ariel had nothing mischievous in his nature, except that he took rather too much pleasure in tormenting an ugly monster called Caliban, for he owed him a grudge because he was the son of his old enemy Sycorax. This Caliban Prospero found in the woods, a strange misshapen thing, far less human in form than an ape: he took him home to his cell, and taught him to speak; and Prospero would have been very kind to him, but the bad nature, which Caliban inherited from his mother Sycorax, would not let him learn anything good or useful: therefore he was employed like a slave, to fetch wood, and do the most laborious offices; and Ariel had the charge of compelling him to these services.

When Caliban was lazy and neglected his work, Ariel (who was invisible to all eyes but Prospero's) would come slyly and pinch him, and sometimes tumble him down in the mire; and then Ariel, in the likeness of an ape, would make mouths at him. Then swiftly changing his shape, in the likeness of an hedgehog he would lie tumbling in Caliban's way, who feared the hedgehog's sharp quills would prick his bare feet. With a variety of such-like vexatious tricks Ariel would often torment him, whenever Caliban neglected the work which Prospero commanded him to do.

Having these powerful spirits obedient to his will, Prospero could by their means command the winds and the waves of the sea. By his orders they raised a violent storm, in the midst of which, and struggling with the wild sea-waves that every moment threatened to swallow it up, he shewed his daughter a fine large ship, which he told her was full of living beings like themselves. "O my dear father," said she, "if by your art you have raised this dreadful storm, have pity on their sad distress. See! the vessel will be dashed to pieces. Poor souls! they will all perish. If I had power, I would sink the sea beneath the earth, rather than the good ship should be destroyed, with all the precious souls within her."

"Be not so amazed, daughter Miranda," said Prospero; "there is no harm done. I have so ordered it that no person in the ship shall receive any hurt. What I have done has been in care of you, my dear child. You are ignorant who you are, or where you came from, and you know no more of me, but that I am your father, and live in this poor cave. Can you remember a time before you came to this cell? I think you cannot, for you were not then three years of age."

"Certainly I can, sir," replied Miranda.

"By what?" asked Prospero: "by any other house or person? Tell me what you can remember, my child."

Miranda said, "It seems to me like the remembrance of a dream. But had I not once four or five women who attended upon me?"

Prospero answered, "You had, and more. How is it that this still lives in your mind? Do you remember how you came here?"

"No, sir," said Miranda, "I remember nothing more."

"Twelve years ago, Miranda," continued Prospero, "I was Duke of Milan, and you were a princess and my only heir. I had a younger brother, whose name was Antonio, to whom I trusted everything; and as I was fond of retirement and deep study, I commonly left the management of my state affairs to your uncle, my false brother (for so indeed he proved). I, neglecting all worldly ends, buried among my books, did dedicate my whole time to the bettering of my mind. My brother Antonio, being thus in possession of my power, began to think himself the duke indeed. The opportunity I gave him of making himself popular among my subjects, awakened in his bad nature a proud ambition to deprive me of my dukedom; this he soon effected with the aid of the King of Naples, a powerful prince, who was my enemy."

"Wherefore," said Miranda, "did they not that hour destroy us?"

"My child," answered her father, "they durst not, so dear was the love that my people bore me. Antonio carried us on board a ship, and when we were some leagues out at sea, he forced us into a small boat, without either tackle, sail, or mast: there he left us as he thought to perish. But a kind lord of my court, one Gonzalo, who loved me, had privately placed in the boat, water, provisions, apparel, and some books which I prize above my dukedom."

"O my father," said Miranda, "what a trouble must I have been to you then!"

"No, my love," said Prospero, "you were a little cherul that did preserve me. Your innocent smiles made me to bea up against my misfortunes. Our food lasted till we landed or this desert island, since when my chief delight has been in teaching you, Miranda, and well have you profited by my in structions."

"Heaven thank you, my dear father," said Miranda "Now pray tell me, sir, your reason for raising this sea storm."

"Know then," said her father, "that by means of this storm my enemies, the King of Naples and my cruel brother, are cast ashore upon this island."

Having so said, Prospero gently touched his daughter with his magic wand, and she fell fast asleep: for the spirit Ariel just then presented himself before his master, to give an account of the tempest, and how he had disposed of the ship's company; and, though the spirits were always invisible to Miranda, Prospero did not choose she should hear him holding converse (as would seem to her) with the empty air.

"Well, my brave spirit," said Prospero to Ariel, "how have you performed your task?"

Ariel gave a lively description of the storm, and of the terror of the mariners; and how the king's son, Ferdinand, was the first who leaped into the sea; and his father thought he saw his dear son swallowed up by the waves, and lost. "But he is safe," said Ariel, "in a corner of the isle, sitting with his arms folded sadly, lamenting the loss of the king his father, whom he concludes drowned. Not a hair of his head is injured, and his princely garments, though drenched in the sea-waves, look fresher than before."

"That's my delicate Ariel," said Prospero. "Bring him hither: my daughter must see this young prince. Where is the king, and my brother?"

"I left them," answered Ariel, "searching for Ferdinand, whom they have little hopes of finding, thinking they saw him perish. Of the ship's crew not one is missing; though each one thinks himself the only one saved: and the ship, though invisible to them, is safe in the harbour."

"Ariel," said Prospero, "thy charge is faithfully performed; but there is more work yet."

"Is there more work?" said Ariel. "Let me remind you, master, you have promised me my liberty. I pray, remember, I have done you worthy service, told you no lies, made no mistakes, served you without grudge, or grumbling."

"How now," said Prospero. "You do not recollect what a torment I freed you from. Have you forgot the wicked witch Sycorax, who with age and envy was almost bent double? Where was she born? Speak: tell me."

"Sir, in Algiers," said Ariel.

"O was she so?" said Prospero. I must recount what you have been, which I find you do not remember. This bad witch Sycorax, for her witchcrafts, too terrible to enter human hearing, was banished from Algiers, and here left by the sailors; and because you were a spirit too delicate to execute her wicked commands, she shut you up in a tree, where I found you howling. This torment, remember, I did free you from."

"Pardon me, dear master," said Ariel, ashamed to seem ungrateful; "I will obey your commands."

"Do so," said Prospero, "and I will set you free." He then gave orders what farther he would have him to do, and away went Ariel, first to where he had left Ferdinand, and found him still sitting on the grass in the same melancholy posture.

"O my young gentleman," said Ariel, when he saw him, "I will soon move you. You must be brought, I find, for the lady Miranda to have a sight of your pretty person. Come, sir, follow me." He then began singing,

> "Full fathom five thy father lies;
>   Of his bones are coral made;
> Those are pearls that were his eyes:
>   Nothing of him that doth fade,
> But doth suffer a sea-change
> Into something new and strange.
> Sea-nymphs hourly ring his knell.
> Hark, now I hear them, ding-dong bell."

This strange news of his lost father soon roused the prince from the stupid fit into which he had fallen. He followed in amazement the sound of Ariel's voice, till it led him to Prospero and Miranda, who were setting under the shade of a large tree. Now, Miranda had never seen a man before, except her own father.

"Miranda," said Prospero, "tell me what you are looking at yonder."

"O father," said Miranda, in a strange surprise, "surely that is a spirit. Lord! how it looks about! Believe me, sir, it is a beautiful creature. Is it not a spirit?"

"No, girl," answered her father; "it eats, and sleeps, and has senses such as we have. This young man you see was in the ship. He is somewhat altered by grief, or you might call him a handsome person. He has lost his companions, and is wandering about to find them."

Miranda, who thought all men had grave faces and gray beards like her father, was delighted with the appearance of this beautiful young prince; and Ferdinand seeing such a lovely lady in this desert place, and from the strange sounds he had heard expecting nothing but wonders, thought he was upon an inchanted island, and that Miranda was the goddess of the place, and as such he began to address her.

She timidly answered, she was no goddess, but a simple maid, and was going to give an account of herself, when Prospero interrupted her. He was well pleased to find they admired each other, for he plainly perceived they had (as we say) fallen in love at first sight: but to try Ferdinand's constancy, he resolved to throw some difficulties in their way: therefore advancing forward, he addressed the prince with a stern air, telling him, he came to the island as a spy to take it from him who was the lord of it. "Follow me," said he, "I will tie you, neck and feet together. You shall drink sea-water; shell-fish, withered roots, and husks of acorns shall be your food." "No," said Ferdinand, "I will resist such entertainment till I see a more powerful enemy," and drew his sword; but Prospero, waving his magic wand, fixed him to the spot where he stood, so that he had no power to move.

Miranda hung upon her father, saying, "Why are you so ungentle? Have pity, sir; I will be his surety. This is the second man I ever saw, and to me he seems a true one."

"Silence," said her father, "one word more will make me chide you, girl! What! an advocate for an impostor! You think there are no more such fine men, having seen only him and Caliban. I tell you, foolish girl, most men as far excel this, as he does Caliban." This he said to prove his daughter's constancy; and she replied, "My affections are most humble. I have no wish to see a goodlier man."

"Come on, young man," said Prospero to the prince, "you have no power to disobey me."

"I have not, indeed," answered Ferdinand; and not knowing it was by magic he was deprived of all power of resistance, he was astonished to find himself so strangely compelled to follow Prospero; looking back on Miranda as long as he could see her, he said, as he went after Prospero into the cave, "My spirits are all bound up, as if I were in a dream; but this man's threats, and the weakness which I feel, would seem light to me, if from my prison I might once a day behold this fair maid."

Prospero kept Ferdinand not long confined within the cell: he soon brought out his prisoner, and set him a severe task to perform, taking care to let his daughter know the hard labor he had imposed on him, and then pretending to go into his study he secretly watched them both.

Prospero had commanded Ferdinand to pile up some heavy logs of wood. King's sons not being much used to laborious work, Miranda soon after found her lover almost dying with fatigue. "Alas!" said she, "do not work so hard; my father is at his studies, he is safe for these three hours, pray, rest yourself."

"O my dear lady," said Ferdinand, "I dare not. I must finish my task before I take my rest."

"If you will sit down," said Miranda, "I will carry your logs the while." But this Ferdinand would by no means agree to. Instead of a help, Miranda became a hindrance, for they began a long conversation, so that the business of log-carrying went on very slowly.

Prospero, who had enjoined Ferdinand this task merely as a trial of his love, was not at his books, as his daughter supposed, but was standing by them invisible, to overhear, what they said.

Ferdinand inquired her name, which she told him, saying it was against her father's express command she did so.

Prospero only smiled at this first instance of his daughter's disobedience, for having by his magic art caused his daughter to fall in love so suddenly, he was not angry that she shewed her love by forgetting to obey his commands. And he listened well pleased to a long speech of Ferdinand, in which he professed to love her above all the ladies he ever saw.

In answer to his praises of her beauty, which he said exceeded all the women in the world, she replied, "I do not remember the face of any woman, nor have I seen any more men than you, my good friend, and my dear father. How features are abroad I know not; but believe me, sir, I would not wish any companion in the world but you, nor can my imagination form any shape but yours that I could like. But, sir, I fear I talk to you too freely, and my father's precepts I forget."

At this Prospero smiled, and nodded his head, as much as to say, "This goes on exactly as I could wish; my girl will be queen of Naples."

And then Ferdinand, in another fine long speech (for young princes speak in courtly phrases), told the innocent Miranda he was heir to the crown of Naples, and that she should be his queen.

"Ah! sir," said she, "I am a fool to weep at what I am glad of. I will answer you in plain and holy innocence. I am your wife, if you will marry me."

Prospero prevented Ferdinand's thanks by appearing visible before them.

"Fear nothing, my child," said he; "I have overheard, and approve of all you have said. And Ferdinand, if I have too severely used you, I will make you rich amends, by giving you my daughter. All your vexations were but my trials of your love, and you have nobly stood the test. Then as my gift, which your true love has worthily purchased, take my daughter, and do not smile that I boast she is above all praise." He then, telling them that he had business which required his presence, desired they would sit down and talk together, till he returned; and this command Miranda seemed not at all disposed to disobey.

When Prospero left them, he called his spirit Ariel, who quickly appeared before him, eager to relate what he had done with Prospero's brother and the king of Naples. Ariel said he had left them almost out of their senses with fear at the strange things he had caused them to see and hear. When fatigued with wandering about, and famished for want of food, he had suddenly set before them a delicious banquet, and then, just as they were going to eat, he appeared visible before them in the shape of a harpy, an ugly monster with wings, and the feast vanished away. Then, to their utter amazement, this seeming harpy spoke to them, reminding them of their cruelty in driving Prospero from his dukedom, and leaving him and his infant daughter to perish in the sea; saying, that for this cause these terrors were suffered to afflict them.

The king of Naples, and Antonio the false brother, repented the injustice they had done to Prospero: and Ariel told his master he was certain their penitence was sincere, and that he, though a spirit, could not but pity them.

"Then bring them hither, Ariel," said Prospero: "if you, who are but a spirit, feel for their distress, shall not I, who am a human being like themselves, have compassion on them? Bring them quickly, my dainty Ariel."

Ariel soon returned with the king, Antonio, and old Gonzalo in their train, who had followed him wondering at the wild music he played in the air to draw them on to his master's presence. This Gonzalo was the same who had so kindly provided Prospero formerly with books and provisions, when his wicked brother left him, as he thought, to perish in an open boat in the sea.

Grief and terror had so stupefied their senses, that they did not know Prospero. He first discovered himself to the good old Gonzalo, calling him the preserver of his life; and then his brother and the king knew that he was the injured Prospero.

Antonio with tears and sad words of sorrow and true repentance implored his brother's forgiveness, and the king expressed his sincere remorse for having assisted Antonio to depose his brother: and Prospero forgave them; and, upon their engaging to restore his dukedom, he said to the king of Naples "I have a gift in store for you too"; and opening a door, showed him his son Ferdinand, playing at chess with Miranda.

Nothing could exceed the joy of the father and the son at this unexpected meeting, for they each thought the other drowned in the storm.

"O wonder!" said Miranda, "what noble creatures these are; it must surely be a brave world that has such people in it."

The king of Naples was almost as much astonished at the beauty and excellent graces of the young Miranda as his son had been. "Who is this maid?" said he; "she seems the goddess that has parted us, and brought us thus together." "No, sir," answered Ferdinand, smiling to find his father had fallen into the same mistake that he had done when he first saw

Miranda, "she is a mortal, but by immortal Providence she is mine; I chose her when I could not ask you, my father, for your consent, not thinking you were alive. She is the daughter of this Prospero, who is the famous duke of Milan, of whose renown I have heard so much, but never saw him till now: of him I have received a new life: he has made himself to me a second father, giving me this dear lady."

"Then I must be her father," said the king: "but oh! how oddly will it sound, that I must ask my child forgiveness."

"No more of that," said Prospero: "let us not remember our troubles past, since they so happily have ended." And then Prospero embraced his brother, and again assured him of his forgiveness; and said that a wise, over-ruling Providence had permitted that he should be driven from his poor dukedom of Milan, that his daughter might inherit the crown of Naples, for that by their meeting in this desert island it had happened, that the king's son had loved Miranda.

These kind words which Prospero spoke, meaning to comfort his brother, so filled Antonio with shame and remorse, that he wept and was unable to speak: and the kind old Gonzalo wept to see this joyful reconciliation, and prayed for blessings on the young couple.

Prospero now told them that their ship was safe in the harbour, and the sailors all on board her, and that he and his daughter would accompany them home the next morning. "In the meantime," said he, "partake of such refreshments as my poor cave affords; and for your evening's entertainment I will relate the history of my life from my first landing in this desert island." He then called for Caliban to prepare some food, and set the cave in order; and the company were astonished at the uncouth form and savage appearance of this ugly monster, who (Prospero said) was the only attendant he had to wait upon him.

Before Prospero left the island, he dismissed Ariel from his service, to the great joy of that lively little spirit; who, though he had been a faithful servant to his master, was always longing to enjoy his free liberty to wander uncontrolled in the air, like a wild bird, under green trees, among pleasant fruits, and sweet-smelling flowers. "My quaint Ariel," said Prospero to the little sprite when he made him free, "I shall miss you; yet you shall have your freedom." "Thank you, my dear master," said Ariel; "but give me leave to attend your ship home with prosperous gales, before you bid farewell to the assistance of your faithful spirit; and then, master, when I am free, how merrily I shall live!" Here Ariel sung this pretty song:

"Where the bee sucks, there suck I;
In a cowslip's bell I lie:
There I couch when owls do cry.
On the bat's back I do fly
After summer merrily.
Merrily, merrily, shall I live now
Under the blossom that hangs on the bough."

Prospero then buried deep in the earth his magical books, and wand, for he was resolved never more to make use of the magic art. And having thus overcome his enemies, and being reconciled to his brother and the king of Naples, nothing now remained to complete his happiness, but to revisit his native land, to take possession of his dukedom, and to witness the happy nuptials of his daughter Miranda and prince Ferdinand, which the king said should be instantly celebrated with great splendor on their return to Naples. At which place, under the safe convoy of the spirit Ariel, they, after a pleasant voyage, soon arrived.

———

A Midsummer Night's Dream

THERE was a law in the city of Athens, which gave to its citizens the power of compelling their daughters to marry whomsoever they pleased: for upon a daughter's refusing to marry the man her father had chosen to be her husband, the father was empowered by this law to cause her to be put to death; but as fathers do not often desire the death of their own daughters, even though they do happen to prove a little refractory, this law was seldom or never put in execution, though perhaps the young ladies of that city were not unfrequently threatened by their parents with the terrors of it.

There was one instance however of an old man, whose name was Egeus, who actually did come before Theseus (at that time the reigning duke of Athens), to complain that his daughter Hermia, whom he had commanded to marry Demetrius, a young man of a noble Athenian family, refused to obey him, because she loved another young Athenian, named Lysander. Egeus demanded justice of Theseus, and desired that this cruel law might be put in force against his daughter.

Hermia pleaded in excuse for her disobedience, that Demetrius had formerly professed love for her dear friend

Helena, and that Helena loved Demetrius to distraction; but this honourable reason which Hermia gave for not obeying her father's command, moved not the stern Egeus.

Theseus, though a great and merciful prince, had no power to alter the laws of his country; therefore he could only give Hermia four days to consider of it: and at the end of that time, if she still refused to marry Demetrius, she was to be put to death.

When Hermia was dismissed from the presence of the duke, she went to her lover Lysander, and told him the peril she was in, and that she must either give up him and marry Demetrius, or lose her life in four days.

Lysander was in great affliction at hearing these evil tidings; but recollecting that he had an aunt who lived at some distance from Athens, and that at the place where she lived the cruel law could not be put in force against Hermia (this law not extending beyond the boundaries of the city), he proposed to Hermia, that she should steal out of her father's house that night, and go with him to his aunt's house, where he would marry her. "I will meet you," said Lysander, "in the wood a few miles without the city; in that delightful wood, where we have so often walked with Helena in the pleasant month of May."

To this proposal Hermia joyfully agreed; and she told no one of her intended flight but her friend Helena. Helena (as maidens will do foolish things for love) very ungenerously resolved to go and tell this to Demetrius, though she could hope no benefit from betraying her friend's secret, but the poor pleasure of following her faithless lover to the wood; for she well knew that Demetrius would go thither in pursuit of Hermia.

The wood, in which Lysander and Hermia proposed to meet, was the favourite haunt of those little beings known by the name of *Fairies*.

Oberon, the king, and Titania, the queen, of the Fairies, with all their tiny train of followers, in this wood held their midnight revels.

Between this little king and queen of spirits there happened, at this time, a sad disagreement: they never met by moonlight in the shady walks of this pleasant wood, but they were quarrelling, till all their fairy elves would creep into acorn cups and hide themselves for fear.

The cause of this unhappy disagreement was Titania's refusing to give Oberon a little changeling boy, whose mother had been Titania's friend; and upon her death the fairy queen stole the child from its nurse, and brought him up in the woods.

The night on which the lovers were to meet in this wood, as Titania was walking with some of her maids of honour, she met Oberon attended by his train of fairy courtiers.

"Ill met by moonlight, proud Titania," said the fairy king. The queen replied, "What, jealous Oberon, is it you? Fairies, skip hence; I have forsworn his company." "Tarry, rash fairy," said Oberon; "am I not thy lord? Why does Titania cross her Oberon? Give me your little changeling boy to be my page."

"Set your heart at rest," answered the queen; "your whole fairy kingdom buys not the boy of me." She then left her lord in great anger. "Well, go your way," said Oberon; "before the morning dawns I will torment you for this injury."

Oberon then sent for Puck, his chief favourite and privy counsellor.

Puck (or, as he was sometimes called, Robin Goodfellow) was a shrewd and knavish sprite, and used to play comical pranks in the neighbouring villages; sometimes getting into the dairies and skimming the milk, sometimes plunging his light and airy form into the butter-churn, and while he was dancing his fantastic shape in the churn, in vain the dairy-maid would labour to change her cream into butter: nor had the village swains any better success; whenever Puck chose to play his freaks in the brewing-copper, the ale was sure to be spoiled. When a few good neighbours were met to drink some comfortable ale together, Puck would jump into the bowl of ale in the likeness of a roasted crab, and when some old goody was going to drink, he would bob against her lips, and spill the ale over her withered chin; and presently after, when the same old dame was gravely seating herself to tell her neighbours a sad and melancholy story, Puck would slip her three-legged stool from under her, and down toppled the poor old woman, and then the old gossips would hold their sides and laugh at her, and swear they never wasted a merrier hour.

"Come hither, Puck," said Oberon to this little merry

wanderer of the night; "fetch me the flower which maids call *Love in Idleness*; the juice of that little purple flower laid on the eyelids of those who sleep, will make them, when they awake, doat on the first thing they see. Some of the juice of that flower I will drop on the eyelids of my Titania when she is asleep; and the first thing she looks upon when she opens her eyes she will fall in love with, even though it be a lion, or a bear, a meddling monkey, or a busy ape: and before I will take this charm from off her sight, which I can do with another charm I know of, I will make her give me that boy to be my page."

Puck, who loved mischief to his heart, was highly diverted with this intended frolic of his master, and ran to seek the flower; and while Oberon was waiting the return of Puck he observed Demetrius and Helena enter the wood: he over-heard Demetrius reproaching Helena for following him, and after many unkind words on his part, and gentle expostula-tions from Helena, reminding him of his former love and professions of true faith to her, he left her (as he said) to the mercy of the wild beasts, and she ran after him as swiftly as she could.

The fairy king, who was always friendly to true lovers, felt great compassion for Helena; and perhaps, as Lysander said they used to walk by moonlight in this pleasant wood, Oberon might have seen Helena in those happy times when she was beloved by Demetrius. However that might be, when Puck returned with the little purple flower, Oberon said to his favourite, "Take a part of this flower: there has been a sweet Athenian lady here, who is in love with a disdainful youth; if you find him sleeping, drop some of the love-juice in his eyes, but contrive to do it when she is near him, that the first thing he sees when he awakes may be this despised lady. You will know the man by the Athenian garments which he wears." Puck promised to manage this matter very dexterously; and then Oberon went, unperceived by Titania, to her bower, where she was preparing to go to rest. Her fairy bower was a bank, where grew wild thyme, cowslips, and sweet violets under a canopy of woodbine, muskroses, and eglantine. There Titania always slept some part of the night; her coverlet the enameled skin of a snake, which, though a small mantle, was wide enough to wrap a fairy in.

He found Titania giving orders to her fairies, how they were to employ themselves while she slept. "Some of you," said her majesty, "must kill cankers in the musk-rose-buds, and some wage war with the bats for their leathern wings, to make my small elves coats; and some of you keep watch that the clamorous owl, that nightly hoots, comes not near me; but first sing me to sleep." Then they began to sing this song:

> "You spotted snakes with double tongue,
> Thorny hedgehogs, be not seen;
> Newts and blind-worms, do no wrong,
> Come not near our Fairy Queen.
> Philomel, with melody,
> Sing in your sweet lullaby,
> Lulla, lulla, lullaby; lulla, lulla, lullaby:
> Never harm, nor spell, nor charm,
> Come our lovely lady nigh;
> So good-night with lullaby."

The Presentation of the Book to Queen Elizabeth, 1807

MOST·SVRE·THE·GODDESS·ON·WHOM·THESE·AIRS·ATTEND!

The Tempest—Tale the First

When the fairies had sung their queen asleep with this pretty lullaby, they left her, to perform the important services she had enjoined them. Oberon then softly drew near his Titania, and dropped some of the love-juice on her eyelids, saying,

"What thou seest, when thou dost wake,
Do it for thy true-love sake."

But to return to Hermia, who made her escape out of her father's house that night, to avoid the death she was doomed to for refusing to marry Demetrius. When she entered the wood, she found her dear Lysander waiting for her, to conduct her to his aunt's house; but before they had passed half through the wood, Hermia was so much fatigued, that Lysander, who was very careful of this dear lady, who had proved her affection for him even by hazarding her life for his sake, persuaded her to rest till morning on a bank of soft moss, and lying down himself on the ground at some little distance, they soon fell fast asleep. Here they were found by Puck, who seeing a handsome young man asleep, and perceiving that his clothes were made in the Athenian fashion, and that a pretty lady was sleeping near him, concluded that this must be the Athenian maid and her disdainful lover whom Oberon had sent him to seek; and he naturally enough conjectured that as they were alone together, she must be the first thing he would see when he awoke; so without more ado, he proceeded to pour some of the juice of the little purple flower into his eyes. But it so fell out, that Helena came that way, and, instead of Hermia, was the first object Lysander beheld when he opened his eyes; and, strange to relate, so powerful was the love-charm, all his love for Hermia vanished away, and Lysander fell in love with Helena.

Had he first seen Hermia when he awoke, the blunder Puck committed would have been of no consequence, for he could not love that faithful lady too well; but for poor Lysander to be forced by a fairy love-charm to forget his own true Hermia, and to run after another lady, and leave Hermia asleep quite alone in a wood at midnight, was a sad chance indeed.

Thus this misfortune happened. Helena, as has been before related, endeavoured to keep pace with Demetrius when he ran away so rudely from her; but she could not continue this unequal race long, men being always better runners in a long race than ladies. Helena soon lost sight of Demetrius; and as she was wandering about dejected and forlorn, she arrived at the place where Lysander was sleeping. "Ah," said she, "this is Lysander lying on the ground: is he dead or asleep?" Then gently touching him, she said, "Good sir, if you are alive, awake." Upon this Lysander opened his eyes, and (the love-charm beginning to work) immediately addressed her in terms of extravagant love and admiration; telling her, she as much excelled Hermia in beauty as a dove does a raven, and that he would run through fire for her sweet sake; and many more such lover-like speeches.

Helena, knowing Lysander was her friend Hermia's lover, and that he was solemnly engaged to marry her, was in the utmost rage when she heard herself addressed in this manner;

for she thought (well she might) that Lysander was making a jest of her. "Oh!" said she, "why was I born to be mocked and scorned by every one? Is it not enough, is it not enough, young man, that I can never get a sweet look or a kind word from Demetrius; but you, sir, must pretend in this disdainful manner to court me? I thought, Lysander, you were a lord of more true gentleness." Saying these words in great anger, she ran away; and Lysander followed her, quite forgetful of his own Hermia, who was still asleep.

When Hermia awoke, she was in a sad fright at finding herself alone. She wandered about the wood, not knowing what was become of Lysander, or which way to go to seek for him. In the meantime Demetrius, not being able to find Hermia and his rival Lysander, and fatigued with his fruitless search, was observed by Oberon fast asleep. Oberon had learned, by some questions he had asked of Puck, that he had applied the love-charm to the wrong person's eyes; and now having found the person first intended, he touched the eyelids of the sleeping Demetrius with the love-juice, and he instantly awoke; and the first thing he saw being Helena, he, as Lysander had done before, began to address love-speeches to her; and just at that moment Lysander, followed by Hermia (for through Puck's unlucky mistake it was now become Hermia's turn to run after her lover), made his appearance; and then Lysander and Demetrius, both speaking together, made love to Helena, they being each one under the influence of the same potent charm.

The astonished Helena thought that Demetrius, Lysander,

and her once dear friend Hermia, were all in a plot together to make a jest of her.

Hermia was as much surprised as Helena: she knew not why Lysander and Demetrius, who both before loved her, were now become the lovers of Helena; and to Hermia the matter seemed to be no jest.

The ladies, who before had always been the dearest of friends, now fell to high words together.

"Unkind Hermia," said Helena, "it is you have set Lysander on, to vex me with mock praises; and your other lover Demetrius, who used almost to spurn me with his foot, have you not bid him call me Goddess, Nymph rare, precious, and celestial? He would not speak thus to me whom he hates, if you did not set him on to make a jest of me. Unkind Hermia, to join with men in scorning your poor friend. Have you forgot our school-day friendship? How often, Hermia, have we two, sitting on one cushion, both singing one song, with our needles working the same flower, both on the same sampler wrought; growing up together in fashion of a double cherry, scarcely seeming parted? Hermia, it is not friendly in you, it is not maidenly, to join with men in scorning your poor friend."

"I am amazed at your passionate words," said Hermia: "I scorn you not; it seems you scorn me." "Aye, do," returned Helena, "persevere, counterfeit serious looks, and make mouths at me when I turn my back; then wink at each other, and hold the sweet jest up. If you had any pity, grace, or manners, you would not use me thus."

While Helena and Hermia were speaking these angry words to each other, Demetrius and Lysander left them, to fight together in the wood for the love of Helena.

When they found the gentlemen had left them, they departed, and once more wandered weary in the wood in search of their lovers.

As soon as they were gone, the fairy king, who with little Puck had been listening to their quarrels, said to him, "This is your negligence, Puck; or did you do this wilfully?" "Believe me, king of shadows," answered Puck, "it was a mistake: did not you tell me I should know the man by his Athenian garments? However, I am not sorry this has happened, for I think their jangling makes excellent sport." "You heard," said Oberon, "that Demetrius and Lysander are gone to seek a convenient place to fight in. I command you to overhang the night with a thick fog, and lead these quarrelsome lovers so astray in the dark, that they shall not be able to find each other. Counterfeit each of their voices to the other, and with bitter taunts provoke them to follow you, while they think it is their rival's tongue they hear. See you do this, till they are so weary that they can go no farther; and when you find they are asleep, drop the juice of this other flower into Lysander's eyes, and when he awakes he will forget his new love for Helena, and return to his old passion for Hermia; and then the two fair ladies may each one be happy with the man she loves; and they will think all that has passed a vexatious dream. About this quickly, Puck; and I will go and see what sweet love my Titania has found."

Titania was still sleeping, and Oberon, seeing a clown near her, who had lost his way in the wood, and was likewise asleep: "This fellow," said he, "shall be my Titania's true-love"; and clapping an ass's head over the clown's, it seemed to fit him as well as if it had grown upon his own shoulders. Though Oberon fixed the ass's head on very gently, it awakened him, and rising up, unconscious of what Oberon had done to him, he went toward the bower where the fairy queen slept.

"Ah! what angel is that I see!" said Titania, opening her eyes, and the juice of the little purple flower beginning to take effect: "Are you as wise as you are beautiful?"

"Why, mistress," said the foolish clown, "if I have wit enough to find the way out of this wood, I have enough to serve my turn."

"Out of the wood do not desire to go," said the enamoured queen. "I am a spirit of no common rate. I love you. Go with me, and I will give you fairies to attend upon you."

She then called four of her fairies: their names were Pease-blossom, Cobweb, Moth, and Mustard-seed.

"Attend," said the queen, "upon this sweet gentleman: hop in his walks, and gambol in his sight; feed him with grapes and apricots, and steal for him the honey-bags from the bees. Come, sit with me," said she to the clown, "and let me play with your amiable hairy cheeks, my beautiful ass! and kiss your fair large ears, my gentle joy!"

"Where is Pease-blossom?" said the ass-headed clown; not much regarding the fairy-queen's courtship, but very proud of his new attendants.

"Here, sir," said little Pease-blossom.

"Scratch my head," said the clown. "Where is Cobweb?"

"Here, sir," said Cobweb.

"Good Mr. Cobweb," said the foolish clown, "kill me the red humble-bee on the top of that thistle yonder; and, good Mr. Cobweb, bring me the honey-bag. Do not fret yourself too much in the action, Mr. Cobweb, and take care the honey-bag break not; I should be sorry to have you over-flown with a honey-bag. Where is Mustard-seed?"

"Here, sir," said Mustard-seed; "what is your will?"

"Nothing," said the clown, "good Mr. Mustard-seed, but to help Mr. Pease-blossom to scratch; I must go to a barber's, Mr. Mustard-seed, for methinks I am marvelous hairy about the face."

"My sweet love," said the queen, "what will you have to eat? I have a venturous fairy shall seek the squirrel's hoard, and fetch you some new nuts."

"I had rather have a handful of dried pease," said the clown, who with his ass's head had got an ass's appetite. "But, I pray, let none of your people disturb me, for I have a mind to sleep."

"Sleep then," said the queen, "and I will wind you in my arms. O how I love you! How I doat upon you!"

When the fairy king saw the clown sleeping in the arms of his queen, he advanced within her sight, and reproached her with having lavished her favours upon an ass.

This she could not deny, as the clown was then sleeping

within her arms, with his ass's head crowned by her with flowers.

When Oberon had teased her for some time, he again demanded the changeling-boy; which she, ashamed of being discovered by her lord with her new favourite, did not dare to refuse him.

Oberon, having thus obtained the little boy he had so long wished for to be his page, took pity on the disgraceful situation into which, by his merry contrivance, he had brought his Titania, and threw some of the juice of the other flower into her eyes; and the fairy-queen immediately recovered her senses, and wondered at her late dotage, saying how she now loathed the sight of the strange monster.

Oberon likewise took the ass's head from off the clown, and left him to finish his nap with his own fool's head upon his shoulders.

Oberon and his Titania being now perfectly reconciled, he related to her the history of the lovers, and their midnight quarrels; and she agreed to go with him, and see the end of their adventures.

The fairy king and queen found the lovers and their fair ladies, at no great distance from each other, sleeping on a grass-plot; for Puck, to make amends for his former mistake, had contrived with the utmost diligence to bring them all to the same spot, unknown to each other; and he had carefully removed the charm from off the eyes of Lysander with the antidote the fairy king gave to him.

Hermia first awoke, and finding her lost Lysander asleep

so near her, was looking at him and wondering at his strange inconstancy. Lysander presently opening his eyes, and seeing his dear Hermia, recovered his reason, which the fairy charm had before clouded, and with his reason his love for Hermia; and they began to talk over the adventures of the night, doubting if these things had really happened, or if they had both been dreaming the same bewildering dream.

Helena and Demetrius were by this time awake; and a sweet sleep having quieted Helena's disturbed and angry spirits, she listened with delight to the professions of love, which Demetrius still made to her, and which, to her surprise as well as pleasure, she began to perceive were sincere.

These fair night-wandering ladies, now no longer rivals, became once more true friends; all the unkind words which had passed were forgiven, and they calmly consulted together what was best to be done in their present situation. It was soon agreed that, as Demetrius had given up his pretensions to Hermia, he should endeavour to prevail upon her father to revoke the cruel sentence of death which had been passed against her. Demetrius was preparing to return to Athens for this friendly purpose, when they were surprised with the sight of Egeus, Hermia's father, who came to the wood in pursuit of his runaway daughter.

When Egeus understood that Demetrius would not now marry his daughter, he no longer opposed her marriage with Lysander, but gave his consent that they should be wedded on the fourth day from that time, being the same day on which Hermia had been condemned to lose her life; and on that same day Helena joyfully agreed to marry her beloved and now faithful Demetrius.

The fairy king and queen, who were invisible spectators of this reconciliation, and now saw the happy ending of the lovers' history brought about through the good offices of Oberon, received so much pleasure, that these kind spirits resolved to celebrate the approaching nuptials with sports and revels throughout their fairy kingdom.

And now, if any are offended with this story of fairies and their pranks, as judging it incredible and strange, they have only to think that they have been asleep and dreaming, and that all these adventures were visions which they saw in their sleep: and I hope none of my readers will be so unreasonable as to be offended with a pretty, harmless Midsummer Night's Dream.

Tale the Third

The Winter's Tale

LEONTES, king of Sicily, and his queen, the beautiful and virtuous Hermione, once lived in the greatest harmony together. So happy was Leontes in the love of this excellent lady, that he had no wish ungratified, except that he sometimes desired to see again, and to present to his queen, his old companion and school-fellow, Polixenes, king of Bohemia. Leontes and Polixenes were brought up together from their infancy, but being by the death of their fathers called to reign over their respective kingdoms, they had not met for many years, though they frequently interchanged gifts, letters, and loving embassies.

At length, after repeated invitations, Polixenes came from Bohemia to the Sicilian court, to make his friend Leontes a visit.

{41}

At first this visit gave nothing but pleasure to Leontes. He recommended the friend of his youth to the queen's particular attention, and seemed in the presence of his dear friend and old companion to have his felicity quite completed. They talked over old times; their school-days and their youthful pranks were remembered, and recounted to Hermione, who always took a cheerful part in these conversations.

When after a long stay, Polixenes was preparing to depart, Hermione, at the desire of her husband, joined her entreaties to his that Polixenes would prolong his visit.

And now began this good queen's sorrow; for Polixenes refusing to stay at the request of Leontes, was won over by Hermione's gentle and persuasive words to put off his departure for some weeks longer. Upon this, although Leontes had so long known the integrity and honourable principles of his friend Polixenes, as well as the excellent disposition of his virtuous queen, he was seized with an ungovernable jealousy. Every attention Hermione showed to Polixenes, though by her husband's particular desire, and merely to please him, increased the unfortunate king's jealousy; and from being a loving and true friend, and the best and fondest of husbands, Leontes became suddenly a savage and inhuman monster. Sending for Camillo, one of the lords of his court, and telling him of the suspicion he entertained, he commanded him to poison Polixenes.

Camillo was a good man; and he, well knowing that the jealousy of Leontes had not the slightest foundation in truth, instead of poisoning Polixenes, acquainted him with the king his master's orders, and agreed to escape with him out of the Sicilian dominions; and Polixenes, with the assistance of Camillo, arrived safe in his own kingdom of Bohemia, where Camillo lived from that time in the king's court, and became the chief friend and favourite of Polixenes.

The flight of Polixenes enraged the jealous Leontes still more; he went to the queen's apartment, where the good lady was sitting with her little son Mamillus, who was just beginning to tell one of his best stories to amuse his mother, when the king entered, and taking the child away, sent Hermione to prison.

Mamillus, though but a very young child, loved his mother tenderly; and when he saw her so dishonoured, and found she was taken from him to be put into a prison, he took it deeply to heart, and drooped and pined away by slow degrees, losing his appetite and his sleep, till it was thought his grief would kill him.

The king, when he had sent his queen to prison, commanded Cleomenes and Dion, two Sicilian lords, to go to Delphos, there to inquire of the oracle at the temple of Apollo, if his queen had been unfaithful to him.

When Hermione had been a short time in prison, she was brought to bed of a daughter; and the poor lady received much comfort from the sight of her pretty baby, and she said to it, "My poor little prisoner, I am as innocent as you are."

Hermione had a kind friend in the noble-spirited Paulina,

who was the wife of Antigonus, a Sicilian lord: and when the Lady Paulina heard her royal mistress was brought to bed, she went to the prison where Hermione was confined; and she said to Emilia, a lady who attended upon Hermione, "I pray you, Emilia, tell the good queen, if her majesty dare trust me with her little babe, I will carry it to the king its father; we do not know how he may soften at the sight of his innocent child." "Most worthy madam," replied Emilia, "I will acquaint the queen with your noble offer; she was wishing to-day that she had any friend who would venture to present the child to the king." "And tell her," said Paulina, "that I will speak boldly to Leontes in her defence." "May you be for ever blessed," said Emilia, "for your kindness to our gracious queen!" Emilia then went to Hermione, who joyfully gave up her baby to the care of Paulina, for she had feared that no one would dare venture to present the child to its father.

Paulina took the new-born infant, and forcing herself into the king's presence, notwithstanding her husband, fearing the king's anger, endeavoured to prevent her, she laid the babe at its father's feet, and Paulina made a noble speech to the king in defence of Hermione, and she reproached him severely for his inhumanity, and implored him to have mercy on his innocent wife and child. But Paulina's spirited remonstrances only aggravated Leontes' displeasure, and he ordered her husband Antigonus to take her from his presence.

When Paulina went away, she left the little baby at its

father's feet, thinking, when he was alone with it, he would look upon it, and have pity on its helpless innocence.

The good Paulina was mistaken; for no sooner was she gone than the merciless father ordered Antigonus, Paulina's husband, to take the child, and carry it out to sea, and leave it upon some desert shore to perish.

Antigonus, unlike the good Camillo, too well obeyed the orders of Leontes; for he immediately carried the child on ship-board, and put out to sea, intending to leave it on the first desert coast he could find.

So firmly was the king persuaded of the guilt of Hermione, that he would not wait for the return of Cleomenes and Dion, whom he had sent to consult the oracle of Apollo at Delphos; but before the queen was recovered from her lying-in, and from her grief for the loss of her precious baby, he had her brought to a public trial before all the lords and nobles of his court. And when all the great lords, the judges, and all the nobility of the land were assembled together to try Hermione, and that unhappy queen was standing as a prisoner before her subjects to receive their judgment, Cleomenes and Dion entered the assembly, and presented to the king the answer of the oracle sealed up; and Leontes commanded the seal to be broken, and the words of the oracle to be read aloud, and these were the words: *"Hermione is innocent, Polixenes blameless, Camillo a true subject, Leontes a jealous tyrant, and the king shall live without an heir if that which is lost be not found."* The king would give no credit to the words of the oracle: he said it was a falsehood invented by the queen's friends, and he desired the judge to proceed in the trial of the queen; but while Leontes was speaking, a man entered and told him that the Prince Mamillus, hearing his mother was to be tried for her life, struck with grief and shame, had suddenly died.

Hermione, upon hearing of the death of this dear affectionate child, who had lost his life in sorrowing for her misfortune, fainted; and Leontes, pierced to the heart by the news, began to feel pity for his unhappy queen, and he ordered Paulina, and the ladies who were her attendants, to take her away, and use means for her recovery. Paulina soon returned, and told the king that Hermione was dead.

When Leontes heard that the queen was dead, he repented of his cruelty to her; and now that he thought his ill usage had broken Hermione's heart, he believed her innocent; and he now thought the words of the oracle were true, as he knew "if that which was lost was not found," which he concluded was his young daughter, he should be without an heir, the young Prince Mamillus being dead; and he would give his kingdom now to recover his lost daughter: and Leontes gave himself up to remorse, and passed many years in mournful thoughts and repentant grief.

The ship in which Antigonus carried the infant princess out to sea was driven by a storm upon the coast of Bohemia, the very kingdom of the good King Polixenes. Here Antigonus landed, and here he left the little baby.

Antigonus never returned to Sicily to tell Leontes where he had left his daughter, for as he was going back to the ship a bear came out of the woods and tore him to pieces; a just punishment on him for obeying the wicked order of Leontes.

The child was dressed in rich clothes and jewels; for Hermione had made it very fine when she sent it to Leontes, and Antigonus had pinned a paper to its mantle, with the name of *Perdita* written thereon, and words obscurely intimating its high birth and untoward fate.

This poor deserted baby was found by a shepherd. He was a humane man, and so he carried the little Perdita home to his wife, who nursed it tenderly; but poverty tempted the shepherd to conceal the rich prize he had found: therefore he left that part of the country, that no one might know where he got his riches, and with part of Perdita's jewels he bought herds of sheep, and became a wealthy shepherd. He brought up Perdita as his own child, and she knew not she was any other than a shepherd's daughter.

The little Perdita grew up a lovely maiden; and though she had no better education than that of a shepherd's daughter, yet so did the natural graces she inherited from her royal mother shine forth in her untutored mind, that no one from her behaviour would have known she had not been brought up in her father's court.

Polixenes, the king of Bohemia, had an only son, whose name was Florizel. As this young prince was hunting near the shepherd's dwelling he saw the old man's supposed daughter; and the beauty, modesty, and queen-like deportment of Perdita caused him instantly to fall in love with her. He soon, under the name of Doricles, and in the disguise of a private gentleman, became a constant visitor at the old shepherd's house.

Florizel's frequent absence from court alarmed Polixenes; and setting people to watch his son, he discovered his love for the shepherd's fair daughter.

Polixenes then called for Camillo, the faithful Camillo, who had preserved his life from the fury of Leontes; and desired Camillo to accompany him to the house of the shepherd, the supposed father of Perdita.

Polixenes and Camillo, both in disguise, arrived at the old shepherd's dwelling while they were celebrating the feast of sheep-shearing: and though they were strangers, yet at the sheep-shearing every guest being made welcome, they were invited to walk in and join in the general festivity.

Nothing but mirth and jollity was going forward. Tables were spread, and great preparations were making for the rustic feast. Some lads and lasses were dancing on the green before the house, while others of the young men were buying ribands, gloves, and such toys of a peddler at the door.

While this busy scene was going forward, Florizel and Perdita sat quietly in a retired corner, seemingly more pleased with the conversation of each other than desirous of engaging in the sports and silly amusements of those around them.

The king was so disguised that it was impossible his son

could know him; he therefore advanced near enough to hear the conversation. The simple yet elegant manner in which Perdita conversed with his son did not a little surprise Polixenes: he said to Camillo, "This is the prettiest low-born lass I ever saw; nothing she does or says but looks like something greater than herself, too noble for this place."

Camillo replied, "Indeed she is the very queen of curds and cream."

"Pray, my good friend," said the king to the old shepherd, "what fair swain is that talking with your daughter?" "They call him Doricles," replied the shepherd. "He says he loves my daughter; and to speak truth, there is not a kiss to choose which loves the other best. If young Doricles can get her, she shall bring him that he little dreams of": meaning the remainder of Perdita's jewels; which, after he had bought herds of sheep with part of them, he had carefully hoarded up for her marriage portion.

Polixenes then addressed his son. "How now, young man!" said he; "your heart seems full of something that takes off your mind from feasting. When I was young, I used to load my love with presents; but you have let the peddler go, and have bought your lass no toy."

The young prince, who little thought he was talking to the king his father, replied, "Old sir, she prizes not such trifles; the gifts which Perdita expects from me are locked up in my heart." Then turning to Perdita, he said to her, "O hear me, Perdita, before this ancient gentleman, who it seems was once himself a lover; he shall hear what I profess." Florizel then called upon this old stranger to be a witness to a solemn promise of marriage which he made to Perdita, saying to Polixenes, "I pray you, mark our contract."

"Mark your divorce, young sir," said the king, discovering himself. Polixenes then reproached his son for daring to contract himself to this low-born maiden, calling Perdita "shepherd's brat, sheep-hook," and other disrespectful names; and threatening, if ever she suffered his son to see her again, he would put her, and the old shepherd her father, to a cruel death.

The king then left them in great wrath, and ordered Camillo to follow him with prince Florizel.

When the king had departed, Perdita, whose royal nature was roused by Polixenes' reproaches, said, "Though we are all undone, I was not much afraid; and once or twice I was about to speak, and tell him plainly that the self-same sun which shines upon his palace hides not his face from our cottage, but looks on both alike." Then sorrowfully she said, "But now I am awakened from this dream, I will queen it no farther. Leave me, sir; I will go milk my ewes, and weep."

The kind-hearted Camillo was charmed with the spirit and propriety of Perdita's behaviour; and perceiving that the young prince was too deeply in love to give up his mistress at the command of his royal father, he thought of a way to befriend the lovers, and at the same time to execute a favourable scheme he had in his mind.

Camillo had long known that Leontes, the king of Sicily, was become a true penitent; and though Camillo was now the favoured friend of king Polixenes, he could not help wishing once more to see his late royal master and his native home. He therefore proposed to Florizel and Perdita, that they should accompany him to the Sicilian court, where he would engage Leontes should protect them, till, through his mediation they could obtain pardon from Polixenes, and his consent to their marriage.

To this proposal they joyfully agreed; and Camillo, who conducted everything relative to their flight, allowed the old shepherd to go along with them.

The shepherd took with him the remainder of Perdita's jewels, her baby clothes, and the paper which he had found pinned to her mantle.

After a prosperous voyage, Florizel and Perdita, Camillo and the old shepherd, arrived in safety at the court of Leontes. Leontes, who still mourned his dead Hermione and his lost child, received Camillo with great kindness, and gave a cordial welcome to prince Florizel. But Perdita, whom Florizel introduced as his princess, seemed to engross all Leontes' attention: perceiving a resemblance between her and his dead queen Hermione, his grief broke out afresh, and he said, such a lovely creature might his own daughter have been, if he had not so cruelly destroyed her. "And then, too," said he to Florizel, "I lost the society and friendship of your brave father, whom I now desire more than my life once again to look upon."

When the old shepherd heard how much notice the king had taken of Perdita, and that he had lost a daughter, who was exposed in infancy, he fell to comparing the time when he found the little Perdita with the manner of its exposure, the jewels and other tokens of its high birth; from all which it was impossible for him not to conclude, that Perdita and the king's lost daughter were the same.

Florizel and Perdita, Camillo and the faithful Paulina, were present when the old shepherd related to the king the manner in which he had found the child, and also the circumstance of Antigonus' death, he having seen the bear seize upon him. He showed the rich mantle in which Paulina remembered Hermione had wrapped the child; and he produced a jewel which she remembered Hermione had tied about Perdita's neck; and he gave up the paper which Paulina knew to be the writing of her husband; it could not be doubted that Perdita was Leontes' own daughter: but oh! the noble struggles of Paulina, between sorrow for her husband's death and joy that the oracle was fulfilled, in the king's heir, his long-lost daughter, being found! When Leontes heard that Perdita was his daughter, the great sorrow that he felt that Hermione was not living to behold her child made him that he could say nothing for a long time but, "O thy mother, thy mother!"

Paulina interrupted this joyful yet distressful scene, with saying to Leontes, that she had a statue, newly finished by that rare Italian master, Julio Romano, which was such a perfect resemblance of the queen that would his majesty be pleased to go to her house and look upon it, he would almost be ready to think it was Hermione herself. Thither then they all went; the king anxious to see the semblance of his Hermione, and Perdita longing to behold what the mother she never saw did look like.

When Paulina drew back the curtain which concealed this famous statue, so perfectly did it resemble Hermione, that all the king's sorrow was renewed at the sight: for a long time he had no power to speak or move.

"I like your silence, my liege," said Paulina; "it the more shews your wonder. Is not this statue very like your queen?"

At length the king said, "O, thus she stood, even with such majesty, when I first wooed her. But yet, Paulina, Hermione was not so aged as this statue looks." Paulina replied, "So much the more the carver's excellence, who has made the statue as Hermione would have looked had she been living now. But let me draw the curtain, sire, lest presently you think it moves."

The king then said, "Do not draw the curtain! Would I were dead! See, Camillo, would you not think it breathed? Her eye seems to have motion in it." "I must draw the curtain, my liege," said Paulina. "You are so transported, you will persuade yourself the statue lives." "O, sweet Paulina," said Leontes, "make me think so twenty years together! Still methinks there is an air comes from her. What fine chisel could ever yet cut breath? Let no man mock me, for I will kiss her." "Good my lord, forbear!" said Paulina. "The ruddiness upon her lips is wet; you will stain your own with oily painting. Shall I draw the curtain?" "No, not these twenty years," said Leontes.

Perdita, who all this time had been kneeling, and beholding in silent admiration the statue of her matchless mother, said now, "And so long could I stay here, looking upon my dear mother."

"Either forbear this transport," said Paulina to Leontes, "and let me draw the curtain; or prepare yourself for more amazement. I can make the statue move indeed; aye, and descend from off the pedestal, and take you by the hand. But then you will think, which I protest I am not, that I am assisted by some wicked powers."

"What you can make her do," said the astonished king, "I am content to look upon. What you can make her speak, I am content to hear; for it is as easy to make her speak as move."

Paulina then ordered some slow and solemn music, which she had prepared for the purpose, to strike up; and to the amazement of all the beholders, the statue came down from off the pedestal, and threw its arms around Leontes' neck. The statue then began to speak, praying for blessings on her husband, and on her child, the newly found Perdita.

No wonder that the statue hung upon Leontes' neck, and blessed her husband and her child. No wonder; for the statue was indeed Hermione herself, the real, and living queen.

Paulina had falsely reported to the king the death of Hermione, thinking that the only means to preserve her royal mistress's life; and with the good Paulina, Hermione had lived ever since, never choosing Leontes should know she was living, till she heard Perdita was found; for though she had long forgiven the injuries which Leontes had done to herself, she could not pardon his cruelty to his infant daughter.

His dead queen thus restored to life, his lost daughter found, the long-sorrowing Leontes could scarcely support the excess of his own happiness.

Nothing but congratulations and affectionate speeches were heard on all sides. Now the delighted parents thanked prince Florizel for loving their lowly-seeming daughter; and now they blessed the good old shepherd for preserving their child. Greatly did Camillo and Paulina rejoice, that they had lived to see so good an end of all their faithful services.

And as if nothing should be wanting to complete this strange and unlooked-for joy, king Polixenes himself now entered the palace.

When Polixenes first missed his son and Camillo, knowing that Camillo had long wished to return to Sicily, he conjectured he should find the fugitives here; and, following them with all speed, he happened to arrive just at this, the happiest moment of Leontes' life.

Polixenes took a part in the general joy; he forgave his friend Leontes the unjust jealousy he had conceived against him, and they once more loved each other with all the warmth of their first boyish friendship. And there was no fear that Polixenes would now oppose his son's marriage with Perdita. She was no "sheep-hook" now, but the heiress of the crown of Sicily.

Thus have we seen the patient virtues of the long-suffering Hermione rewarded. That excellent lady lived many years with her Leontes and her Perdita, the happiest of mothers and of queens.

Much Ado About Nothing

THERE lived in the palace at Messina two ladies whose names were Hero and Beatrice. Hero was the daughter, and Beatrice the niece of Leonato, the governor of Messina.

Beatrice was of a lively temper, and loved to divert her cousin Hero, who was of a more serious disposition, with her sprightly sallies. Whatever was going forward was sure to make matter of mirth for the light-hearted Beatrice.

At the time the history of these ladies commences, some young men of high rank in the army, as they were passing through Messina on their return from a war that was just ended, in which they had distinguished themselves by their great bravery, came to visit Leonato. Among these were Don Pedro, the prince of Arragon, and his friend Claudio, who was a lord of Florence; and with them came the wild and witty Benedick, and he was a lord of Padua.

These strangers had been at Messina before, and the hospitable governor introduced them to his daughter and his niece as their old friends and acquaintance.

Benedick, the moment he entered the room, began a lively conversation with Leonato and the prince. Beatrice, who liked not to be left out of any discourse, interrupted Benedick by saying, "I wonder that you will still be talking, Signor Benedick; nobody marks you." Benedick was just such another rattlebrain as Beatrice, yet he was not pleased at this free salutation: he thought it did not become a well-bred lady to be so flippant with her tongue; and he remembered, when he was last at Messina, that Beatrice used to select him to make her merry jests upon. And as there is no one who so little likes to be made a jest of as those who are apt to take the same liberty themselves, so it was with Benedick and Beatrice; these two sharp wits never met in former times, but a perfect war of raillery was kept up between them, and they always parted mutually displeased with each other. Therefore when Beatrice stopped him in the middle of his discourse by telling him nobody marked what he was saying, Benedick, affecting not to have observed before that she was present, said, "What, my dear lady Disdain, are you yet living?" And now war broke out afresh between them, and a long jangling argument ensued, during which Beatrice, although she knew he had so well approved his valour in the late war, said that she would eat all he had killed there: and observing the prince take delight in Benedick's conversation, she called him "the prince's jester." This sarcasm sunk deeper into the mind of Benedick than all Beatrice had said before. The hint she gave him that he was a coward, by saying she would eat all he had killed, he did not regard, knowing himself to be a brave man: but there is nothing that great wits so much dread as the imputation of buffoonery, because the charge comes sometimes a little too near the truth: therefore Benedick perfectly hated Beatrice when she called him "the prince's jester."

The modest lady Hero was silent before the noble guests; and while Claudio was attentively observing the improvement which time had made in her beauty, and was contemplating the exquisite graces of her fine figure (for she was an admirable young lady), the prince was highly amused with listening to the humorous dialogue between Benedick and Beatrice; and he said in a whisper to Leonato, "This is a pleasant-spirited young lady. She were an excellent wife for Benedick." Leonato replied to this suggestion, "O my lord, my lord, if they were but a week married, they would talk themselves mad." But though Leonato thought they would make a discordant pair, the prince did not give up the idea of matching these two keen wits together.

When the prince returned with Claudio from the palace, he found that the marriage he had devised between Benedick and Beatrice was not the only one projected in that good company, for Claudio spoke in such terms of Hero, as made the prince guess at what was passing in his heart; and he liked it well, and he said to Claudio, "Do you affect Hero?" To this question Claudio replied, "O my lord, when I was last at Messina, I looked upon her with a soldier's eye, that liked, but had no leisure for loving; but now, in this happy time of peace, thoughts of war have left their places vacant in my mind, and in their room come thronging soft and delicate thoughts, all prompting me how fair young Hero is, reminding me that I liked her before I went to the wars." Claudio's confession of his love for Hero so wrought upon the prince, that he lost no time in soliciting the consent of Leonato to accept of Claudio for a son-in-law. Leonato agreed to this proposal, and the prince found no great difficulty in persuading the gentle Hero herself to listen to the suit of the noble Claudio, who was a lord of rare endowments, and highly accomplished; and Claudio, assisted by his kind prince, soon prevailed upon Leonato to fix an early day for the celebration of his marriage with Hero.

Claudio was to wait but a few days before he was to be married to his fair lady; yet he complained of the interval being tedious, as indeed most young men are impatient, when they are waiting for the accomplishment of any event they have set their hearts upon: the prince, therefore, to make the time seem short to him, proposed, as a kind of merry pastime, that they should invent some artful scheme to make Benedick and Beatrice fall in love with each other. Claudio entered with great satisfaction into this whim of the prince, and Leonato promised them his assistance, and even Hero said she would do any modest office to help her cousin to a good husband.

The device the prince invented was, that the gentlemen should make Benedick believe that Beatrice was in love with him, and that Hero should make Beatrice believe that Benedick was in love with her.

The prince, Leonato, and Claudio began their operations first, and, watching an opportunity when Benedick was quietly seated reading in an arbour, the prince and his assistants took their station among the trees behind the arbour, so near that Benedick could not choose but hear all they said; and after some careless talk, the prince said, "Come hither,

Leonato. What was it you told me the other day—that your niece Beatrice was in love with signior Benedick? I did never think that lady would have loved any man." "No, nor I either, my lord," answered Leonato. "It is most wonderful that she should so doat on Benedick, whom she in all outward behaviour seemed ever to dislike." Claudio confirmed all this, by saying that Hero had told him Beatrice was so in love with Benedick that she would certainly die of grief, if he could not be brought to love her; which Leonato and Claudio seemed to agree was impossible, he having always been such a railer against all fair ladies, and in particular against Beatrice.

The prince affected to hearken to all this with great compassion for Beatrice, and he said, "It were good that Benedick were told of this." "To what end?" said Claudio; "he would but make sport of it, and torment the poor lady worse." "And if he should," said the prince, "it were a good deed to hang him; for Beatrice is an excellent sweet lady, and exceeding wise in everything but in loving Benedick." Then the prince motioned to his companions that they should walk on, and leave Benedick to meditate upon what he had overheard.

Benedick had been listening with great eagerness to this conversation; and he said to himself when he heard Beatrice loved him, "Is it possible? Sits the wind in that corner?" And when they were gone, he began to reason in this manner with himself. "This can be no trick! they were very serious, and they have the truth from Hero, and seem to pity the lady. Love me! Why, it must be requited! I did never think to marry. But when I said I should die a bachelor, I did not think I should live to be married. They say the lady is virtuous and fair. She is so. And wise in everything but in loving me. Why this is no great argument of her folly. But here comes Beatrice. By this day, she is a fair lady. I do spy some marks of love in her." Beatrice now approached him, and said with her usual tartness, "Against my will I am sent to bid you come in to dinner." Benedick, who never felt himself disposed to speak so politely to her before, replied, "Fair Beatrice, I thank you for your pains": and when Beatrice, after two or three more rude speeches, left him, Benedick thought he observed a concealed meaning of kindness under the uncivil words she uttered, and he said aloud, "If I do not take pity on her, I am a villain. If I do not love her, I am a Jew. I will go get her picture."

The gentleman being thus caught in the net they had spread for him, it was now Hero's turn to play her part with Beatrice; and for this purpose she sent for Ursula and Margaret, two gentlewomen who attended upon her, and she said to Margaret, "Good Margaret, run to the parlour; there you will find my cousin Beatrice talking with the prince and Claudio. Whisper in her ear, that I and Ursula are walking in the orchard, and that our discourse is all of her. Bid her steal into that pleasant arbour, where honey-suckles, ripened by the sun, like ungrateful minions, forbid the sun to enter." This arbour, into which Hero desired Margaret to entice Beatrice, was the very same pleasant arbour where Benedick had so lately been an attentive listener. "I will make her come, I warrant, presently," said Margaret.

WHAT · ANGEL · WAKES · ME · FROM · MY · FLOWERY · BED

A Midsummer Night's Dream—Tale the Second

THIS·BOND·DOTH·GIVE·THEE·HERE·NO·JOT·OF·BLOOD

The Merchant of Venice—Tale the Seventh

Hero, then taking Ursula with her into the orchard, said to her, "Now, Ursula, when Beatrice comes, we will walk up and down this alley, and our talk must be only of Benedick, and when I name him, let it be your part to praise him more than ever man did merit. My talk to you must be how Benedick is in love with Beatrice. Now begin; for look where Beatrice like a lap-wing runs close by the ground, to hear our conference." They then began; Hero saying, as if in answer to something which Ursula had said, "No, truly, Ursula. She is too disdainful; her spirits are as coy as wild birds of the rock." "But are you sure," said Ursula, "that Benedick loves Beatrice so entirely?" Hero replied, "So says the prince, and my lord Claudio, and they intreated me to acquaint her with it; but I persuaded them, if they loved Benedick, never to let Beatrice know of it." "Certainly," replied Ursula, "it were not good she knew his love, lest she made sport of it." "Why to say truth," said Hero, "I never yet saw a man, how wise soever, or noble, young or rarely featured, but she would dispraise him." "Sure, sure, such carping is not commendable," said Ursula. "No," replied Hero, "but who dare tell her so? if I should speak, she would mock me into air." "O you wrong your cousin," said Ursula: "she cannot be so much without true judgment, as to refuse so rare a gentleman as signior Benedick." "He hath an excellent good name," said Hero: "indeed he is the first man in Italy, always excepting my dear Claudio." And now, Hero giving her attendant a hint that it was time to change the discourse, Ursula said, "And when are you to be married, madam?" Hero then told her, that she was to be married to Claudio the next day, and desired she would go in with her, and look at some new attire, as she wished to consult with her on what she would wear on the morrow. Beatrice, who had been listening with breathless eagerness to this dialogue, when they went away, exclaimed "What fire is in my ears? Can this be true? Farewel contempt, and scorn and maiden pride, adieu! Benedick, love on! I will requite you, taming my wild heart to your loving hand."

It must have been a pleasant sight to see these old enemies converted into new and loving friends; and to behold their first meeting after being cheated into mutual liking by the merry artifice of the good-humoured prince. But a sad reverse in the fortunes of Hero must now be thought of. The morrow, which was to have been her wedding-day, brought sorrow on the heart of Hero and her good father Leonato.

The prince had a half-brother, who came from the wars along with him to Messina. This brother (his name was Don John) was a melancholy, discontented man, whose spirits seemed to labour in the contriving of villainies. He hated the prince his brother, and he hated Claudio, because he was the prince's friend, and determined to prevent Claudio's marriage with Hero, only for the malicious pleasure of making Claudio and the prince unhappy: for he knew the prince had set his heart upon this marriage, almost as much as Claudio himself: and to effect this wicked purpose, he employed one Borachio, a man as bad as himself, whom he encouraged with the offer of a great reward. Thus Borachio paid his court to Margaret, Hero's attendant; and Don John, knowing this, prevailed upon him to make Margaret promise to talk with him from her lady's chamber-window that night, after Hero was asleep, and also to dress herself in Hero's clothes, the better to deceive Claudio into the belief that it was Hero; for that was the end he meant to compass by this wicked plot.

Don John then went to the prince and Claudio, and told them that Hero was an imprudent lady, and that she talked with men from her chamber-window at midnight. Now this was the evening before the wedding, and he offered to take them that night, where they should themselves hear Hero discoursing with a man from her window; and they consented to go along with him, and Claudio said, "If I see anything to-night why I should not marry her, to-morrow in the congregation, where I intended to wed her, there will I shame her." The prince also said, "And as I assisted you to obtain her, I will join with you to disgrace her."

When Don John brought them near Hero's chamber that night, they saw Borachio standing under the window, and they saw Margaret looking out of Hero's window, and heard her talking with Borachio; and Margaret being dressed in the same clothes they had seen Hero wear, the prince and Claudio believed it was the lady Hero herself.

Nothing could equal the anger of Claudio, when he had made (as he thought) this discovery. All his love for the innocent Hero was at once converted into hatred, and he resolved to expose her in the church, as he had said he would, the next day; and the prince agreed to this, thinking no punishment could be too severe for the naughty lady, who talked with a man from her window the very night before she was going to be married to the noble Claudio.

The next day, when they were all met to celebrate the marriage, and Claudio and Hero were standing before the priest, and the priest, or friar as he was called, was proceeding to pronounce the marriage-ceremony, Claudio, in the most passionate language, proclaimed the guilt of the blameless Hero, who, amazed at the strange words he uttered, said meekly,

"Is my lord well, that he does speak so wide?"

Leonato, in the utmost horror, said to the prince,

"My lord, why speak not you?" "Why should I speak?" said the prince; "I stand dishonoured, that have gone about to link my dear friend to an unworthy woman. Leonato, upon my honour, myself, my brother, and this grieved Claudio, did see and hear her last night at midnight talk with a man at her chamber-window."

Benedick, in astonishment at what he heard, said, "This looks not like a nuptial."

"True, O God!" replied the heart-struck Hero; and then this hapless lady sunk down in a fainting fit, to all appearance dead. The prince and Claudio left the church, without staying to see if Hero would recover, or at all regarding the distress into which they had thrown Leonato. So hard-hearted had their anger made them.

Benedick remained, and assisted Beatrice to recover Hero from her swoon, saying, "How does the lady?" "Dead, I think," replied Beatrice in great agony, for she loved her cousin; and knowing her virtuous principles, she believed nothing of what she had heard spoken against her. Not so the poor old father; he believed the story of his child's shame, and it was piteous to hear him lamenting over her, as she lay like one dead before him, wishing she might never more open her eyes.

But the ancient friar was a wise man, and full of observation on human nature, and he had attentively marked the lady's countenance when she heard herself accused, and noted a thousand blushing shames to start into her face, and then he saw an angel-like whiteness bear away those blushes, and in her eye he saw a fire that did belie the error that the prince did speak against her maiden truth, and he said to the sorrowing father, "Call me a fool; trust not my reading, nor my observation; trust not my age, my reverence, nor my calling; if this sweet lady lie not guiltless here under some biting error."

When Hero recovered from the swoon into which she had fallen, the friar said to her, "Lady, what man is he you are accused of?" Hero replied, "They know that do accuse me; I know of none": then turning to Leonato, she said, "O my father, if you can prove that any man has ever conversed with me at hours unmeet, or that I yesternight changed words with any creature, refuse me, hate me, torture me to death."

"There is," said the friar, "some strange misunderstanding in the prince and Claudio"; and then he counselled Leonato, that he should report that Hero was dead; and he said, that the death-like swoon in which they had left Hero, would make this easy of belief; and he also advised him, that he should put on mourning, and erect a monument for her, and do all rites that appertain to a burial. "What shall become of this?"

said Leonato; "what will this do?" The friar replied, "This report of her death shall change slander into pity: that is some good; but that is not all the good I hope for. When Claudio shall hear she died upon hearing his words, the idea of her life shall sweetly creep into his imagination. Then shall he mourn, if ever love had interest in his heart, and wish he had not so accused her. Yea, though he thought his accusation truer."

Benedick now said, "Leonato, let the friar advise you; and though you know how well I love the prince and Claudio, yet on my honour I will not reveal this secret to them."

Leonato, thus persuaded, yielded; and he said sorrowfully, "I am so grieved, that the smallest twine may lead me." The kind friar then led Leonato and Hero away to comfort and console them, and Beatrice and Benedick remained alone; and this was the meeting from which their friends, who contrived the merry plot against them, expected so much diversion; those friends who were now overwhelmed with affliction, and from whose minds all thoughts of merriment seemed for ever banished.

Benedick was the first who spoke, and he said, "Lady Beatrice, have you wept all this while?" "Yea, and I will weep a while longer," said Beatrice. "Surely," said Benedick, "I do believe your fair cousin is wronged." "Ah!" said Beatrice, "how much might that man deserve of me who would right her!" Benedick then said, "Is there any way to show such friendship? I do love nothing in the world so well as you: is not that strange?" "It were as possible," said Beatrice, "for me to say I loved nothing in the world so well as you; but believe me not, and yet I lie not. I confess nothing, nor I deny nothing. I am sorry for my cousin." "By my sword," said Benedick, "you love me, and I protest I love you. Come, bid me do anything for you." "Kill Claudio," said Beatrice. "Ha! not for the wide world," said Benedick; for he loved his friend Claudio, and he believed he had been imposed upon. "Is not Claudio a villain that has slandered, scorned, and dishonoured my cousin?" said Beatrice: "O that I were a man!" "Hear me, Beatrice!" said Benedick. But Beatrice would hear nothing in Claudio's defence; and she continued to urge on Benedick to revenge her cousin's wrongs: and she said, "Talk with a man out of the window; a proper saying! Sweet Hero! she is wronged; she is slandered; she is undone. O that I were a man for Claudio's sake! or that I had any friend, who would be a man for my sake! but valour is melted into courtesies and compliments. I cannot be a man with wishing, therefore I will die a woman with grieving." "Tarry, good Beatrice," said Benedick: "by this hand, I love you." "Use it for my love some other way than swearing by it," said Beatrice. "Think you on your soul, that Claudio has wronged Hero?" asked Benedick. "Yea," answered Beatrice; "as sure as I have a thought, or a soul." "Enough," said Benedick; "I am engaged; I will challenge him. I will kiss your hand, and so leave you. By this hand, Claudio shall render me a dear account! As you hear from me, so think of me. Go, comfort your cousin."

While Beatrice was thus powerfully pleading with Benedick, and working his gallant temper by the spirit of her angry words to engage in the cause of Hero, and fight even with his dear friend Claudio, Leonato was challenging the prince and Claudio to answer with their swords the injury they had done his child, who, he affirmed, had died for grief. But they respected his age and his sorrow, and they said, "Nay, do not quarrel with us, good old man." And now came Benedick, and he also challenged Claudio to answer with his sword the injury he had done to Hero: and Claudio and the prince said to each other, "Beatrice has set him on to do this." Claudio nevertheless must have accepted this challenge of Benedick, had not the justice of Heaven at the moment brought to pass a better proof of the innocence of Hero than the uncertain fortune of a duel.

While the prince and Claudio were yet talking of the challenge of Benedick, a magistrate brought Borachio as a prisoner before the prince. Borachio had been overheard talking with one of his companions of the mischief he had been employed by Don John to do.

Borachio made a full confession to the prince in Claudio's hearing, that it was Margaret dressed in her lady's clothes that he had talked with from the window, whom they had mistaken for the lady Hero herself; and no doubt remained on the minds of Claudio and the prince of the innocence of Hero. If a doubt had remained, it must have been removed by the flight of Don John, who, finding his villainies were detected, fled from Messina to avoid the just anger of his brother.

The heart of Claudio was sorely grieved, when he found he had falsely accused Hero, who, he thought, died upon hearing his cruel words; and the memory of his beloved

Hero's image came over him, in the rare semblance that he loved it first; and the prince asking him if what he heard did not run like iron through his soul, he answered, that he felt as if he had taken poison while Borachio was speaking.

And the repentant Claudio implored forgiveness of the old man Leonato for the injury he had done his child; and promised, that whatever penance Leonato would lay upon him for his fault in believing the false accusation against his betrothed wife, for her dear sake he would endure it.

The penance Leonato enjoined him was, to marry the next morning a cousin of Hero's, who, he said, was now his heir, and in person very like Hero. Claudio, regarding the solemn promise he made to Leonato, said he would marry this unknown lady, even though she were an Ethiop; but his heart was very sorrowful, and he passed that night in tears, and in remorseful grief, at the tomb which Leonato had erected for Hero.

When the morning came, the prince accompanied Claudio to the church, where the good friar, and Leonato and his niece, were already assembled, to celebrate a second nuptial; and Leonato presented to Claudio his promised bride; and she wore a mask, that Claudio might not discover her face. And Claudio said to the lady in the mask, "Give me your hand, before this holy friar; I am your husband, if you will marry me." "And when I lived I was your other wife," said this unknown lady; and, taking off her mask, she proved to be no niece (as was pretended), but Leonato's very daughter, the lady Hero herself. We may be sure that this proved a most agreeable surprise to Claudio, who thought her dead, so that he could scarcely for joy believe his eyes: and the prince, who was equally amazed at what he saw, exclaimed, "Is not this Hero, Hero that was dead?" Leonato replied, "She died, my lord, but while her slander lived." The friar promised them an explanation of this seeming miracle after the ceremony was ended; and was proceeding to marry them, when he was interrupted by Benedick, who desired to be married at the same time to Beatrice. Beatrice making some demur to this match, and Benedick challenging her with her love for him, which he had learned from Hero, a pleasant explanation took place; and they found that they had both been tricked into a belief of love, which had never existed and had become lovers in truth by the power of a false jest: but the affection, which a merry invention had cheated them into, was grown too powerful to be shaken by a serious explanation; and since Benedick proposed to marry, he was resolved to think nothing to the purpose that the world could say against it; and he merrily kept up the jest, and swore to Beatrice, that he took her but for pity, and because he heard she was dying of love for him; and Beatrice protested, that she yielded but upon great persuasion, and partly to save his life, for she heard he was in a consumption. So these two mad wits were reconciled, and made a match of it, after Claudio and Hero were married; and to complete the history, Don John, the contriver of the villainy, was taken in his flight, and brought back to Messina; and a brave punishment it was to this gloomy and discontented man, to see the joy and feastings which, by the disappointment of his plots, took place at the palace in Messina.

Tale the Fifth

As You Like It

DURING the time that France was divided into provinces (or dukedoms as they were called), there reigned in one of these provinces an usurper who had deposed and banished his elder brother, the lawful duke.

The duke, who was thus driven from his dominions, retired with a few faithful followers to the forest of Arden; and here the good duke lived with his loving friends, who had put themselves into a voluntary exile for his sake, while their land and revenues enriched the false usurper; and custom soon made the life of careless ease they led here more sweet to them than the pomp and uneasy splendor of a courtier's life. Here they lived like the old Robin Hood of England, and to this forest many noble youths daily resorted from the court, and did fleet the time carelessly, as they did in the golden age. In the summer they lay along under the fine shade of the large forest trees, marking the playful sports of the wild deer; and so fond were they of these poor dappled fools, who seemed to be the native inhabitants of the forest, that it grieved them to be forced to kill them to supply themselves with venison for their food. When the cold winds of winter made the duke feel the change of his adverse fortune, he would endure it patiently and say, "These chilling winds, which blow upon my body, are true counsellors, they do not flatter, but represent truly to me my condition; and though they bite sharply, their tooth is nothing like so keen as that of unkindness and ingratitude. I find that, howsoever men speak against adversity, yet some sweet uses are to be extracted from it; like the jewel, precious for medicine, which is taken from the head of the venomous and despised toad." In this manner did the patient duke draw a useful moral from every thing that he saw; and by the help of this moralizing turn, in that life of his, remote from public haunts, he could find tongues in trees, books in the running brooks, sermons in stones, and good in every thing.

The banished duke had an only daughter, named Rosalind, whom the usurper, Duke Frederick, when he banished her father, still retained in his court as a companion for his own daughter Celia. A strict friendship subsisted between these ladies, which the disagreement between their fathers did not in the least interrupt, Celia striving by every kindness in her power to make amends to Rosalind for the injustice of her own father in deposing the father of Rosalind; and whenever the thoughts of her father's banishment, and her own dependence on the false usurper, made Rosalind melancholy, Celia's whole care was to comfort and console her.

One day, when Celia was talking in her usual kind manner to Rosalind, saying, "I pray you, Rosalind, my sweet cousin, be merry," a messenger entered from the duke, to tell them that if they wished to see a wrestling-match, which was just going to begin, they must come instantly to the court before the palace; and Celia, thinking it would amuse Rosalind, agreed to go and see it.

In those times wrestling, which is only practised now by country clowns, was a favourite sport even in the courts of princes, and before fair ladies and princesses. To this wrestling-match therefore Celia and Rosalind went. They found that it was likely to prove a very tragical sight; for a large and powerful man, who had long been practised in the art of wrestling, and had slain many men in contests of this kind, was just going to wrestle with a very young man, who, from his extreme youth and inexperience in the art, the beholders all thought would certainly be killed.

When the duke saw Celia and Rosalind, he said, "How now, daughter and niece, are you crept hither to see the wrestling? You will take little delight in it, there is such odds in the men: in pity to this young man, I would wish to persuade him from wrestling. Speak to him, ladies, and see if you can move him."

The ladies were well pleased to perform this humane office, and first Celia entreated the young stranger that he would desist from the attempt; and then Rosalind spoke so kindly to him, and with such feeling consideration for the danger he was about to undergo, that instead of being persuaded by her gentle words to forego his purpose, all his thoughts were bent to distinguish himself by his courage in this lovely lady's eyes. He refused the request of Celia and Rosalind in such graceful and modest words, that they felt still more concern for him; he concluded his refusal by saying, "I am sorry to deny such fair and excellent ladies anything. But let your fair eyes and gentle wishes go with me to my trial, wherein if I be conquered, there is one shamed that was never gracious; if I am killed, there is one dead that is willing to die. I shall do my friends no wrong, for I have none to lament me; the world no injury, for in it I have nothing; for I only fill up a place in the world which may be better supplied when I have made it empty."

And now the wrestling-match began. Celia wished the young stranger might not be hurt; but Rosalind felt most for him. The friendless state which he said he was in, and that he wished to die, made Rosalind think that he was like herself, unfortunate; and she pitied him so much, and so deep an interest she took in his danger while he was wrestling, that she might almost be said at that moment to have fallen in love with him.

The kindness shewn this unknown youth by these fair and noble ladies gave him courage and strength, so that he performed wonders; and in the end completely conquered his antagonist, who was so much hurt, that for a while he was unable to speak or move.

The Duke Frederick was much pleased with the courage and skill shewn by this young stranger; and desired to know his name and parentage, meaning to take him under his protection.

The stranger said his name was Orlando, and that he was the youngest son of sir Rowland de Boys.

Sir Royland de Boys, the father of Orlando, had been dead some years; but when he was living, he had been a true subject and dear friend of the banished duke: therefore, when Frederick heard Orlando was the son of his banished brother's friend, all his liking for this brave young man was changed into displeasure, and he left the place in very ill humour. Hating to hear the very name of any of his brother's friends, and yet still admiring the valour of the youth, he said, as he went out, that he wished Orlando had been the son of any other man.

Rosalind was delighted to hear that her new favourite was the son of her father's old friend; and she said to Celia, "My father loved sir Rowland de Boys, and if I had known this young man was his son, I would have added tears to my entreaties before he should have ventured."

The ladies then went up to him; and seeing him abashed by the sudden displeasure shewn by the duke, they spoke kind and encouraging words to him; and Rosalind, when they were going away, turned back to speak some more civil things to the brave young son of her father's old friend; and taking a chain from off her neck, she said, "Gentleman, wear this for me. I am out of suits with fortune, or I would give you a more valuable present."

When the ladies were alone, Rosalind's talk being still of

Orlando, Celia began to perceive her cousin had fallen in love with the handsome young wrestler, and she said to Rosalind, "Is it possible you should fall in love so suddenly?" Rosalind replied, "The duke, my father, loved his father dearly." "But," said Celia, "does it therefore follow that you should love his son dearly? for then I ought to hate him, for my father hated his father; yet I do not hate Orlando."

Frederick being enraged at the sight of sir Rowland de Boys' son, which reminded him of the many friends the banished duke had among the nobility, and having been for some time displeased with his niece, because the people praised her for her virtues and pitied her for her good father's sake, his malice suddenly broke out against her; and while Celia and Rosalind were talking of Orlando, Frederick entered the room, and with looks full of anger ordered Rosalind instantly to leave the palace, and follow her father into banishment; telling Celia, who in vain pleaded for her, that he had only suffered Rosalind to stay upon her account. "I did not then," said Celia, "entreat you to let her stay; for I was too young at that time to value her; but now that I know her worth, and that we so long have slept together, rose at the same instant, learned, played, and eat together, I cannot live out of her company." Frederick replied, "She is too subtle for you; her smoothness, her very silence, and her patience, speak to the people, and they pity her. You are a fool to plead for her, for you will seem more bright and virtuous when she is gone; therefore open not your lips in her favour, for the doom which I have past upon her is irrevocable."

When Celia found she could not prevail upon her father to let Rosalind remain with her, she generously resolved to accompany her; and, leaving her father's palace that night, she went along with her friend to seek Rosalind's father, the banished duke, in the forest of Arden.

Before they set out, Celia considered that it would be unsafe for two young ladies to travel in the rich clothes they then wore: she therefore proposed that they should disguise their rank by dressing themselves like country maids. Rosalind said it would be a still greater protection if one of them was to be dressed like a man; and so it was quickly agreed on between them, that as Rosalind was the tallest, she should wear the dress of a young countryman, and Celia should be habited like a country lass, and that they should say they were brother and sister, and Rosalind said she would be called Ganimed, and Celia chose the name of Aliena.

In this disguise, and taking their money and jewels to defray their expenses, these fair princesses set out on their long travel; for the forest of Arden was a long way off, beyond the boundaries of the duke's dominions.

The lady Rosalind (or Ganimed as she must now be called) with her manly garb seemed to have put on a manly courage. The faithful friendship Celia had shown in accompanying Rosalind so many weary miles made the new brother, in recompense for this true love, exert a cheerful spirit, as if he were indeed Ganimed, the rustic and stout-hearted brother of the gentle village maiden, Aliena.

When at last they came to the forest of Arden, they no

longer found the convenient inns and good accommodations they had met with on the road; and being in want of food and rest, Ganimed, who had so merrily cheered his sister with pleasant speeches and happy remarks, all the way, now owned to Aliena that he was so weary, he could find it in his heart to disgrace his man's apparel, and cry like a woman; and Aliena declared she could go no farther; and then again Ganimed tried to recollect that it was a man's duty to comfort and console a woman, as the weaker vessel: and to seem courageous to his new sister, he said, "Come, have a good heart, my sister Aliena; we are now at the end of our travel, in the forest of Arden. "But feigned manliness and forced courage would no longer support them; for though they were in the forest of Arden, they knew not where to find the duke: and here the travel of these weary ladies might have come to a sad conclusion, for they might have lost themselves, and have perished for want of food; but, providentially, as they were sitting on the grass, almost dying with fatigue and hopeless of any relief, a countryman chanced to pass that way, and Ganimed once more tried to speak with a manly boldness, saying, "Shepherd, if love or gold can in this desert place procure us entertainment, I pray you bring us where me may rest ourselves; for this young maid, my sister, is much fatigued with travelling, and faints for want of food."

The man replied, that he was only servant to a shepherd, and that his master's house was just going to be sold, and therefore they would find but poor entertainment; but that if they would go with him, they should be welcome to what there was. They followed the man, the near prospect of re-lief giving them fresh strength; and bought the house and sheep of the shepherd, and took the man who conducted them to the shepherd's house, to wait on them; and being by this means so fortunately provided with a neat cottage, and well supplied with provisions, they agreed to stay here till they could learn in what part of the forest the duke dwelt.

When they were rested after the fatigue of their journey, they began to like their new way of life, and almost fancied themselves the shepherd and shepherdess they feigned to be; yet sometimes Ganimed remembered he had once been the same lady Rosalind who had so dearly loved the brave Or-lando, because he was the son of old sir Rowland, her father's friend; and though Ganimed thought that Orlando was many miles distant, even so many weary miles as they had travelled, yet it soon appeared that Orlando was also in the forest of Arden: and in this manner this strange event came to pass.

Orlando was the youngest son of sir Rowland de Boys, who, when he died, left him (Orlando being then very young) to the care of his eldest brother Oliver, charging Oliver, on his blessing, to give his brother a good education, and pro-vide for him as became the dignity of their ancient house. Oliver proved an unworthy brother; and disregarding the commands of his dying father, he never put his brother to school, but kept him at home untaught and entirely neglected. But in his nature and in the noble qualities of his mind Or-lando so much resembled his excellent father, that without any advantages of education he seemed like a youth who had been bred with the utmost care; and Oliver so envied the fine person and dignified manners of his untutored brother, that at last he wished to destroy him; and to effect this he set on people to persuade him to wrestle with the famous wrestler who, as has been before related, had killed so many men. Now it was this cruel brother's neglect of him which made Orlando say he wished to die, being so friendless.

When, contrary to the wicked hopes he had formed, his brother proved victorious, his envy and malice knew no bounds, and he swore he would burn the chamber where Orlando slept. He was overheard making this vow by one that had been an old and faithful servant to their father, and that loved Orlando because he resembled sir Rowland. This old man went out to meet him when he returned from the duke's palace, and when he saw Orlando, the peril his dear young master was in made him break out into these passionate exclamations: "O my gentle master, my sweet master, O you memory of old sir Rowland! why are you virtuous? why are you gentle, strong, and valiant? and why would you be so fond to overcome the famous wrestler? Your praise is come too swiftly home before you." Orlando, wondering what all this meant, asked him what was the matter? and then the old man told him how his wicked brother, envying the love all people bore him, and now hearing the fame he had gained by his victory in the duke's palace, intended to destroy him by setting fire to his chamber that night; and in conclusion, advised him to escape the danger he was in by instant flight: and knowing Orlando had no money, Adam (for that was the good old man's name) had brought out with him his own little hoard, and he said, "I have five hundred crowns, the thrifty hire I saved under your father, and laid by to be provision for me when my old limbs should become unfit for service; take that, and He that doth the ravens feed be comfort to my age! Here is the gold; all this I give to you: let me be your servant; though I look old, I will do the service of a younger man in all your business and necessities. "O good old man!" said Orlando, "how well appears in you the constant service of the old world? You are not for the fashion of these times. We will go along together, and before your youthful wages are spent I shall light upon some means for both our maintenance."

Together, then, this faithful servant and his loved master set out; and Orlando and Adam travelled on, uncertain what course to pursue, till they came to the forest of Arden, and there they found themselves in the same distress for want of food that Ganimed and Aliena had been. They wandered on, seeking some human habitation, till they were almost spent with hunger and fatigue. Adam at last said, "O my dear master, I die for want of food—I can go no farther!" He then laid himself down, thinking to make that place his grave, and bade his dear master farewel. Orlando, seeing him in this weak state, took his old servant up in his arms, and carried him under the shelter of some pleasant trees; and he said to him, "Cheerly, old Adam, rest your weary limbs here a while, and do not talk of dying!"

Orlando then searched about to find some food, and he happened to arrive at that part of the forest where the duke was; and he and his friends were just going to eat their dinner, this royal duke being seated on the grass, under no other canopy than the shady cover of some large trees.

Orlando, whom hunger had made desperate, drew his sword, intending to take their meat by force, and said, "Forbear, and eat no more; I must have your food!" The duke asked him if distress had made him so bold, or if he were a rude despiser of good manners? On this Orlando said, he was dying with hunger; and then the duke told him he was welcome to sit down and eat with them. Orlando, hearing him speak so gently, put up his sword, and blushed with shame at the rude manner in which he had demanded their food. "Pardon me, I pray you," said he: "I thought that all things had been savage here, and therefore I put on the countenance of stern command; but whatever men you are, that in this desert, under the shade of melancholy boughs, lose and neglect the creeping hours of time: if ever you have looked on better days; if ever you have been where bells have knolled to church; if you have ever sate at any good man's feast; if ever from your eyelids you have wiped a tear, and know what it is to pity or be pitied, may gentle speeches now move you to do me human courtesy!" The duke replied, "True it is that we are men (as you say) who have seen better days, and though we have now our habitation in this wild forest, we have lived in towns and cities, and have with holy bell been knolled to church, have sate at good men's feasts, and from our eyes have wiped the drops which sacred pity has engendered: therefore sit you down, and take of our refreshment as much as will minister to your wants." "There is an old poor man," answered Orlando, "who has limped after me many a weary step in pure love, oppressed at once with two sad infirmities, age and hunger; till he be satisfied, I must not touch a bit." "Go, find him out, and bring him hither," said the duke; "we will forbear to eat till you return." Then Orlando went like a doe to find its fawn and give it food; and presently returned, bringing Adam in his arms; and the duke said, "Set down your venerable burthen; you are both welcome": and they fed the old man, and cheered his heart, and he revived, and recovered his health and strength again.

The duke enquired who Orlando was, and when he found that he was the son of his old friend, sir Rowland de Boys, he took him under his protection, and Orlando and his old servant lived with the duke in the forest.

Orlando had not been in the forest many days before Ganimed and Aliena arrived there and (as has been before related) bought the shepherd's cottage.

Ganimed and Aliena were strangely surprised to find the name of Rosalind carved on the trees, and love-sonnets fastened to them, all addressed to Rosalind: and while they were wondering how this could be, they met Orlando, and they perceived the chain which Rosalind had given him about his neck.

Orlando little thought that Ganimed was the fair princess Rosalind, who, by her noble condescension and favour, had so

won his heart, that he passed his whole time in carving her
name upon the trees, and writing sonnets in praise of her
beauty: but being much pleased with the fraceful air of this
pretty shepherd-youth, he entered into conversation with him,
and he thought he saw a likeness in Ganimed to his beloved
Rosalind, but that he had none of the dignified deportment
of that noble lady; for Ganimed assumed the forward manners
often seen in youths when they are between boys and men,
and with much archness and humour talked to Orlando of a
certain lover, "who," said he, "haunts our forest, and spoils
our young trees with carving Rosalind upon their barks; and
he hangs odes upon hawthorns, and elegies on brambles, all
praising this same Rosalind. If I could find this lover, I
would give him some good counsel that would soon cure him
of his love."

Orlando confessed that he was the fond lover of whom he
spoke, and asked Ganimed to give him the good counsel he
talked of. The remedy Ganimed proposed and the counsel
he gave him, was that Orlando should come every day to the
cottage where he and his sister Aliena dwelt: "And then,"
said Ganimed, "I will feign myself to be Rosalind, and you
shall feign to court me in the same manner as you would do
if I were Rosalind, and then I will imitate the fantastic ways
of whimsical ladies to their lovers, till I make you ashamed
of your love; and this is the way I propose to cure you."
Orlando had no great faith in the remedy, yet he agreed to
come very day to Ganimed's cottage, and feign a playful
courtship; and every day Orlando visited Ganimed and

Aliena, and Orlando called the shepherd Ganimed his Rosalind, and every day talked over all the fine words and flattering compliments which young men delight to use when they court their mistresses. It does not appear, however, that Ganimed made any progress in curing Orlando of his love for Rosalind.

Though Orlando thought all this was but a sportive play (not dreaming that Ganimed was his very Rosalind), yet the opportunity it gave him of saying all the fond things he had in his heart, pleased his fancy almost as well as it did Ganimed's, who enjoyed the secret jest in knowing these fine love-speeches were all addressed to the right person.

In this manner many days passed pleasantly on with these young people; and the good-natured Aliena, seeing it made Ganimed happy, let him have his own way, and was diverted at the mock courtship, and did not care to remind Ganimed that the lady Rosalind had not yet made herself known to the duke her father, whose place of resort in the forest they had learned from Orlando. Ganimed met the duke one day, and had some talk with him, and the duke asked of what parentage he came. Ganimed answered, that he came of as good a parentage as he did; which made the duke smile, for he did not suspect the pretty shepherd-boy came of royal lineage. Then seeing the duke look well and happy, Ganimed was content to put off all further explanation for a few days longer.

One morning, as Orlando was going to visit Ganimed, he saw a man lying asleep on the ground, and a large green snake

had twisted itself about his neck. The snake, seeing Orlando
approach, glided away among the bushes. Orlando went
nearer, and then he discovered a lioness lie couching, with
her head on the ground, with a cat-like watch, waiting till
the sleeping man awaked (for it is said the lions will prey on
nothing that is dead or sleeping). It seemed as if Orlando
was sent by Providence to free the man from the danger of
the snake and lioness: but when Orlando looked in the man's
face, he perceived that the sleeper, who was exposed to this
double peril was his own brother Oliver, who had so cruelly
used him, and had threatened to destroy him by fire; and he
was almost tempted to leave him a prey to the hungry lioness:
but brotherly affection and the gentleness of his nature soon
overcame his first anger against his brother; and he drew his
sword, and attacked the lioness, and slew her, and thus preserved his brother's life both from the venomous snake and
from the furious lioness: but before Orlando could conquer
the lioness, she had torn one of his arms with her sharp claws.

While Orlando was engaged with the lioness Oliver awaked,
and perceiving that his brother Orlando, whom he had so cruelly treated, was saving him from the fury of a wild beast at
the risk of his own life, shame and remorse at once seized him,
and he repented of his unworthy conduct, and besought with
many tears his brother's pardon for the injuries he had done
him. Orlando rejoiced to see him so penitent, and readily
forgave him: and they embraced each other, and from that
hour Oliver loved Orlando with a true brotherly affection,
though he had come to the forest bent on his destruction.

The wound in Orlando's arm having bled very much, he found himself too weak to go to visit Ganimed, and therefore he desired his brother to go and tell Ganimed, "whom," said Orlando, "I in sport do call my Rosalind," the accident which had befallen him.

Thither then Oliver went, and told to Ganimed and Aliena how Orlando had saved his life: and when he had finished the story of Orlando's bravery, and his own providential escape, he owned to them that he was Orlando's brother, who had so cruelly used him; and then he told them of their reconciliation.

The sincere sorrow that Oliver expressed for his offences made such a lively impression on the kind heart of Aliena, that she instantly fell in love with him; and Oliver observing how much she pitied the distress he told her he felt for his fault, he as suddenly fell in love with her. But while love was stealing into the hearts of Aliena and Oliver, he was no less busy with Ganimed, who hearing of the danger Orlando had been in, and that he was wounded by the lioness, fainted: and when he recovered, he pretended he had counterfeited the swoon in the imaginary character of Rosalind, and Ganimed said to Oliver, "Tell your brother Orlando how well I counterfeited a swoon." But Oliver saw by the paleness of his complexion that he did really faint, and much wondering at the weakness of the young man, he said, "Well, if you did counterfeit, take a good heart, and counterfeit to be a man." "So I do," replied Ganimed (truly), "but I should have been a woman by right."

Oliver made this visit a very long one, and when at last he returned back to his brother, he had much news to tell him: for besides the account of Ganimed's fainting at the hearing that Orlando was wounded, Oliver told him how he had fallen in love with the fair shepherdess Aliena, and that she had lent a favourable ear to his suit, even in this their first interview; and he talked to his brother, as of a thing almost settled, that he should marry Aliena, saying, that he so well loved her, that he would live here as a shepherd, and settle his estate and house at home upon Orlando.

"You have my consent," said Orlando. "Let your wedding be to-morrow, and I will invite the duke and his friends. Go and persuade your shepherdess to agree to this: she is now alone; for look here comes her brother." Oliver went to Aliena; and Ganimed, whom Orlando had perceived approaching, came to enquire after the health of his wounded friend.

When Orlando and Ganimed began to talk over the sudden love which had taken place between Oliver and Aliena, Orlando said he had advised his brother to persuade his fair shepherdess to be married on the morrow, and then he added how much he could wish to be married on the same day to his Rosalind.

Ganimed, who well approved of this arrangement, said, that if Orlando really loved Rosalind as well as he professed to do, he should have his wish: for on the morrow he would engage to make Rosalind appear in her own person, and also that Rosalind should be willing to marry Orlando.

This seemingly wonderful event, which, as Ganimed was the lady Rosalind, he could so easily perform, he pretended he would bring to pass by the aid of magic, which he said he had learned of an uncle who was a famous magician.

The fond lover Orlando, half believing and half doubting what he heard, asked Ganimed if he spoke in sober meaning. "By my life I do," said Ganimed; "therefore put on your best clothes, and bid the duke and your friends to your wedding; for if you desire to be married to-morrow to Rosalind, she shall be here."

The next morning, Oliver having obtained the consent of Aliena, they came into the presence of the duke, and with them also came Orlando.

They being all assembled to celebrate this double marriage, and as yet only one of the brides appearing, there was much of wondering and conjecture, but they mostly thought that Ganimed was making a jest of Orlando.

The duke, hearing it was his own daughter that was to be brought in this strange way, asked Orlando if he believed the shepherd-boy could really do what he had promised; and while Orlando was answering that he knew not what to think, Ganimed entered and asked the duke, if he brought his daughter, whether he would consent to her marriage with Orlando. "That I would," said the duke, "if I had kingdoms to give with her." Ganimed then said to Orlando, "And you say you will marry her if I bring her here?" "That I would," said Orlando, "if I were king of many kingdoms."

Ganimed and Aliena then went out together, and Ganimed throwing off his male attire, and being once more dressed in woman's apparel, quickly became Rosalind without the power of magic; and Aliena, changing her country garb for her own rich clothes, was with as little trouble transformed into the lady Celia.

While they were gone, the duke said to Orlando, that he thought the shepherd Ganimed very like his daughter Rosalind; and Orlando said, he also had observed the resemblance.

They had no time to wonder how all this would end, for Rosalind and Celia in their own clothes entered; and no longer pretending that it was by the power of magic that she came there, Rosalind threw herself on her knees before her father, and begged his blessing. It seemed so wonderful to all present that she should so suddenly appear, that it might well have passed for magic; but Rosalind would no longer trifle with her father, and told him the story of her banishment, and of her dwelling in the forest as a shepherd-boy, her cousin Celia passing as her sister.

The duke ratified the consent he had already given to the marriage; and Orlando and Rosalind, Oliver and Celia, were married at the same time. And though their wedding could not be celebrated in this wild forest with any of the parade or splendour usual on such occasions, yet a happier wedding-day was never passed: and while they were eating their venison under the cool shade of the pleasant trees, as if nothing should be wanting to complete the felicity of this good duke and the true lovers, an unexpected messenger arrived to tell the duke the joyful news, that his dukedom was restored to him.

The usurper, enraged at the flight of his daughter Celia, and hearing that every day men of great worth resorted to the forest of Arden to join the lawful duke in his exile, much envying that his brother should be so highly respected in his adversity, put himself at the head of a large force, and advanced to the forest, intending to seize his brother, and put him, with all his faithful followers, to the sword, but by a wonderful interposition of Providence, this bad brother was converted from his evil intention: for just as he entered the skirts of the wild forest he was met by an old religious man, a hermit, with whom he had much talk, and who in the end completely turned his heart from his wicked design. Thenceforward he became a true penitent, and resolved, relinquishing his unjust dominion, to spend the remainder of his days in a religious house. The first act of his newly-conceived penitence was to send a messenger to his brother (as has been related), to offer to restore to him his dukedom, which he had usurped so long, and with it the lands and revenues of his friends, the faithful followers of his adversity.

This joyful news, as unexpected as it was welcome, came opportunely to heighten the festivity and rejoicings at the wedding of the princesses. Celia complimented her cousin on this good fortune which had happened to the duke, Rosalind's father, and wished her joy very sincerely, though she herself was no longer heir to the dukedom, but by this restoration which her father had made, Rosalind was now the heir: so completely was the love of these two cousins unmixed with anything of jealousy or envy.

The duke had now an opportunity of rewarding those true friends who had staid with him in his banishment; and these worthy followers, though they had patiently shared his adverse fortune, were very well pleased to return in peace and prosperity to the palace of their lawful duke.

Tale the Sixth

The Two Gentlemen of Verona

THERE lived in the city of Verona two young gentlemen, whose names were Valentine and Protheus, between whom a firm and uninterrupted friendship had long subsisted. They pursued their studies together, and their hours of lesiure were always passed in each other's company, except when Protheus visited a lady he was in love with; and these visits to his mistress, and this passion of Protheus for the fair Julia, were the only topics on which these two friends disagreed: for Valentine, not being himself a lover, was sometimes a little weary of hearing his friend for ever talking of his Julia, and then he would laugh at Protheus, and in pleasant terms ridicule the passion of love, and declare that no such idle fancies should ever enter his head, greatly preferring (as he said) the free and happy life that he led, to the anxious hopes and fears of the lover Protheus.

One morning Valentine came to Protheus to tell him that they must for a time be separated, for that he was going to Milan. Protheus, unwilling to part with his friend, used many arguments to prevail upon Valentine not to leave him; but Valentine said, "Cease to persuade me, my loving Protheus. I will not, like a sluggard, wear out my youth in idleness at home. Home-keeping youths have ever homely wits. If your affection were not chained to the sweet glances of your hon-oured Julia, I would entreat you to accompany me, to see the wonders of the world abroad; but since you are a lover, love on still and may your love be prosperous!"

They parted with mutual expressions of unalterable friendship. "Sweet Valentine, adieu!" said Protheus; "think on me, when you see some rare object worthy of notice in your travels, and wish me partaker of your happiness."

Valenine began his journey that same day toward Milan, and when his friend had left him, Protheus sat down to write a letter to Julia, which he gave to her maid Lucetta to deliver to her mistress.

Julia loved Protheus as well as he did her, but she was a lady of a noble spirit, and she thought it did not become her maiden dignity too easily to be won; therefore she affected to be insensible of his passion, and gave him much uneasiness in the prosecution of his suit.

And when Lucetta offered the letter to Julia, she would not receive it, and chid her maid for taking letters from

Protheus, and ordered her to leave the room. But she so much wished to see what was written in the letter, that she soon called in her maid again, and when Lucetta returned, she said, "What o'clock is it?" Lucetta, who knew her mistress more desired to see the letter than to know the time of day, without answering her question, again offered the rejected letter. Julia, angry that her maid should thus take the liberty of seeming to know what she really wanted, tore the letter in pieces, and threw it on the floor, ordering her maid once more out of the room. As Lucetta was retiring, she stooped to pick up the fragments of the torn letter; but Julia, who meant not so to part with them, said in pretended anger, "Go, get you gone, and let the papers lie; you would be fingering them to anger me."

Julia then began to piece together as well as she could the torn fragments. She first made out these words, "Love-wounded Protheus"; and lamenting over these and such-like loving words, which she made out though they were all torn asunder, or, she said, *wounded* (the expression "Love-wounded Protheus," giving her that idea), she talked to these kind words, telling them she would lodge them in her bosom as in a bed, till their wounds were healed, and that she would kiss each several piece, to make amends.

In this manner she went on talking with a pretty, lady-like childishness, till finding herself unable to make out the whole, and vext at her own ingratitude in destroying such sweet and loving words, as she called them, she wrote a much kinder letter to Protheus than she had ever done before.

Protheus was greatly delighted at receiving this favourable answer to his letter; and while he was reading it, he exclaimed, "Sweet love, sweet lines, sweet life!" In the midst of his raptures he was interrupted by his father. "How now!" said the old gentleman; "what letter are you reading there?"

"My lord," replied Protheus, "it is a letter from my friend Valentine, at Milan."

"Lend me the letter," said his father; "let me see what news."

"There is no news, my lord," said Protheus, greatly alarmed, "but that he writes how well beloved he is of the duke of Milan, who daily graces him with favours, and how he wishes me with him, the partner of his fortune."

"And how stand you affected to his wish?" asked the father.

"As one relying on your lordship's will, and not depending on his friendly wish," said Protheus.

Now it happened that Protheus' father had just been talking with a friend on this very subject: his friend had said, he wondered his lordship suffered his son to spend his youth at home, while most men were sending their sons to seek preferment abroad. "Some," said he, "to the wars, to try their fortunes there, and some to discover islands far away, and some to study in foreign universities; and there is his companion Valentine, he is gone to the duke of Milan's court. Your son is fit for any of these things, and it will be a great disadvantage to him in his riper age not to have travelled in his youth."

Protheus' father thought the advice of his friend was very good, and upon Protheus telling him that Valentine "wished him with him, the partner of his fortune," he at once determined to send his son to Milan; and without giving Protheus any reason for this sudden resolution, it being the usual habit of this positive old gentleman to command his son, not reason with him, he said: "My will is the same as Valentine's wish"; and seeing his son look astonished, he added, "Look not amazed, that I so suddenly resolve you shall spend some time in the duke of Milan's court; for what I will I will, and there is an end. To-morrow be in readiness to go. Make no excuses; for I am peremptory."

Protheus knew it was of no use to make objections to his father, who never suffered him to dispute his will; and he blamed himself for telling his father an untruth about Julia's letter, which had brought upon him the sad necessity of leaving her.

Now that Julia found she was going to lose Protheus for so long a time, she no longer pretended indifference; and they bade each other a mournful farewel with many vows of love and constancy. Protheus and Julia exchanged rings, which they both promised to keep for ever in remembrance of each other; and thus, taking a sorrowful leave, Protheus set out on his journey to Milan, the abode of his friend, Valentine.

Valentine was in reality what Protheus had feigned to his father, in high favour with the duke of Milan; and another event had happened to him, of which Protheus did not even dream, for Valentine had given up the freedom of which he used so much to boast, and was become as passionate a lover as Protheus.

She who had wrought this wondrous change in Valentine, was the lady Silvia, daughter of the duke of Milan, and she also loved him; but they concealed their love from the duke, because although he showed much kindness for Valentine, and invited him every day to his palace, yet he designed to marry his daughter to a young courtier whose name was Thurio. Silvia despised this Thurio, for he had none of the fine sense and excellent qualities of Valentine.

These two rivals, Thurio and Valentine, were one day on a visit to Silvia, and Valentine was entertaining Silvia with turning every thing Thurio said into ridicule, when the duke himself entered the room, and told Valentine the welcome news of his friend Protheus' arrival. Valentine said, "If I had wished a thing, it would have been to have seen him here!" and then he highly praised Protheus to the duke, saying, "My lord, though I have been a truant of my time, yet hath my friend made use and fair advantage of his days, and is complete in person as in mind, in all good grace to grace a gentleman."

"Welcome him, then, according to his worth," said the duke; "Silvia, I speak to you, and you, sir Thurio; for Valentine, I need not bid him do so." They were here interrupted by the entrance of Protheus, and Valentine introduced him to Silvia, saying, "Sweet lady, entertain him to be my fellow-servant to your ladyship."

When Valentine and Protheus had ended their visit, and were alone together, Valentine said: "Now, tell me how all does from whence you came? How does your lady, and how thrives your love?" Protheus replied, "My tales of love used to weary you. I know you joy not in a love-discourse."

"Aye, Protheus," returned Valentine, "but that life is altered now. I have done penance for condemning love. For in revenge of my contempt of Love, Love has chased sleep from my enthralled eyes. O gentle Protheus, Love is a mighty lord, and hath so humbled me that I confess there is no woe like his correction, nor no such joy on earth as in his service. I now like no discourse except it be of love. Now I can break my fast, dine, sup, and sleep upon the very name of love."

This acknowledgment of the change which love had made in the disposition of Valentine was a great triumph to his friend Protheus. But *"friend"* Protheus must be called no longer, for the same all-powerful deity Love, of whom they were speaking (yea, even while they were talking of the change he had made in Valentine), was working in the heart of Protheus; and he, who had till this time been a pattern of true love and perfect friendship, was now, in one short interview with Silvia, become a false friend and a faithless lover: for at the first sight of Silvia, all his love for Julia vanished away like a dream, nor did his long friendship for Valentine deter him from endeavouring to supplant him in her affections; and although, as it will always be, when people of dispositions naturally good become unjust, he had many scruples, before he determined to forsake Julia, and become the rival of Valentine, yet he at length overcame his sense of duty, and yielded himself up, almost without remorse, to his new unhappy passion.

Valentine imparted to him in confidence the whole history of his love, and how carefully they had concealed it from the duke her father, and told him, that despairing of ever being able to obtain his consent, he had prevailed upon Silvia to leave her father's palace that night, and go with him to Mantua; then he shewed Protheus a ladder of ropes, by help of which he meant to assist Silvia to get out of one of the windows of the palace after it was dark.

Upon hearing this faithful recital of his friend's dearest secrets, it is hardly possible to be believed, but so it was, that Protheus resolved to go to the duke and disclose the whole to him.

This false friend began his tale with many artful speeches to the duke, such, as that by the laws of friendship he ought to conceal what he was going to reveal, but that the gracious favour the duke had shewn him, and the duty he owed his grace, urged him to tell that, which else no wordly good should draw from him: he then told all he had heard from Valentine, not omitting the ladder of ropes, and the manner in which Valentine meant to conceal them under a long cloak.

The duke thought Protheus quite a miracle of integrity, in that he preferred telling his friend's intention rather than he would conceal an unjust action; highly commended him, and promised him not to let Valentine know from whom he had learned this intelligence, but by some artifice to make Valentine betray the secret himself. For this purpose the duke awaited the coming of Valentine in the evening, whom he soon saw hurrying toward the palace, and he perceived somewhat was wrapped within his cloak, which he concluded was the rope-ladder.

The duke upon this stopped him, saying, "Whither away so fast, Valentine?" "May it please your grace," said Valentine, "there is a messenger, that stays to bear my letters to my friends, and I am going to deliver them." Now this falsehood of Valentine's had no better success in the event than the untruth Protheus told his father.

"Be they of much import?" said the duke.

"No more, my lord," said Valentine, "than to tell my father I am well and happy at your grace's court."

"Nay, then," said the duke, "no matter: stay with me a while. I wish your counsel about some affairs that concern me nearly." He then told Valentine an artful story, as a prelude to draw his secret from him, saying, that Valentine knew he wished to match his daughter with Thurio, but that she was stubborn and disobedient to his commands, "neither regarding," said he, "that she is my child, nor fearing me as if I were her father. And I may say to thee, this pride of hers has drawn my love from her. I had thought my age should have been cherished by her childlike duty. I now am resolved to take a wife, and turn her out to whosoever will take her in. Let her beauty be her wedding dower, for me and my possessions she esteems not."

Valentine, wondering where all this would end, made answer, "And what would your grace have me do in all this?"

"Why," said the duke, "the lady I would wish to marry is nice and coy, and does not much esteem my aged eloquence. Besides, the fashion of courtship is much changed since I was young: now I would willingly have you to be my tutor to instruct me how I am to woo."

Valentine gave him a general idea of the modes of courtship then practised by young men, when they wished to win a fair lady's love, such as presents, frequent visits, and the like.

The duke replied to this, that the lady did refuse a present which he sent her, and that she was so strictly kept by her father, that no man might have access to her by day.

"Why, then," said Valentine, "you must visit her by night."

"But at night," said the artful duke, who was now coming to the drift of his discourse, "her doors are fast locked."

Valentine then unfortunately proposed, that the duke should get into the lady's chamber at night by means of a ladder of ropes, saying, he would procure him one fitting for that purpose; and in conclusion advised him to conceal this ladder of ropes under such a cloak as that which he now wore. "Lend me your cloak," said the duke, who had feigned this long story on purpose to have a pretence to get off the cloak: so, upon saying these words, he caught hold of Valentine's cloak, and throwing it back, he discovered not only the ladder of ropes, but also a letter of Silvia's which he instantly opened, and read; and this letter contained a full account of their intended elopement. The duke, after upbraiding Valentine for his ingratitude in thus returning the favour he had shewn him, by endeavouring to steal away his daughter, banished him from the court and city of Milan for ever; and Valentine was forced to depart that night, without even seeing Silvia.

While Protheus at Milan was thus injuring Valentine, Julia at Verona was regretting the absence of Protheus; and her regard for him at last so far overcame her sense of propriety, that she resolved to leave Verona, and seek her lover at Milan; and to secure herself from danger on the road, she dressed her maid Lucetta and herself in men's clothes, and they set out in this disguise, and arrived at Milan, soon after Valentine was banished from that city through the treachery of Protheus.

Julia entered Milan about noon, and she took up her abode at an inn; and her thoughts being all on her dear Protheus, she entered into conversation with the innkeeper, or host, as he was called, thinking by that means to learn some news of Protheus.

The host was greatly pleased that this handsome young gentleman (as he took her to be), who from his appearance, he concluded was of high rank, spoke so familiarly to him; and being a good-natured man, he was sorry to see him look so melancholy; and to amuse his young guest he offered to take him to hear some fine music, with which, he said, a gentleman that evening was going to serenade his mistress.

The reason Julia looked so very melancholy was that she did not well know what Protheus would think of the imprudent step she had taken; for she knew he had loved her for her noble maiden-pride and dignity of character, and she feared she should lower herself in his esteem: and this it was that made her wear a sad and thoughtful countenance.

She gladly accepted the offer of the host to go with him, and hear the music; for she secretly hoped she might meet Protheus by the way.

But when she came to the palace whither the host conducted her, a very different effect was produced to what the kind host intended; for there, to her heart's sorrow, she beheld her lover, the inconstant Protheus, serenading the lady Silvia with music, and addressing discourse of love and admiration to her. And Julia overheard Silvia from a window talk with Protheus, and reproach him for forsaking his own true lady, and for his ingratitude to his friend Valentine: and then Silvia left the window, not choosing to listen to his music and his fine speeches; for she was a faithful lady to her banished Valentine, and abhorred the ungenerous conduct of his false friend Protheus.

Though Julia was in despair at what she had just witnessed, yet did she still love the truant Protheus; and hearing that he had lately parted with a servant, she contrived with the assistance of her host, the friendly innkeeper, to hire herself to Protheus as a page; and Protheus knew not she was Julia, and he sent her with letters and presents to her rival Silvia, and he even sent by her the very ring she gave him as a parting gift at Verona.

When she went to that lady with the ring, she was most glad to find that Silvia utterly rejected the suit of Protheus;

and Julia, or the page Sebastian, as she was called, entered into conversation with Silvia about Protheus' first love, the forsaken lady Julia. She, putting in (as one may say) a good word for herself, said she knew Julia; as well she might, being herself the Julia of whom she spoke: telling how fondly Julia loved her master Protheus, and how his unkind neglect would grieve her: and then she with a pretty equivocation went on: "Julia is about my height, and of my complexion, the colour of her eyes and hair the same as mine"; and indeed Julia looked a most beautiful youth in her boy's attire. Silvia was moved to pity this lovely lady, who was so sadly forsaken by the man she loved; and when Julia offered the ring which Protheus had sent, refused it, saying, "The more shame for him that he sends me that ring; I will not take it, for I have often heard him say his Julia gave it to him. I love thee, gentle youth, for pitying her, poor lady! Here is a purse; I give it you for Julia's sake." These comfortable words coming from her kind rival's tongue cheered the drooping heart of the disguised lady.

But to return to the banished Valentine; who scrace knew which way to bend his course, being unwilling to return home to his father a disgraced and banished man: as he was wandering over a lonely forest, not far distant from Milan, where he had left his heart's dear treasure, the lady Silvia, he was set upon by robbers, who demanded his money.

Valentine told them, that he was a man crossed by adversity, that he was going into banishment, and that he had no money, the clothes he had on being all his riches.

The robbers, hearing that he was a distressed man, and being struck with his noble air and manly behaviour, told him, if he would live with them, and be their chief, or captain, they would put themselves under his command; but that if he refused to accept their offer, they would kill him.

Valentine, who cared little what became of himself, said, he would consent to live with them and be their captain, provided they did no outrage on women or poor passengers.

Thus the noble Valentine became, like Robin Hood, of whom we read in ballads, a captain of robbers and outlawed banditti; and in this situation he was found by Silvia, and in this manner it came to pass.

Silvia, to avoid a marriage with Thurio, whom her father insisted upon her no longer refusing, came at last to the resolution of following Valentine to Mantua, at which place she had heard her lover had taken refuge; but in this account she was misinformed, for he still lived in the forest among the robbers, bearing the name of their captain, but taking no part in their depredations, and using the authority which they had imposed upon him in no other way, than to compel them to shew compassion to the travellers they robbed.

Silvia contrived to effect her escape from her father's palace in company with a worthy old gentleman whose name was Eglamour, whom she took along with her for protection on the road. She had to pass through the forest where Valentine and the banditti dwelt; and one of these robbers seized on Silvia, and would also have taken Eglamour, but he escaped.

The robber who had taken Silvia, seeing the terror she was in, bid her not be alarmed, for that he was only going to carry her to a cave where his captain lived, and that she need not be afraid, for their captain had an honourable mind, and always shewed humanity to women. Silvia found little comfort in hearing she was going to be carried as a prisoner before the captain of a lawless banditti. "O Valentine," she cried, "this I endure for thee!"

But as the robber was conveying her to the cave of his captain he was stopped by Protheus, who, still attended by Julia in the disguise of a page, having heard of the flight of Silvia, had traced her steps to this forest. Protheus now rescued her from the hands of the robber; but scarce had she time to thank him for the service he had done her, before he began to distress her afresh with his love-suit: and while he was rudely pressing her to consent to marry him, and his page (the forlorn Julia) was standing beside them in great anxiety of mind, fearing lest the great service which Protheus had just done to Silvia should win her to shew him some favour, they were all strangely surprised by the sudden appearance of Valentine, who, having heard his robbers had taken a lady prisoner, came to console and relieve her.

Protheus was courting Silvia, and he was so much ashamed of being caught by his friend, that he was all at once seized with penitence and remorse; and he expressed such a lively sorrow for the injuries he had done to Valentine, that Valentine, whose nature was noble and generous, even to a romantic degree, not only forgave and restored him to his former place in his friendship, but in a sudden flight of heroism he said, "I freely do forgive you; and all the interest I have in Silvia, I give it up to you." Julia, who was standing beside her master as a page, hearing this strange offer, and fearing Protheus would not be able, with this new-found virtue to refuse Silvia, fainted, and they were all employed in recovering her: else would Silvia have been offended at being thus made over to Protheus, though she could scarcely think that Valentine would long persevere in this overstrained and too generous act of friendship. When Julia recovered from the fainting fit, she said, "I had forgot, my master ordered me to deliver this ring to Silvia." Protheus, looking upon the ring, saw that it was the one he gave to Julia, in return for that which he received from her, and which he had sent by the supposed page to Silvia. "How is this?" said he, "this is Julia's ring: how came you by it, boy?" Julia answered, "Julia herself did give it me, and Julia herself hath brought it hither."

Protheus, now looking earnestly upon her, plainly perceived that the page Sebastian was no other than the lady Julia herself: and the proof she had given of her constancy and true love so wrought in him, that his love for her returned into his heart, and he took again his own dear lady, and joyfully resigned all pretensions to the lady Silvia to Valentine, who had so well deserved her.

Protheus and Valentine were expressing their happiness in their reconciliation, and in the love of their faithful ladies, when they were surprised by the sight of the duke of Milan and Thurio, who came there in pursuit of Silvia.

Thurio first approached, and attempted to seize Silvia, saying, "Silvia is mine." Upon this Valentine said to him in a very spirited manner, "Thurio, keep back: if once again you say that Silvia is yours, you shall embrace your death. Here she stands, take but possession of her with a touch! I dare you but to breathe upon my love." Hearing this threat, Thurio, who was a great coward, drew back, and said he cared not for her, and that none but a fool would fight for a girl who loved him not.

The duke, who was a very brave man himself, said now in great anger: "The more base and degenerate in you to take such means for her as you have done, and leave her on such slight conditions." Then turning to Valentine, he said, "I do applaud your spirit, Valentine, and think you worthy of an empress's love. You shall have Silvia, for you have well deserved her." Valentine then with great humility kissed the duke's hand, and accepted the noble present which he had made him of his daughter with becoming thankfulness, taking occasion of this joyful minute to entreat the good-humoured duke to pardon the thieves with whom he had associated in the forest, assuring him, that when reformed and restored to society, there would be found among them many good, and fit for great employment; for the most of them had been banished, like Valentine, for state offences rather than for any black crimes they had been guilty of. To this the ready duke consented: and now nothing remained but that Protheus, the false friend, was ordained, by way of penance for his love-prompted faults, to be present at the recital of the whole story of his loves and falsehoods before the duke; and the shame of the recital to his awakened conscience was judged sufficient punishment: which being done, the lovers, all four, returned back to Milan, and their nuptials were solemnized in presence of the duke, with high triumphs and feasting.

The Merchant of Venice

SHYLOCK, the Jew, lived at Venice: he was an usurer, who had amassed an immense fortune by lending money at great interest to Christian merchants. Shylock, being a hard-hearted man, exacted the payment of the money he lent with such severity, that he was much disliked by all good men, and particularly by Anthonio, a young merchant of Venice; and Shylock as much hated Anthonio, because he used to lend money to people in distress, and would never take any interest for the money he lent; therefore there was great enmity between this covetous Jew and the generous merchant Anthonio. Whenever Anthonio met Shylock on the Rialto (or Exchange) he used to reproach him with his usuries and hard dealings; which the Jew would bear with seeming patience, while he secretly meditated revenge.

Anthonio was the kindest man that lived, the best conditioned, and had the most unwearied spirit in doing courtesies; indeed, he was one in whom the ancient Roman honour more appeared than in any that drew breath in Italy. He was greatly beloved by all his fellow-citizens; but the friend who was nearest and dearest to his heart was Bassanio, a noble Venetian, who, having but a small patrimony, had nearly exhausted his little fortune by living in too expensive a manner for his slender means, as young men of high rank with small fortunes are too apt to do. Whenever Bassanio wanted money, Anthonio assisted him; and it seemed as if they had but one heart and one purse between them.

One day Bassanio came to Anthonio, and told him that he wished to repair his fortune by a wealthy marriage with a lady whom he dearly loved, whose father, that was lately dead, had left her sole heiress to a large estate; and that in her father's lifetime he used to visit at her house, when he thought he had observed this lady had sometimes from her eyes sent speechless messages, that seemed to say he would be no unwelcome suitor; but not having money to furnish himself with an appearance befitting the lover of so rich an heiress, he besought Anthonio to add to the many favours he had shown him, by lending him three thousand ducats.

Anthonio had no money by him at that time to lend his friend; but expecting soon to have some ships come home laden with merchandise, he said he would go to Shylock, the rich money-lender, and borrow the money upon the credit of those ships.

Anthonio and Bassanio went together to Shylock, and Anthonio asked the Jew to lend him three thousand ducats upon any interest he should require, to be paid out of the merchandise contained in his ships at sea. On this Shylock thought within himself, "If I can once catch him on the hip,

I will feed fat the ancient grudge I bear him; he hates our Jewish nation; he lends out money gratis; and among the merchants he rails at me and my well-earned bargains, which he calls interest. Cursed be my tribe if I forgive him!" Anthonio, finding he was musing within himself and did not answer, and being impatient for money, said, "Shylock, do you hear? will you lend the money?" To this question the Jew replied, "Signor Anthonio, on the Rialto many a time and often you have railed at me about my monies and my usuries, and I have borne it with a patient shrug, for sufferance is the badge of all our tribe; and then you have called me unbeliever, cut-throat dog, and spit upon my Jewish garments, and spurned at me with your foot, as if I were a cur. Well then, it now appears you need my help; and you come to me, and say, *Shylock, lend me monies*. Has a dog money? Is it possible a cur should lend three thousand ducats? Shall I bend low and say, Fair sir, you spit upon me on Wednesday last, another time you called me dog, and for these courtesies I am to lend you monies?" Anthonio replied, "I am as like to call you so again, to spit on you again, and spurn you too. If you will lend me this money, lend it not to me as to a friend, but rather lend it to me as to an enemy, that, if I break, you may with better face exact the penalty." "Why, look you," said Shylock, "how you storm! I would be friends with you, and have your love. I will forget the shames you have put upon me. I will supply your wants, and take no interest for my money." This seemingly kind offer greatly surprised Anthonio; and then Shylock, still pretending kindness, and that all he did was to gain Anthonio's love, again said he would lend him the three thousand ducats, and take no interest for his money; only Anthonio should go with him to a lawyer, and there sign in merry sport a bond, that if he did not repay the money by a certain day, he would forfeit a pound of flesh, to be cut off from any part of his body that Shylock pleased.

"Content," said Anthonio: "I will sign to this bond, and say there is much kindness in the Jew."

Bassanio said Anthonio should not sign to such a bond for him; and still Anthonio insisted that he would sign it, for that before the day of payment came, his ships would return laden with many times the value of the money.

Shylock, hearing this debate, exclaimed, "O father Abraham, what suspicious people these Christians are! Their own hard dealings teach them to suspect the thoughts of others. I pray you tell me this, Bassanio: if he should break this day, what should I gain by the exaction of the forfeiture? A pound of man's flesh, taken from a man, is not so estimable, nor profitable neither, as the flesh of mutton or of beef. I say, to buy his favour I offer this friendship: if he will take it, so; if not, adieu."

At last, against the advice of Bassanio, who, notwithstanding all the Jew had said of his kind intentions, did not like his friend should run the hazard of this shocking penalty for his sake, Anthonio signed the bond, thinking it really was (as the Jew said) merely in sport.

The rich heiress that Bassanio wished to marry lived near

Venice, at a place called Belmont: her name was Portia, and in the graces of her person and her mind she was nothing inferior to that Portia of whom we read, who was Cato's daughter, and the wife of Brutus.

Bassanio, being so kindly supplied with money by his friend Anthonio at the hazard of his life, set out for Belmont with a splendid train, and attended by a gentleman of the name of Gratiano.

Bassanio proving successful in his suit, Portia in a short time consented to accept of him for a husband.

Bassanio confessed to Portia that he had no fortune, and that his high birth and noble ancestry was all that he could boast of; she, who loved him for his worthy qualities, and had riches enough not to regard wealth in a husband, answered with a graceful modesty, that she would wish herself a thousand times more fair, and ten thousand times more rich, to be more worthy of him; and then the accomplished Portia prettily dispraised herself, and said she was an unlessoned girl, unschooled, unpractised, yet not so old but that she could learn, and that she would commit her gentle spirit to be directed and governed by him in all things; and she said, "Myself, and what is mine, to you and yours is now converted. But yesterday, Bassanio, I was the lady of this fair mansion, queen of myself, and mistress over these servants; and now this house, these servants, and myself are yours, my lord; I give them with this ring," presenting a ring to Bassanio.

Bassanio was so overpowered with gratitude and wonder at the gracious manner in which the rich and noble Portia accepted of a man of his humble fortunes, that he could not express his joy and reverence to the dear lady who so honoured him by anything but broken words of love and thankfulness: and taking the ring, he vowed never to part with it.

Gratiano, and Nerissa, Portia's waiting-maid, were in attendance upon their lord and lady, when Portia so gracefully promised to become the obedient wife of Bassanio; and Gratiano, wishing Bassanio and the generous lady joy, desired permission to be married at the same time.

"With all my heart, Gratiano," said Bassanio, "if you can get a wife."

Gratiano then said that he loved the lady Portia's fair waiting gentlewoman, Nerissa, and that she had promised to be his wife, if her lady married Bassanio. Portia asked Nerissa if this was true. Nerissa replied, "Madam, it is so, if you approve of it." Portia willingly consenting, Bassanio pleasantly said, "Then our wedding feast shall be much honoured by your marriage, Gratiano."

The happiness of these lovers was sadly crossed at this moment by the entrance of a messenger, who brought a letter from Anthonio containing fearful tidings. When Bassanio read Anthonio's letter, Portia feared it was to tell him of the death of some dear friend, he looked so pale; and enquiring what was the news which had so distressed him, he said, "O sweet Portia, here are a few of the unpleasantest words that ever blotted paper: gentle lady, when I first imparted my love to you, I freely told you all the wealth I had ran in my veins; but I should have told you that I had less than nothing, being in debt." Bassanio then told Portia what has been here related, of his borrowing the money of Anthonio, and of Anthonio's procuring it of Shylock the Jew, and of the bond by which Anthonio had engaged to forfeit a pound of flesh, if it was not repaid by a certain day; and then Bassanio read Anthonio's letter, the words of which were, "*Sweet Bassanio, my ships are all lost, my bond to the Jew is forfeited, and since in paying it is impossible I should live, I could wish to see you at my death; notwithstanding use your pleasure; if your love for me do not persuade you to come, let not my letter.*" "Oh my dear love," said Portia, "dispatch all business and be gone; you shall have gold to pay the money twenty times over, before this kind friend shall lose a hair by my Bassanio's fault; and as you are so dearly bought, I will dearly love you." Portia then said she would be married to Bassanio before he set out, to give him a legal right to her money; and that same day they were married, and Gratiano was also married to Nerissa; and Bassanio and Gratiano, the instant they were married, set out in great haste for Venice, where Bassanio found Anthonio in prison.

The day of payment being past, the cruel Jew would not accept of the money which Bassanio offered him, but insisted upon having a pound of Anthonio's flesh. A day was appointed to try this shocking cause before the duke of Venice, and Bassanio awaited in dreadful suspense the event of the trial.

When Portia parted with her husband, she spoke cheeringly to him, and bade him bring his dear friend along with him when he returned; yet she feared it would go hard with Anthonio, and when she was left alone, she began to think and consider within herself, if she could by any means be instrumental in saving the life of her dear Bassanio's friend; and notwithstanding, when she wished to honour her Bassanio, she had said to him with such a meek and wife-like grace, that she would submit in all things to be governed by his superior wisdom, yet being now called forth into action by the peril of her honoured husband's friend, she did nothing doubt her own powers, and by the sole guidance of her own true and perfect judgment, at once resolved to go herself to Venice, and speak in Anthonio's defence.

Portia had a relation who was a counsellor in the law; to this gentleman, whose name was Bellario, she wrote, and stating the case to him, desired his opinion, and that with his advice he would also send her the dress worn by a counsellor. When the messenger returned, he brought letters from Bellario of advice how to proceed, and also every thing necessary for her equipment.

Portia dressed herself and her maid Nerissa in men's apparel, and putting on the robes of a counsellor, she took Nerissa along with her as her clerk; and setting out immediately, they arrived at Venice on the very day of the trial. The cause was just going to be heard before the duke and senators of Venice in the senate-house, when Portia entered this high court of justice, and presented a letter from Bellario, in which that learned counsellor wrote to the duke, saying he would have come himself to plead for Anthonio, but that he was prevented by sickness, and he requested that the learned young doctor Balthasar (so he called Portia) might be permitted to plead in his stead. This the duke granted, much wondering at the youthful appearance of the stranger, who was prettily disguised by her counsellor's robes and her large wig.

And now began this important trial. Portia looked around her, and she saw the merciless Jew; and she saw Bassanio, but he knew her not in her disguise. He was standing beside Anthonio, in an agony of distress and fear for his friend.

The importance of the arduous task Portia had engaged in gave this tender lady courage, and she boldly proceeded in the duty she had undertaken to perform; and first of all she addressed herself to Shylock; and allowing that he had a right by the Venetian law to have the forfeit expressed in the bond, she spoke so sweetly of the noble quality of *mercy*, as would have softened any heart but the unfeeling Shylock's; saying, that it dropped as the gentle rain from heaven upon the place beneath; and how mercy was a double blessing, it blessed him that gave, and him that received it; and how it became monarchs better than their crowns, being an attribute of God himself; and that earthly power came nearest to God's in proportion as mercy tempered justice: and she bid Shylock remember that as we all pray for mercy, that same prayer should teach us to shew mercy. Shylock only answered her by desiring to have the penalty forfeited in the bond. "Is he not able to pay the money?" asked Portia. Bassanio then offered the Jew the payment of the three thousand ducats, as many times over as he should desire; which Shylock refusing, and still insisting upon having a pound of Anthonio's flesh, Bassanio begged the learned young counsellor would endeavour to wrest the law a little, to save Anthonio's life. But Portia gravely answered, that laws once established must never be altered. Shylock hearing Portia say that the law might not be altered, it seemed to him that she was pleading in his favour, and he said, "A Daniel is come to judgment! O wise young judge, how I do honour you! How much elder are you than your looks!"

Portia now desired Shylock to let her look at the bond; and when she had read it, she said, "This bond is forfeited and by this the Jew may lawfully claim a pound of flesh, to be by him cut off nearest Anthonio's heart." Then she said to Shylock, "Be merciful; take the money, and bid me tear the bond." But no mercy would the cruel Shylock shew; and he said, "By my soul I swear, there is no power in the tongue of man to alter me." "Why then, Anthonio," said Portia, "you must prepare your bosom for the knife"; and while Shylock was sharpening a long knife with great eagerness, to cut off the pound of flesh, Portia said to Anthonio, "Have you anything to say?" Anthonio with a calm resignation replied, that he had but little to say, for that he had prepared his mind for death. Then he said to Bassanio, "Give me your hand, Bassanio! Fare you well! Grieve not that I am fallen into this misfortune for you. Commend me to your honourable wife, and tell her how I have loved you!" Bassanio in the deepest affliction replied, "Anthonio, I am married to a wife who is as dear to me as life itself; but life itself, my wife, and all the world, are not esteemed with me above your life: I would lose all, I would sacrifice all to this devil here to deliver you."

Portia hearing this, though the kind-hearted lady was not at all offended with her husband for expressing the love he owed to so true a friend as Anthonio in these strong terms, yet could not help answering, "Your wife would give you little thanks, if she were present, to hear you make this offer." And then Gratiano, who loved to copy what his lord did, thought he must make a speech like Bassanio's, and he said, in Nerissa's hearing, who was writing in her clerk's dress by the side of Portia, "I have a wife, whom I protest I love; I wish she were in heaven, if she could but entreat some power there to change the cruel temper of this currish Jew." "It is well you wish this behind her back, else you would have but an unquiet house," said Nerissa.

Shylock now cried out impatiently, "We trifle time; I pray pronounce the sentence." And now all was awful expectation in the court, and every heart was full of grief for Anthonio.

Portia asked if the scales were ready to weigh the flesh; and she said to the Jew, "Shylock, you must have some surgeon by, lest he bleed to death." Shylock, whose whole intent was that Anthonio should bleed to death, said, "It is not so named in the bond." Portia, replied, "It is not so named in the bond, but what of that? It were good you did so much charity." To this all the answer Shylock would make was, "I cannot find it; it is not in the bond." "Then," said Portia, "a pound of Anthonio's flesh is thine. The law allows it, and the court awards it. And you may cut this flesh from off his breast. The law allows it, and the court awards it." Again Shylock exclaimed, "O wise and upright judge! A Daniel is come to judgment!" And then he sharpened his long knife again, and looking eagerly on Anthonio, he said, "Come, prepare!"

"Tarry a little, Jew," said Portia; "there is something else. This bond here gives you no drop of blood; the words expressly are, 'a pound of flesh.' If in the cutting of the pound of flesh you shed one drop of Christian blood, your land and goods are by the law to be confiscated to the State of Venice." Now as it was utterly impossible for Shylock to cut off the pound of flesh without shedding some of Anthonio's blood, this wise discovery of Portia, that it was flesh and not blood that was named in the bond, saved the life of Anthonio; and all admiring the wonderful sagacity of the young counsellor who had so happily thought of this expedient, plaudits resounded from every part of the senate-house; and Gratiano exclaimed, in the words which Shylock had used, "O wise and upright judge! mark, Jew, a Daniel is come to judgment!"

Shylock, finding himself defeated in his cruel intent, said with a disappointed look, that he would take the money; and Bassanio, rejoiced beyond measure at Anthonio's unexpected deliverance, cried out, "Here is the money!" But Portia stopped him, saying, "Softly; there is no haste; the Jew shall have nothing but the penalty: therefore prepare, Shylock, to cut off the flesh; but mind you shed no blood; nor do not cut off more nor less than just a pound; be it more or less by one poor scruple, nay if the scale turn but by the weight of a single hair, you are condemned by the laws of Venice to die, and all your wealth is forfeited to the senate." "Give me my money, and let me go," said Shylock. "I have it ready," said Bassanio; "here it is."

Shylock was going to take the money, when Portia again stopped him, saying, "Tarry, Jew; I have yet another hold upon you. By the laws of Venice, your wealth is forfeited to the State, for having conspired against the life of one of its citizens, and your life lies at the mercy of the duke; therefore down on your knees, and ask him to pardon you."

The duke then said to Shylock, "That you may see the difference of our Christian spirit, I pardon you your life before you ask it; half your wealth belongs to Anthonio, the other half comes to the State."

The generous Anthonio then said that he would give up his share of Shylock's wealth, if Shylock would sign a deed to make it over at his death to his daughter and her husband; for Anthonio knew that the Jew had an only daughter, who had lately married against his consent to a young Christian, named Lorenzo, a friend of Anthonio's, which had so offended Shylock, that he had disinherited her.

The Jew agreed to this: and being thus disappointed in his revenge, and despoiled of his riches, he said, "I am ill. Let me go home: send the deed after me, and I will sign over half my riches to my daughter." "Get thee gone, then," said the duke, "and sign it; and if you repent your cruelty and turn Christian, the State will forgive you the fine of the other half of your riches."

The duke now released Anthonio, and dismissed the court. He then highly praised the wisdom and ingenuity of the young counsellor, and invited him home to dinner. Portia, who meant to return to Belmont before her husband, replied, "I humbly thank your grace, but I must away directly." The duke said he was sorry he had not leisure to stay and dine with him; and turning to Anthonio, he added, "Reward this gentleman; for in my mind you are much indebted to him."

The duke and his senators left the court; and then Bassanio said to Portia, "Most worthy gentleman, I and my friend Anthonio have by your wisdom been this day acquitted of grievous penalties, and I beg you will accept of three thousand ducats due unto the Jew." "And we shall stand indebted to you over and above," said Anthonio, "in love and service evermore."

Portia could not be prevailed upon to accept the money; but upon Bassanio still pressing her to accept of some reward, she said, "Give me your gloves; I will wear them for your sake"; and then Bassanio taking off his gloves, she espied the ring which she had given him upon his finger: now it was the ring the wily lady wanted to get from him, to make a merry jest when she saw Bassanio again, that made her ask him for his gloves; and she said, when she saw the ring, "And for your love I will take this ring from you." Bassanio was sadly

BVT·SCREW·YOVR·COVRAGE·TO·THE·STICKING·PLACE·AND·WE·LL·NOT·FAIL

Macbeth—Tale the Tenth

WHAT—NO·MAN·AT·DOOR·TO·HOLD·MY·STIRRVP·NOR·TO·TAKE·MY·HORSE

The Taming of the Shrew—Tale the Twelfth

distressed, that the counsellor should ask him for the only thing he could not part with, and he replied in great confusion, that he could not give him that ring, because it was his wife's gift, and he had vowed never to part with it; but that he would give him the most valuable ring in Venice, and find it out by proclamation. On this Portia affected to be affronted, and left the court, saying, "You teach me, sir, how a beggar should be answered."

"Dear Bassanio," said Anthonio, "let him have the ring; let my love and the great service he has done for me be valued against your wife's displeasure." Bassanio, ashamed to appear so ungrateful, yielded, and sent Gratiano after Portia, with the ring; and then the *clerk* Nerissa, who had also given Gratiano a ring, she begged his ring, and Gratiano (not choosing to be outdone in generosity by his lord) gave it to her. And there was laughing among these ladies, to think, when they got home, how they would tax their husbands with giving away their rings, and swear that they had given them as a present to some woman.

Portia, when she returned, was in that happy temper of mind which never fails to attend the consciousness of having performed a good action; her cheerful spirit enjoyed everything she saw: the moon never seemed to shine so bright before; and when that pleasant moon was hid behind a cloud, then a light which she saw from her house at Belmont as well pleased her charmed fancy, and she said to Nerissa, "That light we see is burning in my hall; how far that little candle throws its beams; so shines a good deed in a naughty world":

and hearing the sound of music from her house, she said, "Methinks that music sounds sweeter than by day."

And now Portia and Nerissa entered the house, and dressing themselves in their own apparel, they awaited the arrival of their husbands, who soon followed them with Anthonio; and Bassanio presenting his dear friend to the lady Portia, the congratulations and welcomings of that lady were hardly over, when they perceived Nerissa and her husband quarrelling in a corner of the room. "A quarrel already?" said Portia. "What is the matter?" Gratiano replied, "Lady, it is about a paltry ring that Nerissa gave me, with words upon it like the poetry on a cutler's knife: *Love me, and leave me not.*"

"What does the poetry or the value of the ring signify?" said Nerissa. "You swore to me, when I gave it to you, that you would keep it till the hour of death; and now you say you gave it to the lawyer's clerk. I know you gave it to a woman." "By this hand," replied Gratiano, "I gave it to a youth, a kind of boy, a little scrubbed boy no higher than yourself; he was clerk to the young counsellor that by his wise pleading saved Anthonio's life: this prating boy begged it for a fee, and I could not for my life deny him." Portia said, "You were to blame, Gratiano, to part with your wife's first gift. I gave my Lord Bassanio a ring, and I am sure he would not part with it for all the world." Gratiano in excuse for his fault now said, "My Lord Bassanio gave his ring away to the counsellor, and then the boy, his clerk, that took some pains in writing, he begged my ring."

Portia, hearing this, seemed very angry, and reproached

Bassanio for giving away her ring; and she said Nerissa had taught her what to believe, and that she knew some woman had the ring. Bassanio was very unhappy to have so offended his dear lady, and he said with great earnestness, "No, by my honour, no woman had it, but a civil doctor, who refused three thousand ducats of me, and begged the ring, which when I denied him, he went displeased away. What could I do, sweet Portia? I was so beset with shame for my seeming ingratitude, that I was forced to send the ring after him. Pardon me, good lady; had you been there, I think you would have begged the ring of me to give the worthy doctor."

"Ah!" said Anthonio, "I am the unhappy cause of these quarrels."

Portia bid Anthonio not to grieve at that, for that he was welcome notwithstanding; and then Anthonio said, "I once did lend my body for Bassanio's sake; and but for him to whom your husband gave the ring, I should have now been dead. I dare be bound again, my soul upon the forfeit, your lord will never more break his faith with you." "Then you shall be his surety," said Portia; "give him this ring, and bid him keep it better than the other."

When Bassanio looked at this ring, he was strangely surprised to find it was the same he gave away; and then Portia told him, how she was the young counsellor, and Nerissa was her clerk; and Bassanio found, to his unspeakable wonder and delight, that it was by the noble courage and wisdom of his wife that Anthonio's life was saved.

And Portia again welcomed Anthonio, and gave him letters

which by some chance had fallen into her hands, which contained an account of Anthonio's ships, that were supposed lost, being safely arrived in the harbour. So these tragical beginnings of this rich merchant's story were all forgotten in the unexpected good fortune which ensued; and there was leisure to laugh at the comical adventure of the rings, and the husbands that did not know their own wives: Gratiano merrily swearing, in a sort of rhyming speech, that

> "———while he lived, he'd fear no other thing
> So sore, as keeping safe Nerissa's ring."

Tale the Eighth

Cymbeline

DURING the time of Augustus Cæsar, emperor of Rome, there reigned in England (which was then called Britain) a king whose name was Cymbeline.

Cymbeline's first wife died when his three children (two sons and a daughter) were very young. Imogen, the eldest of these children, was brought up in her father's court, but by a strange chance the two sons of Cymbeline were stolen out of their nursery when the eldest was but three years of age, and the youngest quite an infant: and Cymbeline could never discover what was become of them, or by whom they were conveyed away.

Cymbeline was twice married; his second wife was a

wicked, plotting woman, and a cruel stepmother to Imogen, Cymbeline's daughter by his first wife.

The queen, though she hated Imogen, yet wished her to marry a son of her own by a former husband (she also having been twice married): for by this means she hoped upon the death of Cymbeline to place the crown of Britain upon the head of her son Cloten; for she knew that, if the king's sons were not found, the princess Imogen must be the king's heir. But this design was prevented by Imogen herself, who married without the consent or even knowledge of her father or the queen.

Posthumus (for that was the name of Imogen's husband) was the best scholar and most accomplished gentleman of that age. His father died fighting in the wars for Cymbeline, and soon after his birth his mother died also for grief at the loss of her husband.

Cymbeline, pitying the helpless state of this orphan, took Posthumus (Cymbeline having given him that name because he was born after his father's death), and educated him in his own court.

Imogen and Posthumus were both taught by the same masters, and were play-fellows from their infancy: they loved each other tenderly when they were children, and their affection continuing to increase with their years, when they grew up they privately married.

The disappointed queen soon learnt this secret, for she kept spies constantly in watch upon the actions of her daughter-in-law, and she immediately told the king of the marriage of Imogen with Posthumus.

Nothing could exceed the wrath of Cymbeline, when he heard that his daughter had been so forgetful of her high dignity as to marry a subject. He commanded Posthumus to leave Britain, and banished him from his native country for ever.

The queen, who pretended to pity Imogen for the grief she suffered at losing her husband, offered to procure them a private meeting, before Posthumus set out on his journey to Rome, which place he had chosen for his residence in his banishment: This seeming kindness she shewed, the better to succeed in her future designs in regard to her son Cloten; for she meant to persuade Imogen, when her husband was gone, that her marriage was not lawful, being contracted without the consent of the king.

Imogen and Posthumus took a most affectionate leave of each other. Imogen gave her husband a diamond ring which had been her mother's, and Posthumus promised never to part with the ring; and he fastened a bracelet on the arm of his wife, which he begged she would preserve with great care, as a token of his love: They then bid each other farewel, with many vows of everlasting love and fidelity.

Imogen remained a solitary and dejected lady in her father's court, and Posthumus arrived at Rome, the place of his banishment.

Posthumus fell into company at Rome with some gay young men of different nations, who were talking freely of ladies: each one praising the ladies of his own country and his own mistress. Posthumus, who had ever his own dear lady in his mind, affirmed that his wife, the fair Imogen, was the most virtuous, wise, and constant lady in the world.

One of these gentlemen, whose name was Iachimo, being offended that a lady of Britain should be so praised above the Roman ladies, his countrywomen, provoked Posthumus by seeming to doubt the constancy of his so highly-praised wife: and at length, after much altercation, Posthumus consented to a proposal of Iachimo's, that he (Iachimo) should go to Britain, and endeavour to gain the love of the married Imogen. They then laid a wager, that if Iachimo did not succeed in this wicked design, he was to forfeit a large sum of money; but if he could win Imogen's favour, and prevail upon her to give him the bracelet which Posthumus had so earnestly desired she would keep as a token of his love, then the wager was to terminate with Posthumus giving to Iachimo the ring which was Imogen's love-present when she parted with her husband. Such firm faith had Posthumus in the fidelity of Imogen, that he thought he ran no hazard in this trial of her honour.

Iachimo, on his arrival in Britain, gained admittance and a courteous welcome from Imogen, as a friend of her husband; but when he began to make professions of love to her, she repulsed him with disdain, and he soon found that he could have no hope of succeeding in his dishonourable design.

The desire Iachimo had to win the wager made him now have recourse to a stratagem to impose upon Posthumus, and for this purpose he bribed some of Imogen's attendants and was by them conveyed into her bedchamber, concealed in a large trunk, where he remained shut up till Imogen was retired to rest, and had fallen asleep; and then getting out of the trunk, he examined the chamber with great attention, and wrote down everything he saw there, and particularly noticed a mole which he observed upon Imogen's neck, and then softly unloosing the bracelet from her arm, which Posthumus had given to her, he retired into the chest again; and the next day he set off for Rome with great expedition, and boasted to Posthumus that Imogen had given him the bracelet, and likewise permitted him to pass a night in her chamber: and in this manner Iachimo told his false tale; "Her bedchamber," said he, "was hung with tapestry of silk and silver, the story was *the proud Cleopatra when she met her Antony*, a piece of work most bravely wrought."

"This is true," said Posthumus; "but this you might have heard spoken of without seeing."

"Then the chimney," said Iachimo, "is south of the chamber, and the chimney-piece is *Diana bathing;* never saw I figures livelier expressed."

"This is a thing you might have likewise heard," said Posthumus, "for it is much talked of."

Iachimo as accurately described the roof of the chamber, and added, "I had almost forgot her andirons, they were *two winking Cupids* made of silver, each on one foot standing." He then took out the bracelet, and said, "Know you this jewel, sir? She gave me this. She took it from her arm. I see her yet; her pretty action did out-sell her gift, and yet enriched it, too. She gave it me, and said, *she prized it once.*"

He last of all described the mole he had observed upon her neck.

Posthumus, who had heard the whole of this artful recital in an agony of doubt, now broke out into the most passionate exclamations against Imogen. He delivered up the diamond ring to Iachimo, which he had agreed to forfeit to him, if he obtained the bracelet from Imogen.

Posthumus then, in a jealous rage wrote to Pisanio, a gentleman of Britain, who was one of Imogen's attendants, and had long been a faithful friend to Posthumus; and after telling him what proof he had of his wife's disloyalty, he desired Pisanio would take Imogen to Milford-Haven, a seaport of Wales, and there kill her. And at the same time he wrote a deceitful letter to Imogen, desiring her to go with Pisanio, for that finding he could live no longer without seeing her, though he was forbidden, upon pain of death to return to Britain, he would come to Milford-Haven, at which place he begged she would meet him. She, good, unsuspecting lady, who loved her husband above all things, and desired more than her life to see him, hastened her departure with Pisanio, and the same night she received the letter she set out.

When their journey was nearly at an end, Pisanio, who, though faithful to Posthumus, was not faithful to serve him in an evil deed, disclosed to Imogen the cruel order he had received.

Imogen, who, instead of meeting a loving and beloved husband, found herself doomed by that husband to suffer death, was afflicted beyond measure.

Pisanio persuaded her to take comfort, and wait with patient fortitude for the time when Posthumus should see and repent his injustice: in the meantime, as she refused in her distress to return to her father's court, he advised her to dress herself in boy's clothes for more security in travelling; to which advice she agreed, and thought in that disguise she would go over to Rome and see her husband, whom, though he had used her so barbarously, she could not forget to love.

When Pisanio had provided her with her new apparel, he left her to her uncertain fortune, being obliged to return to court; but before he departed he gave her a shial of cordial, which he said the queen had given him as a sovereign remedy in all disorders.

The queen, who hated Pisanio because he was a friend to Imogen and Posthumus, gave him this shial, which she supposed contained poison, she having ordered her physician to give her some poison, to try its effects (as she said) upon animals. But the physician, knowing her malicious disposition, would not trust her with real poison, but gave her a drug which would do no other mischief than causing a person to sleep with every appearance of death for a few hours. This mixture, which Pisanio thought a choice cordial, he gave to Imogen, desiring her, if she found herself ill upon the road, to take it; and so with blessings and prayers for her safety and happy deliverance from her undeserved troubles he left her.

Providence strangely directed Imogen's steps to the dwelling of her two brothers, who had been stolen away in their infancy. Bellarius, who stole them away, was a lord in the court of Cymbeline, and having been falsely accused to the king of treason, and banished from the court, in revenge he stole away the two sons of Cymbeline, and brought them up in a forest, where he lived concealed in a cave. He stole them through revenge, but he soon loved them as tenderly as if they had been his own children, educated them carefully, and they grew up fine youths, their princely spirits leading them to bold and daring actions, and as they subsisted by hunting, they were active and hardy, and were always pressing their supposed father to let them seek their fortune in the wars.

At the cave where these youths dwelt, it was Imogen's fortune to arrive. She had lost her way in a large forest through which her road lay to Milford-Haven (from whence she meant to embark for Rome), and being unable to find any place where she could purchase food, she was with weariness and hunger almost dying; for it is not merely putting on a man's apparel that will enable a young lady, tenderly brought up, to bear the fatigue of wandering about lonely forests like a man. Seeing this cave she entered, hoping to find some one within of whom she could procure food. She found the cave empty, but looking about she discovered some cold meat, and her hunger was so pressing, that she could not wait for an invitation, but sat down and began to eat. "Ah!" said she, talking to herself, "I see a man's life is a tedious one; how tired am I! for two nights together I have made the ground my bed; my resolution helps me, or I should be sick. When Pisanio shewed me Milford-Haven from the mountain-top, how near it seemed!" Then the thoughts of her husband

and his cruel mandate came across her, and she said, "My dear Posthumus, thou art a false one."

The two brothers of Imogen, who had been hunting with their reputed father, Bellarius, were by this time returned home. Bellarius had given them the names of Polidore and Cadwal, and they knew no better, but supposed that Bellarius was their father; but the real names of these princes were Guiderius and Arviragus.

Bellarius entered the cave first, and seeing Imogen, stopped them, saying, "Come not in yet; it eats our victuals, or I should think that it was a fairy."

"What is the matter, sir?" said the young men.

"By Jupiter," said Bellarius again, "there is an angel in the cave, or if not, an earthly paragon." So beautiful did Imogen look in her boy's apparel.

She, hearing the sound of voices, came forth from the cave, and addressed them in these words: "Good masters, do not harm me; before I entered your cave I had thought to have begged or bought what I have eaten. Indeed, I have stolen nothing, nor would I, though I had found gold strewed on the floor. Here is money for my meat, which I would have left on the board when I had made my meal, and parted with prayers for the provider." They refused her money with great earnestness. "I see you are angry with me," said the timid Imogen: "but, sirs, if you kill me for my fault, know that I should have died if I had not made it."

"Whither are you bound?" asked Bellarius, "and what is your name?"

"Fidele is my name," answered Imogen. "I have a kins-man who is bound for Italy: he embarked at Milford-Haven; to whom being going, almost spent with hunger, I am fallen into this offence."

"Prithee, fair youth," said old Bellarius, "do not think us churls, nor measure our good minds by this rude place we live in. You are well encountered; it is almost night. You shall have better cheer before you depart, and thanks to stay and eat it. Boys, bid him welcome."

The gentle youths, her brothers, then welcomed Imogen to their cave with many kind expressions, saying they would love her (or, as they said, *him*) as a brother; and they entered the cave, where (they having killed venison when they were hunting) Imogen delighted them with her neat housewifery, assisting them in preparing their supper; for though it is not the custom now for young women of high birth to understand cookery, it was then, and Imogen excelled in this useful art; and, as her brothers prettily expressed it, Fidele cut their roots in characters, and sauced their broth as if Juno had been sick, and Fidele were her dieter. "And then," said Polidore to his brother, "how angel-like he sings!"

They also remarked to each other, that though Fidele smiled so sweetly, yet so sad a melancholy did overcloud his lovely face, as if grief and patience had together taken pos-session of him.

For these her gentle qualities (or perhaps it was their near relationship, though they knew it not) Imogen (or, as the boys called her, *Fidele*) became the doating-piece of her brothers, and she scarcely less loved them, thinking that but for the memory of her dear Posthumus, she could live and die in the cave with these wild forest youths; and she gladly consented to stay with them, till she was enough rested from the fatigue of travelling to pursue her way to Milford-Haven.

When the venison they had taken was all eaten, and they were going out to hunt for more, Fidele could not accompany them, because she was unwell. Sorrow, no doubt, for her husband's cruel usage, as well as the fatigue of wandering in the forest, was the cause of her illness.

They then bid her farewel, and went to their hunt, praising all the way the noble parts and graceful demeanour of the youth Fidele.

Imogen was no sooner left alone than she recollected the cordial Pisanio had given her, and drank it off, and presently fell into a sound and dead-like sleep.

When Bellarius and her brothers returned from hunting, Polidore went first into the cave, and supposing her asleep, pulled off his heavy shoes, that he might tread softly and not awake her; so did true gentleness spring up in the minds of these princely foresters: but he soon discovered that she could not be awakened by any noise, and concluded her to be dead, and Polidore lamented over her with dear and brotherly regret, as if they had never from their infancy been parted.

Bellarius also proposed to carry her out into the forest, and there celebrate her funeral with songs and solemn dirges, as was then the custom.

Imogen's two brothers then carried her to a shady covert,

and there laying her gently on the grass, they sang repose to her departed spirit, and covering her over with leaves and flowers, Polidore said, "While summer lasts and I live here, Fidele, I will daily strew thy sad grave. The pale primrose, that flower most like thy face; the bluebell, like thy clear veins; and the leaf of eglantine, which is not sweeter than was thy breath: all these I will strew over thee. Yea, and the furred moss in winter, when there are no flowers to cover thy sweet corse."

When they had finished her funeral obsequies, they departed very sorrowful.

Imogen had not been long left alone, when, the effect of the sleepy drug going off, she awakened, and easily shaking off the slight covering of leaves and flowers they had thrown over her, she arose, and imagining she had been dreaming, she said, "I thought I was a cave-keeper, and cook to honest creatures; how came I here, covered with flowers?" Not being able to find her way back to the cave, and seeing nothing of her new companions, she concluded it was certainly all a dream; and once more Imogen set out on her weary pilgrimage, hoping at last she should find her way to Milford-Haven, and thence get a passage in some ship bound for Italy; for all her thoughts were still with her husband Posthumus, whom she intended to seek in the disguise of a page.

But great events were happening at this time, of which Imogen knew nothing; for a war had suddenly broken out between the Roman emperor Augustus Cæsar, and Cymbeline the king of Britain: and a Roman army had landed to invade

Britain, and was advanced into the very forest over which Imogen was journeying. With this army came Posthumus.

Though Posthumus came over to Britain with the Roman army, he did not mean to fight on their side against his own countrymen, but intended to join the army of Britain, and fight in the cause of his king who had banished him.

He still believed Imogen false to him; yet the death of her he had so fondly loved, and by his own orders, too (Pisanio having written him a letter to say he had obeyed his command, and that Imogen was dead) sat heavy on his heart, and therefore he returned to Britain, desiring either to be slain in battle, or to be put to death by Cymbeline for returning home from banishment.

Imogen, before she reached Milford-Haven, fell into the hands of the Roman army; and her presence and deportment recommending her, she was made a page to Lucius, the Roman general.

Cymbeline's army now advanced to meet the enemy, and when they entered this forest, Polidore and Cadwal joined the king's army. The young men were eager to engage in acts of valour, though they little thought they were going to fight for their own royal father; and old Bellarius went with them to the battle. He had long since repented of the injury he had done to Cymbeline in carrying away his sons; and having been a warrior in his youth, he gladly joined the army to fight for the king he had so injured.

And now a great battle commenced between the armies, and the Britons would have been defeated, and Cymbeline himself killed, but for the extraordinary valour of Posthumus, and Bellarius, and the two sons of Cymbeline. They rescued the king, and saved his life, and so entirely turned the fortune of the day, that the Britons gained the victory.

When the battle was over, Posthumus, who had not found the death he sought for, surrendered himself up to one of the officers of Cymbeline, willing to suffer the death which was to be his punishment if he returned from banishment.

Imogen and the master she served were taken prisoners, and brought before Cymbeline, as was also her old enemy Iachimo, who was an officer in the Roman army; and when these prisoners were before the king, Posthumus was brought in to receive his sentence of death; and at this strange juncture of time, Bellarius with Polidore and Cadwal were also brought before Cymbeline, to receive the rewards due to the great services they had by their valour done for the king. Pisanio, being one of the king's attendants, was likewise present.

Therefore there was now standing in the king's presence (but with very different hopes and fears) Posthumus, and Imogen, with her new master the Roman general; the faithful servant Pisanio, and the false friend Iachimo; and likewise the two lost sons of Cymbeline, with Bellarius who had stolen them away.

The Roman general was the first who spoke; the rest stood silent before the king, though there was many a beating heart amongst them.

Imogen saw Posthumus and knew him, though he was in the disguise of a peasant; but he did not know her in her male attire: and she knew Iachimo, and she saw a ring on his finger which she perceived to be her own, but she did not know him as yet to have been the author of all her troubles: and she stood before her own father a prisoner of war.

Pisanio knew Imogen, for it was he who had dressed her in the garb of a boy. "It is my mistress," thought he; "since she is living, let the time run on to good or bad." Bellarius knew her too, and softly said to Cadwal, "Is not this boy revived from death?" "One sand," replied Cadwal, "does not more resemble another than that sweet rosy lad is like the dead Fidele." "The same dead thing alive," said Polidore. "Peace, peace," said Bellarius; "if it were he, I am sure he would have spoken to us." "But we saw him dead," again whispered Polidore. "Be silent," replied Bellarius.

Posthumus waited in silence to hear the welcome sentence of his own death; and he resolved not to disclose to the king that he had saved his life in the battle, lest that should move Cymbeline to pardon him.

Lucius, the Roman general, who had taken Imogen under his protection as his page, was the first (as has been before said) who spoke to the king. He was a man of high courage, and noble dignity, and this was his speech to the king:

"I hear you take no ransom for your prisoners, but doom them all to death; I am a Roman, and with a Roman heart will suffer death. But there is one thing for which I would entreat." Then bringing Imogen before the king, he said, "This boy is a Briton born. Let him be ransomed. He is my page. Never master had a page so kind, so duteous, so diligent on all occasions, so true, so nurse-like. He hath done no Briton wrong, though he hath served a Roman. Save him, if you spare no one besides."

Cymbeline looked earnestly on his daughter Imogen.

He knew her not in that disguise; but it seemed that all-powerful nature spake in his heart, for he said, "I have surely seen him, his face appears familiar to me. I know not why or wherefore I say, Live, boy; but I give you your life, and ask of me what boon you will, and I will grant it you. Yea, even though it be the life of the noblest prisoner I have."

"I humbly thank your highness," said Imogen.

What was then called granting a boon was the same as a promise to give any one thing, whatever it might be, that the person on whom that favour was conferred chose to ask for. They all were attentive to hear what thing the page would ask for, and Lucius her master said to her, "I do not beg my life, good lad, but I know that is what you will ask for." "No, no, alas!" said Imogen, "I have other work in hand, good master; your life I cannot ask for."

This seeming want of gratitude in the boy astonished the Roman general.

Imogen then fixing her eye on Iachimo, demanded no other boon than this, that Iachimo should be made to confess when he had the ring he wore on his finger.

Cymbeline granted her this boon, and threatened Iachimo with the torture if he did not confess how he came by the diamond ring on his finger.

Iachimo then made a full acknowledgment of all his villainy, telling, as has been before related, the whole story of his wager with Posthumus, and how he had succeeded in imposing upon his credulity.

What Posthumus felt at hearing this proof of the innocence of his lady cannot be expressed. He instantly came forward, and confessed to Cymbeline the cruel sentence which he had enjoined Pisanio to execute upon the princess: exclaiming wildly, "O Imogen, my queen, my life, my wife! O Imogen, Imogen, Imogen!"

Imogen could not see her beloved husband in this distress without discovering herself, to the unutterable joy of Posthumus, who was thus relieved from a weight of guilt and woe, and restored to the good graces of the dear lady he had so cruelly treated.

Cymbeline, almost as much overwhelmed as he with joy at finding his lost daughter so strangely recovered, received her to her former place in his fatherly affection, and not only gave her husband Posthumus his life, but consented to acknowledge him for his son-in-law.

Bellarius chose this time of joy and reconciliation to make his confession. He presented Polidore and Cadwal to the king, telling him they were his two lost sons Guiderius and Arviragus.

Cymbeline forgave old Bellarius; for who could think of punishment at a season of such universal happiness: To find his daughter living, and his lost sons in the persons of his young deliverers, that he had seen so bravely fight in his defence, was unlooked-for joy indeed!

Imogen was now at leisure to perform good services for her late master, the Roman general, Lucius, whose life the king her father readily granted at her request; and by the mediation of the same Lucius a peace was concluded between the Romans and the Britons, which was kept inviolate many years.

How Cymbeline's wicked queen, through despair of bringing her projects to pass, and touched with remorse of conscience, sickened and died, having first lived to see her foolish son Cloten slain in a quarrel which he had provoked, are events too tragical to interrupt this happy conclusion by more than merely touching upon. It is sufficient that all were made happy, who were deserving; and even the treacherous Iachimo, in consideration of his villainy having missed its final aim, was dismissed without punishment.

Tale the Ninth

King Lear

LEAR, king of Britain, had three daughters; Gonerill, wife to the duke of Albany; Regan, wife to the duke of Cornwall; and Cordelia, a young maid, for whose love the king of France and duke of Burgundy were joint suitors, and were at this time making stay for that purpose in the court of Lear.

The old king, worn out with age and the fatigues of government, he being more than fourscore years old, determined to take no further part in state affairs, but to leave the management to younger strengths, that he might have time to prepare for death, which must at no long period ensue. With this intent he called his three daughters to him, to know from their own lips which of them loved him best, that he might part his kingdom among them in such proportions as their affection for him should seem to deserve.

Gonerill, the eldest, declared that she loved her father more than words could give out, that he was dearer to her than the light of her own eyes, dearer than life and liberty, with a deal of such professing stuff, which is easy to counterfeit where there is no real love, only a few fine words delivered with confidence being wanted in that case. The king, delighted to hear from her own mouth this assurance of her love, and thinking truly that her heart went with it, in a fit of fatherly fondness bestowed upon her and her husband one third of his ample kingdom.

Then calling to him his second daughter, he demanded what she had to say. Regan, who was made of the same hollow metal as her sister, was not a whit behind in her professions, but rather declared that what her sister had spoken came short of the love which she professed to bear for his highness: insomuch that she found all other joys dead, in comparison with the pleasure which she took in the love of her dear king and father.

Lear blest himself in having such loving children, as he thought; and could do no less, after the handsome assurances which Regan had made, than bestow a third of his kingdom upon her and her husband, equal in size to that which he had already given away to Gonerill.

Then turning to his youngest daughter Cordelia, whom he called his joy, he asked what she had to say; thinking, no doubt that she would glad his ears with the same loving speeches which her sisters had uttered, or rather that her expressions would be so much stronger than theirs, as she had always been his darling, and favoured by him above either of them. But Cordelia, disgusted with the flattery of her sisters, whose hearts she knew were far from their lips, and seeing that all their coaxing speeches were only intended to wheedle the old king out of his dominions, that they and their husbands might reign in his lifetime, made no other reply but this, that she loved his majesty according to her duty, neither more nor less.

The king, shocked with this appearance of ingratitude in his favourite child, desired her to consider her words, and to mend her speech, lest it should mar her fortunes.

Cordelia then told her father, that he was her father, that he had given her breeding, and loved her, that she returned those duties back as was most fit, and did obey him, love him, and most honour him. But that she could not frame her mouth to such large speeches as her sisters had done, or promise to love nothing else in the world. Why had her sisters husbands, if (as they said) they had no love for anything but their father? If she should ever wed, she was sure the lord to whom she gave her hand would want half her love, half of her care and duty; she should never marry like her sisters, to love her father all.

Cordelia, who in earnest loved her old father even almost as extravagantly as her sisters pretended to do, would have plainly told him so at any other time, in more daughter-like and loving terms, and without these qualifications, which did indeed sound a little ungracious: but after the crafty flattering speeches of her sisters, which she had seen could draw such extravagant rewards, she thought the handsomest thing she could do was to love and be silent. This put her affection out of suspicion of mercenary ends, and shewed that she loved, but not for gain; and that her professions, the less ostentatious they were, had so much the more of truth and sincerity than her sisters'.

This plainness of speech, which Lear called pride, so enraged the old monarch—who in his best of times always shewed much of spleen and rashness, and in whom the doatage incident to old age had so clouded over his reason, that he could not discern truth from flattery, nor a gay painted speech from words that came from the heart— that in a fury of resentment he retracted the third part of his kingdom which yet remained, and which he had reserved for Cordelia, and gave it away from her, sharing it equally between her two sisters and their husbands, the dukes of Albany and Cornwall: whom he now called to him, and in presence of all his courtiers, bestowing a coronet between them, invested them jointly with all the power, revenue, and execution of government, only retaining to himself the name of king; all the rest of royalty he resigned: with this reservation, that himself, with a hundred knights for his attendants, was to be maintained by monthly course in each of his daughter's palaces in turn.

So preposterous a disposal of his kingdom, so little guided by reason, and so much by passion, filled all his courtiers with astonishment and sorrow; but none of them had the courage to interpose between this incensed king and his wrath, except the earl of Kent, who was beginning to speak a good word for Cordelia, when the passionate Lear on pain of death commanded him to desist: but the good Kent was not so to be repelled. He had been ever loyal to Lear, whom he had honoured as a king, loved as a father, followed as a master: and had never esteemed his life further than as a pawn to wage against his royal master's enemies, nor feared to lose it when Lear's safety was the motive: nor now that Lear was most his own enemy did this faithful servant of the king forget his old principles, but manfully opposed Lear, to do Lear good; and was unmannerly only because Lear was mad. He had been a most faithful counsellor, in times past to the king, and he besought him now, that he would see with his eyes (as he had done in many weighty matters), and go by his advice still; and in his best consideration recall this hideous rashness: for he would answer with his life his judgment, that Lear's youngest daughter did not love him least, nor were those empty-hearted whose low sound gave no token of hollowness. When power bowed to flattery, honour was bound to plainness. For Lear's threats, what could he do to him, whose life was already at his service? that should not hinder duty from speaking.

The honest freedom of this good earl of Kent only stirred up the king's wrath the more, and like a frantic patient who kills his physician, and loves his mortal disease, he banished this true servant, and allotted him but five days to make his preparations for departure; but if on the sixth his hated per-

son was found within the realm of Britain, that moment was
to be his death. And Kent bade farewel to the king, and said,
that since he chose to shew himself in such fashion, it was but
banishment to stay there: and before he went, he recommended Cordelia to the protection of the gods, the maid who
had so rightly thought, and so discreetly spoken; and only
wished that her sisters' large speeches might be answered with
deeds of love: and then he went, as he said, to shape his old
course to a new country.

The king of France and duke of Burgundy were now called
in to hear the determination of Lear about his youngest
daughter, and to know whether they would persist in their
courtship to Cordelia, now that she was under her father's
displeasure, and had no fortune but her own person to recommend her; and the duke of Burgundy declined the match, and
would not take her to wife upon such conditions; but the king
of France, understanding what the nature of the fault had
been which had lost her the love of her father, that it was
only a tardiness of speech, and the not being able to frame
her tongue to flattery like her sisters, took this young maid
by the hand, and saying that her virtues were a dowry above
a kingdom, bade Cordelia to take farewel of her sisters, and
of her father, though he had been unkind, and she should go
with him, and be queen of him and of fair France, and reign
over fairer possessions than her sisters: and he called the duke
of Burgundy in contempt a waterish duke, because his love
for this young maid had in a moment run all away like water.

Then Cordelia with weeping eyes took leave of her sisters,

and besought them to love their father well, and make good their professions: and they sullenly told her not to prescribe to them, for they knew their duty; but to strive to content her husband, who had taken her (as they tauntingly expressed it) as Fortune's alms. And Cordelia with a heavy heart departed, for she knew the cunning of her sisters, and she wished her father in better hands than she was about to leave him in.

Cordelia was no sooner gone, than the devilish dispositions of her sisters began to shew themselves in their true colours. Even before the expiration of the first month, which Lear was to spend by agreement with his eldest daughter Gonerill, the old king began to find out the difference between promises and performances. This wretch having got from her father all that he had to bestow, even to the giving away of the crown from off his head, began to grudge even those small remnants of royalty which the old man had reserved to himself, to please his fancy with the idea of being still a king. She could not bear to see him and his hundred knights. Every time she met her father, she put on a frowning countenance; and when the old man wanted to speak with her, she would feign sickness or any thing to be rid of the sight of him; for it was plain that she esteemed his old age a useless burden, and his attendants an unnecessary expense: not only she herself slackened in her expressions of duty to the king, but by her example, and (it is to be feared) not without her private instructions, her very servants affected to treat him with neglect, and would either refuse to obey his orders, or still more contemptuously pretend not to hear them. Lear could not but perceive this alteration in the behaviour of his daughter, but he shut his eyes against it as long as he could, as people commonly are unwilling to believe the unpleasant consequences which their own mistakes and obstinacy have brought upon them.

True love and fidelity are no more to be estranged by *ill*, than falsehood and hollow-heartedness can be conciliated by *good usage*. This eminently appears in the instance of the good earl of Kent, who, though banished by Lear, and his life made forfeit if he were found in Britain, chose to stay and abide all consequences, as long as there was a chance of his being useful to the king his master. See to what mean shifts and disguises poor loyalty is forced to submit sometimes; yet it counts nothing base or unworthy, so as it can but do service where it owes an obligation! In the disguise of a serving-man, all his greatness and pomp laid aside, this good earl proffered his services to the king, who not knowing him to be Kent in that disguise, but pleased with a certain plainness, or rather bluntness in his answers which the earl put on (so different from that smooth oily flattery which he had so much reason to be sick of, having found the effects not answerable in his daughter), a bargain was quickly struck, and Lear took Kent into his service by the name of Caius, as he called himself, never suspecting him to be his once great favourite, the high and mighty earl of Kent.

This Caius quickly found means to show his fidelity and love to his royal master: for Gonerill's steward that same day behaving in a disrespectful manner to Lear, and giving him saucy looks and language, as no doubt he was secretly encouraged to do by his mistress, Caius not enduring to hear so open an affront put upon majesty, made no more ado but presently tript up his heels, and laid the unmannerly slave in the kennel: for which friendly service Lear became more and more attached to him.

Nor was Kent the only friend Lear had. In his degree, and as far as so insignificant a personage could shew his love, the poor fool, or jester, that had been of his palace while Lear had a palace, as it was the custom of kings and great personages at that time to keep a fool (as he was called) to make them sport after serious business:—this poor fool clung to Lear after he had given away his crown, and by his witty sayings would keep up his good humour; though he could not refrain sometimes from jeering at his master, for his imprudence, in uncrowning himself, and giving all away to his daughters: at which time, as he rhymingly expressed it, these daughters

> "For sudden joy did weep,
> And he for sorrow sung,
> That such a king should play bo-peep,
> And go the fools among."

And in such wild sayings, and scraps of songs, of which he had plenty, this pleasant honest fool poured out his heart even in the presence of Gonerill herself, in many a bitter taunt and jest which cut to the quick; such as comparing the king to the hedge-sparrow, who feeds the young of the cuckoo till they grow old enough, and then has its head bit off for its pains: and saying, that an ass may know when the cart draws the horse (meaning that Lear's daughters, that ought to go behind, now ranked before their father); and that Lear was no longer Lear, but the shadow of Lear: for which free speeches he was once or twice threatened to be whipt.

The coolness and falling off of respect which Lear had begun to perceive, were not all which this foolish-fond father was to suffer from his unworthy daughter: she now plainly told him that his staying in her palace was inconvenient so long as he insisted upon keeping up an establishment of a hundred knights; that this establishment was useless and expensive, and only served to fill her court with riot and feastings; and she prayed him that he would lessen their number, and keep none but old men about him, such as himself, and fitting his age.

Lear at first could not believe his eyes or ears, nor that it was his daughter who spoke so unkindly. He could not believe that she who had received a crown from him could seek to cut off his train, and grudge him the respect due to his old age. But she persisting in her undutiful demand, the old man's rage was so excited, that he called her a detested kite, and said that she had spoke an untruth: and so indeed she did, for the hundred knights were all men of choice behaviour and sobriety of manners, skilled in all particulars of duty, and not given to rioting and feasting as she said. And he bid his horses to be prepared, for he would go to his other daughter, Regan, he and his hundred knights: and he spoke of ingratitude, and said it was a marble-hearted devil, and shewed more hideous in a child than the sea-monster. And he cursed

LOOK · THOV · BVT · SWEET · AND · I · AM · PROOF · AGAINST · THEIR · ENMITY

Romeo and Juliet—Tale the Seventeenth

DO·YOV·SEE·NOTHING·THERE ～ NOTHING·AT·ALL·YET·ALL·THAT·IS·I·SEE

Hamlet, Prince of Denmark—Tale the Eighteenth

his eldest daughter Gonerill so as was terrible to hear: praying that she might never have a child, or if she had, that it might live to return that scorn and contempt upon her, which she had shewn to him: that she might feel how sharper than a serpent's tooth it was to have a thankless child. And Gonerill's husband, the duke of Albany, beginning to excuse himself for any share which Lear might suppose he had in the unkindness, Lear would not hear him out, but in a rage ordered his horses to be saddled, and set out with his followers for the abode of Regan, his other daughter. And Lear thought to himself, how small the fault of Cordelia (if it was a fault) now appeared, in comparison with her sister's, and he wept; and then he was ashamed that such a creature as Gonerill should have so much power over his manhood as to make him weep.

Regan and her husband were keeping their court in great pomp and state at their palace: and Lear despatched his servant Caius with letters to his daughter, that she might be prepared for his reception, while he and his train followed after. But it seems that Gonerill had been beforehand with him, sending letters also to Regan, accusing her father of waywardness and ill humours, and advising her not to receive so great a train as he was bringing with him. This messenger arrived at the same time with Caius, and Caius and he met: and who should it be but Caius's old enemy the steward, whom he had formerly tript up by the heels for his saucy behaviour to Lear. Caius not liking the fellow's look, and suspecting what he came for, began to revile him, and challenged him to fight, which the fellow refusing, Caius, in a fit of honest passion, beat him soundly, as such a mischief-maker and carrier of wicked messages deserved: which coming to the ears of Regan and her husband, they ordered Caius to be put in the stocks, though he was a messenger from the king her father, and in that character demanded the highest respect: so that the first thing the king saw when he entered the castle was his faithful servant Caius sitting in that disgraceful situation.

This was but a bad omen of the reception which he was to expect; but a worse followed, when upon inquiry for his daughter and her husband, he was told they were weary with travelling all night, and could not see him: and when lastly, upon his insisting in a positive and angry manner to see them, they came to greet him, whom should he see in their company but the hated Gonerill, who had come to tell her own story, and set her sister against the king her father!

This sight much moved the old man, and still more to see Regan take her by the hand: and he asked Gonerill if she was not ashamed to look upon his old white beard? And Regan advised him to go home again with Gonerill and live with her peaceably, dismissing half of his attendants, and to ask her forgiveness; for he was old and wanted discretion, and must be ruled and led by persons that had more discretion than himself. And Lear shewed how preposterous that would sound, if he were to down on his knees, and beg of his own daughter for food and raiment, and he argued against such an unnatural dependence; declaring his resolution never to return with her, but to stay where he was with Regan, he and his hundred knights: for he said that she had not forgot the half of the kingdom which he had endowed her with, and that her eyes were not fierce like Gonerill's but mild and kind. And he said that rather than return to Gonerill with half his train cut off, he would go over to France, and beg a wretched pension of the king there, who had married his youngest daughter without a portion.

But he was mistaken in expecting kinder treatment of Regan than he had experienced from her sister Gonerill. As if willing to outdo her sister in unfilial behaviour, she declared that she thought fifty knights too many to wait upon him: that five-and-twenty were enough. Then Lear, nigh heart-broken, turned to Gonerill, and said that he would go back with her, for her fifty doubled five-and-twenty, and so her love was twice as much as Regan's. But Gonerill excused herself, and said, what need of so many as five-and-twenty? or even ten? or five? when he might be waited upon by her servants, or her sister's servants? So these two wicked daughters, as if they strove to exceed each other in cruelty to their old father who had been so good to them, by little and little would have abated him of all his train, all respect (little enough for him that once commanded a kingdom), which was left him to shew that he had once been a king! Not that a splendid train is essential to happiness, but from a king to a beggar is a hard change, from commanding millions to be without one attendant; and it was the ingratitude in his daughters' denying it, more than what he would suffer by the want of it, which pierced the poor old king to the heart: insomuch that with this double ill usage, and vexation for having so foolishly given away a kingdom, his wits began to be unsettled, and while he said he knew not what, he vowed revenge against those unnatural hags, and to make examples of them that should be a terror to the earth!

While he was thus idly threatening what his weak arm could never execute, night came on, and a loud storm of thunder and lightning with rain; and his daughters still persisting in their resolution not to admit his followers, he called for his horses, and chose rather to encounter the utmost fury of the storm abroad, than stay under the same roof with these ungrateful daughters: and they saying that the injuries which wilful men procure to themselves are their just punishment, suffered him to go in that condition, and shut their doors upon him.

The winds were high, and the rain and storm increased, when the old man sallied forth to combat with the elements, less sharp than his daughters' unkindness. For many miles about there was scarce a bush; and there upon a heath, exposed to the fury of the storm in a dark night, did king Lear wander out, and defy the winds and the thunder: and he bid the winds to blow the earth into the sea, or swell the waves of the sea till they drowned the earth, that no token might remain of any such ungrateful animal as man. The old king was now left with no other companion than the poor fool, who still abided with him, with his merry conceits striving to outjest misfortune, saying, it was but a naughty night to swim in, and truly the king had better go in and ask his daughter's blessing,

"But he that has a little tiny wit,
With heigh ho, the wind and the rain!
Must make content with his fortunes fit
Though the rain it raineth every day,"

and swearing it was a brave night to cool a lady's pride.

Thus poorly accompanied this once great monarch was found by his ever faithful servant the good earl of Kent, now transformed to Caius, who ever followed close at his side, though the king did not know him to be the earl; and he said, "Alas! sir, are you here? creatures that love night, love not such nights as these. This dreadful storm has driven the beasts to their hiding-places. Man's nature cannot endure the affliction or the fear." And Lear rebuked him and said, these lesser evils were not felt, where a greater malady was fixed. When the mind is at ease, the body has leisure to be delicate; but the tempest in his mind did take all feeling else from his senses, but of that which beat at his heart. And he spoke of filial ingratitude, and said it was all one as if the mouth should tear the hand for lifting food to it; for parents were hands and food and every thing to children.

But the good Caius still persisting in his entreaties that the king would not stay out in the open air, at last persuaded him to enter a little wretched hovel which stood upon the heath, where the fool first entering, suddenly ran back terrified, saying that he had seen a spirit. But upon examination this spirit proved to be nothing more than a poor Bedlam-beggar, who had crept into this deserted hovel for shelter, and with his talk about devils frighted the fool, one of those poor lunatics who are either mad, or feign to be so, the better to extort charity from the compassionate country-people; who go about the country, calling themselves poor Tom and poor Turlygood, saying, "Who gives anything to poor Tom?" sticking pins and nails and sprigs of rosemary into their arms to make them bleed; and with such horrible actions, partly by prayers, and partly with lunatic curses, they move or terrify the ignorant country-folks into giving them alms. This poor fellow was such a one; and the king seeing him in so wretched a plight, with nothing but a blanket about his loins to cover his nakedness, could not be persuaded but that the fellow was some father who had given all away to his daughters, and brought himself to that pass: for nothing he thought could bring a man to such wretchedness but the having unkind daughters.

And from this and many such wild speeches which he uttered, the good Caius plainly perceived that he was not in his perfect mind, but that his daughters' ill usage had really made him go mad. And now the loyalty of this worthy earl of Kent shewed itself in more essential services than he had hitherto found opportunity to perform. For with the assistance of some of the king's attendants who remained loyal, he had the person of his royal master removed at daybreak to the castle of Dover, where his own friends and influence, as earl of Kent, chiefly lay: and himself embarking for France, hastened to the court of Cordelia, and did there in such moving terms represent the pitiful condition of her royal father, and set out in such lively colours she inhumanity of her sisters, that this good and loving child with many tears besought the king her husband, that he would give her leave to embark for England with a sufficient power to subdue these cruel daughters and their husbands, and restore the king her father to his throne; which being granted, she set forth, and with a royal army landed at Dover.

Lear, having by some chance escaped from the guardians which the good earl of Kent had put over him to take care of him in his lunacy, was found by some of Cordelia's train, wandering about the fields near Dover, in a pitable condition, stark mad and signing aloud to himself, with a crown upon his head which he had made of straw, and nettles, and other wild weeds that he had picked up in the corn-fields. By the advice of the physicians, Cordelia, though earnestly desirous of seeing her father, was prevailed upon to put off the meeting, till, by sleep and the operation of herbs which they gave him, he should be restored to greater composure. By the aid of these skilful physicians, to whom Cordelia promised all her gold and jewels for the recovery of the old king, Lear was soon in a condition to see his daughter.

A tender sight it was to see the meeting between this father and daughter: to see the struggles between the joy of this poor old king at beholding again his once darling child, and the shame at receiving such filial kindness from her whom he had cast off for so small a fault in his displeasure; both these passions struggling with the remains of his malady, which in his half-crazed brain sometimes made him that he scarce remembered where he was, or who it was that so kindly kissed him and spoke to him: and then he would beg the standers-by not to laugh at him, if he were mistaken in thinking this lady to be his daughter Cordelia! And then to see him fall on his knees to beg pardon of his child; and she, good lady, kneeling all the while to ask a blessing of him, and telling him that it did not become him to kneel, but it was her duty, for she was his child, his true and very child, Cordelia! And she kissed him (as she said) to kiss away all her sisters' unkindness, and said that they might be ashamed of themselves, to turn their old kind father with his white beard out into the cold air, when her enemy's dog, though it had bit her (as she prettily expressed it), should have staid by her fire such a night as that, and warmed himself. And she told her father how she had come from France with a purpose to bring him assistance; and he said, that she must forget and forgive, for he was old and foolish, and did not know what he did; but that to be sure she had great cause not to love him, but her sisters had none. And Cordelia said, that she had no cause, no more than they had.

So we will leave this old king in the protection of this dutiful and loving child, where, by the help of sleep and medicine, she and her physicians at length succeeded in winding up the untuned and jarring senses which the cruelty of his other daughters had so violently shaken. Let us return to say a word or two about those cruel daughters.

These monsters of ingratitude, who had been so false to their own father, could not be expected to prove more faithful to their own husbands. They soon grew tired of paying even the appearance of duty and affection, and in an open way shewed they had fixed their loves upon another. It happened that the object of their guilty loves was the same. It was Edmund, a natural son of the late earl of Gloucester, who by his treacheries had succeeded in disinheriting his brother Edgar, the lawful heir from his earldom, and by his wicked practices was now earl himself: a wicked man, and a fit object for the love of such wicked creatures as Gonerill and Regan. It falling out about this time that the duke of Cornwall, Regan's husband, died, Regan immediately declared her intention of wedding this earl of Gloucester, which rousing the jealousy of her sister, to whom as well as to Regan this wicked earl had at sundry times professed love, Gonerill found means to make away with her sister by poison: but being detected in her practices, and imprisoned by her husband the duke of Albany for this deed, and for her guilty passion for the earl which had come to his ears, she in a fit of disappointed love and rage shortly put an end to her own life. Thus the justice of Heaven at last overtook these wicked daughters.

While the eyes of all men were upon this event, admiring the justice displayed in their deserved deaths, the same eyes were suddenly taken off from this sight to admire at the mysterious ways of the same power in the melancholy fate of the young and virtuous daughter, the lady Cordelia, whose good deeds did seem to deserve a more fortunate conclusion: but it is an awful truth, that innocence and piety are not always successful in this world. The forces which Gonerill and Regan had sent out under the command of the bad earl of Gloucester were victorious, and Cordelia, by the practices of this wicked earl, who did not like that any should stand between him and the throne, ended her life in prison. Thus Heaven took this innocent lady to itself in her young years, after shewing her to the world an illustrious example of filial duty. Lear did not long survive this kind child.

Before he died, the good earl of Kent, who had still attended his old master's steps from the first of his daughters' ill usage to this sad period of his decay, tried to make him understand that it was he who had followed him under the name of Caius; but Lear's care-crazed brain at that time could not comprehend how that could be, or how Kent and Caius could be the same person: so Kent thought it needless to trouble him with explanations at such a time; and Lear soon after expiring, this faithful servant to the king, between age and grief for his old master's vexations, soon followed him to the grave.

How the judgment of heaven overtook the bad earl of Gloucester, whose treasons were discovered, and himself slain in single combat with his brother the lawful earl; and how Gonerill's husband, the duke of Albany, who was innocent of the death of Cordelia, and had never encouraged his lady in her wicked proceedings against her father, ascended the throne of Britain after the death of Lear, is needless here to narrate; Lear and his Three Daughters being dead, whose adventures alone concern our story.

Tale the Tenth

Macbeth

WHEN Duncan the Meek reigned king of Scotland, there lived a great thane, or lord, called Macbeth. This Macbeth was a near kinsman to the king, and in great esteem at court for his valour and conduct in the wars; an example of which he had lately given, in defeating a rebel army assisted by the troops of Norway in terrible numbers.

The two Scottish generals, Macbeth and Banquo, returning victorious from this great battle, their way lay over a blasted heath, where they were stopped by the strange appearance of three figures, like women, except that they had beards, and their withered skins and wild attire made them look not like any earthly creatures. Macbeth first addressed them, when they, seemingly offended, laid each one her choppy finger upon her skinny lips, in token of silence: and the first of them saluted Macbeth with the title of thane of Glamis. The general was not a little startled to find himself known by such creatures; but how much more, when the second of them followed up that salute by giving him the title of thane of Cawdor, to which honour he had no pretensions! and again the third bid him, "All hail! king that shall be hereafter!" Such a prophetic greeting might well amaze him, who knew that while the king's sons lived he could not hope to succeed to the throne. Then turning to Banquo, they pronounced him, in a sort of riddling terms, to be *lesser than Macbeth and greater! not so happy, yet much happier!* and prophesied that though he should never reign, yet his sons after him should be kings in Scotland. They then turned into air and vanished: by which the generals knew them to be the weird sisters, or witches.

While they stood pondering on the strangeness of this adventure, there arrived certain messengers from the king, who were empowered by him to confer upon Macbeth the dignity of thane of Cawdor. An event so miraculously corresponding with the prediction of the witches astonished Macbeth, and he stood wrapt in amazement, unable to make reply to the messengers: and in that point of time swelling hopes arose in his mind, that the prediction of the third witch might in like manner have its accomplishment, and that he should one day reign king in Scotland.

Turning to Banquo, he said, "Do you not hope that your children shall be kings, when what the witches promised to me has so wonderfully come to pass?" "That hope," answered the general, "might enkindle you to aim at the throne; but oftentimes these ministers of darkness tell us truths in little things to betray us into deeds of greatest consequence."

But the wicked suggestions of the witches had sunk too deep into the mind of Macbeth, to allow him to attend to the warnings of the good Banquo. From that time he bent all his thoughts how to compass the throne of Scotland.

Macbeth had a wife, to whom he communicated the strange prediction of the weird sisters, and its partial accomplishment. She was a bad, ambitious woman, and so as her husband and herself could arrive at greatness, she cared not much by what means. She spurred on the reluctant purpose of Macbeth, who felt compunction at the thought of blood, and did not cease to represent the murder of the king as a step absolutely necessary to the fulfillment of the flattering prophecy.

It happened at this time that the king, who out of his royal condescension would oftentimes visit his principal nobility upon gracious terms, came to Macbeth's house, attended by his two sons, Malcolm and Donalbain, and a numerous train of thanes and attendants, the more to honour Macbeth for the triumphal success of his wars.

The castle of Macbeth was pleasantly situated, and the air about it was sweet and wholesome, which appeared by the nests which the martlet, or swallow, had built under all the jutting friezes and buttresses of the building, wherever it found a place of advantage: for where those birds most breed and haunt the air is observed to be delicate. The king entered, well pleased with the place, and not less so with the attentions and respect of his honoured hostess, lady Macbeth, who had the art of covering treacherous purposes with smiles; and could look like the innocent flower, while she was indeed the serpent under it.

The king, being tired with his journey, went early to bed, and in his state-room two grooms of his chamber (as was the custom) slept beside him. He had been unusually pleased with his reception, and had made presents, before he retired, to his principal officers; and among the rest, had sent a rich diamond to Lady Macbeth, greeting her by the name of his most kind hostess.

Now was the middle of night, when over half the world nature seems dead, and wicked dreams abuse men's minds asleep, and none but the wolf and the murderer is abroad. This was the time when lady Macbeth waked to plot the murder of the king. She would not have undertaken a deed so abhorrent to her sex, but that she feared her husband's nature, that it was too full of the milk of human kindness, to do a contrived murder. She knew him to be ambitious, but withal to be scrupulous, and not yet prepared for that height of crime which commonly in the end accompanies inordinate ambition. She had won him to consent to the murder, but she doubted his resolution: and she feared that the natural tenderness of his disposition (more humane than her own) would come between, and defeat the purpose. So with her own hands armed with a dagger, she approached the king's bed; having taken care to ply the grooms of his chamber

so with wine that they slept intoxicated, and careless of
their charge. There lay Duncan, in a sound sleep after the
fatigues of his journey, and as she viewed him earnestly,
there was something in his face, as he slept, which resembled her own father; and she had not the courage to
proceed.

She returned to confer with her husband. His resolution
had begun to stagger. He considered that there were strong
resaons against the deed. In the first place, he was not only
a subject but a near kinsman to the king; and he had been
his host and entertainer that day, whose duty by the laws of
hospitality it was to shut the door against his murderers, not
bear the knife himself. Then he considered how just and
merciful a king this Duncan had been, how clear of offence to
his subjects, how loving to his nobility, and in particular to
him; that such kings are the peculiar care of Heaven, and of
their subjects doubly bound to revenge their deaths. Besides,
by the favours of the king, Macbeth stood high in the opinion
of all sorts of men, and how would those honours be stained by
the reputation of so foul a murder!

In these conflicts of the mind lady Macbeth found her
husband, inclining to the better part, and resolving to proceed no further. But she being a woman not easily shaken
from her evil purpose, began to pour in at his ears words which
infused a portion of her own spirit into his mind, assigning
reason upon reason why he should not shrink from what he
had undertaken; how easy the deed was; how soon it would
be over; and how the action of one short night would give to

all their nights and days to come a sovereign sway and royalty! Then she threw contempt on his change of purpose, and accused him of fickleness and cowardice; and declared that she had given suck, and knew how tender it was to love the babe that milked her, but she would, while it was smiling in her face, have plucked it from her breast, and dashed its brains out, if she had so sworn to do it, so he had sworn to perform that murder. Then she added, how practicable it was to lay the guilt of the deed upon the drunken sleepy grooms. And with the valour of her tongue she so chastised his sluggish resolutions, that he once more summoned up courage to the bloody business.

So, taking the dagger in his hand, he softly stole in the dark to the room where Duncan lay; and as he went, he thought he saw another dagger in the air, with the handle toward him, and on the blade and at the point of it drops of blood: but when he tried to grasp at it, it was nothing but air, a mere phantasm proceeding from his own hot and oppressed brain and the business he had in hand.

Getting rid of this fear, he entered the kings' room, whom he dispatched with one stroke of his dagger. Just as he had done the murder, one of the grooms, who slept in the chamber, laughed in his sleep, and the other cried, "Murder," which woke them both: but they said a short prayer; one of them said, "God bless us!" and the other answered, "Amen"; and addressed themselves to sleep again. Macbeth, who stood listening to them, tried to say, "Amen" when the fellow said "God bless us!" but, though he had most need of a blessing, the word stuck in his throat, and he could not pronounce it.

Again he thought he heard a voice which cried, "Sleep no more; Macbeth doth murder sleep, the innocent sleep, that nourishes life." Still it cried, "Sleep no more," to all the house. "Glamis hath murdered sleep, and therefore Cawdor shall sleep no more, Macbeth shall sleep no more."

With such horrible imaginations Macbeth returned to his listening wife, who began to think he had failed of his purpose, and that the deed was somehow frustrated. He came in so distracted a state, that she reproached him with his want of firmness, and sent him to wash his hands of the blood which stained them, while she took his dagger, with purpose to stain the cheeks of the grooms with blood, to make it seem their guilt.

Morning came, and with it the discovery of the murder, which could not be concealed; and though Macbeth and his lady made great show of grief, and the proofs against the grooms (the dagger being produced against them and their faces smeared with blood) were sufficiently strong, yet the entire suspicion fell upon Macbeth, whose inducements to such a deed were so much more forcible than such poor silly grooms could be supposed to have; and Duncan's two sons fled. Malcolm, the eldest, sought for refuge in the English court; and the youngest, Donalbain, made his escape to Ireland.

The king's son, who should have succeeded him, having thus vacated the throne, Macbeth as next heir was crowned king, and thus the prediction of the weird sisters was literally accomplished.

Though placed so high, Macbeth and his queen could not forget the prophecy of the weird sisters, that, though Macbeth should be king, yet not his children, but the children of Banquo, should be kings after him. The thought of this, and that they had defiled their hands with blood, and done so great crimes, only to place the posterity of Banquo upon the throne, so rankled within them, that they determined to put to death both Banquo and his son, to make void the predictions of the weird sisters, which in their own case had been so remarkably brought to pass.

For this purpose they made a great supper, to which they invited all the chief thanes; and, among the rest, with marks of particular respect, Banquo and his son Fleance were invited. The way by which Banquo was to pass to the palace at night was beset by murderers appointed by Macbeth, who stabbed Banquo; but in the scuffle Fleance escaped. From that Fleance descended a race of monarchs who afterward filled the Scottish throne, ending with James the sixth of Scotland and the first of England, under whom the two crowns of England and Scotland were united.

At the supper the queen, whose manners were in the highest degree affable and royal, played the hostess with a gracefulness and attention which conciliated every one present, and Macbeth discoursed freely with his thanes and nobles, saying that all that was honourable in the country was under his roof, if he had but his good friend Banquo present, whom yet he hoped he should rather have to chide for neglect, than to lament for any mischance. Just at these words the ghost of Banquo, whom he had caused to be murdered, entered the room, and placed himself on the chair which Macbeth was about to occupy. Though Macbeth was a bold man, and one that could have faced the devil without trembling, at this horrible sight his cheeks turned white with fear, and he stood quite unmanned with his eyes fixed upon the ghost. His queen and all the nobles, who saw nothing, but perceived him gazing (as they thought) upon an empty chair, took it for a fit of distraction; and she reproached him, whispering that it was but the same fancy which had made him see the dagger in the air, when he was about to kill Duncan. But Macbeth continued to see the ghost, and gave no heed to all they could say, while he addressed it with distracted words, yet so significant, that his queen, fearing the dreadful secret would be disclosed, in great haste dismissed the guests, excusing the infirmity of Macbeth as a disorder he was often troubled with.

To such dreadful fancies Macbeth was subject. His queen and he had their sleeps afflicted with terrible dreams, and the blood of Banquo troubled them not more than the escape of Fleance, whom now they looked upon as father to a line of kings, who should keep their posterity out of the throne. With these miserable thoughts they found no peace, and Macbeth determined once more to seek out the weird sisters, and know from them the worst.

He sought them in a cave upon the heath, where they,

who knew by foresight of his coming, were engaged in preparing their dreadful charms, by which they conjured up infernal spirits to reveal to them futurity. Their horrid ingredients were toads, bats, and serpents, the eye of a newt and the tongue of a dog, the leg of a lizard and the wing of a night-owl, the scale of a dragon, the tooth of a wolf, the maw of the ravenous salt-sea shark, the mummy of a witch, the root of the poisonous hemlock (this to have effect must be digged in the dark), the gall of a goat, and the liver of a Jew, with slips of the yew-tree that roots itself in graves, and the finger of a dead child: all these were set on to boil in a great kettle, or caldron, which, as fast as it grew too hot, was cooled with a baboon's blood: to these they poured in the blood of a sow that had eaten her young, and they threw into the flame the grease that had sweated from a murderer's gibbet. By these charms they bound the infernal spirits to answer their questions.

It was demanded of Macbeth, whether he would have his doubts resolved by them, or by the masters, the spirits. He, nothing daunted by the dreadful ceremonies which he saw, boldly answered, "Where are they? let me see them." And they called the spirits, which were three. And the first arose in the likeness of an armed head, and he called Macbeth by name, and bid him beware of the thane of Fife; for which caution Macbeth thanked him: for Macbeth had entertained a jealousy of Macduff, the thane of Fife.

And the second spirit arose in the likeness of a bloody child, and he called Macbeth by name, and bid him have no fear, but laugh to scorn the power of man, for none of woman born should have power to hurt him: and he advised him to be bloody, bold, and resolute. "Then live, Macduff!" cried the king; "what need I fear of thee? but yet I will make assurance doubly sure. Thou shalt not live; that I may tell pale-hearted fear it lies, and sleep in spite of thunder."

That spirit being dismissed, a third arose in the form of a a child crowned with a tree in his hand. He called Macbeth, by name, and comforted him against conspiracies, saying, that he should never be vanquished, until the wood of Birnam to Dunsinane Hill should come against him. "Sweet bodements! good!" cried Macbeth; "who can unfix the forest, and move it from its earth-bound roots? I see I shall live the usual period of man's life, and not be cut off by a violent death. But my heart throbs to know one thing. Tell me, if your art can tell so much, if Banquo's issue shall ever reign in this kingdom?" Here the caldron sunk into the ground, and a noise of music was heard, and eight shadows, like kings, passed by Macbeth, and Banquo last, who bore a glass which shewed the figures of many more, and Banquo all bloody smiled upon Macbeth, and pointed to them; by which Macbeth knew that these were the posterity of Banquo, who should reign after him in Scotland: and the witches, with a sound of soft music, and with dancing, making a shew of duty and welcome to Macbeth, vanished. And from this time the thoughts of Macbeth were all bloody and dreadful.

The first thing he heard when he got out of the witches'
cave, was, that Macduff, thane of Fife, had fled to England,
to join the army which was forming against him under Malcom, the eldest son of the late king, with intent to dis-
place Macbeth, and set Malcolm, the right heir, upon the
throne. Macbeth, stung with rage, set upon the castle
of Macduff, and put his wife and children, whom the
thane had left behind, to the sword, and extended the
slaughter to all who claimed the least relationship to
Macduff.

These and such-like deeds alienated the minds of all his
chief nobility from him. Such as could, fled to join with
Malcolm and Macduff, who were now approaching with a
powerful army which they had raised in England; and the
rest secretly wished success to their arms, though for fear of
Macbeth they could take no active part. His recruits went
on slowly. Everybody hated the tyrant, nobody loved or
honoured him, but all suspected him, and he began to envy the
condition of Duncan whom he had murdered, who slept
soundly in his grave, against whom treason had done its
worst: steel nor poison, domestic malice nor foreign levies,
could hurt him any longer.

While these things were acting, the queen, who had been
the sole partner in his wickedness, in whose bosom he could
sometimes seek a momentary repose from those terrible dreams
which afflicted them both nightly, died, it is supposed by her
own hand, unable to bear the remorse of guilt, and public
hate; by which event he was left alone, without a soul to love

or care for him, or a friend to whom he could confide his wicked purposes.

He grew careless of life, and wished for death; but the near approach of Malcolm's army roused in him what remained of his ancient courage, and he determined to die (as he expressed it) "with armour on his back." Besides this, the hollow promises of the witches had filled him with false confidence, and he remembered the sayings of the spirits, that none of woman born was to hurt him, and that he was never to be vanquished till Birnam Wood should come to Dunsinane, which he thought could never be. So he shut himself up in his castle, whose impregnable strength was such as defied a siege: here he sullenly awaited the approach of Malcolm. When, upon a day, there came a messenger to him, pale and shaking with fear, almost unable to report that which he had seen: for he averred that as he stood upon his watch on the hill, he looked toward Birnam, and to his thinking the wood began to move! "Liar and slave," cried Macbeth, "if thou speakest false thou shalt hang alive upon the next tree, till famine end thee. If thy tale be true, I care not if thou dost as much by me": for Macbeth now began to faint in resolution, and to doubt the equivocal speeches of the spirits. He was not to fear till Birnam Wood should come to Dunsinane: and now a wood did move! "However," said he, "if this which he avouches be true, let us arm and out. There is no flying hence, nor staying here. I begin to be weary of the sun, and wish my life at an end." With these desperate speeches he sallied forth upon the besiegers, who had now come up to the castle.

The strange appearance, which had given the messenger an idea of a wood moving, is easily solved. When the besieging army marched through the wood of Birnam, Malcolm, like a skilful general, instructed his soldiers to hew down every one a bough and bear it before him, by way of concealing the true numbers of his host. This marching of the soldiers with boughs had at a distance the appearance which had frightened the messenger. Thus were the words of the spirit brought to pass in a sense different from that in which Macbeth had understood them, and one great hold of his confidence was gone.

And now a severe skirmishing took place, in which Macbeth, though feebly supported by those who called themselves his friends, but in reality hated the tyrant and inclined to the party of Malcom and Macduff, yet fought with the extreme of rage and valour, cutting to pieces all who were opposed to him, till he came to where Macduff was fighting. Seeing Macduff, and remembering the caution of the spirit who had counselled him to avoid Macduff above all men, he would have turned, but Macduff, who had been seeking him through the whole fight, opposed his turning, and a fierce contest ensued; Macduff giving him many foul reproaches for the murder of his wife and children. Macbeth, whose soul was charged enough with blood of that family already, would still have declined the combat; but Macduff still urged him to it, calling him tyrant, murderer, hell-hound, and villain.

Then Macbeth remembered the words of the spirit, how

none of woman born should hurt him; and smiling confidently he said to Macduff, "Thou losest thy labour, Macduff. As easily thou mayest impress the air with thy sword, as make me vulnerable. I bear a charmed life, which must not yield to one of woman born."

"Despair thy charm," said Macduff, "and let that lying spirit, whom thou hast served, tell thee that Macduff was never born of woman, never as the ordinary manner of men is to be born, but was untimely taken from his mother."

"Accursed be the tongue which tells me so," said the trembling Macbeth, who felt his last hold of confidence give way; "and let never man in future believe the lying equivocations of witches and juggling spirits, who deceive us in words which have double senses, and while they keep their promise literally, disappoint our hopes with a different meaning. I will not fight with thee."

"Then live!" said the scornful Macduff; "we will have a shew of thee, as men shew monsters, and a painted board, on which shall be written, 'Here men may see the tyrant!'"

"Never," said Macbeth, whose courage returned with despair; "I will not live to kiss the ground before young Malcolm's feet, and to be baited with the curses of the rabble. Though Birnam Wood be come to Dunsinane, and thou opposed to me wast never born of woman, yet I willl try the last." With these frantic words he threw himself upon Macduff, who, after a severe struggle, in the end overcame him, and cutting off his head, made a present of it to the young and lawful king, Malcolm; who took upon him the govern-ment which by the machinations of the usurper, he had so long been deprived of, and ascended the throne of Duncan the Meek amid the acclamations of the nobles and the people.

All's Well That Ends Well

BERTRAM, count of Rossilion, had newly come to his title and estate, by the death of his father. The king of France loved the father of Bertram, and when he heard of his death, he sent for his son to come immediately to his royal court in Paris; intending, for the friendship he bore the late count, to grace young Bertram with his especial favour and protection.

Bertram was living with his mother, the widowed countess, when Lafeu, an old lord of the French court, came to conduct Bertram to the king. The king of France was an absolute monarch, and the invitation to court was in the form of a royal mandate, or positive command, which no subject, of what high dignity soever might disobey; therefore though the countess, in parting with this dear son, seemed a second time to bury her husband, whose loss she had so lately mourned, yet she dared not keep him a single day, but gave instant orders for his departure. Lafeu, who came to fetch him, tried to comfort the countess for the loss of her late lord, and her son's absence; and he said, in a courtier's flattering manner, that the king was so kind a prince, she would find in his majesty a husband, and that he would be a father to her son: meaning only that the good king would befriend the fortunes of Bertram. Lafeu told the countess that the king had fallen into a sad malady, which was pronounced by his physicians to be incurable. The lady expressed great sorrow on hearing this account of the king's ill health, and said, she wished the father of Helena (a young gentlewoman who was present in attendance upon her) were living, for that she doubted not he could have cured his majesty of his disease. And she told Lafeu something of the history of Helena, saying she was the only daughter of the famous physician Gerard de Narbon, and that he had recommended his daughter to her care when he was dying, so that since his death, she had taken Helena under her protection; then the countess praised the virtuous disposition and excellent qualities of Helena, saying she inherited these virtues from her worthy father. While she was speaking, Helena wept in sad and mournful silence, which made the countess gently reprove her for too much grieving for her father's death.

Bertram now bade his mother farewel. The countess parted with this dear son with tears and many blessings, and commended him to the care of Lafeu, saying, "Good my lord, advise him, for he is an unseasoned courtier."

Bertram's last words were spoken to Helena, but they were words of mere civility, wishing her happiness; and he concluded his short farewel to her with saying, "Be comfortable to my mother your mistress, and make much of her."

Helena had long loved Bertram, and when she wept in sad and mournful silence, the tears she shed were not for Gerard de Narbon. Helena loved her father, but in the present feeling of a deeper love, the object of which she was about to lose, she had forgotten the very form and features of her dead father, her imagination presenting no image to her mind but Bertram's.

Helena had long loved Bertram, yet she always remembered that he was the Count of Rossilion, descended from the most ancient family in France. She of humble birth. Her parents of no note at all. His ancestors all noble. And therefore she looked up to the high-born Bertram, as to her master and to her dear lord, and dared not form any wish but to live his servant, and so living to die his vassal. So great the distance seemed to her between his height of dignity and her lowly fortunes, that she would say, "It were all one that I should love a bright peculiar star, and think to wed it, Bertram is so far above me."

Bertram's absence filled her eyes with tears, and her heart with sorrow; for though she loved without hope, yet it was a pretty comfort to her to see him every hour, and Helena would sit and look upon his dark eye, his arched brow, and the curls of his fine hair, till she seemed to draw his portrait on the tablet of her heart, that heart too capable of retaining the memory of every line in the features of that loved face.

Gerard de Narbon, when he died, left her no other portion than some prescriptions of rare and well proved virtue, which by deep study and long experience in medicine he had collected, as sovereign and almost infallible remedies. Among the rest there was one set down as an improved medicine for the disease under which Lafeu said the king at that time languished; and when Helena heard of the king's complaint, she who till now had been so humble and so hopeless, formed an ambitious project in her mind to go herself to Paris, and undertake the cure of the king. But though Helena was the possessor of this choice prescription, it was unlikely, as the king as well as his physicians were of opinion that his disease was incurable, that they would give credit to a poor unlearned virgin, if she should offer to perform a cure. The firm hopes that Helena had of succeeding, if she might be permitted to make the trial, seemed more than even her father's skill warranted, though he was the most famous physician of his time; for she felt a strong faith that this good medicine was sanctified by all the luckiest stars in heaven, to be the legacy that should advance her fortune, even to the high dignity of being count Rossilion's wife.

Bertram had not been long gone, when the countess was informed by her steward, that he had overheard Helena talking to herself, and that he understood from some words she uttered, she was in love with Bertram, and had thought of following him to Paris. The countess dismissed the steward with thanks, and desired him to tell Helena she wished to speak with her. What she had just heard of Helena brought the remembrance of days long past into the mind of the countess, those days probably when her love for Bertram's father first began; and she said to herself, "Even so it was with me when I was young. Love is a thorn that belongs to the rose of youth; for in the season of youth, if ever we are nature's children, these faults are ours, though then we think not they are faults." While the countess was thus meditating on the loving errors of her own youth, Helena entered, and she said to her, "Helena, you know I am a mother to you." Helena replied, "You are my honourable mistress." "You are my daughter," said the countess again; "I say I am your mother. Why do you start and look pale at my words?" With looks of alarm and confused thoughts, fearing the countess suspected her love, Helena still replied, "Pardon me, madam, you are not my mother; the count Rossilion cannot be my brother, nor I your daughter." "Yet, Helena," said the countess, "you might be my daughter-in-law; and I am afraid that is what you mean to be, the words *mother* and *daughter* so disturb you. Helena, do you love my son?" "Good madam, pardon me," said the affrighted Helena. Again the countess repeated her question. "Do you love my son?" "Do not you love him, madam?" said Helena. The countess replied, "Give me not this evasive answer, Helena. Come, come, disclose the state of your affections, for your love has to the full appeared." Helena on her knees now owned her love, and with shame and terror implored the pardon of her noble mistress; and with words expressive of the sense she had of the inequality between their fortunes, she protested Bertram did not know she loved him, comparing her humble unaspiring love to a poor Indian, who adores the sun, that looks upon his worshipper but knows of him no more. The countess asked Helena if she had not lately an intent to go to Paris? Helena owned the deisgn she had formed in her mind, when she heard Lafeu speak of the king's illness. "This was your motive for wishing to go to Paris," said the countess, "was it? Speak truly." Helena honestly answered, "My lord your son made me to think of this; else Paris, and the medicine, and the king, had from the conversation of my thoughts been absent then." The countess heard the whole of this confession without saying a word either of approval or of blame, but she strictly questioned Helena as to the probability of the medicine being useful to the king. She found that it was the most prized by Gerard de Narbon of all he possessed, and that he had given it to his daughter on his death-bed; and remembering the solemn promise she had made at that awful hour in regard to this young maid, whose destiny, and the life of the king himself, seemed to depend on the execution of a project (which though conceived by the fond suggestions of a loving maiden's thoughts, the countess knew not but it might be the unseen workings of Providence to bring to pass the recovery of the king, and to lay the foundation of the future fortunes of Gerard de Narbon's daughter), free leave she gave to Helena to pursue her own way, and generously furnished her with ample means and suitable attendants, and Helena set out for

Paris with the blessings of the countess, and her kindest wishes for her success.

Helena arrived at Paris, and by the assistance of her friend the old Lord Lafeu, she obtained an audience of the king. She had still many difficulties to encounter, for the king was not easily prevailed on to try the medicine offered him by this fair young doctor. But she told him she was Gerard de Narbon's daughter (with whose fame the king was well acquainted), and she offered the precious medicine as the darling treasure which contained the essence of all her father's long experience and skill, and she boldly engaged to forfeit her life, if it failed to restore his majesty to perfect health in the space of two days. The king at length consented to try it, and in two days time Helena was to lose her life if the king did not recover; but if she succeeded, he promised to give her the choice of any man throughout all France (the princes only excepted) whom she could like for an husband; the choice of an husband being the fee Helena demanded, if she cured the king of his disease.

Helena did not deceive herself in the hope she conceived of the efficacy of her father's medicine. Before two days were at an end, the king was restored to perfect health, and he assembled all the young noblemen of his court together, in order to confer the promised reward of an husband upon his fair physician; and he desired Helena to look round on this youthful parcel of noble bachelors, and choose her husband. Helena was not slow to make her choice, for among these young lords she saw the count Rossilion, and turning to Bertram, she said, "This is the man. I dare not say, my lord, I take you, but I give me and my service ever whilst I live into your guiding power." "Why then," said the king, "young Bertram, take her; she is your wife." Bertram did not hesitate to declare his dislike to this present of the king's of the self-offered Helena, who, he said, was a poor physician's daughter, bred at his father's charge, and now living a dependant on his mother's bounty. Helena heard him speak these words of rejection and of scorn, and she said to the king, "That you are well, my lord, I am glad. Let the rest go." But the king would not suffer his royal command to be so slighted; for the power of bestowing their nobles in marriage was one of the many privileges of the kings of France; and that same day Bertram was married to Helena, a forced and uneasy marriage to Bertram, and of no promising hope to the poor lady, who, though she gained the noble husband she had hazarded her life to obtain, seemed to have won but a splendid blank, her husband's love not being a gift in the power of the king of France to bestow.

Helena was no sooner married, than she was desired by Bertram to apply to the king for him for leave of absence from court; and when she brought him the king's permission for his departure, Bertram told her that as he was not prepared for this sudden marriage, it had much unsettled him, and therefore she must not wonder at the course he should pursue. If Helena wondered not, she grieved, when she found it was his intention to leave her. He ordered her to go home to his mother. When Helena heard this unkind command, she replied, "Sir, I can say nothing to this, but that I am your most obedient servant, and shall ever with true observance seek to eke out that desert, wherein my homely stars have failed to equal my great fortunes." But this humble speech of Helena's did not at all move the haughty Bertram to pity his gentle wife, and he parted from her without even the common civility of a kind farewel.

Back to the countess then Helena returned. She had accomplished the purport of her journey, she had preserved the life of the king, and she had wedded her heart's dear lord, the count Rossilion; but she returned back a dejected lady to her noble mother-in-law, and as soon as she entered the house, she received a letter from Bertram which almost broke her heart.

The good countess received her with a cordial welcome, as if she had been her son's own choice, and a lady of a high degree, and she spoke kind words, to comfort her for the unkind neglect of Bertram in sending his wife home on her bridal day alone. But this gracious reception failed to cheer the sad mind of Helena, and she said, "Madam, my lord is gone, for ever gone." She then read these words out of Bertram's letter: *When you can get the ring from my finger, which never shall come off, then call me husband, but in such a Then I write a Never.* "This is a dreadful sentence!" said Helena. The countess begged her to have patience, and said, now Bertram was gone, she should be her child, and that she deserved a lord, that twenty such rude boys as Bertram might tend upon, and hourly call her mistress. But in vain by respectful condescension and kind flattery this matchless mother tried to soothe the sorrows of her daughter-in-law. Helena still kept her eyes fixt upon the letter, and cried out in an agony of grief, *Till I have no wife I have nothing in France.* The countess asked her if she found those words in the letter? "Yes, madam," was all poor Helena could answer.

The next morning Helena was missing. She left a letter to be delivered to the countess after she was gone, to acquaint her with the reason of her sudden absence: in this letter she informed her, that she was so much grieved at having driven Bertram from his native country and his home, that to atone for her offence she had undertaken a pilgrimage to the shrine of St. Jaques le Grand, and concluded with requesting the countess to inform her son that the wife he so hated had left his house for ever.

Bertram, when he left Paris, went to Florence, and there became an officer in the duke of Florence's army, and after a successful war, in which he distinguished himself by many brave actions, Bertram received letters from his mother, containing the acceptable tidings that Helena would no more disturb him; and he was preparing to return home, when Helena herself, clad in pilgrim's weeds, arrived at the city of Florence.

Florence was a city through which the pilgrims used to pass on their way to St. Jaques le Grand; and when Helena arrived at this city, she heard that a hospitable widow dwelt there, who used to receive into her house the female pilgrims that were going to visit the shrine of that saint, giving them lodging and kind entertainment. To this good lady therefore Helena went, and the widow gave her a courteous welcome, and invited her to see whatever was curious in that famous city, and told her that if she would like to see the duke's army, she would take her where she might have a full view of it. "And you will see a countryman of yours," said the widow; "his name is count Rossilion, who has done worthy service in the duke's wars." Helena wanted no second invitation, when she found Bertram was to make a part of the show. She accompanied her hostess; and a sad and mournful pleasure it was to her to look once more upon her dear husband's face. "Is he not a handsome man?" said the widow. "I like him well," replied Helena with great truth. All the way they walked, the talkative widow's discourse was all of Bertram; she told Helena the story of Bertram's marriage, and how he had deserted the poor lady his wife, and entered into the duke's army to avoid living with her. To this account of her own misfortunes Helena patiently listened, and when it was ended, the history of Bertram was not yet done, for then the widow began another tale, every word of which sunk deep into the mind of Helena; for the story she now told was of Bertram's love for her daughter.

Though Bertram did not like the marriage forced on him by the king, it seems he was not insensible to love, for since he had been stationed with the army at Florence, he had fallen in love with Diana, a fair young gentlewoman, the daughter of this widow who was Helena's hostess; and every night, with music of all sorts, and songs composed in praise of

Diana's beauty, he would come under her window, and solicit her love: and all his suit to her was that she would permit him to visit her by stealth after the family were retired to rest; but Diana would by no means be persuaded to grant this improper request, nor give any encouragement to his suit, knowing him to be a married man: for Diana had been brought up under the counsels of a prudent mother, who, though she was now in reduced circumstances, was well-born, and descended from the noble family of the Capulets.

All this the good lady related to Helena, highly praising the virtuous principles of her discreet daughter, which she said were entirely owing to the excellent education and good advice she had given her; and she farther said, that Bertram had been particularly importunate with Diana to admit him to the visit he so much desired that night, because he was going to leave Florence early next morning.

Though it grieved Helena to hear of Bertram's love for the widow's daughter, yet from this story the ardent mind of Helena conceived a project (nothing discouraged at the ill success of her former one) to recover her truant lord. She disclosed to the widow, that she was Helena, the deserted wife of Bertram, and requested that her kind hostess and her daughter suffer this visit from Bertram to take place, and allow her to pass herself upon Bertram for Diana; telling them, her chief motive for desiring to have this secret meeting with her husband was to get a ring from him, which he had said if ever she was in possession of, he would acknowledge her as his wife.

The widow and her daughter promised to assist her in this affair, partly moved by pity for this unhappy forsaken wife, and partly won over to her interest by the promises of reward which Helena made them, giving them a purse of money in earnest of her future favour. In the course of that day Helena caused information to be sent to Bertram, that she was dead, hoping that when he thought himself free to make a second choice by the news of her death, he would offer marriage to her in her feigned character of Diana. And if she could obtain the ring and this promise too, she doubted not she should make some future good come of it.

In the evening, after it was dark, Bertram was admitted into Diana's chamber, and Helena was there ready to receive him. The flattering compliments and love-discourse he addressed to Helena were precious sounds to her, though she knew they were meant for Diana; and Bertram was so well pleased with her that he made her a solemn promise to be her husband, and to love her forever; which she hoped would be prophetic of a real affection, when he should know it was his own wife, the despised Helena, whose conversation had so delighted him.

Bertram never knew how sensible a lady Helena was, else perhaps he would not have been so regardless of her; and seeing her every day, he had entirely overlooked her beauty, a face we are accustomed to see constantly losing the effect which is caused by the first sight either of beauty or of plainness; and of her understanding it was impossible he should judge, because she felt such reverence, mixed with her love for him, that she was always silent in his presence; but now that her future fate, and the happy ending of all her love-projects, seemed to depend on her leaving a favourable impression on the mind of Bertram from this night's interview, she exerted all her wit to please him; and the simple graces of her lively conversation and the endearing sweetness of her manners so charmed Bertram, that he vowed she should be his wife. Helena begged the ring from off his finger as a token of his regard, and he gave it to her; and in return for this ring, which it was of such importance to her to possess, she gave him another ring, which was one the king had made her a present of. Before it was light in the morning, she sent Bertram away; and he immediately set out on his journey toward his mother's house.

Helena prevailed on the widow and Diana to accompany her to Paris, their farther assistance being necessary to the full accomplishment of the plan she had formed. When they arrived there, they found the king was gone upon a visit to the countess of Rossilion, and Helena followed the king with all the speed she could make.

The king was still in perfect health, and his gratitude to her who had been the means of his recovery was so lively in his mind, that the moment he saw the countess of Rossilion, he began to talk of Helena, calling her a precious jewel that was lost by the folly of her son; but seeing the subject distressed the countess, who sincerely lamented the death of Helena, he said, "My good lady, I have forgiven and forgotten all." But the good-natured old Lafeu, who was present, and could not bear that the memory of his favourite Helena should be so lightly passed over, said, "This I must say, the young lord did great offence to his majesty, his mother, and his lady; but to himself he did the greatest wrong of all, for he has lost a wife whose beauty astonished all eyes, whose words took all ears captive, whose deep perfection made all hearts wish to serve her." The king said, "Praising what is lost makes the remembrance dear. Well—call him hither"; meaning Bertram, who now presented himself before the king: and, on his expressing deep sorrow for the injuries he had done to Helena, the king, for his dead father's and his admirable mother's sake, pardoned him, and restored him once more to his favour. But the gracious countenace of the king was soon changed toward him, for he perceived that Bertram wore the very ring upon his finger which he had given to Helena; and he well remembered that Helena had called all the saints in heaven to witness she would never part with that ring, unless she sent it to the king himself upon some great disaster befalling her; and Bertram, on the king's questioning him how he came by the ring, told an improbable story of a lady throwing it to him out of a window, and denied ever having seen Helena since the day of their marriage. The king, knowing Bertram's dislike to his wife, feared he had destroyed her; and he ordered his guards to seize Bertram, saying, "I am wrapt in dismal thinking, for I fear the life of Helena was foully snatched." At this moment Diana and her mother entered, and presented a petition to the king, wherein they begged his majesty to exert his royal power to compel Bertram to marry Diana, he having made her a solemn promise of marriage. Bertram, fearing the king's anger, denied he had made any such promise; and then Diana produced the ring (which Helena had put into her hands) to confirm the truth of her words; and she said that she had given Bertram the ring he then wore, in exchange for that, at the time he vowed to marry her. On hearing this, the king ordered the guards to seize her also; and her account of the ring differing from Bertram's, the king's suspicions were confirmed; and he said, if they did not confess how they came by this ring of Helena's, they should be both put to death. Diana requested her mother might be permitted to fetch the jeweller of whom she bought the ring, which being granted, the widow went out, and presently returned leading in Helena herself.

The good countess, who in silent grief had beheld her son's danger, and had even dreaded that the suspicion of his having destroyed his wife might possibly be true, finding her dear Helena, whom she loved with even a maternal affection, was still living, felt a delight she was hardly able to support; and the king, scarce believing for joy that it was Helena, said, "Is this indeed the wife of Bertram that I see?" Helena, feeling herself yet an unacknowledged wife, replied, "No, my good lord, it is but the shadow of a wife you see, the name and not the thing." Bertram cried out, "Both, both! O pardon!" "O my lord," said Helena, "when I personated this fair maid, I found you wondrous kind; and look, here is your letter!"— reading to him in a joyful tone those words, which she had once repeated so sorrowfully, *When from my finger you can get this ring—*" This is done, it was to me you gave the ring. Will you be mine, now you are doubly won?" Bertram replied, "If you can make it plain that you were the lady I talked with that night, I will love you dearly, ever, ever dearly." This was no difficult task, for the widow and Diana came with Helena purposely to prove this fact; and the king was so well pleased with Diana for the friendly assistance she had rendered the dear lady he so truly valued for the service she had done him, that he promised her also a noble husband: Helena's history giving him a hint that it was a suitable reward for kings to bestow upon fair ladies when they perform notable services.

Thus Helena at last found that her father's legacy was indeed sanctified by the luckiest stars in heaven; for she was now the beloved wife of her dear Bertram, the daughter-in-law of her noble mistress, and herself the countess of Rossilion.

The Taming of the Shrew

KATHERINE, the shrew, was the eldest daughter of
Baptista, a rich gentleman of Padua. She was a lady
of such an ungovernable spirit and fiery temper, such a loud-
tongued scold, that she was known in Padua by no other name
than Katherine the Shrew. It seemed very unlikely, indeed,
impossible, that any gentleman would ever be found who
would venture to marry this lady, and therefore Baptista was
much blamed for deferring his consent to many excellent
offers that were made to her gentle sister Bianca, putting off
all Bianca's suitors with this excuse, that when the eldest
sister was fairly off his hands, they should have free leave to
address young Bianca.

It happened however that a gentleman, named Petruchio
came to Padua, purposely to look out for a wife, who, nothing
discouraged by these reports of Katherine's temper, and hearing she was rich and handsome, resolved upon marrying this
famous termagant, and taming her into a meek and manage-
able wife. And truly none was so fit to set about this herculean
labour as Petruchio, whose spirit was as high as Katherine's,
and he was a witty and most happy-tempered humourist,

and withal so wise, and of such a true judgment, that he well knew how to feign a passionate and furious deportment, when his spirits were so calm that himself could have laughed merrily at his own angry feigning, for his natural temper was careless and easy; the boisterous airs he assumed when he became the husband of Katherine being but in sport, or, more properly speaking, affected by his excellent discernment, as the only means to overcome in her own way the passionate ways of the furious Katherine.

A courting then Petruchio went to Katherine the Shrew, and first of all he applied to Baptista, her father, for leave to woo his *gentle daughter* Katherine, as Petruchio called her, saying archly that having heard of her bashful modesty and mild behaviour, he had come from Verona to solicit her love. Her father, though he wished her married, was forced to confess Katherine would ill answer this character, it being soon apparent of what manner of gentleness she was composed, for her music-master rushed into the room to complain that the gentle Katherine, his pupil, had broken his head with her lute for presuming to find fault with her performance; which, when Petruchio heard, he said, "It is a brave wench; I love her more than even, and long to have some chat with her"; and hurrying the old gentleman for a positive answer, he said, "My business is in haste, signior Baptista, I cannot come every day to woo. You knew my father. He is dead, and has left me heir to all his lands and goods. Then tell me, if I get your daughter's love, what dowry you will give with her." Baptista thought his manner was somewhat blunt for a lover; but being glad to get Katherine married, he answered that he would give her twenty thousand crowns for her dowry, and half his estate at his death: so this odd match was quickly agreed on, and Baptista went to apprize his shrewish daughter of her lover's addresses, and sent her in to Petruchio to listen to his suit.

In the mean time Petruchio was settling with himself the mode of courtship he should pursue: and he said, "I will woo her with some spirit when she comes. If she rails at me, why then I will tell her she sings as sweetly as a nightingale; and if she frowns, I will say she looks as clear as roses newly washed with dew. If she will not speak a word, I will praise the eloquence of her language; and if she bids me leave her, I will give her thanks as if she bid me stay with her a week." Now the stately Katherine entered, and Petruchio first addressed her with "Good morrow, Kate, for that is your name, I hear." Katherine, not liking this plain salutation, said disdainfully, "They call me Katherine who do speak to me." "You lie," replied the lover; "for you are called plain Kate, and bonny Kate, and sometimes Kate the Shrew; but, Kate, you are the prettiest Kate in Christendom, and therefore, Kate, hearing your mildness praised in every town, I am come to woo you for my wife."

A strange courtship they made of it. She in loud and angry terms showing him how justly she had gained the name of shrew, while he still praised her sweet and courteous words till at length, hearing her father coming, he said (intending to make as quick a wooing as possible), "Sweet Katherine, let us set this idle chat aside, for your father has consented that you shall be my wife, your dowry is agreed on, and whether you will or no, I will marry you."

And now Baptista entering, Petruchio told him his daughter had received him kindly, and that she had promised to be married the next Sunday. This Katherine denied, saying she would rather see him hanged on Sunday, and reproached her father for wishing to wed her to such a mad-cap ruffian as Petruchio. Petruchio desired her father not to regard her angry words, for they had agreed she should seem reluctant before him, but that when they were alone he had found her very fond and loving; and he said to her, "Give me your hand, Kate; I will go to Venice to buy you fine apparel against our wedding-day. Provide the feast, father, and bid the wedding guests. I will be sure to bring rings, fine array, and rich clothes, that my Katherine may be fine; and kiss me, Kate, for we will be married on Sunday."

On the Sunday all the wedding guests were assembled, but they waited long before Petruchio came, and Katherine wept for vexation to think that Petruchio had only been making a jest of her. At last, however, he appeared, but he brought none of the bridal finery he had promised Katherine, nor was he dressed himself like a bridegroom, but in strange, disordered attire, as if he meant to make a sport of the serious business he came about; and his servant and the very horses on which they rode were in like manner in mean and fantastic fashion habited.

Petruchio could not be persuaded to change his dress; he

said Katherine was to be married to him, and not to his
clothes; and finding it was in vain to argue with him, to the
church they went, he still behaving in the same mad way, for
when the priest asked Petruchio if Katherine should be his
wife, he swore so loud that she should, that all-amazed the
priest let fall his book, and as he stooped to take it up, this
mad-brained bridegroom gave him such a cuff, that down
fell the priest and his book again. And all the while they were
being married he stampt and swore so, that the high-spirited
Katherine trembled and shook with fear. After the ceremony
was over, while they were yet in the church, he called for wine,
and drank a loud health to the company, and threw a sop
which was at the bottom of the glass full in the sexton's face,
giving no other reason for this strange act, than that the
sexton's beard grew thin and hungerly, and seemed to ask the
sop as he was drinking. Never sure was there such a mad
marriage; but Petruchio did but put this wildness on, the
better to succeed in the plot he had formed to tame his shrewish wife.

Baptista had provided a sumptuous marriage feast, but
when they returned from church, Petruchio, taking hold of
Katherine, declared his intention of carrying his wife home instantly; and no remonstrance of his father-in-law, or angry
words of the enraged Katherine, could make him change his
purpose; he claimed a husband's right to dispose of his wife
as he pleased, and away he hurried Katherine off: he seemed
so daring and resolute that no one dared attempt to stop
him.

Petruchio mounted his wife upon a miserable horse, lean and lank, which he had picked out for the purpose, and himself and his servant no better mounted, they journeyed on through rough and miry ways, and ever when this horse of Katherine's stumbled, he would storm and swear to the poor jaded beast, who could scarce crawl under his burden, as if he had been the most passionate man alive.

At length, after a weary journey, during which Katherine had heard nothing but the wild ravings of Petruchio at the servant and the horses, they arrived at his house. Petruchio welcomed her kindly to her home, but he resolved she should have neither rest nor food that night. The tables were spread, and supper soon served; but Petruchio, pretending to find fault with every dish, threw the meat about the floor, and ordered the servants to remove it away, and all this he did, as he said, in love for his Katherine, that she might not eat meat that was not well dressed. And when Katherine weary and supperless retired to rest, he found the same fault with the bed, throwing the pillows and bed-clothes about the room, so that she was forced to sit down in a chair, where if she chanced to drop asleep, she was presently awakened by the loud voice of her husband, storming at the servants for the ill-making of his wife's bridal-bed.

The next day Petruchio pursued the same course, still speaking kind words to Katherine, but when she attempted to eat, finding fault with everything that was set before her, throwing the breakfast on the floor as he had done the supper; and Katherine, the haughty Katherine, was fain to beg the servants would bring her secretly a morsel of food, but they being instructed by Petruchio, replied they dared not give her anything unknown to their master. "Ah," said she, "did he marry me to famish me? Beggars that come to my father's door have food given them. But I, who never knew what it was to entreat for any thing, am starved for want of food, giddy for want of sleep, with oaths kept waking, and with brawling fed, and that which vexes me more than all, he does it under the name of perfect love, pretending that if I sleep or eat, it were present death to me." Here her soliloquy was interrupted by the entrance of Petruchio: he, not meaning she should be quite starved, had brought her a small portion of meat, and he said to her, "How fares my sweet Kate? Here, love, you see how diligent I am, I have dressed your meat myself. I am sure this kindness merits thanks. What, not a word? Nay then you love not the meat, and all the pains I have taken is to no purpose." He then ordered the servant to take the dish away. Extreme hunger, which had abated the pride of Katherine, made her say, though angered to the heart, "I pray you let it stand." But this was not all Petruchio intended to bring her to, and he replied, "The poorest service is repaid with thanks, and so shall mine before you touch the meat." On this Katherine brought out a reluctant "I thank you, sir." And now he suffered her to make a slender meal, saying, "Much good may it do your gentle heart, Kate; eat apace! And now, my honey love, we will return to your father's house, and revel it as bravely as the best, with silken coats and caps and golden rings, with ruffs and scarfs and fans and double change of finery"; and to make her believe he really intended to give her these gay things, he called in a taylor and a haberdasher, who brought some new clothes he had ordered for her, and then giving her plate to the servant to take away, before she had half satisfied her hunger, he said, "What, have you dined?" The haberdasher presented a cap, saying, "Here is the cap your worship bespoke"; on which Petruchio began to storm afresh, saying, the cap was moulded in a porringer, and that it was no bigger than a cockle or walnut shell, desiring the haberdasher to take it away and make a bigger. Katherine said, "I will have this; all gentlewomen wear such caps as these." "When you are gentle," replied Petruchio, "you shall have one too, and not till then." The meat Katherine had eaten had a little revived her fallen spirits, and she said, "Why sir, I trust I may have leave to speak, and speak I will. I am no child, no babe; your betters have endured to hear me say my mind; and if you cannot, you had better stop your ears." Petruchio would not hear these angry words, for he had happily discovered a better way of managing his wife than keeping up a jangling argument with her; therefore his answer was, "Why, you say true, it is a paltry cap, and I love you for not liking it." "Love me, or love me not," said Katherine, "I like the cap, and I will have this cap or none." "You say you wish to see the gown," said Petruchoi, still affecting to misunderstand her. The taylor then came forward and shewed her a fine gown he had made for her. Petruchio, whose intent was that she should have neither cap nor gown, found as much fault with that. "O mercy, Heaven!" said he, "what stuff is here! What, do you call this a sleeve? it is like a demi-cannon, carved up and down like an apple-tart." The taylor said, "You bid me make it according to the fashion of the times"; and Katherine said she never saw a better fashioned gown. This was enough for Petruchio, and privately desiring these people might be paid for their goods, and excuses made to them for the seemingly strange treatment he bestowed upon them, he with fierce words and furious gestures drove the taylor and the haberdasher out of the room: and then, turning to Katherine, he said, "Well, come, my Kate, we will go to your father's even in these mean garments we now wear." And then he ordered his horses, affirming they should reach Baptista's house by dinner-time, for that it was but seven o'clock. Now it was not early morning, but the very middle of the day, when he spoke this; therefore Katherine ventured to say, though modestly, being almost overcome by the vehemence of his manner, "I dare assure you, sir, it is two o'clock, and will be supper-time before we get there." But Petruchio meant that she should be so completely subdued, that she should assent to everything he said, before he carried her to her father; and therefore, as if he were lord even of the sun, and could command the hours, he said it should be what time he pleased to have it, before he set forward; "For," said he, "whatever I say or do you still are crossing it. I will not go to-day, and when I go, it shall be what o'clock I say it is." Another day Katherine was forced to practise her newly-found obedience, and not till he had brought her proud spirit to such a perfect subjection, that she dared not remember there was such a word as contradiction, would Petruchio allow her to go to her father's house; and even while they were upon their journey thither, she was in danger of being turned back again, only because she happened to hint it was the sun, when he affirmed the moon shone brightly at noon-day. "Now, by my mother's son," said he, "and that is myself, it shall be the moon, or stars, or what I list, before I journey to your father's house." He then made as if he were going back again; but Katherine, no longer Katherine the Shrew, but the obedient wife, said, "Let us go forward, I pray, now we have come so far, and it shall be the sun, or moon, or what you please, and if you please to call it a rush candle henceforth, I vow it shall be so for me." This he was resolved to prove, therefore he said again, "I say it is the moon." "I know it is the moon," replied Katherine. "You lie, it is the blessed sun," said Petruchio. "Then it is the blessed sun," replied Katherine; "but sun it is not, when you say it is not. What you will have it named even so it is, and so it ever shall be for Katherine." Now then he suffered her to proceed on her journey; but further to try if this yielding humour would last, he addressed an old gentleman they met on the road as if he had been a young woman, saying to him, "Good morrow, gentle mistress"; and asked Katherine if she had ever beheld a fairer gentlewoman, praising the red and white of the old man's cheeks, and comparing his eyes to two bright stars; and again he addressed him, saying, "Fair, lovely maid, once more good day to you!" and said to his wife, "Sweet Kate, embrace her for her beauty's sake." The now completely vanquished Katherine quickly adopted her husband's opinion, and made her speech in like sort to the old gentleman, saying to him, "Young budding virgin, you are fair, and fresh, and sweet: whither are you going, and where is your dwelling? Happy are the parents of so fair a child." "Why, how now, Kate," said Petruchio; "I hope you are not mad. This is a man, old and wrinkled, faded and withered, and not a maiden, as you say he is." On this Katherine said, "Pardon me, old gentleman; the sun has so dazzled my eyes, that every thing I look on seemeth green. Now I perceive you are a reverend father: I hope you will pardon me for my sad mistake." "Do, good old grandsire," said Petruchio, "and tell us which way you are travelling. We shall be glad of your good company, if you are going our way." The old gentleman replied, "Fair sir, and you my merry mistress, your strange encounter has much amazed me. My name is Vincentio, and I am going to visit a son of mine who lives at Padua." Then Petruchio knew the old gentleman to be the father of Lucentio, a young gentleman who was to be married to Baptista's younger daughter, Bianca, and he made Vincentio very happy by telling him the rich marriage his son was about to make; and they all journeyed on pleasantly together till they came to Baptista's house, where there was a large company assembled to celebrate the wedding of Bianca and Lucentio, Baptista having willingly consented to the marriage of Bianca when he had got Katherine off his hands.

When they entered, Baptista welcomed them to the wedding feast, and there was present also another newly-married pair.

Lucentio, Bianca's husband, and Hortensio, the other new-married man, could not forbear sly jests, which seemed to hint at the shrewish disposition of Petruchio's wife, and these fond bridegrooms seemed highly pleased with the mild tempers of the ladies they had chosen, laughing at Petruchio for his less fortunate choice. Petruchio took little notice of their jokes till the ladies were retired after dinner, and then he perceived Baptista himself joined in the laugh against him; for when Petruchio affirmed that his wife would prove more obedient than theirs, the father of Katherine said, "Now, in good sadness, son Petruchio, I fear you have got the veriest shrew of all." "Well," said Petruchio, "I say no, and therefore for assurance that I speak the truth, let us each one send for his wife, and he whose wife is most obedient to come at first when she is sent for shall win a wager which we will propose." To this the other two husbands willingly consented, for they were quite confident that their gentle wives would prove more obedient than the headstrong Katherine; and they proposed a wager of twenty crowns, but Petruchio merrily said he would lay as much as that upon his hawk or hounds, but twenty times as much upon his wife. Lucentio and Hortensio raised the wager to an hundred crowns, and Lucentio first sent his servant to desire Bianca would come to him. But the servant returned, and said, "Sir, my mistress sends you word she is busy and cannot come." "How," said Petruchio, "does she say she is busy and cannot come? Is that and answer for a wife?" Then they laughed at him, and said, it would be well if Katherine did not send him a worse answer. And now it was Hortensio's turn to send for his wife; and he said to his servant, "Go, and entreat my wife to come to me." "Oh ho! entreat her!" said Petruchio. "Nay, then she needs must come." "I am afraid, sir," said Hortensio, "your wife will not be entreated." But presently this civil husband looked a little blank, when the servant returned without his mistress; and he said to him, "How now! Where is my wife?" "Sir," said the servant, "my mistress says you have some goodly jest in hand, and therefore she will not come. She bids you come to her." "Worse and worse!" said Petruchio; and then he sent his servant, saying, "Sirrah, go to your mistress, and tell her I command her to come to me." The company had scarcely time to think she would not obey this summons, when Baptista, all in amaze, exclaimed, "Now, by my hollidam, here comes Katherine!" and she entered, saying meekly to Petruchio, "What is your will, sir, that you send for me?" "Where is your sister and Hortensio's wife?" said he. Katherine replied, "They sit conferring by the parlour-fire." "Go, fetch them hither," said Petruchio. Away went Katherine without reply to perform her husband's command. "Here is a wonder," said Lucentio, "if you talk of a wonder." "And so it is," said Hortensio; "I marvel what it bodes." "Marry, peace it bodes," said Petruchio, "and love, and quiet life, and right supremacy; and to be short, every thing that is sweet and happy." Katherine's father, over-joyed to see this reformation in his daughter, said, "Now, fair befall thee, son Petruchio! you have won the wager, and I will add another twenty thousand crowns to her dowry, as if she were another daughter, for she is changed as if she had never been." "Nay," said Petruchio, "I will win the wager better yet, and show more signs of her new-built virtue and obedience." Katherine now entering with the two ladies, he continued, "See where she comes, and brings your froward wives as prisoners to her womanly persuasion. Katherine, that cap of yours does not become you; off with that bauble, and throw it under foot." Katherine instantly took off her cap, and threw it down. "Lord!" said Hortensio's wife, "may I never have a cause to sigh till I am brought to such a silly pass!" And Bianca, she too said, "Fie, what foolish duty call you this?" On this Bianca's husband said to her, "I wish your duty were as foolish too! The wisdom of your duty, fair Bianca, has cost me an hundred crowns since dinner-time." "The more fool you," said Bianca, "for laying on my duty." "Katherine," said Petruchio, "I charge you tell these head-strong women what duty they owe their lords and husbands." And, to the wonder of all present, the reformed shrewish lady spoke as eloquently in praise of the wife-like duty of obedience as she had practised it implicitly in a ready submission to Petruchio's will. And Katherine once more became famous in Padua, not as heretofore, as Katherine the Shrew, but as Katherine the most obedient and duteous wife in Padua.

The Comedy of Errors

THE States of Syracuse and Ephesus being at variance, there was a cruel law made at Ephesus, ordaining that if any merchant of Syracuse was seen in the city of Ephesus, he was to be put to death, unless he could pay a thousand marks for the ransom of his life.

Ægeon, an old merchant of Syracuse, was discovered in the streets of Ephesus, and brought before the duke, either to pay this heavy fine, or to receive sentence of death.

Ægeon had no money to pay the fine, and the duke, before he pronounced the sentence of death upon him, desired him to relate the history of his life, and to tell for what cause he had ventured to come to the city of Ephesus, which it was death for any Syracusan merchant to enter.

Ægeon said, that he did not fear to die, for sorrow had made him weary of his life, but that a heavier task could not have been imposed upon him, than to relate the events of his unfortunate life. He then began his own history in the following words.

"I was born at Syracuse, and brought up to the profession of a merchant. I married a lady with whom I lived very happily, but being obliged to go to Epidamnium, I was detained there by my business six months, and then, finding I should be obliged to stay some time longer, I sent for my wife, who, as soon as she arrived, was brought to bed of two sons, and what was very strange, they were both so exactly alike, that it was impossible to distinguish the one from the other. At the same time that my wife was brought to bed of these twin-boys, a poor woman in the inn where my wife lodged was brought to bed of two sons, and these twins were as much like each other as my two sons were. The parents of these children being exceeding poor, I bought the two boys, and brought them up to attend upon my sons.

"My sons were very fine children, and my wife was not a little proud of two such boys: and she daily wishing to return home, I unwilling agreed, and in an evil hour we got on shipboard; for we had not sailed above a league from Epidamnium before a dreadful storm arose, which continued with such violence, that the sailors, seeing no chance of saving the ship, crowded into the boat to save their own lives, leaving us alone in the ship, which we every moment expected would be destroyed by the fury of the storm.

"The incessant weeping of my wife, and the piteous complaints of the pretty babes, who not knowing what to fear, wept for fashion, because they saw their mother weep, filled me with terror for them, though I did not for myself fear death; and all my thoughts were bent to contrive means for their safety; I tied my youngest son to the end of a small spare mast, such as seafaring men provide against storms; at the other end I bound the youngest of the twin-slaves, and at the same time I directed my wife how to fasten the other children in like manner to another mast. She thus having the care of the two eldest children and I of the two younger, we bound ourselves separately to these masts with the children; and but for this contrivance we had all been lost, for the ship split on a mighty rock and was dashed in pieces, and we clinging to these slender masts were supported above the water, where I, having the care of two children, was unable to assist my wife, who, with the other children, was soon separated from me; but while they were yet in my sight they were taken up by a boat of fishermen, from Cornith (as I supposed), and seeing them in safety, I had no care, but to struggle with the wild sea-waves, to preserve my dear son and the youngest slave. At length we in our turn were taken up by a ship, and the sailors, knowing me, gave us kind welcome and assistance, and landed us in safety at Syracuse; but from that sad hour I have never known what became of my wife and eldest child.

"My youngest son, and now my only care, when he was eighteen years of age, began to be inquisitive after his mother and his brother, and often importuned me that he might take his attendant, the young slave, who had also lost his brother, and go in search of them: at length I unwillingly gave consent, for though I anxiously desired to hear tidings of my wife and eldest son, yet in sending my younger one to find them, I hazarded the loss of him also. It is now seven years since my son left me; five years I have past in travelling through the world in search of him: I have been in farthest Greece, and through the bounds of Asia, and coasting homeward I landed here in Ephesus, being unwilling to leave any place unsought that harbours men; but this day must end the story of my life, and happy should I think myself in my death, if I were assured my wife and sons were living."

Here the hapless Ægeon ended the account of his misfortunes; and the duke, pitying this unfortunate father, who had brought upon himself this great peril by his love for his lost son, said, if it were not against the laws, which his oath and dignity did not permit him to alter, he would freely pardon him; yet, instead of dooming him to instant death, as the strict letter of the law required, he would give him that day, to try if he could beg or borrow the money to pay the fine.

This day of grace did seem no great favour to Ægeon, for not knowing any man in Ephesus, there seemed to him but little chance that any stranger would lend or give him a thousand marks to pay the fine: and helpless and hopeless of any relief, he retired from the presence of the duke in the custody of a jailer.

Ægeon supposed he knew no person in Ephesus; but here, at the very time he was in danger of losing his life through the careful search he was making after his youngest son, that son and his eldest son also were both in the city of Ephesus.

Ægeon's sons, besides being exactly alike in face and person, were both named alike, being both called Antipholis, and the two twin slaves were also both named Dromio. Ægeon's youngest son, Antipholis of Syracuse, he whom the old man had come to Ephesus to seek, happened to arrive at Ephesus with his slave Dromio that very same day that Ægeon did; and he being also a merchant of Syracuse, he would have been in the same danger that his father was, but by good fortune he met a friend who told him the peril an old merchant of Syracuse was in, and advised him to pass for a merchant of Epidamnium: this Antipholis agreed to do, and he was sorry to hear one of his own countrymen was in this danger, **but he** little thought this old merchant was his own father.

The oldest son of Ægeon (who must be called Antipholis of Ephesus, to distinguish him from his brother, Antipholis of Syracuse) had lived at Epheus twenty years, and, being a rich man, was well able to have paid the money for the ransom of his father's life; but Antipholis knew nothing of his father, being so young when he was taken out of the sea with his mother by the fishermen, that he only remembered he had been so preserved, but he had no recollection of either his father or his mother; the fishermen who took up this Antipholis and his mother and the young slave Dromio having carried the two children away from her (to the great grief of that unhappy lady), intending to sell them.

Antipholis and Dromio were sold by them to 'duke Menaphon, a famous warrior, who was uncle to the duke of Ephesus, and he carried the boys to Ephesus when he went to visit the duke his nephew.

The duke of Ephesus taking a liking to young Antipholis, when he grew up, made him an officer in his army, in which he distinguished himself by his great bravery in the wars, where he saved the life of his patron the duke, who rewarded his merit by marrying him to Adriana, a rich lady of Ephesus; with whom he was living (his slave Dromio still attending him) at the time his father came there.

Antipholis of Syracuse, when he parted with his friend, who advised him to say he came from Epidamnium, gave his slave Dromio some money to carry to the inn where he intended to dine, and in the mean time he said he would walk about and view the city, and observe the manners of the people.

Dromio was a pleasant fellow, and when Antipholis was dull and melancholy he used to divert himself with the odd humours and merry jests of his slave, so that the freedoms of speech he allowed in Dromio were greater than is usual between masters and their servants.

When Antipholis of Syracuse had sent Dromio away, he stood a while thinking over his solitary wanderings in search of his mother and his brother, and his brother, of whom in no place where he landed could he hear the least tidings; and he said sorrowfully to himself, "I am like a drop of water in the ocean, which seeking to find its fellow-drop, loses itself in the wide sea. So I unhappily, to find a mother and a brother, do lose myself."

While he was thus meditating on his weary travels, which had hitherto been so useless, Dromio (as he thought) returned. Antipholis, wondering that he came back so soon, asked him where he had left the money. Now it was not his own Dromio, but the twin brother that lived with Antipholis of Ephesus, that he spoke to. The two Dromios and the two Antipholises were still as much alike as Ægeon had said they were in their infancy; therefore no wonder Antipholis thought it was his own slave returned, and asked him why he came back so soon. Dromio replied, "My mistress sent me to bid you come to dinner. The capon burns, and the pig falls from the spit, and the meat will be all cold if you do not come home." "These jests are out of season," said Antipholis: "where did you leave the money?" Dromio still answering, that his mistress had sent him to fetch Antipholis to dinner: "What mistress?" said Antipholis. "Why your worship's wife, sir," replied Dromio. Antipholis having no wife, he was very angry with Dromio, and said, "Because I familiarly some-times chat with you, you presume to jest with me in this free manner. I am not in a sportive humour now: where is the money? we being strangers here, how dare you trust so great a charge from your own custody?" Dromio hearing his master, as he thought him, talk of their being strangers, supposing Antipholis was jesting, replied merrily, "I pray you, sir, jest as you sit at dinner: I had no charge but to fetch you home, to dine with my mistress and her sister." Now Antipholis lost all patience, and beat Dromio, who ran home, and told his mistress, that his master had refused to come to dinner, and said that he had no wife.

Adriana, the wife of Antipholis of Ephesus, was very angry, when she heard that her husband said he had no wife; for she was of a jealous temper, and she said her husband meant that he loved another lady better than herself; and she began to fret, and say unkind words of jealousy and reproach of her husband; and her sister Luciana, who lived with her, tried in vain to persuade her out of her groundless suspicions.

Antipholis of Syracuse went to the inn, and found Dromio with the money in safety there, and seeing his own Dromio, he was going again to chide him for his free jests, when Adriana came up to him, and not doubting that it was her husband she saw, she began to reproach him for looking strange upon her (as well he might, never having seen this angry lady before); and then she told him how well he loved her before they were married, and that now he loved some other lady instead of her. "How comes it now, my husband," said she, "O, how comes it, that I have lost your love?" "Plead you to me, fair dame?" said the astonished Antipholis. It was in vain he told her he was not her husband, and that he had been in

Ephesus but two hours, she insisted on his going home with her, and Antipholis at last, being unable to get away, went with her to his brother's house, and dined with Adriana and her sister, the one calling him husband and the other brother, he, all amazed, thinking he must have been married to her in his sleep, or that he was sleeping now. And Dromio, who followed them, was no less surprised, for the cook-maid, who was his brother's wife, also claimed him for her husband.

While Antipholis of Syracuse was dining with his brother's wife, his brother, the real husband, returned home to dinner with his slave Dromio; but the servants would not open the door, because their mistress had ordered them not to admit any company; and when they repeatedly knocked, and said they were Antipholis and Dromio, the maids laughed at them, and said that Antipholis was at dinner with their mistress, and Dromio was in the kitchen; and though they almost knocked the door down, they could not gain admittance, and at last Antipholis went away very angry, and strangely surprised at hearing a gentleman was dining with his wife.

When Antipholis of Syracuse had finished his dinner, he was so perplexed at the lady's still persisting in calling him husband, and at hearing that Dromio had also been claimed by the cook-maid, that he left the house, as soon as he could find any pretense to get away; for though he was very much pleased with Luciana, the sister, yet the jealous-tempered Adriana he disliked very much, nor was Dromio at all better satisfied with his fair wife in the kitchen; therefore both master and man were glad to get away from their new wives as fast as they could.

The moment Antipholis of Syracuse had left the house, he was met by a goldsmith, who mistaking him, as Adriana had done, for Antipholis of Ephesus, gave him a gold chain, calling him by his name; and when Antipholis would have refused the chain, saying it did not belong to him, the goldsmith replied he made it by his own orders; and went away, leaving the chain in the hand of Antipholis, who ordered his man Dromio to get his things on board a ship, not choosing to stay in a place any longer, where he met with such strange adventures that he surely thought himself bewitched.

The goldsmith who had given the chain to the wrong Antipholis was arrested immediately after for a sum of money he owed; and Antipholis, the married brother, to whom the goldsmith thought he had given the chain, happened to come to the place where the officer was arresting the goldsmith, who, when he saw Antipholis, asked him to pay for the gold chain he had just delivered to him, the price amounting to nearly the same sum as that for which he had been arrested. Antipholis denying the having received the chain, and the goldsmith persisting to declare that he had but a few minutes before given it to him, they disputed this matter a long time, both thinking they were right, for Antipholis knew the goldsmith never gave him the chain, and, so like were the two brothers, the goldsmith was as certain he had delivered the chain into his hands, till at last the officer took the gold-smith away to prison for the debt he owed, and at the same time the goldsmith made the officer arrest Antipholis for the price of the chain; so that at the conclusion of their dispute, Antipholis and the merchant were both taken away to prison together.

As Antipholis was going to prison, he met Dromio of Syracuse, his brother's slave, and mistaking him for his own, he ordered him to go to Adriana, his wife, and tell her to send the money for which he was arrested. Dromio wondering that his master should send him back to the strange house where he dined, and from which he had just before been in such haste to depart, did not dare to reply, though he came to tell his master the ship was ready to sail; for he saw Antipholis was in no humour to be jested with. Therefore he went away, grumbling, within himself that he must return to Adriana's house, "Where," said he, "Dowsabel claims me for a husband: but I must go, for servants must obey their masters' commands."

Adriana gave him the money, and as Dromio was returning, he met Antipholis of Syracuse, who was still in amaze at the surprising adventures he met with; for his brother being well known in Ephesus, there was hardly a man he met in the streets but saluted him as an old acquaintance: some offered him money which they said was owing to him, some invited him to come and see them, and some gave him thanks for kindnesses they said he had done them, all mistaking him for his brother. A taylor showed him some silks he had bought for him, and insisted upon taking measure of him for some clothes.

Antipholis began to think he was among a nation of sorcerers and witches, and Dromio did not at all relieve his master from his bewildered thoughts by asking him how he got free from the officer who was carrying him to prison, and giving him the purse of gold which Adriana had sent to pay the debt with. This talk of Dromio's of the arrest, and of a prison, and of the money he had brought from Adriana, perfectly confounded Antipholis, and he said, "This fellow Dromio is certainly distracted, and we wander here in illusions"; and quite terrified at his own confused thoughts, he cried out, "Some blessed power deliver us from this strange place!"

And now another stranger came up to him, and she was a lady, and she too called him Antipholis and told him he had dined with her that day, and asked him for a gold chain which she said he had promised to give her. Antipholis now lost all patience, and calling her a sorceress, he denied that he had ever promised her a chain, or dined with her, or had ever seen her face before that moment. The lady persisted in affirming he had dined with her, and had promised her a chain, which Antipholis still denying, she farther said, that she had given him a valuable ring, and if he would not give her the gold chain, she insisted upon having her own ring again. On this Antipholis became quite frantic, and again calling her sorceress and witch, and denying all knowledge of her and her ring, ran away from her, leaving her astonished at his words and his wild looks, for nothing to her appeared more certain than that he had dined with her, and that she had given him a ring, in consequence of his promising to make her a present of a gold chain. But this lady had fallen into the same mistake the others had done, for she had taken him for his brother: the married Antipholis had done all the things she taxed this Antipholis with.

When the married Antipholis was denied entrance into his own house (those within supposing him to be already there), he had gone away very angry, believing it to be one of his wife's jealous freaks, to which she was very subject, and remembering that she had often falsely accused him of visiting other ladies, he to be revenged on her for shutting him out of his own house, determined to go and dine with this lady, and she receiving him with great civility, and his wife having so highly offended him, Antipholis promised to give her a gold chain, which he had intended as a present for his wife; it was the same chain which the goldsmith by mistake had given to his brother. The lady liked so well the thoughts of having a fine gold chain, that she gave the married Antipholis a ring; which when, as she supposed (taking his brother for him), he denied, and said he did not know her, and left her in such a wild passion, she began to think he was certainly out of his senses; and presently she resolved to go and tell Adriana that her husband was mad. And while she was telling it to Adriana, he came, attended by the jailer, who allowed him to come home to get the money to pay the debt, for the purse of money which Adriana had sent by Dromio, and he had delivered to the other Antipholis.

Adriana believed the story the lady told her of her husband's madness must be true, when he reproached her for shutting him out of his own house; and remembering how he had protested all dinner-time that he was not her husband, and had never been in Ephesus till that day, she had no doubt that he was mad; she therefore paid the jailer the money, and having discharged him, she ordered her servants to bind her husband with ropes, and had him conveyed into a dark room, and sent for a doctor to come and cure him of his madness: Antipholis all the while hotly exclaiming against this false accusation, which the exact likeness he bore to his brother had brought upon him. But his rage only the more confirmed them in the belief that he was mad; and Dromio persisting in the same story, they bound him also, and took him away along with his master.

Soon after Adriana had put her husband into confinement, a servant came to tell her, that Antipholis and Dromio must have broken loose from their keepers, for that they were both walking at liberty in the next street. On hearing this, Adriana ran out to fetch him home, taking some people with her to secure her husband again; and her sister went along with her. When they came to the gates of a convent in their neighbourhood, there they saw Antipholis and Dromio, as they thought, being again deceived by the likeness of the twin brothers.

Antipholis of Syracuse was still beset with the perplexities this likeness had brought upon him. The chain which the goldsmith had given was about his neck, and the goldsmith was reproaching him for denying that he had it, and refusing to pay for it, and Antipholis was protesting that the goldsmith freely gave him the chain in the morning, and that from that hour he had never seen the goldsmith again.

And now Adriana came up to him, and claimed him as her lunatic husband, who had escaped from his keepers; and the men she brought with her were going to lay violent hands on Antipholis and Dromio; but they ran into the convent, and Antipholis begged the abbess to give him shelter in her house.

And now came out the lady abbess herself to enquire into the cause of this disturbance. She was a grave and venerable lady, and wise to judge of what she saw, and she would not too hastily give up the man who had sought protection in her house; so she strictly questioned the wife about the story she told of her husband's madness, and she said, "What is the cause of this sudden distemper of your husband's? Has he lost his wealth at sea? Or is it the death of some dear friend that has distrubed his mind?" Adriana replied, that no such things as these had been the cause. "Perhaps," said the abbess, "he has fixed his affections on some other lady than you his wife; and that has driven him into this state." Adriana said she had long thought the love of some other lady was the cause of his frequent absences from home. Now it was not his love for another, but the teasing jealousy of his wife's temper, that often obliged Antipholis to leave his home; and (the abbess suspecting this from the vehemence of Adriana's manner) to learn the truth, she said, "You should have reprehended him for this." "Why so I did," replied Adriana. "Aye," said the abbess, "but perhaps not enough." Adriana, willing to convince the abbess that she had said enough to Antipholis on this subject, replied, "It was the constant subject of our conversation: in bed I would not let him sleep for speaking of it. At table I would not let him eat for speaking of it. When I was alone with him, I talked of nothing else; and in company I gave him frequent hints of it. Still all my talk was how vile and bad it was in him to love any lady better than me."

The lady abbess, having drawn this full confession from the jealous Adriana, now said, "And therefore comes it that your husband is mad. The venomous clamour of a jealous woman is a more deadly poison than a mad dog's tooth. It seems his sleep was hindered by your railing; no wonder that his head is light; and his meat was sauced with your upbraidings; unquiet meals make ill digestions, and that has thrown him into this fever. You say his sports were disturbed by your brawls; being debarred from the enjoyment of society and recreation, what could ensue but dull melancholy and comfortless despair? The consequence is then, that your jealous fits have made your husband mad."

Luciana would have excused her sister, saying, she always reprehended her husband mildly; and she said to her sister, "Why do you hear these rebukes without answering them?" But the abbess had made her so plainly perceive her fault, that she could only answer, "She has betrayed me to my own reproof."

Adriana, though ashamed of her own conduct, still insisted on having her husband delivered up to her; but the abbess would suffer no person to enter her house, nor would she deliver up this unhappy man to the care of the jealous wife, determining herself to use gentle means for his recovery, and she retired into her house again, and ordered her gates to be shut against them.

During the course of this eventful day, in which so many errors had happened from the likeness the twin brothers bore to each other, old Ægeon's day of grace was passing away, it being now near sunset; and at sunset he was doomed to die, if he could not pay the money.

The place of his execution was near this convent, and here he arrived just as the abbess retired into the convent; the duke attending in person, that if any offered to pay the money, he might be present to pardon him.

Adriana stopped this melancholy procession, and cried out to the duke for justice, telling him that the abbess had refused to deliver up her lunatic husband to her care. While she was speaking, her real husband and his servant Dromio, who had got loose, came before the duke to demand justice, complaining that his wife had confined him on a false charge of lunacy; and telling in what manner he had broken his bands, and eluded the vigilance of his keepers. Adriana was strangely surprised to see her husband, when she thought he had been within the convent.

Ægeon seeing his son, concluded this was the son who had left him to go in search of his mother and his brother; and he felt secure that this dear son would readily pay the money demanded for his ransom. He therefore spoke to Antipholis in words of fatherly affection, with joyful hope that he should now be released. But to the utter astonishment of Ægeon, his son denied all knowledge of him, as well he might, for this Antipholis had never seen his father since they were separated in the storm in his infancy; but while the poor old Ægeon was in vain endeavouring to make his son acknowledge him, thinking surely that either his griefs and the anxieties he had suffered had so strangely altered him that his son did not know him, or else that he was ashamed to acknowledge his father in his misery; in the midst of this perplexity the lady abbess and the other Antipholis and Dromio came out, and the wondering Adriana saw two husbands and two Dromios standing before her.

And now these riddling errors, which had so perplexed them all, were clearly made out. When the duke saw the two Antipholises and the two Dromios both so exactly alike, he at once conjectured aright of these seeming mysteries, for he remembered the story Ægeon had told him in the morning; and he said, these men must be the two sons of Ægeon and their twin slaves.

But now an unlooked-for joy indeed completed the history of Ægeon; and the tale he had in the morning told in sorrow, and under sentence of death, before the setting sun went down was brought to a happy conclusion, for the venerable lady abbess made herself known to be the long-lost wife of Ægeon, and the fond mother of the two Antipholises.

When the fishermen took the eldest Antipholis and Dromio away from her, she entered a nunnery, and by her wise and virtuous conduct she was at length made lady abbess of this convent, and in discharging the rites of hospitality to an unhappy stranger she had unknowingly protected her own son.

Joyful congratulations and affectionate greetings between these long-separated parents and their children made them for a while forget that Ægeon was yet under sentence of death: but when they were become a little calm, Antipholis of Ephesus offered the duke the ransom money for his father's life; but the duke freely pardoned Ægeon, and would not take the money. And the duke went with the abbess and her newly-found husband and children into the convent, to hear this happy family discourse at leisure of the blessed ending of their adverse fortunes. And the two Dromios' humble joy must not be forgotten; they had their congratulations and greetings too, and each Dromio pleasantly complimented his brother on his good looks, being well pleased to see his own person (as in a glass) shew so handsome in his brother.

Adriana had so well profited by the good counsel of her mother-in-law, that she never after cherished unjust suspicions, or was jealous of her husband.

Antipholis of Syracuse married the fair Luciana, the sister of his brother's wife; and the good old Ægeon, with his wife and sons, lived at Ephesus many years. Nor did the unravelling of these perplexities so entirely remove every ground of mistake for the future, but that sometimes, to remind them of adventures past, comical blunders would happen, and the one Antipholis, and the one Dromio, be mistaken for the other, making altogether a pleasant and diverting Comedy of Errors.

Tale the Fourteenth

Measure for Measure

IN the city of Vienna there once reigned a duke of such a
mild and gentle temper, that he suffered his subjects to
neglect the laws with impunity; and there was in particular
one law, the existence of which was almost forgotten, the
duke never having put it in force during his whole reign.
This was a law dooming any man to the punishment of death,
who should live with a woman that was not his wife; and this
law through the lenity of the duke being utterly disregarded,
the holy institution of marriage became neglected, and complaints were every day made to the duke by the parents of
the young ladies in Vienna, that their daughters had been
seduced from their protection, and were living as the companions of single men.

The good duke perceived with sorrow this growing evil among his subjects; but he thought that a sudden change in himself from the indulgence he had hitherto shown, to the strict severity requisite to check this abuse, would make his people (who had hitherto loved him) consider him as a tyrant; therefore he determined to absent himself a while from his dukedom and depute another to the full exercise of his power, that the law against these dishonourable lovers might be put in effect, without giving offence by an unusual severity in his own person.

Angelo, a man who bore the reputation of a saint in Vienna for his strict and rigid life, was chosen by the duke as a fit person to undertake this important charge; and when the duke imparted his design to lord Escalus, his chief counsellor, Escalus said, "If any man in Vienna be of worth to undergo such ample grace and honour, it is lord Angelo." And now the duke departed from Vienna under pretence of making a journey into Poland, leaving Angelo to act as the lord deputy in his absence; but the duke's absence was only a feigned one, for he privately returned to Vienna, habited like a friar, with intent to watch unseen the conduct of the saintly-seeming Angelo.

It happened just about the time that Angelo was invested with his new dignity, that a gentleman, whose name was Claudio, had seduced a young lady from her parents; and for this offence, by command of the new lord deputy, Claudio was taken up and committed to prison, and by virtue of the old law which had been so long neglected, Angelo sentenced

Claudio to be beheaded. Great interest was made for the pardon of young Claudio, and the good old lord Escalus himself interceded for him. "Alas," said he, "this gentleman whom I would save had an honourable father, for whose sake I pray you pardon the young man's transgression." But Angelo replied, "We must not make a scarecrow of the law, setting it up to frighten birds of prey, till custom, finding it harmless, makes it their perch, and not their terror. Sir, he must die."

Lucio, the friend of Claudio, visited him in the prison, and Claudio said to him, "I pray you, Lucio, do me this kind service. Go to my sister Isabel, who this day proposes to enter the convent of Saint Clare; acquaint her with the danger of my state: implore her that she make friends with the strict deputy; bid her go herself to Angelo. I have great hopes in that; for she can discourse with prosperous art, and well she can persuade; besides, there is a speechless dialect in youthful sorrow, such as moves men."

Isabel, the sister of Claudio, had, as he said, that day entered upon her novitiate in the convent, and it was her intent after passing through her probation as a novice, to take the veil, and she was enquiring of a nun concerning the rules of the convent, when they heard the voice of Lucio, who, as he entered that religious house, said, "Peace be in this place!" "Who is it that speaks?" said Isabel. "It is a man's voice," replied the nun: "Gentle Isabel, go to him and learn his business; you may, I may not. When you have taken the veil, you must not speak with men but in the presence of the prioress; then if you speak, you must not shew your face, or if you shew you face, you must not speak." "And have you nuns no farther privileges?" said Isabel. "Are not these large enough?" replied the nun. "Yes, truly," said Isabel: "I speak not as desiring more, but rather wishing a more strict restraint upon the sisterhood, the votarists of Saint Clare." Again they heard the voice of Lucio, and the nun said, "He calls again. I pray you answer him." Isabel then went out to Lucio, and in answer to his salutation, said, "Peace and prosperity! Who is it that calls?" Then Lucio, approaching her with revenerence, said, "Hail, virgin, if such you be, as the roses in your cheeks proclaims you are no less! can you bring me to the sight of Isabel, a novice of this place, and the fair sister to her unhappy brother Claudio?" "Why her unhappy brother?" said Isabel, "let me ask, for I am that Isabel, and his sister." "Fair and gentle lady," he replied, "your brother kindly greets you by me; he is in prison." "Woe is me! for what?" said Isabel. Lucio then told her, Claudio was imprisoned for seducing a young maiden. "Ah," said she, "I fear it is my cousin Juliet." Juliet and Isabel were not related, but they called each other cousin in remembrance of their school-days friendship; and as Isabel knew that Juliet loved Claudio, she feared she had been led by her affection for him into this transgression. "She it is," replied Lucio. "Why then let my brother marry Juliet," said Isabel. Lucio replied, that Claudio would gladly marry Juliet, but that the lord deputy had sentenced him to die for his offence; "unless," said he, "you have the grace by your fair prayer to soften

Angelo, and that is my business between you and your poor brother." "Alas," said Isabel, "what poor ability is there in me to do him good? I doubt I have no power to move Angelo." "Our doubts are traitors," said Lucio, "and make us lose the good we might often win, by fearing to attempt it. Go to lord Angelo! When maidens sue, and kneel, and weep, men give like gods." "I will see what I can do," said Isabel; "I will but stay to give the prioress notice of the affair, and then I will go to Angelo. Commend me to my brother: soon at night I will send him word of my success."

Isabel hastened to the palace, and threw herself on her knees before Angelo, saying, "I am a woeful suitor to your honour, if it will please your honour to hear me." "Well, what is your suit?" said Angelo. She then made her petition in the most moving terms for her brother's life. But Angelo said, "Maiden, there is no remedy; your brother is sentenced, and he must die." "O just, but severe law!" said Isabel: "I had a brother then—Heaven keep your honour!" and she was about to depart. But Lucio, who had accompanied her, said, "Give it not over so; return to him again, entreat him, kneel down before him, hang upon his gown. You are too cold; if you should need a pin, you could not with a more tame tongue desire it." Then again Isabel on her knees implored for mercy. "He is sentenced," said Angelo: "it is too late." "Too late!" said Isabel: "Why, no; I that do speak a word, may call it back again. Believe this, my lord, no ceremony that to great ones belongs, not the king's crown, nor the deputed sword, the marshal's truncheon, nor the judge's robe, becomes them with one half so good a grace as mercy does." "Pray you begone," said Angelo. But still Isabel entreated; and she said, "If my brother had been as you, and you as he, you might have slipt like him, but he like you would not have been so stern. I would to Heaven I had your power, and you were Isabel. Should it then be thus? No, I would tell you what it were to be a judge, and what a prisoner." "Be content, fair maid!" said Angelo: "it is the law, not I, condemns your brother. Were he my kinsman, my brother, or my son, it should be thus with him. He must die to-morrow." "To-morrow?" said Isabel: "Oh, that is sudden: spare him, spare him; he is not prepared for death. Even for our kitchens we kill the fowl in season; shall we serve Heaven with less respect than we minister to our gross selves? Good, good, my lord, bethink you, none have died for my brother's offence, though many have committed it. So you would be the first that gives this sentence, and he the first that suffers it. Go to your own bosom, my lord; knock there, and ask your heart what it does know that is like my brother's fault; if it confess a natural guiltiness, such as his is, let it not sound a thought against my brother's life!" Her last words more moved Angelo than all she had before said, for the beauty of Isabel had raised a guilty passion in his heart, and he began to form thoughts of dishonourable love, such as Claudio's crime had been; and the conflict in his mind made him turn away from Isabel: but she called him back, saying, "Gentle my lord, turn back; hark, how I will bribe you. Good my lord, turn back!" "How, bribe me!" said Angelo, astonished that she should think of offering him a bribe. "Aye," said Isabel, "with such gifts that Heaven itself shall share with you; not with golden treasures, or those glittering stones, whose price is either rich or poor as fancy values them, but with true prayers that shall be up to Heaven before sunrise— prayers from preserved souls, from fasting maids whose minds are dedicated to nothing temporal." "Well, come to me to-morrow," said Angelo. And for this short respite of her brother's life, and for this permission that she might be heard again, she left him with the joyful hope that she might at last prevail over his stern nature: and as she went away, she said, "Heaven keep your honour safe! Heaven save your honour!" Which, when Angelo heard, he said within his heart, "Amen, I would be saved from thee and from thy virtues": and then, affrighted at his own evil thoughts, he said, "What is this? What is this? Do I love her, that I desire to hear her speak again, and feast upon her eyes? What is it I dream on? The cunning enemy of mankind, to catch a saint, with saints does bait the hook. Never could an immodest woman once stir my temper, but this virtuous woman subdues me quite. Even till now, when men were fond, I smiled, and wondered at them."

In the guilty conflict in his mind Angelo suffered more that night, than the prisoner he had so severely sentenced; for in the prison Claudio was visited by the good duke, who in his friar's habit taught the young man the way to heaven, preaching to him the words of penitence and peace. But Angelo felt all the pangs of irresolute guilt: now wishing to seduce Isabel from the paths of innocence and honour, and now suffering remorse and horror for a crime as yet but intentional. But in the end his evil thoughts prevailed; and he who had so lately started at the offer of a bribe, resolved to tempt this maiden with so high a bribe as she might not be able to resist, even with the precious gift of her dear brother's life.

When Isabel came in the morning, Angelo desired she might be admitted alone to his presence; and being there, he said to her, if she would yield to him her virgin honour, and transgress even as Juliet had done with Claudio, he would give her her brother's life: "For," said he, "I love you, Isabel." "My brother," said Isabel, "did so love Juliet, and yet you tell me he shall die for it." "But," said Angelo, "Claudio shall not die, if you will consent to visit me by stealth at night, even as Juliet left her father's house at night to come to Claudio." Isabel in amazement at his words, that he should tempt her to the same fault for which he passed sentence of death upon her brother, said, "I would do as much for my poor brother as for myself, that is, were I under sentence of death, the impression of keen whips I would wear as rubies, and go to my death as to a bed that longing I had been sick for, ere I would yield myself up to this shame." And then she told him, she hoped he only spoke these words to try her virtue. But he said, "Believe me on my honour, my words express my purpose." Isabel, angered to the heart to hear him use the word honour to express such dishonourable purposes, said, "Ha! little honour, to be much believed; and most pernicious purpose. I will proclaim thee, Angelo; look for it! Sign me a present pardon for my brother, or I will tell the world aloud what man thou art!" "Who will believe you, Isabel?" said Angelo; "my unsoiled name, the austereness of my life, my word vouched against yours, will outweigh your accusation. Redeem your brother by yielding to my will, or he shall die to-morrow. As for you, say what you can, my false will overweigh your true story. Answer me to-morrow."

"To whom should I complain? Did I tell this, who would believe me?" said Isabel, as she went towards the dreary prison where her brother was confined. When she arrived there, her brother was in pious conversation with the duke, who in his friar's habit, had also visited Juliet, and brought these guilty lovers to a proper sense of their fault; and unhappy Juliet with tears and a true remorse confessed, that she was more to blame than Claudio, in that she willingly consented to his dishonourable solicitations.

As Isabel entered the room where Claudio was confined, she said, "Peace be here, grace, and good company!" "Who is there?" said the disguised duke: "come in; the wish deserves a welcome." "My business is a word or two with Claudio," said Isabel. Then the duke left them together, and desired the provost, who had the charge of the prisoners, to place him where he might overhear their conversation.

"Now, sister, what is the comfort?" said Claudio. Isabel told him he must prepare for death on the morrow. "Is there no remedy?" said Claudio. "Yes, brother," replied Isabel, "there is, but such a one, as if you consented to it would strip your honour from you, and leave you naked." "Let me know the point," said Claudio. "O, I do fear you, Claudio!" replied his sister; "and I quake, lest you should wish to live, and more respect the trifling term of six or seven winters added to your life, than your perpetual honour! Do you dare to die! The sense of death is most in apprehension, and the poor beetle that we tread upon, feels a pang as great as when a giant dies." "Why do you give me this shame?" said Claudio. "Think you I can fetch a resolution from flowery tenderness? If I must die, I will encounter darkness as a bride, and hug it in my arms." "These spoke my brother," said Isabel; "there my father's grave did utter forth a voice. Yes, you must die; yet, would you think it, Claudio; this outward sainted deputy, if I would yield to him my virgin honour, would grant your life. O, were it but my life, I would lay it down for your deliverance as frankly as a pin!" "Thanks, dear Isabel," said Claudio. "Be ready to die to-morrow," said Isabel. "Death is a fearful thing," said Claudio. "And shamed life a hateful," replied his sister. But the thoughts of death overcame the constancy of Claudio's temper, and terrors, such as the guilty only at their deaths do know, assailing him, he cried out, "Sweet sister, let me live! The sin you do to save a brother's life, nature dispenses with the deed so far, that it becomes a virtue." "O faithless coward! O dishonest wretch!" said Isabel: "would you preserve your life by your sister's shame? O fie, fie, fie! I thought, my brother, you had in you such a mind of honour, that had you twenty heads to render up on twenty blocks, you would have yielded them up all before your sister should stoop to such dishonour." "Nay, hear me, Isabel!" said Claudio. But what he would have said in defence of his weakness, in desiring to live by the dishonour of his virtuous sister, was interrupted by the entrance of the duke; who said, "Claudio, I have overheard what has passed between you and your sister. Angelo had never the purpose to corrupt her; what he said has only been to make trial of her virtue. She having the truth of honour in her, has given him that gracious denial which he is most glad to receive. There is no hope that he will pardon you; therefore pass your hours in prayer, and make ready for death." Then Claudio repented of his weakness, and said, "Let me ask my sister's pardon! I am so out of love with life, that I will sue to be rid of it." And Claudio retired, overwhelmed with shame and sorrow for his fault.

The duke being now alone with Isabel, commended her virtuous resolution saying, "The hand that made you fair, has made you good." "O," said Isabel, "how much is the good duke deceived in Angelo! if ever he return, and I can speak to him, I will discover his government." Isabel knew not that she was even now making the discovery she threatened. The duke replied, "That shall not be much amiss; yet, as the matter now stands, Angelo will repel your accusation; therefore lend an attentive ear to my advisings. I believe that you may most righteously do a poor wronged lady a merited benefit, redeem your brother from the angry law, do no stain to your own most gracious person, and much please the absent duke, if peradvertune he shall ever return to have notice of this business." Isabel said, she had a spirit to do anything he desired, provided it was nothing wrong. "Virtue is bold, and never fearful," said the duke: and then he asked her, if she had ever heard of Mariana, the sister of Frederick, the great soldier who was drowned at sea. "I have heard of the lady," said Isabel, "and good words went with her name." "This lady," said the duke, "is the wife of Angelo; but her marriage dowry was on board the vessel in which her brother perished, and mark how heavily this befell to the poor gentle-woman! for, besides the loss of a most noble and renowned brother, who in his love toward her was the most kind and natural, in the wreck of her fortune she lost the affections of her husband, the well-seeming Angelo; who pretending to dis-cover some dishonour in this honourable lady (though the true cause was the loss of her dowry), left her in her tears, and dried not one of them with his comfort. His unjust unkind-ness, that in all reason should have quenched her love, has, like an impediment in the current, made it more unruly, and Mariana loves her cruel husband with the full continuance of her first affection." The duke then more plainly unfolded his plan. It was, that Isabel should go to lord Angelo, and seem-ingly consent to come to him as he desired, at midnight; that by this means she would obtain the promised pardon; and that Mariana should go in her stead to the appointment, and pass herself upon Angelo, in the dark for Isabel. "Nor, gentle daughter," said the feigned friar, "fear you to do this thing; Angelo is her husband; and to bring them thus together is no sin." Isabel being pleased with this project, departed to do as he directed her; and he went to apprize Mariana of their intention. He had before this time visited this unhappy lady in his assumed character, giving her religious instruction and friendly consolation, at which times he had learned her sad story from her own lips; and now she, looking upon him as a holy man, readily consented to be directed by him in his undertaking.

When Isabel returned from her interview with Angelo, to the house of Mariana, where the duke had appointed her to meet him, he said, "Well met, and in good time; what is the news from this good deputy?" Isabel related the manner in which she had settled the affair. "Angelo," said she, "has a garden surrounded with a brick wall, on the western side of which is a vineyard, and to the vineyard is a gate." And then she showed to the duke and Mariana two keys that Angelo had given her; and she said, "This bigger key opens the vineyard gate; this other a little door which leads from the vineyard to the garden. There I have made my promise at the dead of the night to call upon him, and have got from him his word of assurance for my brother's life. I have taken a due and wary note of the place, and with whispering and most guilty diligence he shewed me the way twice over." "Are there no other tokens agreed upon between you, that Mariana must observe?" said the duke. "No, none," said Isabel, "only to go when it is dark. I have told him my time can be but short; for I have made him think a servant comes along with me, and that this servant is persuaded I come about my brother." The duke commended her discreet management, and she turning to Mariana, said, "Little have you to say to Angelo, when you depart from him, but, soft and low *Remember now my brother!*"

Mariana was that night conducted to the appointed place by Isabel, who rejoiced that she had, as she supposed, by this device preserved both her brother's life and her own honour. But that her brother's life was safe the duke was not well satisfied, and therefore at midnight he again repaired to the prison, and it was well for Claudio that he did so, else would Claudio have that night been beheaded; for soon after the duke entered the prison, an order came from the cruel deputy commanding that Claudio should be beheaded, and his head sent to him by five o'clock in the morning. But the duke persuaded the provost to put off the execution of Claudio, and to deceive Angelo by sending him the head of a man who died that morning in the prison. And to prevail upon the provost to agree to this, the duke, whom still the provost suspected not to be anything more or greater than he seemed, shewed the provost a letter written with the duke's hand, and sealed with his seal, which when the provost saw, he concluded this friar must have some secret order from the absent duke, and therefore he consented to spare Claudio; and he cut off the dead man's head, and carried it to Angelo.

Then the duke, in his own name, wrote to Angelo a letter, saying that certain accidents had put a stop to his journey, and that he should be in Vienna by the following morning, requiring Angelo to meet him at the entrance of the city, there to deliver up his authority; and the duke also commanded it to be proclaimed, that if any of his subjects craved redress for injustice, they should exhibit their petitions in the street on his first entrance into the city.

Early in the morning Isabel came to the prison, and the duke, who there awaited her coming, for secret reasons thought it good to tell her that Claudio was beheaded; therefore when Isabel inquired if Angelo had sent the pardon for her brother, he said, "Angelo has released Claudio from his world. His head is off, and sent to the deputy." The much-grieved sister cried out, "O, unhappy Claudio, wretched Isabel, injurious world, most wicked Angelo!" The seeming friar bid her take comfort, and when she was become a little calm, he acquainted her with the near prospect of the duke's return, and told her in what manner she should proceed in preferring her complaint against Angelo; and he bade her not to fear if the cause should seem to go against her for a while. Leaving Isabel sufficiently instructed, he next went to Mariana, and gave her counsel in what manner she also should act.

Then the duke laid aside his friar's habit, and in his own royal robes, amid a joyful crowd of his faithful subjects assembled to greet his arrival, entered the city of Vienna, where he was met by Angelo, who delivered up his authority in the proper form. And there came Isabel, in the manner of a petitioner for redress, and said, "Justice, most royal duke! I am the sister of one Claudio, who for the seducing a young maid was condemned to lose his head. I made my suit to lord Angelo for my brother's pardon. It were needless to tell your grace how I prayed and kneeled, how he repelled me, and how I replied; for this was of much length. The vile conclusion I now begin with grief and shame to utter. Angelo would not but by my yielding to his dishonourable love release my brother; and after much debate within myself, my sisterly remorse overcame my virtue, and I did yield to him. But the next morning betimes, Angelo, forfeiting his promise, sent a warrant for my poor brother's head!" The duke affected to disbelieve her story; and Angelo said that grief for her brother's death, who had suffered by the due course of the law, had disordered her senses. And now another suitor approached, which was Mariana; and Mariana said, "Noble prince, as there comes light from heaven, and truth from breath, as there is sense in truth, and truth in virtue, I am this man's wife, and, my good lord, the words of Isabel are false, for the night she says she was with Angelo, I passed that night with him in the garden-house. As this is true, let me in safety rise, or else for ever be fixed here a marble monument." Then did Isabel appeal for the truth of what she had said to Friar Lodowick, that being the name the duke had assumed in his disguise. Isabel and Mariana had both obeyed his instructions in what they said, the duke intending that the innocence of Isabel should be plainly proved in that public manner before the whole city of Vienna; but Angelo little thought that it was from such a cause that they thus differed in their story, and he hoped from their contradictory evidence to be able to clear himself from the accusation of Isabel; and he said, assuming the look of offended innocence, "I did but smile till now; but, good my lord, my patience here is touched, and I perceive these poor distracted women are but the instruments of some greater one, who sets them on. Let me have way, my lord, to find this practice out. "Aye, with all my heart," said the duke, "and punish them to the height of your pleasure. You, lord Escalus, sit with lord Angelo, lend him your pains to discover this abuse; the friar is sent for that set them on, and when he comes, do with your injuries as may seem best in any chastisement. I for a while will leave you, but stir not you, lord Angelo, till you have well determined upon this slander." The duke then went away, leaving Angelo well pleased to be deputed judge and umpire in his own cause. But the duke was absent only while he threw off his royal robes and put on his friar's habit; and in that disguise again he presented himself before Angelo and Escalus: and the good old Escalus, who thought Angelo had been falsely accused, said to the supposed friar, "Come, sir, did you set these women on to slander lord Angelo?" He replied, "Where is the duke? It is he should hear me speak." Escalus said, "The duke is in us, and we will hear you. Speak justly." "Boldly at least," retorted the friar: and then he blamed the duke for leaving the cause of Isabel in the hands of him she had accused, and spoke so freely of many corrupt practices he had observed, while, as he said, he had been a looker-on in Vienna, that Escalus threatened him with the torture for speaking words against the State, and for censuring the conduct of the duke, and ordered him to be taken away to prison. Then, to the amazement of all present, and to the utter confusion of Angelo, the supposed friar threw off his disguise, and they saw it was the duke himself.

The duke first addressed Isabel. He said to her, "Come hither, Isabel. Your friar is now your prince, but with my habit I have not changed my heart. I am still devoted to your service." "O give me pardon," said Isabel, "that I, your vassal, have employed and troubled your unknown sovereignty." He answered that he had most need of forgiveness from her for not having prevented the death of her brother;—for not yet would he tell her that Claudio was living; meaning first to make a farther trial of her goodness. Angelo now knew the duke had been a secret witness of his bad deeds, and he said, "O my dread lord, I should be guiltier than my guiltiness, to think I can be undiscernible, when I perceive your grace, like power divine, has looked upon my actions. Then, good prince, no longer prolong my shame, but let my trial be my confession. Immediate sentence and death is all the grace I beg." The duke replied, "Angelo, thy faults are manifest. We do condemn thee to the very block where Claudio stooped to death; and with like haste away with him; and for his possessions, Mariana, we do instate and widow you withal, to buy you a better husband." "O my dear lord," said Mariana, "I crave no other, nor no better man": and then on her knees, even as Isabel had begged the life of Claudio, did this kind wife of an ungrateful husband beg the life of Angelo; and she said, "Gentle my liege, O good my lord! Sweet Isabel, take my part! Lend me your knees, and, all my life to come, I will lend you, all my life, to do you service!" The duke said, "Against all sense you importune me. Should Isabel kneel down to beg for mercy, her brother's ghost would break his paved bed, and take her hence in horror." Still Mariana said, "Isabel, sweet Isabel, do but kneel by me, hold up your hand, say nothing! I will speak all. They say, best men are moulded out of faults, and for the most part become much the better for being a little bad. So may my husband. Oh, Isabel, will you not lend a knee?" The duke then said, "He dies for Claudio." But much pleased was the good duke, when his own Isabel, from whom he expected all gracious and honourable acts, kneeled down before him, and said, "Most bounteous sir, look, if it please you, on this man condemned, as if my brother lived. I partly think a due sincerity governed his deeds, till he did look on me. Since it is so, let him not die! My brother had but justice, in that he did the thing for which he died."

The duke, as the best reply he could make to this noble petitioner for her enemy's life, sending for Claudio from his prison-house, where he lay doubtful of his destiny, presented to her this lamented brother living; and he said to Isabel, "Give me your hand, Isabel; for your lovely sake I pardon Claudio. Say you will be mine, and he shall be my brother too." By this time lord Angelo perceived he was safe; and the duke, observing his eye to brighten up a little, said, "Well, Angelo, look that you love your wife; her worth has obtained your pardon: joy to you Mariana! Love her, Angelo! I have confessed her, and know her virtue." Angelo remembered, when drest in a little brief authority, how hard his heart had been, and felt how sweet is mercy.

The duke commanded Claudio to marry Juliet, and offered himself again to the acceptance of Isabel, whose virtuous and noble conduct had won her prince's heart. Isabel, not having taken the veil was free to marry; and the friendly offices, while hid under the disguise of a humble friar, which the noble duke had done for her, made her with grateful joy accept the honour he offered her; and when she became Duchess of Vienna, the excellent example of the virtuous Isabel worked such a complete reformation among the young ladies of that city, that from that time none fell into the transgression of Juliet, the repentant wife of the reformed Claudio. And the mercy-loving duke long reigned with his beloved Isabel, the happiest of husbands and of princes.

Twelfth Night, or What You Will

SEBASTIAN and his sister Viola, a young gentleman and lady of Messaline, were twins, and (which was accounted a great wonder) from their birth they so much resembled each other, that, but for the difference in their dress, they could not be known apart. They were both born in one hour, and in one hour they were both in danger of perishing, for they were shipwrecked on the coast of Illyria as they were making a sea-voyage together. The ship, on board of which they were, split on a rock in a violent storm, and a very small number of the ship's company escaped with their lives. The captain of the vessel, with a few of the sailors that were saved, got to land in a small boat, and with them they brought Viola safe on shore, where she, poor lady, instead of rejoicing at her own deliverance, began to lament her brother's loss; but the captain comforted her with the assurance that he had seen her brother, when the ship split, fasten himself to a strong mast, on which, as long as he could see anything of him for the distance, he perceived him borne up above the waves. Viola was much consoled by the hope this account gave her, and now considered how she was to dispose of herself in a strange country, so far from home; and she asked the captain if he knew anything of Illyria. "Aye, very well, madam," replied the captain, "for I was born not three hours' travel from this place." "Who governs here?" said Viola. The captain told her, Illyria was governed by Orsino, a duke noble in nature as well as dignity. Viola said, she had heard her father speak of Orsino, and that he was unmarried then." "And he is so now," said the captain; "or was so very lately, for but a month ago I went from here, and then it was the general talk (as you know what great ones do the people will prattle of) that Orsino sought the love of fair Olivia, a virtuous maid, the daughter of a count who died twelve months ago, leaving Olivia to the protection of her brother, who shortly after died also; and for the love of this dear brother, they say, she has adjured the sight and company of men." Viola, who was herself in such a sad affliction for her brother's loss, wished she could live with this lady, who so tenderly mourned a brother's death. She asked the captain if he could introduce her to Olivia, saying she would willingly serve this lady. But he replied, this would be a hard thing to accomplish, because the lady Olivia would admit no person into her house since her brother's death, not even the duke himself. Then Viola formed another project in her mind, which was, in a man's habit, to serve the duke Orsino as a page. It was a strange fancy in a young lady to put on male attire, and pass for a boy; but the forlorn and unprotected state of Viola, who was young and of uncommon beauty, alone, and in a foreign land, must plead her excuse.

She having observed a fair behaviour in the captain, and that he shewed a friendly concern for her welfare, intrusted him with her design, and he readily engaged to assist her. Viola gave him money, and directed him to furnish her with suitable apparel, ordering her clothes to be made of the same colour and in the same fashion her brother Sebastian used to wear, and when she was dressed in her manly garb she looked so exactly like her brother, that some strange errors happened by means of their being mistaken for each other; for, as will afterward appear, Sebastian was also saved.

Viola's good friend, the captain, when he had transformed this pretty lady into a gentleman, having some interest at court, got her presented to Orsino under the feigned name of Cesario. The duke was wonderfully pleased with the address and graceful deportment of this handsome youth, and made Cesario one of his pages, that being the office Viola wished to obtain: and she so well fulfilled the duties of her new station, and shewed such a ready observance and faithful attachment to her lord, that she soon became his most favoured attendant. To Cesario Orsino confided the whole history of his love for the lady Olivia. To Cesario he told the long and unsuccessful suit he had made to one, who, rejecting his long services, and despising his person, refused to admit him to her presence; and for the love of this lady who had so unkindly treated him, the noble Orsino, forsaking the sports of the field, and all manly exercises in which he used to delight, passed his hours in ignoble sloth, listening to the effeminate sounds of soft music, gentle airs, and passionate love-songs;

and neglecting the company of the wise and learned lords with whom he used to associate, he was now all day long conversing with young Cesario. Unmeet companion no doubt his grave courtiers thought Cesario was for their once noble master, the duke Orsino.

It is a dangerous matter for young maidens to be the confidants of handsome young dukes; which Viola too soon found to her sorrow, for all that Orsino told her he endured for Olivia, she presently perceived she suffered for the love of him: and much it moved her wonder, that Olivia could be so regardless of this her peerless lord and master, whom she thought no one should behold without the deepest admiration, and she ventured gently to hint to Orsino, that it was pity he should affect a lady, who was so blind to his worthy qualities; and she said, "If a lady were to love you, my lord, as you love Olivia (and perhaps there may be one who does), if you could not love her in return, would you not tell her that you could not love, and must not she be content with this answer?" But Orsino would not admit of this reasoning, for he denied that it was possible for any woman to love as he did. He said no woman's heart was big enough to hold so much love, and therefore it was unfair to compare the love of any lady for him, to his love for Olivia. Now though Viola had the utmost deference for the duke's opinions, she could not help thinking this was not quite true, for she thought her heart had full as much love in it as Orsino's had; and she said, "Ah, but I know, my lord." "What do you know, Cesario?" said Orsino. "Too well I know," replied Viola, "what love women may owe to men. They are as true of heart as we are. My father had a daughter loved a man, as I perhaps, were I a woman, should love your lordship." "And what is her history?" said Orsino. "A blank, my lord," replied Viola: "she never told her love, but let concealment, like a worm in the bud, prey on her damask cheek. She pined in thought, and with a green and yellow melancholy, she sat like Patience on a monument, smiling at grief." The duke enquired if this lady died of her love, but to this question Viola returned an evasive answer; as probably she had feigned the story, to speak words expressive of the secret love and silent grief she suffered for Orsino.

While they were talking, a gentleman entered whom the duke had sent to Olivia, and he said, "So please you, my lord, I might not be admitted to the lady, but by her handmaid she returned you this answer: Until seven years hence, the element itself shall not behold her face; but like a cloistress she will walk veiled, watering her chamber with her tears for the sad remembrance of her dead brother." On hearing this the duke exclaimed, "O she that has a heart of this fine frame, to pay this debt of love to a dead brother, how will she love when the rich golden shaft has touched her heart!" And then he said to Viola, "You know, Cesario, I have told you all the secrets of my heart; therefore, good youth, go to Olivia's house. Be not denied access; stand at the doors, and tell her there your fixed foot shall grow till you have audience." "And if I do speak to her, my lord, what then?" said Viola. "O then," replied Orsino, "unfold to her the passion of my love. Make a long discourse to her of my dear faith. It will well become you to act my woes, for she will attend more to you than to one of graver aspect."

Away then went Viola; but not willingly did she undertake this courtship, for she was to woo a lady to become a wife to him she wished to marry: but having undertaken the affair, she performed it with fidelity; and Olivia soon heard that a youth was at her door who insisted upon being admitted to her presence. "I told him," said the servant, "that you were sick: he said he knew you were, and therefore he came to speak with you. I told him that you were asleep: he seemed to have a foreknowledge of that too, and said, that therefore he must speak with you. What is to be said to him, lady? for he seems fortified against all denial, and will speak with you, whether you will or no." Olivia, curious to see who this peremptory messenger might be, desired he might be admitted; and throwing her veil over her face, she said she would once more hear Orsino's embassy, not doubting but that he came from the duke, by his importunity. Viola entering, put on the most manly air she could assume, and affecting the fine courtier's language of great men's pages, she said to the veiled lady, "Most radiant, exquisite, and matchless beauty, I pray you tell me if you are the lady of the house; for I should be sorry to cast away my speech upon another; for besides that it is excellently well penned, I have taken great pains to learn it." "Whence come you, sir?" said Olivia. "I can say little more than I have studied," replied Viola; "and that question is out of my part." "Are you a comedian?"

said Olivia. "No," replied Viola; "and yet I am not that which I play"; meaning, that she, being a woman, feigned herself to be a man. And again she asked Olivia if she were the lady of the house. Olivia said she was; and then Viola, having more curiosity to see her rival's features than haste to deliver her master's message, said, "Good madam, let me see your face." With this bold request Olivia was not averse to comply: for this haughty beauty, whom the duke Orsino had loved so long in vain, at first sight conceived a passion for the supposed page, the humble Cesario.

When Viola asked to see her face, Olivia said, "Have you any commission from your lord and master to negotiate with my face?" And then, forgetting her determination to go veiled for seven long years, she drew aside her veil, saying, "But I will draw the curtain and shew the picture. Is it not well done?" Viola replied, "It is beauty truly mixed; the red and white upon your cheeks is by Nature's own cunning hand laid on. You are the most cruel lady living, if you will lead these graces to the grave, and leave the world no copy." "O sir," replied Olivia, "I will not be so cruel. The world may have an inventory of my beauty. As, *item*, two lips, indifferent red; *item*, two gray eyes, with lids to them; one neck; one chin, and so forth. Were you sent here to praise me?" Viola replied, "I see you what you are: you are too proud, but you are fair. My lord and master loves you. O such a love could but be recompensed, though you were crowned the queen of beauty; for Orsino loves you with adoration and with tears, with groans that thunder love, and sighs of fire."

"Your lord," said Olivia, "knows well my mind. I cannot love him; yet I doubt not he is virtuous; I know him to be noble and of high estate, of fresh and spotless youth. All voices proclaim him learned, courteous, and valiant; yet I cannot love him, he might have taken his answer long ago." "If I did love you as my master does," said Viola, "I would make me a willow cabin at your gates, and call upon your name. I would write complaining sonnets on Olivia, and sing them in the dead of the night; your name should sound among the hills, and I would make Echo, the babbling gossip of the air, cry out *Olivia*. O you should not rest between the elements of earth and air, but you should pity me." "You might do much," said Olivia; "what is your parentage?" Viola replied, "Above my fortunes, yet my state is well. I am a gentleman." Olivia now reluctantly dismissed Viola, saying, "Go to your master, and tell him, I cannot love him. Let him send no more, unless perchance you come again to tell me how he takes it." And Viola departed, bidding the lady farewel by the name of Fair Cruelty. When she was gone, Olivia repeated the words, "*Above my fortunes, yet my state is well. I am a gentleman.*" And she said aloud, "I will be sworn he is; his tongue, his face, his limbs, action, and spirit, plainly shew he is a gentleman." And then she wished Cesario was the duke; and perceiving the fast hold he had taken on her affections, she blamed herself for her sudden love; but the gentle blame which people lay upon their own faults has no deep root; and presently the noble lady Olivia so far forgot the inequality between her fortunes and those of this seeming page, as well as the maidenly reserve which is the chief ornament of a lady's character, that she resolved to court the love of young Cesario, and sent a servant after him with a diamond ring, under the pretense that he had left it with her as a present from Orsino. She hoped, by thus artfully making Cesario a present of the ring, she should give him some intimation of her design; and truly it did make Viola suspect; for knowing that Orsino had sent no ring by her, she began to recollect that Olivia's looks and manner were expressive of admiration, and she presently guessed her master's mistress had fallen in love with her. "Alas," said she, "the poor lady might as well love a dream. Disguise I see is wicked, for it has caused Olivia to breathe as fruitless sighs for me, as I do for Orsino."

Viola returned to Orsino's palace, and related to her lord the ill success of the negotiation, repeating the command of Olivia, that the duke should trouble her no more. Yet still the duke persisted in hoping that the gentle Cesario would in time be able to persuade her to shew some pity, and therefore he bade him he should go to her again the next day. In the mean time, to pass away the tedious intervals, he commanded a song which he loved to be sung; and he said, "My good Cesario, when I heard that song last night, methought it did relieve my passion much. Mark it, Cesario, it is old and plain. The spinsters and the knitters when they sit in the sun, and the young maids that weave their thread with bone, chaunt this song. It is silly, yet I love it, for it tells of the innocence of love in the old times."

SONG

"Come away, come away, Death,
    And in sad cypress let me be laid;
Fly away, fly away, breath,
    I am slain by a fair cruel maid.
My shrowd of white stuck all with yew, O prepare it.
My part of death no one so true did share it.

"Not a flower, not a flower sweet,
    On my black coffin let there be strown:
Not a friend, not a friend greet
    My poor corpse, where my bones shall be thrown,
A thousand thousand sighs to save, lay me O where
Sad true lover never find my grave, to weep there."

Viola did not fail to mark the words of the old song, which in such true simplicity described the pangs of unrequited love, and she bore testimony in her countenance of feeling what the song expressed. Her sad looks were observed by Orsino, who said to her, "My life upon it, Cesario, though you are so young, your eye has looked upon some face that it loves; has it not, boy?" "A little, with your leave," replied Viola. "And what kind of woman, and of what age is she?" said Orsino. "Of your age, and of your complexion, my lord," said Viola; which made the duke smile to hear this fair young boy loved a woman so much older than himself, and of a man's dark complexion; but Viola secretly meant Orsino, and not a woman like him.

When Viola made her second visit to Olivia, she found no difficulty in gaining access to her. Servants soon discover when their ladies delight to converse with handsome young messengers; and the instant Viola arrived, the gates were thrown wide open, and the duke's page was shewn into Olivia's apartment with great respect; and when Viola told Olivia that she was come once more to plead in her lord's behalf, this lady said, "I desire you never to speak of him again; but if you would undertake another suit, I had rather hear you solicit, than music from the spheres." This was pretty plain speaking, but Olivia soon explained herself still more plainly, and openly confessed her love; and when she saw displeasure with perplexity expressed in Viola's face, she said, "O what a deal of scorn looks beautiful in the contempt and anger of his lip! Cesario, by the roses of the spring, by maidhood, honour, and by truth, I love you so, that, in spite of your pride, I have neither wit nor reason to conceal my passion. But in vain the lady wooed; Viola hastened from her presence, threatening never more to come to plead Orsino's love; and all the reply she made to Olivia's fond solicitations was, a declaration of a resolution *Never to love any woman.*

No sooner had Viola left the lady than a claim was made upon her valour. A gentleman, a rejected suitor of Olivia, who had learned how that lady had favoured the duke's messenger, challenged him to fight a duel. What should poor Viola do, who, though she carried a manlike outside, had a true woman's heart, and feared to look on her own sword!

When she saw her formidable rival advancing towards her with his sword drawn, she began to think of confessing that she was a woman; but she was relieved at once from her terror, and the shame of such a discovery, by a stranger that was passing by, who made up to them, and as if he had been long known to her, and were her dearest friend, said to her opponent, "If this young gentleman has done offence, I will take the fault on me; and if you offend him, I will for his sake defy you." Before Viola had time to thank him for his protection, or to enquire the reason of his kind interference, her new friend met with an enemy where his bravery was of no use to him; for the officers of justice coming up in that instant, apprehended the stranger in the duke's name to answer for an offence he had committed some years before; and he said to Viola, "This comes with seeking you"; and then he asked her for a purse, saying, "Now my necessity makes me ask for my purse, and it grieves me much more for what I cannot do for you, than for what befalls myself. You stand amazed, but be of comfort." His words did indeed amaze Viola, and she protested she knew him not, nor had ever received a purse from him; but for the kindness he had just shewn her, she offered him a small sum of money, being nearly the whole she possessed. And now the stranger spoke severe things, charging her with ingratitude and unkindness. He said, "This youth whom you see here, I snatched from the jaws of death, and for his sake alone I came to Illyria, and have fallen into this danger." But the officers cared little for hearkening to the complaints of their prisoner, and they hurried him off, saying, "What is that to us?" And as he was carried away, he called Viola by the name of Sebastian, reproaching the supposed Sebastian for disowning his friend, as long as he was within hearing. When Viola heard herself called Sebastian, though the stranger was taken away too hastily for her to ask an explanation, she conjectured that this seeming mystery might arise from her being mistaken for her brother; and she began to cherish hopes that it was her brother whose life this man said he had preserved. And so indeed it was. The stranger, whose name was Anthonio, was a sea-captain. He had taken Sebastian up into his ship, when, almost exhausted with fatigue, he was floating on the mast to which he had fastened himself in the storm. Anthonio conceived such a friendship for Sebastian, that he resolved to accompany him whithersoever he went; and when the youth expressed a curiosity to visit Orsino's court, Anthonio, rather than part from him, come to Illyria, though he knew, if his person should be known there, his life would be in danger, because in a sea-fight he had once dangerously wounded the duke Orsino's nephew. This was the offence for which he was now made a prisoner.

Anthonio and Sebastian had landed together but a few hours before Anthonio met Viola. He had given his purse to Sebastian, desiring him to use it freely if he saw anything he wished to purchase, telling him he would wait at the inn, while Sebastian went to view the town: but Sebastian not returning at the time appointed, Anthonio had ventured out to look for him, and Viola being dressed the same, and in face so exactly resembling her brother, Anthonio drew his sword (as he thought) in defence of the youth he had saved, and when Sebastian (as he supposed) disowned him, and denied him his own purse, no wonder he accused him of ingratitude.

Viola, when Anthonio was gone, fearing a second invitation to fight, slunk home as fast as she could. She had not been long gone, when her adversary thought he saw her return; but it was her brother Sebastian who happened to arrive at this place, and he said, "Now, sir, have I met you again? There's for you"; and struck him a blow. Sebastian was no coward; he returned the blow with interest, and drew his sword.

A lady now put a stop to this duel, for Olivia came out of the house, and she too mistaking Sebastian for Cesario, invited him to come into her house, expressing much sorrow at the rude attack he had met with. Though Sebastian was as much surprised at the courtesy of this lady as at the rudeness of his unknown foe, yet he went very willingly into the house, and Olivia was delighted to find Cesario (as she thought him) become more sensible of her attentions; for though their features were exactly the same, there was none of the contempt and anger to be seen in his face, which she had complained of when she told her love to Cesario.

Sebastian did not at all object to the fondness the lady lavished on him. He seemed to take it in very good part, yet he wondered how it had come to pass, and he was rather inclined to think Olivia was not in her right senses; but perceiving that she was mistress of a fine house, and that she ordered her affairs and seemed to govern her family discreetly, and that in all but her sudden love for him she appeared in the full possession of her reason, he well approved of the courtship, and Olivia finding Cesario in this good humour, and fearing he might change his mind, proposed that, as she had a priest in the house, they should be instantly married. Sebastian assented to this proposal; and when the marriage ceremony was over, he left his lady for a short time, intending to go and tell his friend Anthonio the good fortune that he had met with. In the mean time Orsino came to visit Olivia; and at the moment he arrived before Olivia's house, the officers of justice brought their prisoner, Anthonio, before the duke. Viola was with Orsino, her master; and when Anthonio saw Viola, whom he still imagined to be Sebastian, he told the duke in what manner he had rescued the youth from the perils of the sea; and after fully relating all the kindness he had really shewn to Sebastian, he ended his complaint with saying, that for three months, both day and night, this ungrateful youth had been with him. But now the lady Olivia coming forth from her house, the duke could no longer attend to Anthonio's story; and he said, "Here comes the countess: now Heaven walks on earth! but for thee, fellow, thy words are madness. Three months has this youth attended on me": and then he ordered Anthonio to be taken aside. But Orsino's heavenly countess soon gave the duke cause to accuse Cesario as much of ingratitude as Anthonio had done, for all the words he could hear Olivia speak were words of kindness to Cesario: and when he found his page had obtained this high place in Olivia's favour, he threatened him with all the terrors of his just revenge; and as he was going to depart he called Viola to follow him, saying, "Come, boy, with me. My thoughts are ripe for mischief." Though it seemed in his jealous rage he was going to doom Viola to instant death, yet her love made her no longer a coward, and she said she would most joyfully suffer death to give her master ease. But Olivia would not so lose her husband, and she cried, "Where goes my Cesario?" Viola replied, "After him I love more than my life." Olivia however prevented their departure by loudly proclaiming that Cesario was her husband, and sent for the priest, who declared that not two hours had passed since he had married the lady Olivia to this young man. In vain Viola protested she was not married to Olivia; the evidence of that lady and the priest made Orsino believe that his page had robbed him of the treasure he prized above his life. But thinking that it was past recall, he was bidding farewel to his faithless mistress, and the *young dissembler*, her husband, as he called Viola, warning her never to come in his sight again, when (as it seemed to them) a miracle appeared! for another Cesario entered, and addressed Olivia as his wife. This new Cesario was Sebastian, the real husband of Olivia; and when their wonder had a little ceased at seeing two persons with the same face, the same voice, and the same habit, the brother and sister began to question each other, for Viola could scarce be persuaded that her brother was living, and Sebastian knew not how to account for the sister he supposed drowned being found in the habit of a young man. But Viola presently acknowledged that she was indeed Viola and his sister under that disguise.

When all the errors were cleared up which the extreme likeness between this twin brother and sister had occasioned, they laughed at the lady Olivia for the pleasant mistake she had made in falling in love with a woman; and Olivia shewed no dislike to her exchange, when she found she had wedded the brother instead of the sister.

The hopes of Orsino were for ever at an end by this marriage of Olivia, and with his hopes all his fruitless love seemed to vanish away, and all his thoughts were fixed on the event of this favourite, young Cesario, being changed into a fair lady. He viewed Viola with great attention, and he remembered how very handsome he had always thought Cesario was, and he concluded she would look very beautiful in a woman's attire; and then he remembered how often she had said *she loved him*, which at the time seemed only the dutiful expressions of a faithful page, but now he guessed that something more was meant, for many of her pretty sayings, which were like riddles to him, came now into his mind, and he no sooner remembered all these things than he resolved to make Viola his wife; and he said to her (he still could not help calling her *Cesario* and *boy*), "Boy, you have said to me a thousand times that you should never love a woman like to me, and for the faithful service you have done for me so much beneath your soft and tender breeding, and since you have called me master so long, you shall now be your master's mistress, and Orsino's true duchess."

Olivia, perceiving Orsino was making over that heart, which she had so ungraciously rejected, to Viola, invited them to enter her house, and offered the assistance of the good priest, who had married her to Sebastian in the morning, to perform the same ceremony in the remaining part of the day for Orsino and Viola. Thus the twin brother and sister were both wedded on the same day; the storm and shipwreck, which had separated them, being the means of bringing to pass their high and mighty fortunes. Viola was the wife of Orsino, the duke of Illyria, and Sebastian the husband of the rich and noble countess, the lady Olivia.

POOR · HONEST · LORD BROVGHT · LOW · BY · HIS · OWN · HEART
VNDONE · BY · GOODNESS

Tale the Sixteenth

Timon of Athens

TIMON, a lord of Athens, in the enjoyment of a princely
fortune, affected a humour of liberality which knew no
limits. His almost infinite wealth could not flow in so fast,
but he poured it out faster upon all sorts and degrees of
people. Not the poor only tasted of his bounty, but great
lords did not disdain to rank themselves among his dependents and followers. His table was resorted to by all the lux-
urious feasters, and his house was open to all comers and
goers, at Athens. His large wealth combined with his free and
prodigal nature to subdue all hearts to his love; men of all
minds and dispositions tendered their services to lord Timon,
from the glass-faced flatterer, whose face reflects as in a mirror
the present humour of his patron, to the rough and unbending
cynic, who, affecting a contempt of men's persons, and an in-

difference to worldly things, yet could not stand out against the gracious manners and munificent soul of lord Timon, but would come (against his nature) to partake of his royal entertainments, and return most rich in his own estimation if he had received a nod or a salutation from Timon.

If a poet had composed a work which wanted a recommendatory introduction to the world, he had no more to do but to dedicate it to lord Timon, and the poem was sure of a sale, besides a present purse from the patron, and daily access to his house and table. If a painter had a picture to dispose of, he had only to take it to lord Timon, and pretend to consult his taste as to the merits of it; nothing more was wanting to persuade the liberal-hearted lord to buy it. If a jeweller had a stone of price, or a mercer rich costly stuffs, which for their costliness lay upon his hands, lord Timon's house was a ready mart, always open where they might get off their wares or their jewellery at any price, and the good-natured lord would thank them into the bargain, as if they had done him a piece of courtesy in letting him have the refusal of such precious commodities. So that by this means his house was thronged with superfluous purchases, of no use but to swell uneasy and ostentatious pomp; and his person was still more inconveniently beset with a crowd of these idle visitors, lying poets, painters, sharking tradesmen, lords, ladies, needy courtiers, and expectants, who continually filled his lobbies, raining their fulsome flatteries in whispers in his ears, sacrificing to him with adulation as to a god, making sacred the very stirrup by which he mounted his horse, and seeming as though they drank the free air but through his permission and bounty.

Some of these daily dependents were young men of birth, who (their means not answering to their extravagance) had been put in prison by creditors, and redeemed thence by lord Timon; these young prodigals thenceforward fastened upon his lordship, as if by common sympathy he were necessarily endeared to all such spendthrifts and loose livers, who not being able to follow him in his wealth, found it easier to copy him in prodigality, and copious spending of what was not their own. One of these flesh-flies was Ventidius, for whose debts unjustly contracted Timon but lately had paid down the sum of five talents.

But among this confluence, this great flood of visitors, none were more conspicuous than the makers of presents and givers of gifts. It was fortunate for these men, if Timon took a fancy to a dog or a horse, or any piece of cheap furniture which was theirs. The thing so praised, whatever it was, was sure to be sent the next morning with the compliments of the giver for lord Timon's acceptance, and apologies for the un- worthiness of the gift; and this dog or horse, or whatever it might be, did not fail to produce, from Timon's bounty, who would not be outdone in gifts, perhaps twenty dogs or horses, certainly presents of far richer worth, as these pre- tended donors knew well enough, and that their false presents were but the putting out of so much money at large and speedy interest. In this way lord Lucius had lately sent to Timon a present of four milk-white horses trapped in silver, which this cunning lord had observed Timon upon some occasion to commend; and another lord, Lucullus, had bestowed upon him in the same pretended way of free gift a brace of greyhounds, whose make and fleetness Timon had been heard to admire: these presents the easy-hearted lord accepted without suspicion of the dishonest views of the presenters; and the givers of course were rewarded with some rich return, a diamond or some jewel of twenty times the value of their false and mercenary donation.

Sometimes these creatures would go to work in a more direct way, and with gross and palpable artifice, which yet the credulous Timon was too blind to see, would affect to admire and praise something that Timon possessed, a bargain that he had bought, or some late purchase which was sure to draw from this yielding and soft-hearted lord a gift of the thing commended, for no service in the world done for it but the easy expense of a little cheap and obvious flattery. In this way Timon but the other day had given to one of these mean lords the bay courser which he himself rode upon, because his lordship had been pleased to say that it was a handsome beast and went well; and Timon knew that no man ever justly praised what he did not wish to possess. For lord Timon weighed his friends' affection with his own, and so fond was he of bestowing, that he could have dealt kingdoms to these supposed friends, and never have been weary.

Not that Timon's wealth all went to enrich these wicked flatterers; he could do noble and praiseworthy actions; and when a servant of his once loved the daughter of a rich Athenian, but could not hope to obtain her by reason that in wealth and rank the maid was so far above him, lord Timon freely bestowed upon his servant three Athenian talents, to make his fortune equal with the dowry which the father of the young maid demanded of him who should be her husband. But for the most part, knaves and parasites had the command of his fortune, false friends whom he did not know to be such, but, because they flocked around his person, he thought they must needs love him; and because they smiled and flattered him, he thought surely that his conduct was approved by all the wise and good. And when he was feasting in the midst of all these flatterers and mock friends, when they were eating him up, and draining his fortunes dry with large draughts of richest wines drunk to his health and prosperity, he could not perceive the difference of a friend from a flatterer, but to his deluded eyes (made proud with the sight), it seemed a precious comfort to have so many, like brothers commanding one another's fortunes (though it was his own fortune which paid all the cost), and with joy they would run over at the spectacle of such, as it appeared to him, truly festive and fraternal meeting.

But while he thus outwent the very heart of kindness, and poured out his bounty, as if Plutus, the god of gold, had been but his steward; while thus he proceeded without care of stop, so senseless of expense that he would neither enquire how he could maintain it, nor cease his wild flow of riot; his riches, which were not infinite, must needs melt away before a prodigality which knew no limits. But who should tell him so?

his flatterers? they had an interest in shutting his eyes. In vain did his honest steward Flavius try to represent to him his condition, laying his accounts before him, begging of him, praying of him, with an importunity that on any other occasion would have been unmannerly in a servant, beseeching him with tears, to look into the state of his affairs. Timon would still put him off, and turn the discourse to something else; for nothing is so deaf to remonstrance as riches turned to poverty, nothing so unwilling to believe its situation, nothing is so incredulous to its own true state, and hard to give credit to a reverse. Often had this good steward, this honest creature, when all the rooms of Timon's great house have been choked up with riotous feeders at his master's cost, when the floors have wept with drunken spilling of wine, and every apartment has blazed with lights and resounded with music and feasting, often had he retired by himself to some solitary spot, and wept faster than the wine ran from the wasteful casks within, to see the mad bounty of his lord, and to think, when the means were gone which brought him praises from all sorts of people, how quickly the breath would be gone of which the praise was made; praises won in feasting would be lost in fasting, and at one cloud of winter-showers these flies would disappear.

But now the time was come that Timon could shut his ears no longer to the representations of this faithful steward. Money must be had; and when he ordered Flavius to sell some of his land for that purpose, Flavius informed him, what he had in vain endeavoured at several times before to make him listen to, that most of his land was already sold or forfeited, and that all he possessed at present was not enough to pay the one half of what he owed. Struck with wonder at this representation, Timon hastily replied, "My lands extended from Athens to Lacedemon." "O my good lord," said Flavius, "the world is but a world, and has bounds; were it all yours to give it in a breath, how quickly were it gone!"

Timon consoled himself that no villainous bounty had yet come from him, that if he had given his wealth away unwisely, it had not been bestowed to feed his vices, but to cherish his friends; and he bade the kind-hearted steward (who was weeping) to take comfort in the assurance that his master could never lack means while he had so many noble friends; and this infatuated lord persuaded himself that he had nothing to do but to send and borrow, to use every man's fortune (that had ever tasted his bounty) in this extremity, as freely as his own. Then with a cheerful look, as if confident of the trial, he severally despatched messengers to lord Lucius, to lords Lucullus and Sempronius, men upon whom he had lavished his gifts in past times without measure or moderation; and to Ventidius, whom he had lately released out of prison by paying his debts, and who by the death of his father was now come into the possession of an ample fortune, and well enabled to require Timon's courtesy; to request of Ventidius the return of those five talents which he had paid for him, and of each of these noble lords the loan of fifty talents: nothing doubting that their gratitude would supply his wants (if he needed it) to the amount of five hundred times fifty talents.

Lucullus was the first applied to. This mean lord had been dreaming overnight of a silver bason and cup, and when Timon's servant was announced, his sordid mind suggested to him that his was surely a making out of his dream, and that Timon had sent him such a present: but when he understood the truth of the matter, and that Timon wanted money, the quality of his faint and watery friendship shewed itself, for with many protestations he vowed to the servant that he had long foreseen the ruin of his master's affairs, and many a time he come to dinner to tell him of it, and had come again to supper, to try to persuade him to spend less, but he would take no counsel nor warning by his coming: and true it was that he had been a constant attender (as he said) at Timon's feasts, as he had in greater things tasted his bounty, but that he ever came with that intent, or gave good counsel or reproof to Timon, was a base unworthy lie, which he suitably followed up with meanly offering the servant a bribe, to go home to his master and tell him that he had not found Lucullus at home.

As little success had the messenger who was sent to lord Lucius. This lying lord, who was full of Timon's meat, and enriched almost to bursting with Timon's costly presents, when he found the wind changed, and the fountain of so much bounty suddenly stopt, at first could hardly believe it; but on its being confirmed, he affected great regret that he should not have it in his power to serve lord Timon, for unfortunately (which was a base falsehood) he had made a great purchase the day before, which had quite disfurnished him of the means at present, the more beast he, he called himself, to put it out of his power to serve so good a friend; and he counted it one of his greatest afflictions that his ability should fail him to pleasure such an honourble gentleman.

Who can call any man friend that dips in the same dish with him? just of this metal is every flatterer. In the recollection of everybody Timon had been a father to this Lucius, had kept up his credit with his purse; Timon's money had gone to pay the wages of his servants, to pay the hire of the labourers who had sweat to build the fine houses which Lucius's pride had made necessary to him: yet, oh! the monster which man makes himself when he proves ungrateful! this Lucius now denied to Timon a sum, which, in respect of what Timon had bestowed on him, was less than charitable men afford to beggars.

Sempronius and every one of those mercenary lords to whom Timon applied in their turn, returned the same evasive answer or direct denial; even Ventidius, the redeemed and now rich Ventidius, refused to assist him with the loan of those five talents which Timon had not lent, but generously given him in his distress.

Now was Timon as much avoided in his poverty as he had been courted and resorted to in his riches. Now the same tongues which had been loudest in his praises, extolling him as bountiful, liberal, and open-handed, were not ashamed to censure that very bounty as folly, that liberaltiy as profuseness, though it had shewn itself folly in nothing so truly as in the selection of such unworthy creatures as themselves for its objects. Now was Timon's princely mansion forsaken, and become a shunned and hated place, a place for men to pass by, not a place as formerly where every passenger must stop and taste of his wine and good cheer; now, instead of being thronged with feasting and tumultuous guests, it was beset with impatient and clamourous creditors, usurers, extortioners, fierce and intolerable in their demands, pleading bonds, interest, mortgages, iron-hearted men that would take no denial nor putting off, that Timon's house was now his jail, which he could not pass, nor go in nor out for them; one demanding his due of fifty talents, another bringing in a bill of five thousand crowns, which if he would tell out his blood by drops, and pay them so, he had not enough in his body to discharge, drop by drop.

In this desperate and irremediable state (as it seemed) of his affairs, the eyes of all men were suddenly surprised at a new and incredible luster which this setting sun put forth. Once more lord Timon proclaimed a feast, to which he invited his accustomed guests, lords, ladies, all that was great or fashionable in Athens. Lords Lucius and Lucullus came, Ventidius, Sempronius, and the rest. Who more sorry now than these fawning wretches, when they found (as they thought) that lord Timon's poverty was all pretense, and had been only put on to make trial of their loves, to think that they should not have seen through the artifice at the time, and have had the cheap credit of obliging his lordship? yet who more glad to find the fountain of that noble bounty, which they had thought dried up, still fresh and running?

They came dissembling, protesting, expressing deepest sorrow and shame, that when his lordship sent to them they should have been so unfortunate as to want the present means to oblige so honourable a friend. But Timon begged them not to give such trifles a thought, for he had altogether forgotten it. And these base fawning lords, though they had denied him money in his adversity, yet could not refuse their presence at this new blaze of his returning prosperity. For the swallow follows not summer more willingly than men of these dispositions follow the good fortunes of the great, nor more willingly leaves winter than these shrink from the first appearance of a reverse: such summer birds are men. But now with music and state the banquet of smoking dishes was served up; and when the guests had a little done admiring whence the bankrupt Timon could find means to furnish so costly a feast, some doubting whether the scene they saw was real, as scarce trusting their own eyes; at a signal given, the dishes were uncovered, and Timon's drift appeared: instead of those varieties and far-fetched dainties which they expected, that Timon's epicurean table in past times had so liberally presented, now appeared under the covers of these dishes a preparation more suitable to Timon's poverty, nothing but a little smoke and lukewarm water, fit feast for this knot of mouth-friends, whose professions were indeed smoke, and their hearts lukewarm and slippery as the water with which Timon welcomed his astonished guests, bidding them, "Uncover dogs, and lap"; and before they could recover their surprise, sprinkling it in their faces that they might have enough, and throwing dishes and all after them, who now ran huddling out, lords, ladies, with their caps snatched up in haste, a splendid confusion, Timon pursuing them, still calling them what they were, "Smooth, smiling parasites, destroyers under the mask of courtesy, affable wolves, meek bears, fools of fortune, feast-friends, time-flies." They, crowding out to avoid him, left the house more willingly than they had entered it: some losing their gowns and caps and some their jewels in the hurry, all glad to escape out of the presence of such a mad lord, and the ridicule of his mock banquet.

This was the last feast that ever Timon made, and in it he took farewel of Athens and the society of men, for, after that, he betook himself to the woods, turning his back upon the hated city and upon all mankind, wishing the walls of that detestable city might sink, and their houses fall upon their owners, wishing all plagues which infest humanity, war, outrage, poverty, and diseases, might fasten upon its inhabitants, praying the just gods to confound all Athenians, both young and old, high and low; so wishing, he went to the woods, where he said he should find the unkindest beast much kinder than mankind. He stript himself naked, that he might retain no fashion of a man, and dug a cave to live in, and lived solitary in the manner of a beast, eating the wild roots, and drinking water, flying from the face of his kind, and choosing rather to herd with wild beasts, as more harmless and friendly than man.

What a change from lord Timon the rich, lord Timon the

delight of mankind, to Timon the naked, Timon the man-hater! Where were his flatterers now? Where were his attendants and retinue? Would the bleak air, that boisterous servitor, be his chamberlain, to put his shirt on warm? Would those stiff trees, that had outlived the eagle, turn young and fairy pages to him, to skip on his errands when he bade them? Would the cold brook, when it was iced with winter, administer to him his warm broths and caudles when sick of an over-night's surfeit? Or would the creatures that lived in those wild woods come and lick his hand and flatter him?

Here on a day, when he was digging for roots, his poor sustenance, his spade struck against something heavy, which proved to be gold, a great heap which some miser had probably buried in a time of alarm, thinking to have come again and taken it from its prison, but died before the opportunity had arrived, without making any man privy to the concealment: so it lay, doing neither good nor harm, in the bowels of the earth, its mother, as if it had never come from thence, till the accidental striking of Timon's spade against it once more brought it to light.

Here was a mass of treasure which if Timon had retained his old mind, was enough to have purchased him friends and flatterers again; but Timon was sick of the false world, and the sight of gold was poisonous to his eyes; and he would have restored it to the earth, but that, thinking of the infinite calamities which by means of gold happen to mankind, how the lucre of it causes robberies, oppression, injustice, briberies, violence, and murder among men, he had a pleasure in imagining (such a rooted hatred did he bear to his species) that out of this heap which in digging he had discovered might arise some mischief to plague mankind. And some soldiers passing through the woods near to his cave at that instant, which proved to be a part of the troops of the Athenian captain Alcibiades, who upon some disgust taken against the senators at Athens (the Athenians were ever noted to be a thankless and ungrateful people, giving disgust to their generals and best friends), was marching at the head of the same triumphant army which he had formerly headed in their defence, to war against them: Timon, who liked their business well, bestowed upon their captain the gold to pay his soldiers, requiring no other service from him, than that he should with his conquering army lay Athens level with the ground, and burn, slay, kill all her inhabitants; not sparing the old men for their white beards, for (he said) they were usurers, nor the young children for their seeming innocent smiles, for those (he said) would live, if they grew up, to be traitors; but to steel his eyes and ears against any sights or sounds that might awaken compassion; and not to let the cries of virgins, babes, or mothers, hinder him from making one universal massacre of the city, but to confound them all in his conquest; and when he had conquered, he prayed that the gods would confound him also, the conqueror: so thoroughly did Timon hate Athens, Athenians, and all mankind.

While he lived in this forlorn state, leading a life more brutal than human, he was suddenly surprised one day with the appearance of a man standing in an admiring posture at the door of his cave. It was Flavius, the honest steward, whom love and zealous affection to his master had led to seek him out at his wretched dwelling, and to offer his services; and the first sight of his master, the once noble Timon, in that abject condition, naked as he was born, living in the manner of a beast among beasts, looking like his own sad ruins and a monument of decay, so affected this good servant, that he stood speechless, wrapt up in horror and confounded. And when he found utterance at last to his words, they were so choked with tears, that Timon had much ado to know him again, or to make out who it was that had come (so contrary to the experience he had had of mankind) to offer him service in extremity. And being in the form and shape of a man, he suspected him for a traitor, and his tears for false; but the good servant by so many tokens confirmed the truth of his fidelity, and made it clear that nothing but love and zealous duty to his once dear master had brought him there, that Timon was forced to confess that the world contained one honest man; yet, being in the shape and form of a man, he could not look upon his man's face without abhorrence, or hear words uttered from his man's lips without loathing; and this singly honest man was forced to depart, because he was a man, and because, with a heart more gentle and compassionate than is usual to man, he bore man's detested form and outward feature.

But greater visitants than a poor steward were about to interrupt the savage quiet of Timon's solitude. For now the day was come when the ungrateful lords of Athens sorely repented the injustice which they had done to the noble Timon. For Alcibiades, like an incensed wild boar, was raging at the walls of their city, and with his hot siege threatened to lay fair Athens in the dust. And now the memory of lord Timon's former prowess and military conduct came fresh into their forgetful minds, for Timon had been their general in past times, and was a valiant and expert soldier, who alone of all the Athenians was deemed able to cope with a besieging army such as then threatened them, or to drive back the furious approaches of Alcibiades.

A deputation of the senators was chosen in this emergency to wait upon Timon. To him they come in their extremity, to whom, when he was in extremity, they had shewn but small regard; as if they presumed upon his gratitude whom they had disobliged, and had derived a claim to his courtesy from their own most discourteous and unpiteous treatment.

Now they earnestly beseech him, implore him with tears, to return and save that city, from which their ingratitude had so lately driven him; now they offer him riches, power, dignities, satisfaction for past injuries, and public honours and the public love; their persons, lives, and fortunes, to be at his disposal, if he will but come back and save them. But Timon the naked, Timon the man-hater, was no longer lord Timon, the lord of bounty, the flower of valour, their defence in war, their ornament in peace. If Alcibiades killed his countrymen, Timon cared not. If he sacked fair Athens, and slew her old men and her infants, Timon would rejoice. So he told them; and that there was not a knife in the unruly

camp which he did not prize above the reverendest throat in
Athens.

This was all the answer he vouchsafed to the weeping, disappointed senators; only at parting, he bade them commend
him to his countrymen, and tell them, that to ease them of
their griefs and anxieties, and to prevent the consequences of
fierce Alcibiades' wrath, there was yet a way left, which he
would teach them, for he had yet so much affection left for
his dear countrymen as to be willing to do them a kindness
before his death. These words a little revived the senators,
who hoped that his kindness for their city was returning.
Then Timon told them that he had a tree, which grew near
his cave, which he should shortly have occasion to cut down,
and he invited all his friends in Athens, high or low, of what
degree soever, who wished to shun affliction, to come and take
a taste of his tree before he cut it down; meaning, that they
might come and hang themselves on it, and escape affliction
that way.

And this was the last courtesy, of all his noble bounties,
which Timon shewed to mankind, and this the last sight of
him which his countrymen had: for not many days after, a
poor soldier, passing by the sea-beach, which was at a little
distance from the woods which Timon frequented, found a
tomb on the verge of the sea, with an inscription upon it,
purporting that it was the grave of Timon the man-hater,
who "While he lived, did hate all living men, and dying,
wished a plague might consume all caitiffs left!"

Whether he finished his life by violence, or whether mere

distaste of life and the loathing he had for mankind brought Timon to his conclusion, was not clear, yet all men admired the fitness of his epitaph, and the consistency of his end: dying, as he had lived, a hater of mankind: and some there were who fancied a conceit in the very choice which he made of the sea-beach for his place of burial, where the vast sea might weep for ever upon his grave, as in contempt for the transient and shallow tears of hypocritical and deceitful mankind.

Tale the Seventeenth

Romeo and Juliet

THE two chief families in Verona were the rich Capulets and the Mountagues. There had been an old quarrel between these two families, which was grown to such a height, and so deadly was the enmity between them, that it extended to the remotest kindred, to the followers and retainers of both sides, insomuch that a servant of the house of Mountague could not meet a servant of the house of Capulet, nor a Capulet encounter with a Mountague by chance, but fierce words and sometimes bloodshed ensued; and frequent were the brawls from such accidental meetings, which disturbed the happy quiet of Verona's streets.

Old lord Capulet made a great supper, to which many fair ladies and many noble guests were invited. All the admired beauties of Verona were present, and all comers were made welcome if they were not of the house of Mountague. At this feast of Capulets, Rosaline, beloved of Romeo, son to the old Lord Mountague, was present; and though it was dangerous for a Mountague to be seen in this assembly, yet Benvolio, a friend of Romeo, persuaded the young lord to go to this assembly in the disguise of a mask, that he might see his Rosaline, and see her compare her with some choice beauties of Verona, who (he said) would make him think his swan a crow. Romeo had small faith in Benvolio's words; nevertheless, for the love of Rosaline, he was persuaded to go. For Romeo was a sincere and passionate lover, and one that lost his sleep for love, and fled society to be alone, thinking on Rosaline, who disdained him, and never requited his love with the least show of courtesy or affection; and Benvolio wished to cure his friend of this love by shewing him diversity of ladies and company. To this feast of Capulets then young Romeo with Benvolio and their friend Mercutio went masked. Old Capulet bid them welcome, and told them that ladies who had their toes unplagued with corns would dance with them. And the old man was light-hearted and merry, and said that he had worn a mask when he was young, and could have told a whispering tale in a fair lady's ear. And they fell to dancing, and Romeo was suddenly struck with the exceeding beauty of a lady who danced there, who seemed to him to teach the torches to burn bright, and her beauty to shew by night like a rich jewel worn by a blackamoor: beauty too rich for use, too dear for earth! like a snowy dove trooping with crows (he said), so richly did her beauty and perfections shine above the ladies her companions. While he uttered these praises, he was overheard by Tybalt, a nephew of lord Capulet, who knew him by his voice to be Romeo. And this Tybalt, being of a fiery and passionate temper, could not endure that a Mountague should come under cover of a mask, to fleer and scorn (as he said) at their solemnities. And he stormed and raged exceedingly, and would have struck young Romeo dead. But his uncle, the old lord Capulet, would not suffer him to do any injury at that time, both out of respect to his guests, and because Romeo had borne himself like a gentleman, and all tongues in Verona bragged of him to be a virtuous and well-governed youth. Tybalt, forced to be patient against his will, restrained himself, but swore that this vile Mountague should at another time dearly pay for his intrusion.

The dancing being done, Romeo watched the place where the lady stood; and under favour of his masking habit, which might seem to excuse in part the liberty, he presumed in the gentlest manner to take her by the hand, calling it a shrine, which if he prophaned by touching it, he was a blushing pilgrim, and would kiss it for atonement. "Good pilgrim," answered the lady, "your devotion shews by far too mannerly and too courtly: saints have hands, which pilgrims may touch, but kiss not." "Have not saints lips, and pilgrims too?" said Romeo. "Aye," said the lady, "lips which they must use in prayer." "O then, my dear saint," said Romeo, "hear my prayer and grant it, lest I despair." In such like allusions and loving conceits they were engaged, when the lady was called away to her mother. And Romeo enquiring who her mother was, discovered that the lady whose peerless beauty he was so much struck with, was young Juliet, daughter and heir to the lord Capulet, the great enemy of the Mountagues; and that he had unknowingly engaged his heart to his foe. This troubled him, but it could not dissuade him from loving. As little rest had Juliet, when she found that the gentleman that she had been talking with was Romeo and a Mountague, for she had been suddenly smit with the same hasty and inconsiderate passion for Romeo, which he had conceived for her; and a prodigious birth of love it seemed to her, that she must love her enemy, and that her affections should settle there, where family considerations should induce her chiefly to hate.

It being midnight, Romeo with his companions departed; but they soon missed him, for unable to stay away from the house where he had left his heart, he leaped the wall of an orchard which was at the back of Juliet's house. Here he had not been long, ruminating on his new love, when Juliet appeared above at a window, through which her exceeding beauty seemed to break like the light of the sun in the east; and the moon, which shone in the orchard with a faint light, appeared to Romeo as if sick and pale with grief at the superior luster of this new sun. And she leaning her hand upon her cheek, he passionately wished himself a glove upon that hand, that he might touch her cheek. She all this while thinking herself alone, fetched a deep sigh, and exclaimed, "Ah me!" Romeo; enraptured to hear her speak, said softly, unheard by her, "O speak again, bright angel, for such you appear, being over my head, like a winged messenger from heaven, whom mortals fall back to gaze upon." She, unconscious of being overheard, and full of the new passion which that night's adventure had given birth to, called upon her lover by name (whom she supposed absent): "O Romeo, Romeo!"

said she, "wherefore art thou Romeo? Deny thy father, and refuse thy name, for my sake; or if thou wilt not, be but my sworn love, and I no longer will be a Capulet." Romeo, having this encouragement, would fain have spoken, but he was desirous of hearing more; and the lady continued her passionate discourse with herself (as she thought), still chiding Romeo for being Romeo and a Mountague, and wishing him some other name, or that he would put away the hated name, and for that name, which was no part of himself, he should take all herself. At this loving word Romeo could no longer refrain, but taking up the dialogue as if her words had been addressed to him personally, and not merely in fancy, he bade her call him Love, or by whatever other name she pleased, for he was no longer Romeo, if that name was displeasing to her. Juliet, alarmed to hear a man's voice in the garden, did not at first know who it was, that by favour of the night and darkness had thus stumbled upon the discovery of her secret; but when he spoke again, though her ears had not yet drunk a hundred words of that tongue's uttering, yet so nice is a lover's hearing, that she immediately knew him to be young Romeo, and she expostulated with him on the danger to which he had exposed himself by climbing the orchard walls, for if any of her kinsmen should find him there, it would be death to him, being a Mountague. "Alack," said Romeo, "there is more peril in your eye, than in twenty of their swords. Do you but look kind upon me, lady, and I am proof against their enmity. Better my life should be ended by their hate, than that hated life should be prolonged,

to live without your love." "How came you into this place,"
said Juliet, "and by whose direction?" "Love directed me,"
answered Romeo: "I am no pilot, yet wert thou as far apart
from me, as that vast shore which is washed with the farthest
sea, I should adventure for such merchandise." A crimson
blush came over Juliet's face, yet unseen by Romeo by reason
of the night, when she reflected upon the discovery which she
had made, yet not meaning to make it, of her love to Romeo.
She would fain have recalled her words, but that was impossible; fain would she have stood upon form, and have
kept her lover at a distance, as the custom of discreet ladies
is, to frown and be perverse, and give their suitors harsh
denials at first; to stand off, and affect a coyness or indifference, where they most love, that their lovers may not think
them too lightly or too easily won: for the difficulty of attain-
ment increases the value of the object. But there was no
room in her case for denials, or putting off, or any of the
customary arts of delay and protractive courtship. Romeo
had heard from her own tongue, when she did not dream that
he was near her, a confession of her love. So with an honest
frankness, which the novelty of her situation excused, she
confirmed the truth of what he had before heard, and addressing him by the name of *fair Mountague* (love can
sweeten a sour name), she begged him not to impute her
easy yielding to levity or an unworthy mind, but that he
must lay the fault of it (if it were a fault) upon the accident
of the night which had so strangely discovered her thoughts.
And she added, that though her behaviour to him might

not be sufficiently prudent, measured by the custom of her sex, yet that she would prove more true than many whose prudence was dissembling, and their modesty artificial cunning.

Romeo was beginning to call the heavens to witness that nothing was farther from his thoughts than to impute a shadow of dishonour to such an honoured lady, when she stopped him, begged him not to swear: for although she joyed in him, yet she had no joy of that night's contract; it was too rash, too unadvised, too sudden. But he being urgent with her to exchange a vow of love with her that night, she said that she already had given him hers before he requested it; meaning, when he overheard her confession; but she would retract what she then bestowed, for the pleasure of giving it again, for her bounty was as infinite as the sea, and her love as deep. From this loving conference she was called away by her nurse, who slept with her, and thought it time for her to be in bed, for it was near to daybreak; but hastily returning, she said three or four words more to Romeo, the purport of which was, that if his love was indeed honourable, and his purpose marriage, she would send a messenger to him to-morrow, to appoint a time for their marriage, when she would lay all her fortunes at his feet, and follow him as her lord through the world. While they were settling this point, Juliet was repeatedly called for by her nurse, and went in and returned, and went and returned again, for she seemed as jealous of Romeo going from her, as a young girl of her bird, which she will let hop a little from her hand, and pluck it back with a silken thread; and Romeo was as loath to part as she: for the sweetest music to lovers is the sound of each other's tongues at night. But at last they parted, wishing mutually sweet sleep and rest for that night.

The day was breaking when they parted, and Romeo, who was too full of thoughts of his mistress and that blessed meeting to allow him to sleep, instead of going home, bent his course to a monastery hard by, to find friar Lawrence. The good friar was already up at his devotions, but seeing young Romeo abroad so early, he conjectured rightly, that he had not been a-bed that night, but that some distemper of youthful affection had kept him waking. He was right in imputing the cause of Romeo's wakefulness to love, but he made a wrong guess at the object, for he thought that his love for Rosaline had kept him waking. But when Romeo revealed his new passion for Juliet, and requested the assistance of the friar to marry them that day, the holy man lifted up his eyes and hands in a sort of wonder at the sudden change in Romeo's affections, for he had been privy to all Romeo's love for Rosaline, and his many complaints of her disdain; and he said that young men's love lay not truly in their hearts, but in their eyes. But Romeo replying that he himself had often chidden him for doating on Rosaline, who could not love him again, whereas Juliet both loved and was beloved by him, the friar assented in some measure to his reasons; and thinking that a matrimonial alliance between young Juliet and Romeo might happily be the means of making up the long breach between the Capulets and the Mountagues; which no one more lamented than this good friar, who was a friend to both the families, and had often interposed his mediation to make up the quarrel without effect; partly moved by policy, and partly by his fondness for young Romeo, to whom he could deny nothing, the old man consented to join their hands in marriage.

Now was Romeo blest indeed, and Juliet, who knew his intent from a messenger which she had dispatched according to promise, did not fail to be early at the cell of friar Lawrence, where their hands were joined in holy marriage; the good friar praying the heavens to smile upon that act, and in the union of this young Mountague and young Capulet to bury the old strife and long dissensions of their families.

The ceremony being over, Juliet hastened home, where she staid impatient for the coming of night, at which time Romeo promised to come and meet her in the orchard, where they had met the night before; and the time between seemed as tedious to her as the night before some great festival seems to an impatient child that has got finery which it may not put on till the morning.

That same day about noon, Romeo's friends, Benvolio and Mercutio, walking through the streets of Verona, were met by a party of the Capulets with the impetuous Tybalt at their head. This was the same angry Tybalt who would have fought with Romeo at old lord Capulet's feast. He seeing Mercutio, accused him bluntly of associating with

Romeo, a Mountague. Mercutio, who had as much fire and youthful blood in him as Tybalt, replied to this accusation with some sharpness; and in spite of all Benvolio could say to moderate their wrath, a quarrel was beginning, when Romeo himself passing that way, the fierce Tybalt turned from Mercutio to Romeo, and gave him the disgraceful appellation of villain. Romeo wished to avoid a quarrel with Tybalt above all men, because he was the kinsman of Juliet, and much beloved by her; besides, this young Mountague had never thoroughly entered into the family quarrel, being by nature wise and gentle, and the name of a Capulet, which was his dear lady's name, was now rather a charm to allay resentment, than a watchword to excite fury. So he tried to reason with Tybalt, whom he saluted mildly by the name of *good Capulet*, as if he, though a Mountague, had some secret pleasure in uttering that name: but Tybalt, who hated all Mountagues as he hated hell, would hear no reason, but drew his weapon; and Mercutio, who knew not of Romeo's secret motive for desiring peace with Tybalt, but looked upon his present forbearance as a sort of calm dishonourable submission, with many disdainful words provoked Tybalt to the prosecution of his first quarrel with him; and Tybalt and Mercutio fought, till Mercutio fell, receiving his death's wound while Romeo and Benvolio were vainly endeavouring to part the combatants. Mercutio being dead, Romeo kept his temper no longer, but returned the scornful appellation of villain which Tybalt had given him; and they fought till Tybalt was slain by Romeo. This deadly brawl falling out in the midst of Verona, at noonday, the news of it quickly brought a crowd of citizens to the spot, and among them the old lords Capulet and Mountague, with their wives; and soon arrived the prince himself, who being related to Mercutio, whom Tybalt had slain, and having had the peace of his government often disturbed by these brawls of Mountagues and Capulets, came determined to put the law in strictest force against those who should be found to be offenders. Benvolio, who had been eyewitness to the fray, was commanded by the prince to relate the origin of it, which he did, keeping as near to the truth as he could without injury to Romeo, softening and excusing the part which his friend took in it. Lady Capulet, whose extreme grief for the loss of her kinsman Tybalt made her keep no bounds in her revenge, exhorted the prince to do strict justice upon his murderer, and to pay no attention to Benvolio's representation, who being Romeo's friend, and a Mountague, spoke partially. Thus she pleaded against her new son-in-law, but she knew not yet that he was her son-in-law, and Juliet's husband. On the other hand was to be seen lady Mountague pleading for her son's life, and arguing with some justice that Romeo had done nothing worthy of punishment in taking the life of Tybalt, which was already forfeited to the law by his having slain Mercutio. The prince, unmoved by the passionate exclamations of these women, on a careful examination of the facts, pronounced his sentence, and by that sentence Romeo was banished from Verona.

Heavy news to young Juliet, who had been but a few hours a bride, and now by this decree seemed everlastingly divorced! When the tidings reached her, she at first gave way to rage against Romeo, who had slain her dear cousin: she called him a beautiful tyrant, a fiend angelical, a ravenous dove, a lamb with a wolf's nature, a serpent-heart hid with a flowering face, and other like contradictory names, which denoted the struggles in her mind between her love and her resentment: but in the end love got the mastery, and the tears which she shed for grief that Romeo had slain her cousin turned to drops of joy that her husband lived, whom Tybalt would have slain. Then came fresh tears, and they were altogether of grief for Romeo's banishment. That word was more terrible to her than the death of many Tybalts.

Romeo, after the fray, had taken refuge in friar Lawrence's cell, where he was first made acquainted with the prince's sentence, which seemed to him far more terrible than death. To him it appeared there was no world out of Verona's walls, no living out of the sight of Juliet. Heaven was there where Juliet lived, and all beyond was purgatory, torture, hell. The good friar would have applied the consolation of philosophy to his griefs; but this frantic young man would hear of none, but like a madman he tore his hair, and threw himself all along upon the ground, as he said, to take the measure of his grave. From this unseemly state he was roused by a message from his dear lady, which a little revived him, and then the friar took the advantage to expostulate with him on the unmanly weakness which he had shown. He had slain

Tybalt, but would he also slay himself, slay his dear lady who lived but in his life? The noble form of man, he said, was but a shape of wax, when it wanted the courage which should keep it firm. The law had been lenient to him, that instead of death, which he had incurred, had pronounced by the prince's mouth only banishment. He had slain Tybalt, but Tybalt would have slain him: there was a sort of happiness in that. Juliet was alive, and (beyond all hope) had become his dear wife, therein he was most happy. All these blessings, as the friar made them out to be, did Romeo put from him like a sullen misbehaved wench. And the friar bade him beware, for such as despaired (he said) died miserable. Then when Romeo was a little calmed, he counselled him that he should go that night and secretly take his leave of Juliet, and thence proceed straightways to Mantua, at which place he should sojourn, till the friar found a fit occasion to publish his marriage, which might be a joyful means of reconciling their families; and then he did not doubt but the prince would be moved to pardon him, and he would return with twenty times more joy than he went forth with grief. Romeo was convinced by these wise counsels of the friar, and took his leave to go and seek his lady, purposing to stay with her that night, and by daybreak pursue his journey alone to Mantua; to which place the good friar promised to send him letters from time to time, acquainting him with the state of affairs at home.

That night Romeo passed with his dear wife, gaining secret admission to her chamber from the orchard in which he had heard her confession of love the night before. That had been a night of unmixed joy and rapture; but the pleasures of this night, and the delight which these lovers took in each other's society, were sadly allayed with the prospect of parting, and the fatal adventures of the past day. The unwelcome day-break seemed to come too soon, and when Juliet heard the morning-song of the lark, she would fain have persuaded herself that it was the nightingale, which sings by night; but it was too truly the lark which sung, and a discordant and unpleasing note it seemed to her; and the streaks of day in the east too certainly pointed out that it was time for these lovers to part. Romeo took his leave of his dear wife with a heavy heart, promising to write to her from Mantua every hour in the day; and when he had descended from her chamber-window, as he stood below her on the ground, in that sad foreboding state of mind, in which she was, he appeared to her eyes as one dead in the bottom of a tomb. Romeo's mind misgave him in like manner; but now he was forced hastily to depart, for it was death for him to be found within the walls of Verona after day-break.

This was but the beginning of the tragedy of this pair of star-crossed lovers. Romeo had not been gone many days, before the old lord Capulet proposed a match for Juliet. The husband he had chosen for her, not dreaming that she was married already, was count Paris, a gallant, young, and noble gentleman, no unworthy suitor to the young Juliet, if she had never seen Romeo.

The terrified Juliet was in a sad perplexity at her father's offer. She pleaded her youth unsuitable to marriage, the recent death of Tybalt, which had left her spirits too weak to meet a husband with any face of joy, and how indecorous it would shew for the family of the Capulets to be celebrating a nuptial-feast, when his funeral solemnities were hardly over; she pleaded every reason against the match, but the true one, namely, that she was married already. But lord Capulet was deaf to all her excuses, and in a peremptory manner ordered her to get ready, for by the following Thursday she should be married to Paris: and having found her a husband rich, young, and noble, such as the proudest maid in Verona might joyfully accept, he could not bear that out of an affected coyness, as he construed her denial, she should oppose obstacles to her own good fortune.

In this extremity Juliet applied to the friendly friar, always her counsellor in distress, and he asking her if she had resolution to undertake a desperate remedy, and she answering that she would go into the grave alive, rather than marry Paris, her own dear husband living; he directed her to go home, and appear merry, and give her consent to marry Paris, according to her father's desire, and on the next night, which was the night before the marriage, to drink off the contents of a phial, which he then gave her, the effect of which would be, that for two-and-forty hours after drinking it she should appear cold and lifeless; that when the bridegroom came to fetch her in the morning, he would find her to appearance dead; that then she would be borne, as the manner in that country was, uncovered, on a bier, to be buried in the family vault; that if she could put off womanish fear, and consent to this terrible trial, in forty-two hours after swallow ing the liquid (such was its certain operation) she would be sure to awake, as from a dream; and before she should awake, he would let her husband know their drift, and he should come in the night, and bear her thence to Mantua. Love, and the dread of marrying Paris, gave young Juliet strength to undertake this horrible adventure; and she took the phial of the friar, promising to observe his directions.

Going from the monastery, she met the young count Paris, and modestly dissembling, promised to become his bride. This was joyful news to the lord Capulet and his wife. It seemed to put youth into the old man; and Juliet, who had displeased him exceedingly by her refusal of the count, was his darling again, now she promised to be obedient. All things in the house were in a bustle against the approaching nuptials. No cost was spared to prepare such festival rejoicings as Verona had never before witnessed.

On the Wednesday night Juliet drank off the potion. She had many misgivings, lest the friar, to avoid the blame which might be imputed to him for marrying her to Romeo, had given her poison; but then he was always known for a holy man: then lest she should awake before the time that Romeo was to come for her; whether the terror of the place, a vault full of dead Capulets' bones, and where Tybalt, all bloody, lay festering in his shroud, would not be enough to drive her distracted: again she thought of all the stories she had heard of spirits haunting the places where their bodies were bestowed. But then her love for Romeo, and her aversion for Paris, returned, and she desperately swallowed the draughts, and became insensible.

When young Paris came early in the morning with music, to awaken his bride, instead of a living Juliet, her chamber presented the dreary spectacle of a lifeless corpse. What death to his hopes! What confusion then reigned through the whole house! Poor Paris lamenting his bride, whom most detestable death had beguiled him of, had divorced from him even before their hands were joined. But still more piteous it was to hear the mournings of the old lord and lady Capulet, who having but this one, one poor loving child to rejoice and solace in, cruel death had snatched her from their sight, just as these careful parents were on the point of seeing her advanced (as they thought) by a promising and advantageous match. Now all things that were ordained for the festival were turned from their properties to do the office of a black funeral. The wedding cheer served for a sad burial feast, the bridal hymns were changed to sullen dirges, the sprightly instruments to melancholy bells, and the flowers that should have been strewed in the bride's path, now served but to strew her corse. Now instead of a priest to marry her, a priest was needed to bury her; and she was borne to church indeed, not to augment the cheerful hopes of the living, but to swell the dreary numbers of the dead.

Bad news, which always travels faster than good, now brought the dismal story of his Juliet's death to Romeo at Mantua, before the messenger could arrive who was sent from friar Lawrence to apprise him that these were mock funerals only, and but the shadow and representation of death, and that his dear lady lay in the tomb but for a short while, expecting when Romeo should come to release her from that dreary mansion. Just before, Romeo had been unusually joyful and light-hearted. He had dreamed in the night that he was dead (a strange dream, that gave a dead man leave to think), and that his lady came and found him dead, and breathed such life with kisses in his lips, that he revived, and was an emperor! And now that a messenger came from Verona, he thought surely it was to confirm some good news which his dreams had presaged. But when the contrary to this flattering vision appeared, and that it was his lady who was dead in truth, whom he could not revive by any kisses, he ordered horses to be ready, for he determined that night to visit Verona, and to see his lady in her tomb. And as mischief is swift to enter into the thoughts of desperate men, he called to mind a poor apothecary, whose shop in Mantua he had lately passed, and from the beggarly appearance of the man, who seemed famished, and the wretched show in his shop of empty boxes ranged on dirty shelves, and other tokens of extreme wretchedness, he had said at the time (perhaps having some misgivings that his own disastrous life might haply meet with a conclusion so desperate), "If a man were to need poison, which by the law of Mantua it is death

to sell, here lives a poor wretch who would sell it him."
These words of his now came into his mind, and he sought
out the apothecary, who, after some pretended scruples,
Romeo offering him gold which his poverty could not resist,
sold him a posion, which, if he swallowed, he told him, if
he had the strength of twenty men, would quickly despatch
him.

With this poison he set out for Verona, to have a sight of
his dear lady in her tomb, meaning, when he had satisfied his
sight, to swallow the poison, and be buried by her side. He
reached Verona at midnight, and found the church-yard, in
the midst of which was situated the ancient tomb of the
Capulets. He had provided a light, and a spade, and wrench-
ing iron, and was proceeding to break open the monument,
when he was interrupted by a voice, which by the name of
vile Mountague bade him desist from his unlawful business.
It was the young count Paris, who had come to the tomb of
Juliet at that unseasonable time of night, to strew flowers,
and to weep over the grave of her that should have been his
bride. He knew not what an interest Romeo had in the dead,
but knowing him to be a Mountague, and (as he supposed) a
sworn foe to all the Capulets, he judged that he was come by
night to do some villainous shame to the dead bodies; therefore in angry tone he bade him desist; and as a criminal condemned by the laws of Verona to die if he were found within
the walls of the city, he would have apprehended him. Romeo
urged Paris to leave him, and warned him by the fate of
Tybalt, who lay buried there, not to provoke his anger, or

draw down another sin upon his head, by forcing him to kill him. But the count in scorn refused his warning, and laid hands on him as a felon, which Romeo resisting, they fought, and Paris fell. When Romeo, by the help of a light, came to see who it was that he had slain, that it was Paris, who (he learned on his way from Mantua) should have married Juliet, he took the dead youth by the hand, as one whom misfortune had made a companion, and said that he would bury him in a triumphal grave, meaning in Juliet's grave, which he now opened; and there lay his lady, as one whom Death had no power upon, to change a feature or complexion in her matchless beauty, or as if Death were amourous, and the lean abhorred monster kept her there for his delight; for she lay yet fresh and blooming, as she had fallen to sleep when she swallowed that benumbing potion: and near her lay Tybalt in his bloody shroud, whom Romeo seeing begged pardon of his lifeless corse, and for Juliet's sake called him *cousin*, and said that he was about to do him a favour by putting his enemy to death. Here Romeo took his last leave of his lady's lips, kissing them; and here he shook the burden of his cross stars from his weary body, swallowing that poison which the apothecary had sold him, whose operation was fatal and real, not like that dissembling potion which Juliet had swallowed, the effect of which was now nearly expiring, and she about to awake, to complain that Romeo had not kept his time, or that he had come too soon.

For now the hour was arrived at which the friar had promised that she should awake; and he, having learned that his letters which he had sent to Mantua, by some unlucky detention of the messenger, had never reached Romeo, came himself, provided with a pickaxe and lantern, to deliver the lady from her confinement; but he was surprised to find a light already burning in the Capulets' monument, and to see swords and blood near it, and Romeo and Paris lying breathless by the monument.

Before he could entertain a conjecture to imagine how these fatal accidents had fallen out, Juliet awoke out of her trance, and seeing the friar near her, she remembered the place where she was, and the occasion of her being there, and asked for Romeo: but the friar, hearing a noise, bade her come out of that place of death, and of unnatural sleep, for a greater power than they could contradict had thwarted their intents; and being frighted by the noise of people coming, he fled; but when Juliet saw the cup closed in her true love's hands, she guessed that posoin had been the cause of his end, and she would have swallowed the dregs if any had been left, and she kissed his still warm lips to try if any poison yet did hang upon them: they hearing a nearer noise of people coming, she quickly unsheathed a dagger which she wore, and stabbing herself, died by her true Romeo's side.

The watch by this time had come up to the place. A page belonging to count Paris, who had witnessed the fight between his master and Romeo, had given the alarm, which had spread among the citizens, who went up and down the streets of Verona confusedly, exclaiming, A Paris, a Romeo, a Juliet, as the rumour had imperfectly reached them, till the uproar brought lord Mountague and lord Capulet out of their beds, with the prince, to enquire into the causes of the disturbance. The friar had been apprehended by some of the watch, coming from the church-yard, trembling, sighing, and weeping in a suspicious manner. A great multitude being assembled at the Capulets' monument, the friar was commanded by the prince to deliver what he knew of these strange and disastrous accidents.

And there, in the presence of the old lords Mountague and Capulet, he faithfully related the story of their children's fatal love, the part he took in promoting their marriage, in the hope in that union to end the long quarrels between their families: how Romeo, there dead, was husband to Juliet, and Juliet, there dead, was Romeo's faithful wife: how before he could find a fit opportunity to divulge their marriage, another match was projected for Juliet, who to avoid the crime of a second marriage swallowed the sleeping draught (as he advised), and all thought her dead: how meantime he wrote to Romeo, to come and take her thence when the force of the potion should cease, and by what unfortunate miscarriage of the messenger the letters never reached Romeo: further than this the friar could not follow the story, nor knew more than that coming himself to deliver Juliet from that place of death, he found the count Paris and Romeo slain. The remainder of the transactions was supplied by the narration of the page who had seen Paris and Romeo fight, and by the servant who came with Romeo from Verona, to whom this faithful lover had given letters to be delivered to his father in the event of his death, which made good the friar's words, confessing his marriage with Juliet, imploring the forgiveness of his parents, acknowledging the buying of the poison of the poor apothecary, and his intent in coming to the monument, to die, and lie with Juliet. All these circumstances agreed together to clear the friar from any hand he could be supposed to have had in these complicated slaughters, further than as the unintended consequences of his own well meant, yet too artificial and subtle contrivances.

And the prince, turning to these old lords, Mountague and Capulet, rebuked them for their brutal and irrational enmities, and shewed them what a scourge heaven had laid upon such offences, that it had found means even through the love of their children to punish their unnatural hate. And these old rivals, no longer enemies, agreed to bury their long strife in their children's graves; and lord Capulet requested lord Mountague to give him his hand, calling him by the name of brother, as if in acknowledgment of the union of their families by the marriage of the young Capulet and Mountague; and saying that lord Mountague's hand (in token of reconcilement) was all he demanded for his daughter's jointure: but lord Mountague said that he would give him more, for he would raise her statue of pure gold, that while Verona kept its name, no figure should be so esteemed for its richness and workmanship as that of the true and faithful Juliet. And lord Capulet in return said that he would raise another statue to Romeo. So did these poor old lords, when it was too late, strive to outgo each other in mutual courtesies: while so deadly had been their rage and emnity in past times, that nothing but the fearful overthrow of their children (poor sacrifices to their quarrels and dissensions) could remove the rooted hates and jealousies of these noble families.

Tale the Eighteenth

Hamlet, Prince of Denmark

GERTRUDE, queen of Denmark, becoming a widow by the sudden death of king Hamlet, in less than two months after his death married his brother Claudius, which was noted by all people at the time for a strange act of indiscretion, or unfeelingness, or worse: for this Claudius did no ways resemble her late husband in the qualities of his person or his mind, but was as contemptible in outward appearance, as he was base and unworthy in disposition; and suspicions did not fail to arise in the minds of some, that he had privately made away with his brother, the late king, with the view of marrying his widow, and ascending the throne of Denmark, to the exclusion of young Hamlet, the son of the buried king, and lawful successor to the throne.

But upon no one did this unadvised action of the queen make such impression as upon this young prince, who loved and venerated the memory of his dead father almost to idolatry, and being of a nice sense of honour, and a most exquisite practicer of propriety himself, did sorely take to heart this unworthy conduct of his mother Gertrude: insomuch that, between grief for his father's death and shame for his mother's marriage, this young prince was overclouded with a deep melancholy, and lost all his mirth and all his good looks; all his customary pleasure in books forsook him; his princely exercises and sports, proper to his youth, were no longer acceptable; he grew weary of the world, which seemed to him an unweeded garden, where all the wholesome flowers were choaked up, and nothing but weeds could thrive. Not that the prospect of exclusion from the throne, his lawful inheritance, weighed so much upon his spirits, though that to a young and high-minded prince was a bitter wound and a sore indignity; but what so galled him, and took away all his cheerful spirits, was, that his mother had shewn herself so forgetful to his father's memory: and such a father! who had been to her so loving and gentle a husband! and then she always appeared as loving and obedient a wife to him, and would hang upon him as if her affection grew to him: and now within two months, or as it seemed to young Hamlet, less than two months, she had married again, married his uncle, her dead husband's brother, in itself a highly improper and unlawful marriage, from the nearness of relationship, but made much more so by the indecent haste with which it was concluded, and the unkingly character of the man whom she had chosen to be the partner of her throne and bed. This it was, which, more than the loss of ten kingdoms, dashed the spirits, and brought a cloud over the mind of this honourable young prince.

In vain was all that this mother Gertrude or the king could do or contrive to divert him; he still appeared in court

in a suit of deep black, as mourning for the king his father's
death, which mode of dress he had never laid aside, not even
in compliment to his mother on the day she was married, nor
could he be brought to join in any of the festivities or rejoicings of that (as appeared to him) disgraceful day.

What mostly troubled him was an uncertainty about the
manner of his father's death. It was given out by Claudius,
that a serpent had stung him: but young Hamlet had shrewd
suspicions that Claudius himself was the serpent; in plain
English, that he had murdered him for his crown, and that the
serpent who stung his father did now sit on his throne.

How far he was right in this conjecture, and what he ought
to think of his mother, how far she was privy to this murder,
and whether by her consent or knowledge, or without, it
came to pass, were the doubts which continually harassed and
distracted him.

A rumour had reached the ear of young Hamlet, that an
apparition, exactly resembling the dead king his father, had
been seen by the soldiers upon watch, on the platform before
the palace at midnight, for two or three nights successively.
The figure came constantly clad in the same suit of armour,
from head to foot, which the dead king was known to have
worn: and they who saw it (Hamlet's bosom-friend Horatio
was one) agreed in their testimony as to the time and manner
of its appearance: that it came just as the clock struck twelve;
that it looked pale, with a face more of sorrow than of anger;
that its beard was grisly, and the colour a *sable silvered*, as they
had seen it in his lifetime: that it made no answer when they

spoke to it, yet once they thought it lifted up its head, and addressed itself to motion, as if it were about to speak; but in that moment the morning cock crew, and it shrunk in haste away, and vanished out of their sight.

The young prince, strangely amazed at their relation, which was too consistent and agreeing with itself to disbelieve, concluded that it was his father's ghost which they had seen, and determined to take his watch with the soldiers that night, that he might have a chance of seeing it: for he reasoned with himself, that such an appearance did not come for nothing, but that the ghost had something to impart, and though it had been silent hitherto, yet it would speak to him. And he waited with impatience for the coming of night.

When night came he took his stand with Horatio, and Marcellus, one of the guards, upon the platform, where this apparition was accustomed to walk: and it being a cold night, and the air unusually raw and nipping, Hamlet and Horatio and their companion fell into some talk about the coldness of the night, which was suddenly broken off by Horatio announcing that the ghost was coming.

At the sight of his father's spirit, Hamlet was struck with a sudden surprize and fear. He at first called upon the angels and heavenly ministers to defend them, for he knew not whether it were a good spirit or bad; whether it came for good or for evil: but he gradually assumed more courage; and his father (as it seemed to him) looked upon him so piteously, and as it were desiring to have conversation with him, and did in all respects appear so like himself as he was when he lived, that Hamlet could not help addressing him: he called him by his name, Hamlet, King, Father; and conjured him that he would tell the reason why he had left his grave, where they had seen him quietly bestowed, to come again and visit the earth and the moonlight: and besought him that he would let them know if there was any thing which they could do to give peace to his spirit. And the ghost beckoned to Hamlet, that he should go with him to some more removed place, where they might be alone: and Horatio and Marcellus would have dissuaded the young prince from following it, for they feared lest it should be some evil spirit who would tempt him to the neighbouring sea, or to the top of some dreadful cliff, and there put on some horrible shape which might deprive the prince of his reason. But their counsels and intreaties could not alter Hamlet's determination, who cared too little about life to fear the losing of it; and as to his soul, he said, what could the spirit do to that, being a thing immortal as itself? And he felt as hardy as a lion, and bursting from them who did all they could to hold him, he followed whithersoever the spirit led him.

And when they were alone together the spirit broke silence, and told him that he was the ghost of Hamlet, his father, who had been cruelly murdered, and he told the manner of it; that it was done by his own brother Claudius, Hamlet's uncle, as Hamlet had already but too much suspected, for the hope of succeeding to his bed and crown. That as he was sleeping in his garden, his custom always in the afternoon, this treasonous brother stole upon him in his sleep, and poured the juice of poisonous henbane into his ears, which has such an antipathy to the life of man, that swift as quicksilver it courses through all the veins of the body, baking up the blood, and spreading a crust like leprosy all over the skin: thus sleeping, by a brother's hand he was cut off at once from his crown, his queen, and his life: and he adjured Hamlet, if he did ever his dear father love, that he would revenge his foul murder. And the ghost lamented to his son, that his mother should so fall off from virtue, as to prove false to the wedded love of her first husband, and to marry his murderer: but he cautioned Hamlet, howsoever he proceeded in his revenge against his wicked uncle, by no means to act any violence against the person of his mother, but to leave her to heaven and to the stings and thorns of conscience. And Hamlet promised to observe the ghost's direction in all things, and the ghost vanished.

And when Hamlet was left alone, he took up a solemn resolution, that all he had in his memory, all that he had ever learned by books or observation, should be instantly forgotten by him, and nothing live in his brain but the memory of what the ghost had told him, and enjoined him to do. And Hamlet related the particulars of the conversation which had passed to none but his dear friend Horatio; and he enjoined both to him and Marcellus the strictest secrecy as to what they had seen that night.

The terror which the sight of the ghost had left upon the senses of Hamlet, he being weak and dispirited before, almost unhinged his mind, and drove him beside his reason. And he, fearing that it would continue to have this effect, which might subject him to observation, and set his uncle upon his guard, if he suspected that he was meditating any thing against him, or that Hamlet really knew more of his father's death than he professed, took up a strange resolution, from that time to counterfeit as if he were really and truly mad; thinking that he would be less an object of suspicion when his uncle should believe him incapable of any serious project, and that his real perturbation of mind would be best covered and pass concealed under a disguise of pretended lunacy.

From this time Hamlet affected a certain wildness and strangeness in his apparel, his speech, and behaviour, and did so excellently counterfeit the madman, that the king and queen were both deceived, and not thinking his grief for his father's death a sufficient cause to produce such a distemper, for they knew not of the appearance of the ghost, they concluded that his malady was love, and they thought they had found out the object.

Before Hamlet fell into the melancholy way which has been related, he had dearly loved a fair maid called Ophelia, the daughter of Polonius, the king's chief counsellor in affairs of state. He had sent her letters and rings, and made many tenders of his affection to her, and importuned her with love in honourable fashion; and she had given belief to his vows and importunities. But the melancholy which he fell into latterly had made him neglect her, and from the time he conceived the project of counterfeiting madness, he affected to treat her with unkindness, and a sort of rudeness; but she, good lady, rather than reproach him with being false to her, persuaded herself that it was nothing but the disease in his mind, and no settled unkindness, which had made him less observant of her than formerly; and she compared the faculties of his once noble mind and excellent understanding, impaired as they were with the deep melancholy that oppressed him, to sweet bells which in themselves are capable of most excellent music, but when jangled out of tune, or rudely handled, produce only a harsh and unpleasing sound.

Though the rough business which Hamlet had in hand, the revenging of his father's death upon his murderer, did not suit with the playful state of courtship, or admit of the society of so idle a passion as love now seemed to him, yet it could not hinder but that soft thoughts of his Ophelia would come between, and in one of these moments, when he thought that his treatment of this gentle lady had been unreasonably harsh, he wrote her a letter full of wild starts of passion, and extravagant terms, such as agreed with his supposed madness, but mixed with some gentle touches of affection, which could not but shew to this honoured lady that a deep love for her yet lay at the bottom of his heart. He bade her to doubt the stars were fire, and to doubt that the sun did move, to doubt truth to be a liar, but never to doubt that he loved; with more of such extravagant phrases. This letter Ophelia dutifully shewed to her father, and the old man thought himself bound to communicate it to the king and queen, who from that time supposed that the true cause of Hamlet's madness was love. And the queen wished that the good beauties of Ophelia might be the happy cause of his wildness, for so she hoped that her virtues might happily restore him to his accustomed way again, to both their honours.

But Hamlet's malady lay deeper than she supposed, or than could be so cured. His father's ghost, which he had seen, still haunted his imagination, and the sacred injunction to revenge his murder gave him no rest till it was accomplished. Every hour of delay seemed to him a sin, and a violation of his father's commands. Yet how to compass the death of the king, surrounded as he constantly was with his guards, was no easy matter. Or if it had been, the presence of the queen, Hamlet's mother, who was generally with the king, was a restraint upon his purpose, which he could not break through. Besides, the very circumstance that the usurper was his mother's husband filled him with some remorse, and still blunted the edge of his purpose. The mere act of putting a fellow-creature to death was in itself odious and terrible to a disposition naturally so gentle as Hamlet's was. His very melancholy, and the dejection of spirits he had so long been in, produced an irresoluteness and wavering of purpose, which kept him from proceeding to extremities. Morever, he could not help having some scruples upon his mind, whether the spirit which he had seen was indeed his father, or whether it might not be the devil, who he had heard has power to take any form he pleases, and who might have assumed his father's shape only to take advantage of his weakness and his melancholy, to drive him to the doing of so desperate an act as murder. And he determined that he would have more certain grounds to go upon than a vision of apparition, which might be a delusion.

While he was in this irresolute mind, there came to the court certain players, in whom Hamlet formerly used to take delight, and particularly to hear one of them speak a tragical speech, describing the death of old Priam, king of Troy, with the grief of Hecuba, his queen. Hamlet welcomed his old friends, the players, and remembering how that speech had formerly given him pleasure, requested the player to repeat it; which he did in so lively a manner, setting forth the cruel murder of the feeble old king, with the destruction of his people and city by fire, and the mad grief of the old queen, running barefoot up and down the palace, with a poor clout upon that head where a crown had been, and with nothing but a blanket upon her loins, snatched up in haste, where she had worn a royal robe: but it not only drew tears from all that stood by, who thought they saw the real scene, so livelily was it represented, but even the player himself delivered it with a broken voice and real tears. This put Hamlet upon thinking, if that player could so work himself up to passion by a mere fictitious speech, to weep for one that he had never seen, for Hecuba, that had been dead so many hundred years, a real king and a dear father murdered, was yet so little moved, that this revenge all this while had seemed to have slept in dull and muddy forgetfulness! And while he meditated on actors and acting, and the powerful effects which a good play, represented to the life, has upon the spectator, he remembered the instance of some murderer, who seeing a murder on the stage, was by the mere force of the scene and resemblance of circumstances so affected, that on the spot he confessed the crime which he had committed. And he determined that these players should play something like the murder of his father before his uncle, and he would watch narrowly what effect it might have upon him, and from his looks he would be able to gather with more certainty if he were the murderer or not. To this effect he ordered a play to be prepared, to the representation of which he invited the king and queen.

The story of the play was of a murder done in Vienna upon a duke. The duke's name was Gonzago, his wife Baptista. The play shewed how one Lucianus, a near relation to the duke, poisoned him in his garden for his estate, and how the murderer in a short time after got the love of Gonzago's wife.

At the representation of this play the king, who did not know the trap which was laid for him, was present, with his queen and the whole court: Hamlet sitting attentively near him to observe his looks. The play began with a conversation between Gonzago and his wife, in which the lady made many protestations of love, and of never marrying a second husband, if she should outlive Gonzago; wishing she might be accursed if ever she took a second husband, and adding that no woman ever did so but those wicked women who kill their husbands. Hamlet observed the king, his uncle, change colour at this expression, and that it was as bad as wormwood both to him and to the queen. But when Lucianus, according to the story, came to poison Gonzago sleeping in the garden, the strong resemblance which it bore to his own wicked act upon the late king, his brother, whom he had poisoned in his garden, so struck upon the conscience of this usurper, that he was unable to sit out the rest of the play, but on a sudden calling for light to his chamber, and affecting or partly feeling a sudden sickness, he abruptly left the theatre. The king being departed, the play was given over. Now Hamlet had seen enough to feel satisfied that the words of the ghost were true, and no illusion; and in a fit of gayety, like that which comes over a man who suddenly has some great doubt or scruple resolved, he swore to Horatio that he would take the ghost's word for a thousand pounds. But before he could make up his resolution as to what measures of revenge he should take, now he was certainly informed that his uncle was his father's murderer, he was sent for by the queen, his mother, to a private conference in her closet.

It was by desire of the king that the queen sent for Hamlet, that she might signify to her son how much his late behaviour had displeased them both; and the king, wishing to know all that passed at that conference, and thinking that the too partial report of a mother might let slip some part of Hamlet's words, which it might much import the king to know, Polonius, the old counsellor of state, was ordered to plant himself behind the hangings in the queen's closet, where he might unseen hear all that passed. This artifice was particularly adapted to the disposition of Polonius, who was a man grown old in crooked maxims and policies of state, and delighted to get at the knowledge of matters in an indirect and cunning way.

Hamlet being come to his mother, she began to tax him in the roundest way with his actions and behaviour, and she told him that he had given great offence to *his father*, meaning the king, his uncle, whom, because he had married her, she called Hamlet's father. Hamlet, sorely indignant that she should give so dear and honoured a name, as father seemed to him, to a wretch who was indeed no better than the murderer of his true father, with some sharpness replied, "Mother, *you* have much offended *my father*." The queen said that was but an idle answer. "As good as the question deserved," said Hamlet. The queen asked him if he had forgotten who it was he was speaking to? "Alas!" replied Hamlet, "I wish I could forget. You are the queen, your husband's brother's wife; and you are my mother: I wish you were not what you are." "Nay, then, " said the queen, "if you shew me so little respect, I will set those to you that can speak," and was going to send the king or Polonius to him. But Hamlet would not let her go, now he had her alone, till he had tried if his words could not bring her to some sense of her wicked life; and, taking her by the wrist, he held her fast, and made her sit down. She, affrighted at his earnest manner, and fearful lest in his lunacy he should do her a mischief, cried out: and a voice was heard from behind the hangings, "Help, help, the queen"; which Hamlet hearing, and verily thinking it was the king himself there concealed, he drew his sword, and stabbed at the place where the voice came from, as he would have stabbed a rat that ran there, till the voice ceasing, he concluded the person to be dead. But when he dragged forth the body, it was not the king, but Polonius, the old officious counsellor, that has planted himself as a spy behind the hangings. "Oh, me!" exclaimed the queen, "what a rash and bloody deed have you done!" "A bloody deed, mother," replied Hamlet; "but not so bad as yours, who killed a king and married his brother." Hamlet had gone too far to leave off here. He was now in the humour to speak plainly to his mother, and he pursued it. And though the faults of parents are to be tenderly treated by their children, yet in the case of great crimes the son may have leave to speak even to his own mother with some harshness, so as that harshness is meant for her good, and to turn her from her wicked ways, and not done for the purpose of upbraiding. And now this virtuous prince did in moving terms represent to the queen the heinousness of her offence, in being so forgetful of the dead king, his father, as in so short a space of time to marry with his brother and reputed murderer: such an act as, after the vows which she had sworn to her first husband, was enough to make all vows of women suspected, and all virtue to be accounted hypocrisy, wedding contracts to be less than gamesters' oaths, and religion to be a mockery and a mere form of words. He said she had done such a deed, that the heavens blushed at it, and the earth was sick of her because of it. And he shewed her two pictures, the one of the late king, her first husband, and the other of the present king, her second husband, and he bade her mark the difference: what a grace was on the brow of his father, how like a god he looked! the curls of Apollo, the forehead of Jupiter, the eye of Mars, and a posture like to Mercury newly alighted on some heaven-kissing hill! this man, he said, was her husband. And then he shewed her whom she had got in his stead: how like a blight or a mildew he looked, for so he blasted his wholesome brother. And the queen was sore ashamed that he should so turn her eyes inward upon her soul, which she now saw so black and deformed. And he asked her how she could continue to live with this man, and be a wife to him, who had murdered her first husband and got the crown by as false means as a thief— And just as he spoke, the ghost of his father, such as he was in his life-time, and such as he had lately seen it, entered the room, and Hamlet, in great terror, asked what it would have; and the ghost said that it came to remind him of the revenge he had promised, which Hamlet seemed to have forgot: and the ghost bade him speak to his mother, for the grief and terror she was in would else kill her. It then vanished, and was seen by none but Hamlet, neither could he by pointing to where it stood, or by any description, make his mother perceive it; who was terribly frighted all this while to hear him conversing, as it seemed to her, with nothing: and she imputed it to the disorder of his mind. But Hamlet begged her not to flatter her wicked soul in such a manner as to think that it was his madness, and not her own offences, which had brought his father's spirit again on the earth. And he bade her feel his pulse, how temperately it beat, not like a madman's. And he begged of her with tears to confess herself to heaven for what was past, and for the future to avoid the company of the king, and be no more as a wife to him: and when she should shew herself a mother to him, by respecting his father's memory, he would ask a blessing of her as a son. And she promising to observe his directions, the conference ended.

And now Hamlet was at leisure to consider who it was that in his unfortunate rashness he had killed: and when he came to see that it was Polonius, the father of the lady Ophelia, whom he so dearly loved, he drew apart the dead body, and, his spirits being a little quieter, he wept for what he had done.

This unfortunate death of Polonius gave the king a pretense for sending Hamlet out of the kingdom. He would willingly have put him to death, fearing him as dangerous; but he dreaded the people, who loved Hamlet; and the queen, who, with all her faults, doated upon the prince her son. So this subtle king, under pretense of providing for Hamlet's safety, that he might not be called to account for Polonius' death, caused him to be conveyed on board a ship bound for England, under the care of two courtiers, by whom he dispatched letters to the English court, which at that time was in subjection and paid tribute to Denmark, requiring, for special reasons there pretended, that Hamlet should be put to death as soon as he landed on English ground. Hamlet, suspecting some treachery, in the night-time secretly got at the letters, and skilfully erasing his own name, he in the stead of it put in the names of those two courtiers who had the charge of him, to be put to death: then sealing up the letters, he put them into their place again. Soon after the ship was attacked by pirates, and a sea-fight commenced; in the course of which Hamlet, desirous to shew his valour, with sword in hand singly boarded the enemy's vessel; while his own ship, in a cowardly manner, bore away, and leaving him to his fate, the two courtiers made the best of their way to England, with those letters the sense of which Hamlet had altered to their own deserved destruction.

The pirates, who had the prince in their power, shewed themselves gentle enemies; and knowing whom they had got prisoner, in the hope that the prince might do them a good turn at court in recompense for any favour they might shew him, they set Hamlet on shore at the nearest port in Denmark. From that place Hamlet wrote to the king, acquainting him with the strange chance which had brought him back to his own country, and saying that on the next day he should present himself before his majesty. When he got home, a sad spectacle offered itself the first thing to his eyes.

This was the funeral of the young and beautiful Ophelia, his once dear mistress. The wits of this young lady had begun to turn ever since her poor father's death. That he should die a violent death, and by the hands of the prince whom she loved, so affected this tender young maid, that in a little time she grew perfectly distracted, and would go about giving flowers away to the ladies of the court, and saying that they were for her father's burial, singing songs about love and about death, and sometimes such as had no meaning at all, as if she had no memory of what happened to her. There was a willow which grew slanting over a brook, and reflected the leaves in the stream. To this brook she came one day when she was unwatched, with garlands she had been making, mixed up of daisies and nettles, flowers and weeds together, and clambering up to hang her garland upon the boughs of the willow, a bough broke and precipitated this fair young maid, garland, and all that she had gathered, into the water, where her clothes bore her up for a while, during which she chaunted scraps of old tunes, like one insensible to her own distress, or as if she were a creature natural to that element: but long it was not before her garments, heavy with the wet, pulled her in from her melodious singing to a muddy and miserable death. It was the funeral of this fair maid which her brother Laertes was celebrating, the king and queen and whole court being present, when Hamlet arrived. He knew not what all this shew imported, but stood on one side, not minding to interrupt the ceremony. He saw the flowers strewed upon her grave, as the custom was in maiden burials, which the queen herself threw in; and as she threw them she said, "Sweets to the sweet! I thought to have decked thy bride-bed, sweet maid, not to have strewed thy grave. Thou shouldst have been my Hamlet's wife." And he heard her brother wish that violets might spring from her grave: and he saw him leap into the grave all frantic with grief, and bid the attendants pile mountains of earth upon him, that he might be buried with her. And Hamlet's love for this fair maid came back to him, and he could not bear that a brother should shew so much transport of grief, for he thought that he loved Ophelia better than forty thousand brothers. Then discovering himself, he leaped into the grave where Laertes was, all as frantic or more frantic than he, and Laertes knowing him to be Hamlet, who had been the cause of his father's and his sister's death, grappled him by the throat as an enemy, till the attendants parted them: and Hamlet, after the funeral, excused his hasty act in throwing himself into the grave, as if to brave Laertes; but he said he could not bear that any one should seem to outgo him in grief for the death of the fair Ophelia. And for the time these two noble youths seemed reconciled.

But out of the grief and anger of Laertes for the death of his father and Ophelia, the king, Hamlet's wicked uncle, contrived destruction for Hamlet. He set on Laertes, under cover of peace and reconciliation, to challenge Hamlet to a friendly trial of skill at fencing, which Hamlet accepting, a day was appointed to try the match. At this match all the court was present, and Laertes, by direction of the king, prepared a poisoned weapon. Upon this match great wagers were laid by the courtiers, as both Hamlet and Laertes were known to excel at this sword-play; and Hamlet, taking up the foils chose one, not at all suspecting the treachery of Laertes, or being careful to examine Laertes' weapon, who, instead of a foil or blunted sword, which the laws of fencing require, made use of one with a point, and poisoned. At first Laertes did but play with Hamlet, and suffered him to gain some advantages, which the dissembling king magnified and extolled beyond measure, drinking to Hamlet's success, and wagering rich bets upon the issue: but after a few passes, Laertes growing warm, made a deadly thrust at Hamlet with his poisoned weapon, and gave him a mortal blow. Hamlet incensed, but not knowing the whole of the treachery, in the scuffle exchanged his own innocent weapon for Laertes' deadly one, and with a thrust of Laertes' own sword repaid Laertes home, who was thus justly caught in his own treachery. In this instant the queen shrieked out that she was poisoned. She had inadvertently drunk out of a bowl which the king had prepared for Hamlet, in case that being warm in fencing he should call for drink: into this the treacherous king had infused a deadly poison, to make sure of Hamlet, if Laertes had failed. He had forgotten to warn the queen of the bowl, which she drank of, and immediately died, exclaiming with her last breath that she was poisoned. Hamlet, suspecting some treachery, ordered the doors to be shut, while he sought it out. Laertes told him to seek no further, for he was the traitor; and feeling his life go away with the wound which Hamlet had given him, he made confession of the treachery he had used, and how he had fallen a victim to it: and he told Hamlet of the envenomed point, and said that Hamlet had not half an hour to live, for no medicine could cure him; and begging forgiveness of Hamlet, he died, with his last words accusing the king of being the contriver of the mischief. When Hamlet saw his end draw near, there being yet some venom left upon the sword, he suddenly turned upon his false uncle, and thrust the point of it to his heart, fulfilling the promise which he had made to his father's spirit, whose injunction was now accomplished, and his foul murder revenged upon the murderer. Then Hamlet, feeling his breath fail and life departing, turned to his dear friend Horatio, who had been spectator to this fatal tragedy; and with his dying breath requested him that he would live to tell his story to the word (for Horatio had made a motion as if he would slay himself to accompany the prince in death); and Horatio promised that he would make a true report, as one that was privy to all the circumstances. And, thus satisfied, the noble heart of Hamlet cracked: and Horatio and the bystanders with many tears commended the spirit of their sweet prince to the guardianship of angels. For Hamlet was a loving and a gentle prince, and greatly beloved for his many noble and prince-like qualities; and if he had lived, would no doubt have proved a most royal and complete king to Denmark.

Othello

BRABANTIO, the rich senator of Venice, had a fair daughter, the gentle Desdemona. She was sought to by divers suitors, both on account of her many virtuous qualities and for her rich expectations. But among the suitors of her own clime and complexion she saw none whom she could affect: for this noble lady, who regarded the mind more than the features of men, with a singularity rather to be admired than imitated, had chose for the object of her affections a Moor, a black, whom her father loved, and often invited to his house.

Neither is Desdemona to be altogether condemned for the unsuitableness of the person whom she selected for her lover. Bating that Othello was black, the noble Moor wanted nothing which might recommend him to the affections of the greatest lady. He was a soldier, and a brave one; and by his conduct in bloody wars against the Turks, had risen to the rank of general in the Venetian service, and was esteemed and trusted by the state.

He had been a traveller, and Desdemona (as is the manner of ladies) loved to hear him tell the story of his adventures, which he would run through from his earliest recollection; the battles, sieges, and encounters which he had passed through; the perils he had been exposed to by land and by water; his hairbreath escapes when he had entered a breach, or marched up to the mouth of a cannon; and how he had been taken prisoner by the insolent enemy, and sold to slavery; how he demeaned himself in that state, and how he escaped: all these accounts, added to the narration of the strange things he had seen in foreign countries, the vast wildernesses and romantic caverns, the quarries, the rocks and mountains, whose heads are in the clouds; of the savage nations; the cannibals who are man-eaters, and a race of people in Africa whose heads do grow beneath their shoulders: these travellers' stories would so enchain the attention of Desdemona, that if she were called off at any time by household affairs, she would despatch with all haste that business, and return, and with a greedy ear devour Othello's discourse. And once he took advantage of a pliant hour, and drew from her a prayer, that he would tell her the whole story of his life at large, of which she had heard so much, but only by parts: to which he consented, and beguiled her of many a tear, when he spoke of some distressful stroke which his youth suffered.

His story being done, she gave him for his pains a world of kisses; she swore a pretty oath, that it was all passing strange, and pitiful, wondrous pitiful: she wished (she said) she had not heard it, yet she wished that Heaven had made her such a man: and she thanked him, and told him if he had a friend who loved her, he had only to teach him how to tell his story, and that would woo her. Upon this hint, delivered not with more frankness than modesty, accompanied with a certain bewitching prettiness, and blushes which Othello could not but understand, he spoke more openly of his love, and in this golden opportunity gained the consent of the generous lady Desdemona privately to marry him.

Neither Othello's colour nor his fortune were such, that it could be hoped Brabantio would accept him for a son-in-law. He had left his daughter free; but he did expect that, as the manner of noble Venetian ladies was, she would choose ere long a husband of senatorial rank or expectations: but in this he was deceived; Desdemona loved the Moor, though he was black, and devoted her heart and fortunes to his valiant parts and qualities: so was her heart subdued to an implicit devotion to the man she had selected for a husband, that his very colour, which to all but this discerning lady would have proved an insurmountable objection, was by her esteemed above all the white skins and clear complexions of the young Venetian nobility, her suitors.

Their marriage, which, though privately carried, could not long be kept a secret, came to the ears of the old man, Brabantio, who appeared in a solemn council of the Senate as an accuser of the Moor Othello, who by spells and witch-craft (he maintained) had seduced the affections of the fair Desdemona to marry him, without the consent of her father, and against the obligations of hospitality.

At this juncture of time it happened that the state of Venice had immediate need of the services of Othello, news having arrived that the Turks with mighty preparation had fitted out a fleet, which was bending its course to the island of Cyprus, with intent to regain that strong post from the Venetians, who then held it: in this emergency the state turned its eyes upon Othello, who alone was deemed adequate to conduct the defence of Cyprus against the Turks. So that Othello, now summoned before the senate, stood in their presence at once as a candidate for a great state employment, and as a culprit, charged with offences which by the laws of Venice were made capital.

The age and senatorial character of old Brabantio com-manded a most patient hearing from that grave assembly; but the incensed father conducted his accusation with so much intemperance, producing likelihoods and allegations for proofs, that, when Othello was called upon for his defence he had only to relate a plain tale of the course of his love; which he did with such an artless eloquence, recounting the whole story of his wooing, as we have related it above, and delivered his speech with so noble a plainness (the evidence of truth), that the duke, who sat as chief judge, could not help confessing, that a tale so told would have won his daughter too: and the spells and conjurations, which Othello had used in his courtship, plainly appeared to have been no more than the honest arts of men in love; and the only witchcraft which he had used the faculty of telling a soft tale to win a lady's ear.

This statement of Othello was confirmed by the testimony of the lady Desdemona herself, who appeared in court, and professing a duty to her father for life and education, challenged leave of him to profess a yet higher duty to her lord and husband, even so much as her mother had shewn in preferring him (Brabantio) above *her* father.

The old senator, unable to maintain his plea, called the Moor to him with many expressions of sorrow, and, as an act of necessity, bestowed upon him his daughter, whom, if he had been free to withhold her (he told him) he would with all his heart have kept from him; adding, that he was glad at soul that he had no other child, for this behaviour of Desdemona would have taught him to be a tyrant, and hang clogs on them for her desertion.

This difficulty being got over, Othello, to whom custom had rendered the hardships of a military life as natural as food and rest are to other men, readily undertook the management of the wars in Cyprus; and Desdemona preferring the honour of her lord (though with danger) before the indulgence of those idle delights in which new-married people usually waste their time, chearfully consented to his going.

No sooner were Othello and his lady landed in Cyprus, than news arrived, that a desperate tempest had dispersed the Turkish fleet, and thus the island was secure from any immediate apprehension of an attack. But the war, which

Othello was to suffer, was now beginning; and the enemies, which malice stirred up against this innocent lady, proved in the nature more deadly than strangers or infidels.

Among all the general's friends no one possessed the confidence of Othello more entirely than Cassio. Michael Cassio was a young soldier, a Florentine, gay, amourous, and of pleasing address, favourite qualities with women; he was handsome, and eloquent, and exactly such a person as might alarm the jealousy of a man advanced in years (as Othello in some measure was), who had married a young and beautiful wife: but Othello was as free from jealousy as he was noble, and as incapable of suspecting, as of doing, a base action. He had employed this Cassio in his love affair with Desdemona, and Cassio had been a sort of go-between in his suit: for Othello, fearing that himself had not those soft parts of conversation which please ladies, and finding these qualities in his friend, would often depute Cassio to go (as he phrased it) a courting for him: such innocent simplicity being an honour rather than a blemish to the character of the valiant Moor. So that no wonder if next to Othello himself (but at far distance, as beseems a virtuous wife) the gentle Desdemona loved and trusted Cassio. Nor had the marriage of this couple made any difference in their behaviour to Michael Cassio. He frequented their house, and his free and rattling talk was no unpleasing variety to Othello, who was himself of a more serious temper: for such tempers are observed often to delight in their contraries, as a relief from the oppressive excess of their own: and Desdemona and Cassio would talk and laugh together, as in the days when he went a courting for his friend.

Othello had lately promoted Cassio to be the lieutenant, a place of trust, and nearest to the general's person. This promotion gave great offence to Iago, an older officer, who thought he had a better claim than Cassio, and would often ridicule Cassio, as a fellow fit only for the company of ladies, and one that knew no more of the art of war, or how to set an army in array for battle, than a girl. Iago hated Cassio, and he hated Othello, as well for favouring Cassio, as for an unjust suspicion, which he had lightly taken up against Othello, that the Moor was too fond of Iago's wife Emilia. From these imaginary provocations, the plotting mind of Iago conceived a horrid scheme of revenge, which should involve both Cassio, the Moor, and Desdemona in one common ruin.

Iago was artful, and had studied human nature deeply, and he knew that of all the torments which afflict the mind of man (and far beyond bodily torture), the pains of jealousy were the most intolerable, and had the sorest sting. If he could succeed in making Othello jealous of Cassio, he thought it would be an exquisite plot of revenge, and might end in the death of Cassio or Othello, or both; he cared not.

The arrival of the general and his lady in Cyprus, meeting with the news of the dispersion of the enemy's fleet, made a sort of holiday in the island. Every body gave themselves up to feasting, and making merry. Wine flowed in abundance, and cups went round to the health of the black Othello, and his lady the fair Desdemona.

Cassio had the direction of the guard that night, with a charge from Othello to keep the soldiers from excess in drinking, that no brawl might arise, to fright the inhabitants, or disgust them with the new-landed forces. That night Iago began his deep-laid plans of mischief: under colour of loyalty and love to the general, he enticed Cassio to make rather too free with the bottle (a great fault in an officer upon guard). Cassio for a time resisted, but he could not long hold out against the honest freedom which Iago knew how to put on, but kept swallowing glass after glass (as Iago still plied him with drink and encouraging songs), and Cassio's tongue ran over in praise of the lady Desdemona, whom he again and again toasted, affirming that she was a most exquisite lady: until at last the enemy, which he put into his mouth stole away his brains; and upon some provocation given him by a fellow, whom Iago had set on, swords were drawn, and Montano, a worthy officer, who interfered to appease the dispute, was wounded in the scuffle. The riot now began to be general, and Iago, who had set on foot the mischief, was foremost in spreading the alarm, causing the castle-bell to be rung (as if some dangerous mutiny instead of a slight drunken quarrel had arisen): the alarm-bell ringing awakened Othello, who, dressing in a hurry, and coming to the scene of action, questioned Cassio of the cause. Cassio was now come to himself, the effect of the wine having a little gone off, but was too much ashamed to reply; and Iago, pretending a great reluctance to accuse Cassio, but as it were forced into it by Othello, who insisted to know the truth, gave an account of the whole matter (leaving out his own share in it, which Cassio was too far gone to remember) in such a manner, as while he seemed to make Cassio's offence less, did indeed make it appear greater than it was. The result was, that Othello, who was a strict observer of discipline, was compelled to take away Cassio's place of lieutenant from him.

Thus did Iago's first artifice succeed completely; he had now undermined his hated rival, and thrust him out of his place: but a further use was hereafter to be made of the adventure of this disastrous night.

Cassio, whom this misfortune had entirely sobered, now lamented to his seeming friend Iago that he should have been such a fool as to transform himself into a beast. He was undone, for how could he ask the general for his place again! he would tell him he was a drunkard. He despised himself. Iago, affecting to make light of it, said, that he, or any man living, might be drunk upon occasion; it remained now to make the best of a bad bargain; the general's wife was now the general, and could do anything with Othello; that he were best to apply to the lady Desdemona to mediate for him with her lord; that she was of a frank, obliging disposition, and would readily undertake a good office of this sort, and set Cassio right again in the general's favour; and then this crack in their love would be made stronger than ever. A good advice of Iago, if it had not been given for wicked purposes, which will after appear.

Cassio did as Iago advised him, and made application to the lady Desdemona, who was easy to be won over in any honest suit; and she promised Cassio that she would be his solicitor with her lord, and rather die than give up his cause. This she immediately set about in so earnest and pretty a manner, that Othello, who was mortally offended with Cassio, could not put her off. When he pleaded delay, and that it was too soon to pardon such an offender, she would not be beat back, but insisted that it should be the next night, or the morning after, or the next morning to that at farthest. Then she showed how penitent and humbled poor Cassio was, and that his offence did not deserve so sharp a check. And when Othello still hung back, "What! my lord," said she, "that I should have so much to do to plead for Cassio, Michael Cassio, that came a courting for you, and oftentimes, when I have spoken in dispraise of you, has taken your part? I count this but a little thing to ask of you. When I mean to try your love indeed, I shall ask a weighty matter." Othello could deny nothing to such a pleader, and only requesting that Desdemona would leave the time to him, promised to receive Michael Cassio again into favour.

It happened that Othello and Iago had entered into the room where Desdemona was, just as Cassio, who had been imploring her intercession, was departing at the opposite door; and Iago, who was full of art, said in a low voice, as if to himself, "I like not that." Othello took no great notice of what he said; indeed the conference which immediately took place with his lady put it out of his head; but he remembered it afterwards. For when Desdemona was gone, Iago, as if for mere satisfaction of his thought, questioned Othello whether Michael Cassio, when Othello was courting his lady, knew of his love. To this the general answering in the affirmative, and adding, that he had gone between them very often during the courtship, Iago knitted his brow, as if he had got fresh light of some terrible matter, and cried, "Indeed!" This brought into Othello's mind the words which Iago had let fall upon entering the room and seeing Cassio with Desdemona; and he began to think there was some meaning in all this: for he deemed Iago to be a just man, and full of love and honesty, and what in a false knave would be tricks, in him seemed to be the natural workings of an honest mind, big with something too great for utterance: and Othello prayed Iago to speak what he knew, and to give his worst thoughts words. "And what," said Iago, "if some thoughts very vile should have intruded into my breast, as where is the palace into which foul things do not enter?" Then Iago went on to say, what a pity it were, if any trouble should arise to Othello out of his imperfect observations; that it would not be for Othello's peace to know his thoughts; that people's good names were not to be taken away for slight suspicions; and when Othello's curiosity was raised almost to distraction with these hints and scattered words, Iago, as if in earnest care for Othello's peace of mind, besought him to beware of jealousy: with such art did this villain raise suspicions in the unguarded Othello, by the very caution which he pretended to give him against suspicion. "I know," said Othello, "that my wife is fair, loves company and feasting, is free of speech, sings, plays, and dances well: but where virtue is these qualities are virtuous. I must have proof before I think her dishonest." Then Iago, as if glad that Othello was slow to believe ill of his lady, frankly declared that he had no proof, but begged Othello to observe her behaviour well, when Cassio was by; not to be jealous, nor too secure neither, for that he (Iago) knew the dispositions of the Italian ladies, his country-women, better than Othello could do; and that in Venice the wives let heaven see many pranks they dared not shew their husbands. Then he artfully insinuated, that Desdemona deceived her father in marrying with Othello, and carried it so closely, that the poor old man thought that witchcraft had been used. Othello was much moved with this argument, which brought the matter home to him, for if she had deceived her father, why might she not deceive her husband?

Iago begged pardon for having moved him; but Othello, assuming an indifference, while he was really shaken with inward grief at Iago's words, begged him to go on, which Iago did with many apologies, as if unwilling to produce anything against Cassio, whom he called his friend: he then came strongly to the point, and reminded Othello how Desdemona had refused many suitable matches of her own clime and complexion, and had married him, a Moor, which shewed unnatural in her, and proved her to have a headstrong will: and when her better judgment returned, how probable it was she should fall upon comparing Othello with the fine forms and clear white complexions of the young Italians her country-men. He concluded with advising Othello to put off his reconcilement with Cassio a little longer, and in the meanwhile to note with what earnestness Desdemona should intercede in his behalf; for that much would be seen in that. So mischievously did this artful villain lay his plots to turn the gentle qualities of this innocent lady into her destruction, and make a net for her out of her own goodness to entrap her: first setting Cassio on to entreat her mediation, and then out of that very mediation contriving stratagems for her ruin.

The conference ended with Iago's begging Othello to account his wife innocent, until he had more decisive proof; and Othello promised to be patient: but from that moment the deceived Othello never tasted content of mind. Poppy, nor the juice of mandragora, nor all the sleeping potions in the world, could ever again restore to him that sweet sleep, which he had enjoyed but yesterday. His occupation sickened upon him. He no longer took delight in arms. His heart, that used to be roused at the sight of troops, and banners, and battle-array, and would stir and leap at the sound of a drum, or a trumpet, or a neighing war-horse, seemed to have lost all that pride and ambition, which are a soldier's virtue; and his military ardour and all his old joys forsook him. Sometimes he thought his wife honest, and at times he thought her not so; sometimes he thought Iago just, and at times he thought him not so: then he would wish that he had never known of it; he was not the worse for her loving Cassio, so long as he knew it not: torn in pieces with these distracting thoughts, he once laid hold on Iago's throat, and demanded proof of Desdemona's guilt, or threatened instant death for his having belied her. Iago, feigning indignation that his honesty should be taken for a vice, asked Othello, if he had not sometimes seen a handkerchief spotted with strawberries in his wife's hand. Othello answered, that he had given her such a one, and that it was his first gift. "That same handkerchief," said Iago, "did I see Michael Cassio this day wipe his face with." "If it be as you say," said Othello, "I will not rest till a wide revenge swallow them up: and first, for a token of your fidelity, I expect that Cassio shall be put to death within three days; and for that fair devil [meaning his lady], I will withdraw and devise some swift means of death for her."

Trifles, light as air, are to the jealous proofs as strong as holy writ. A handkerchief of his wife's seen in Cassio's hand, was motive enough to the deluded Othello to pass sentence of death upon them both, without once enquiring how Cassio came by it. Desdemona had never given such a present to Cassio, nor would this constant lady have wronged her lord with doing so naughty a thing as giving his presents to another man; both Cassio and Desdemona were innocent of any offence against Othello; but the wicked Iago, whose spirits never slept in contrivance of villainy, had made his wife (a good, but weak woman) steal this handkerchief from Desdemona, under pretense of getting the work copied, but in reality to drop it in Cassio's way, where he might find it, and give a handle to Iago's suggestion that it was Desdemona's present.

Othello, soon after meeting his wife, pretended that he had a head-ach (as he might indeed with truth), and desired her to lend him her handkerchief to hold his temples. She did so. "Not this," said Othello, "but that handkerchief I gave you." Desdemona had it not about her (for indeed it was stolen as we have related). "How!" said Othello, "this is a fault indeed. That handkerchief an Egyptian woman gave to my mother; the woman was a witch, and could read people's thoughts; she told my mother, while she kept it, it would make her amiable, and my father would love her; but, if she lost it, or gave it away, my father's fancy would turn, and he would lothe her as much as he had loved her. She dying gave it me, and bade me, if I ever married, to give it to my wife. I did so; take heed of it. Make it a darling as precious as your eye." "Is it possible?" said the frighted lady. " 'Tis true"; continued Othello; "it is a magical handkerchief; a sibyl that had lived in the world two hundred years, in a fit of prophetic fury worked it; the silkworms that furnished the silk were hallowed, and it was dyed in mummy of maidens' hearts conserved." Desdemona, hearing the wondrous virtues of the handkerchief, was ready to die with fear, for she plainly perceived she had lost it, and with it, she feared, the affections of her husband. Then Othello started, and looked as if he were going to do some rash thing, and still he demanded the handkerchief, which when she could not produce, she tried to divert her husband from too serious thoughts, and cheerfully told him, she saw all his talk about the handkerchief was only to put her off from her suit about Michael Cassio, whom she went on to praise (as Iago had foretold), till Othello in perfect distraction burst out of the room, and then Desdemona, though unwillingly, began to suspect her lord was jealous.

What cause she could have ministered to him she knew not, and then she accused herself for accusing the noble Othello, and thought to be sure that some untoward news from Venice, or some state troubles, had puddled his spirits, and made his temper not so sweet as formerly. And she said, "Men are not gods, and we must not look for that observance from them when they are married, which they shew us on the bridal day." And she beshrewed herself for so unkindly judging of his unkindness.

Again Othello and Desdemona met, and he accused her more plainly of being unfaithful, and of loving another man, but he did not name whom: and Othello wept, and Desdemona said, "Alas! the heavy day! why do you weep?" And Othello told her, he could have borne all sorts of evils with fortitude—poverty, and disease, and disgrace; but her infidelity had broken his heart: and he called her a weed, that looked so fair, and smelled so sweet, that the sense ached at it; and wished she had never been born. And when he had left her, this innocent lady was so stupefied with wonder at her lord's untrue suspicion of her, that a weight like sleep came over her, and she only desired her attendant to make her bed, and to lay her wedding-sheets upon it, saying that when people teach their babes, they do it by gentle means and easy tasks, and Othello might have chid her so; for in good faith she was but a child when she was chidden. And this was all the complaint which this gentle lady made.

Desdemona being retired to bed, expecting her lord would follow her, soon feel into a slumber, the effect of her troubled spirits, when Othello entered the chamber, full of the black purpose which he had meditated of putting his lady to death. But when he saw her asleep, he thought he would not shed her blood, nor scar that white skin of hers, more white than alabaster. But he was resolved she should die; else (as he said) she would live to betray more men, as she had done him. Then he kissed her for the last time (as he said), and that kiss was so sweet, he must needs kiss her again: and he wept, but he said they were cruel tears.

Desdemona was awakened with his kisses, and she looked upon Othello, and she saw him gnaw his under-lip, and roll his eyes, and she knew he was always fatal when he looked so: and he bade her prepare for death, and to say her prayers, for he would not kill her soul. And this innocent wife, as she lay at his mercy, begged for compassion, and to know her fault, and then he named Cassio, and the handkerchief which (he said) she had given him; and as the guiltless lady was proceeding to clear herself, he suddenly would hear no more, but covering her up in the bedclothes, stifled her till she died.

In this instant of time was brought into the house Cassio, wounded and bleeding, whom Iago had set one of his creatures on to assassinate; but the fellow not succeeding in his attempt to kill Cassio (whom he wounded, but not mortally), and being himself killed by Iago to prevent discovery, in his pockets were found certain letters, which made the guilt of Iago, and the innocence of Cassio, clear beyond all doubt;

and Cassio now came to beg pardon of Othello, and to ask wherein he had offended him, that he had employed Iago to murder him.

This discovery was as a thunderstroke to Othello, who now plainly saw that he was no better than a murderer, and that his wife (poor innocent lady) had been ever faithful to him; the extreme anguish of which discovery making life insupportable, he fell upon his sword, and throwing himself upon the body of his dear injured lady, expired.

These rash acts raised much passion of horror and amazement in the by-standers, for Othello had borne a fair reputation, and till he was wrought upon by the arts of a villain, which his own noble nature never gave him leave to suspect, he was a loving and a doating husband. He had loved, not wisely, but too well; and his manly eyes (when he learned his mistake), though not used to weep on every small occasion, dropt tears as fast as the Arabian trees their gum. And when he was dead all his former merits and his valiant acts were remembered. Nothing now remained for his successor, but to put the utmost censure of the law in force against Iago, who was executed with strict tortures; and to send word to the state of Venice of the lamentable death of their renowned general.

Pericles, Prince of Tyre

PERICLES, prince of Tyre, became a voluntary exile from his dominions, to avert the dreadful calamities which Antiochus, the wicked emperor of Greece, threatened to bring upon his subjects and city of Tyre, in revenge for a discovery which the prince had made of a shocking deed which the emperor had done in secret; as commonly it proves dangerous to pry into the hidden crimes of great ones. Leaving the government of his people in the hands of his able and honest minister, Hellicanus, Pericles set sail from Tyre, thinking to absent himself till the wrath of Antiochus, who was mighty, should be appeased.

The first place which the prince directed his course to was Tharsus; and hearing that the city of Tharsus was at that time suffering under a severe famine, he took with him store of provisions for its relief. On his arrival he found the city reduced to the utmost distress; and he coming like a messenger from heaven with this unhoped-for succour, Cleon, the governor of Tharsus, welcomed him with boundless thanks. Pericles had not been here many days, before letters came from his faithful minister, warning him that it was not safe for him to stay at Tharsus, for Antiochus knew of his abode, and by secret emissaries dispatched for that purpose, sought his life. Upon receipt of these letters Pericles put out to sea again, amidst the blessings and prayers of a whole people who had been fed by his bounty.

He had not sailed far, when his ship was overtaken by a dreadful storm, and every man on board perished except Pericles, who was cast by the sea-waves naked on an unknown shore, where he had not wandered long before he met with some poor fishermen, who invited him to their homes, giving him clothes and provisions. The fishermen told Perciles the name of their country was Pentapolis, and that their king was Symonides, commonly called the good Symonides, because of his peaceable reign and good government. From them he also learned that king Symonides had a fair young daughter, and that the following day was her birth-day, when a grand tournament was to be held at court, many princes and knights being come from all parts to try their skill in arms for the love of Thaisa, this fair princess. While the prince was listening to this account, and secretly lamenting the loss of his good armour, which disabled him from making one among these valiant knights, another fisherman brought in a complete suit of armour that he had taken out of the sea with his fishing-net, which proved to be the very armour he had lost. When Pericles beheld his own armour, he said, "Thanks, Fortune; after all my crosses you give me somewhat to repair myself. This armour was bequeathed to me by my dead father, for whose sake I have so loved it, that whithersoever I went I still have kept it by me, and the rough sea that parted it from me, having now become calm, hath given it back again, for which I thank it, for, since I have my father's gift again, I think my shipwreck no misfortune."

The next day Pericles, clad in his brave father's armour, repaired to the royal court of Symonides, where he performed wonders at the tournament, vanquishing with ease all the brave knights and valiant princes who contended with him in arms for the honour of Thaisa's love. When brave warriors contended at court-tournaments for the love of kings' daughters, if one proved sole victor over all the rest, it was usual for the great lady for whose sake these deeds of valour were undertaken, to bestow all her respect upon the conqueror, and Thaisa did not depart from this custom, for she presently dismissed all the princes and knights whom Pericles had vanquished, and distinguished him by her especial favour and regard, crowning him with the wreath of victory, as king of that day's happiness; and Pericles became a most passionate lover of this beauteous princess from the first moment he beheld her.

The good Symonides so well approved of the valour and

noble qualities of Pericles, who was indeed a most accomplished gentleman, and well learned in all excellent arts, that though he knew not the rank of this royal stranger (for Pericles for fear of Antiochus gave out that he was a private gentleman of Tyre), yet did not Symonides disdain to accept of this valiant unknown for a son-in-law, when he perceived his daughter's affections were firmly fixed upon him.

Pericles had not been many months married to Thaisa, before he received intelligence that his enemy Antiochus was dead; and that his subjects of Tyre, impatient of his long absence, threatened to revolt, and talked of placing Hellicanus upon his vacant throne. This news came from Hellicanus himself, who being a loyal subject to his royal master, would not accept of the high dignity offered him, but sent to let Pericles know their intentions, that he might return home and resume his lawful right. It was matter of great surprise and joy to Symonides to find that his son-in-law (the obscure knight) was the renowned prince of Tyre; yet again he regretted that he was not the private gentleman he supposed him to be, seeing that he must now part with his admired son-in-law, and his beloved daughter, whom he feared to trust to the perils of the sea, because Thaisa was with child; and Pericles himself wished her to remain with her father till after her confinement, but the poor lady so earnestly desired to go with her husband that at last they consented, hoping she would reach Tyre before she was brought to-bed.

The sea was no friendly element to unhappy Pericles, for long before they reached Tyre another dreadful tempest arose, which so terrified Thaisa that she was taken ill, and in a short space of time her nurse Lychorida came to Pericles with a little child in her arms, to tell the sad tidings that his wife died the moment her little babe was born. She held the babe toward its father, saying, "Here is a thing too young for such a place. This is the child of your dead queen." No tongue can tell the dreadful sufferings of Pericles when he heard his wife was dead. As soon as he could speak, he said, "O you gods, why do you make us love your goodly gifts, and then snatch those gifts away?" "Patience, good sir," said Lychorida, "here is all that is left alive of our dead queen, a little daughter, and for your child's sake be more manly. Patience, good sir, even for the sake of this precious charge." Pericles took the new-born infant in his arms, and he said to the little babe, "Now may your life be mild, for a more blusterous birth had never babe! May your condition be mild and gentle, for you have had the rudest welcome that ever prince's child did meet with! May that which follows be happy, for you have had as chiding a nativity as fire, air, water, earth, and heaven could make, to herald you from the womb! Even at the first, your loss," meaning in the death of her mother, "is more than all the joys which you shall find upon this earth, to which you are come a new visitor, shall be able to recompense."

The storm still continuing to rage furiously, and the sailors having a superstition that while a dead body remained in the ship the storm would never cease, they came to Pericles to demand that his queen should be thrown overboard; and they said, "What courage, sir? God save you!" "Courage enough," said the sorrowing prince; "I do not fear the storm; it has done to me its worst: yet for the love of this poor infant, this fresh new sea-farer, I wish the storm was over." "Sir," said the sailors, "your queen must overboard. The sea works high, the wind is loud, and the storm will not abate till the ship be cleared of the dead." Though Pericles knew how weak and unfounded this superstition was, yet he patiently submitted, saying, "As you think meet. Then she must overboard, most wretched queen!" And now this unhappy prince went to take a last view of his dear wife, and as he looked upon his Thaisa, he said, "A terrible childbed hast thou had, my dear; no light, no fire, the unfriendly elements forgot thee utterly, nor have I time to bring thee hallowed to thy grave, but must cast thee scarcely coffined into the sea, where for a monument upon thy bones the humming waters must overwhelm thy corpse, lying with simple shells. O Lychorida, bid Nestor bring me spices, ink, and paper, my casket and my jewels, and bid Nicandor bring me the satin coffin. Lay the babe upon the pillow, and go about this suddenly, Lychorida, while I say a priestly farewel to my Thaisa."

They brought Pericles a large chest, in which (wrapt in a satin shroud) he placed his queen, and sweet-smelling spices he strewed over her, and beside her he placed rich jewels, and a written paper, telling who she was, and praying if haply any one should find the chest which contained the body of his wife, they would give her burial: and then with his own hands he cast the chest into the sea. When the storm was over, Pericles ordered the sailors to make for Tharsus. "For," said Pericles, "the babe cannot hold out till we come to Tyre. At Tharsus I will leave it at careful nursing."

After that tempestuous night when Thaisa was thrown into the sea, and while it was yet early morning, as Cerimon, a worthy gentleman of Ephesus, and a most skilful physician, was standing by the sea-side, his servants brought to him a chest, which they said the sea-waves had thrown on the land. "I never saw," said one of them, "so huge a billow as cast it on our shore." Cerimon ordered the chest to be conveyed to his own house, and when it was opened he beheld with wonder the body of a young and lovely lady; and the sweet-smelling spices, and rich casket of jewels, made him conclude it was some great person who was thus strangely entombed: searching further, he discovered a paper, from which he learned that the corpse which lay as dead before him had been a queen, and wife to Pericles, Prince of Tyre; and much admiring at the strangeness of that accident, and more pitying the husband who had lost this sweet lady, he said, "If you are living, Pericles, you have a heart that even cracks with woe." Then observing attentively Thaisa's face, he saw how fresh and unlike death her looks were; and he said, "They were too hasty that threw you into the sea": for he did not believe her to be dead. He ordered a fire to be made, and proper cordials to be brought, and soft music to be played, which might help to calm her amazed spirits if she should revive; and he said to those who crowded round her, wondering at what they saw, "I pray you, gentlemen, give her air; this queen will live;

she has not been entranced above five hours; and see, she begins to blow into life again; she is alive; behold, her eyelids move; this fair creature will live to make us weep to hear her fate." Thaisa had never died, but after the birth of her little baby had fallen into a deep swoon, which made all that saw her conclude her to be dead; and now by the care of this kind gentleman she once more revived to light and life; and opening her eyes she said, "Where am I? Where is my lord? What world is this?" By gentle degrees Cerimon let her understand what had befallen her; and when he thought she was enough recovered to bear the sight, he shewed her the paper written by her husband, and the jewels; and she looked on the paper, and said, "It is my lord's writing. That I was shipped at sea, I well remember, but whether there delivered of my babe, by the holy gods I cannot rightly say; but since my wedded lord I never shall see again, I will put on a vesta livery, and never more have joy." "Madam," said Cerimon, "if you purpose as you speak, the temple of Diana is not far distant from hence, there you may abide as a vestal. Moreover, if you please, a niece of mine shall there attend you." This proposal was accepted with thanks by Thaisa; and when she was perfectly recovered, Cerimon placed her in the temple of Diana, where she became a vestal or priestess of that goddess, and passed her days in sorrowing for her husband's supposed loss, and in the most devout exercises of those times.

Pericles carried his young daughter (whom he named Marina, because she was born at sea) to Tharsus, intending

to leave her with Cleon, the governor of that city, and his
wife Dionysia, thinking, for the good he had done to them at
the time of their famine, they would be kind to his little
motherless daughter. When Cleon saw prince Pericles, and
heard of the great loss which had befallen him, he said, "O
your sweet queen, that it had pleased Heaven you could have
brought her hither to have blessed my eyes with the sight of
her!" Pericles replied, "We must obey the powers above us.
Should I rage and roar as the sea does in which my Thaisa
lies, yet the end must be as it is. My gentle babe, Marina
here, I must charge your charity with her. I leave her the
infant of your care, beseeching you to give her princely train-
ing." And then turning to Cleon's wife, Dionysia, he said,
"Good madam, make me blessed in your care in bringing up
my child"; and she answered, "I have a child myself who shall
not be more dear to my respect than yours, my lord"; and
Cleon made the like promise, saying, "Your noble services,
prince Pericles, in feeding my whole people with your corn
(for which in their prayers they daily remember you) must in
your child be thought on. If I should neglect your child, my
whole people that were by you relieved would force me to my
duty; but if to that I need a spur, the gods revenge it on me
and mine to the end of generation." Pericles being thus
assured that his child would be carefully attended to, left her
to the protection of Cleon and his wife Dionysia, and with
her he left the nurse Lychorida. When he went away, the
little Marina knew not her loss, but Lychorida wept sadly at
parting with her royal master." "O, no tears, Lychorida,"

said Pericles; "no tears; look to your little mistress, on whose grace you may depend hereafter."

Pericles arrived in safety at Tyre, and was once more settled in the quiet possession of his throne, while his woeful queen, whom he thought dead, remained at Ephesus. Her little babe Marina, whom this hapless mother had never seen, was brought up by Cleon in a manner suitable to her high birth. He gave her the most careful education, so that by the time Marina attained the age of fourteen years, the most deeply-learned men were not more studied in the learning of those times than was Marina. She sung like one immortal, and danced as goddess-like, and with her needle she was so skilful that she seemed to compose nature's own shapes, in birds, fruits, or flowers, the natural roses being scarcely more like to each other than they were to Marina's silken flowers. But when she had gained from education all these graces, which made her the general wonder, Dionysia, the wife of Cleon, became her mortal enemy from jealousy, by reason that her own daughter, from the slowness of her mind, was not able to attain to the perfection wherein Marina excelled: and finding that all praise was bestowed on Marina, whilst her own daughter, who was of the same age and had been educated with the same care as Marina, though not with the same success, was in comparison disregarded, she formed a project to remove Marina out of the way, vainly imagining that her untoward daughter would be more respected when Marina was no more seen. To encompass this she employed a man to murder Marina, and she well timed her wicked design, when Lychorida, the faithful nurse, had just died. Dionysia was discoursing with the man she had commanded to commit this murder, when the young Marina was weeping over the dead Lychorida. Leoline, the man she employed to do this bad deed, though he was a very wicked man, could hardly be persuaded to undertake it, so had Marina won all hearts to love her. He said, "She is a goodly creature!" "The fitter then the gods should have her," replied her merciless enemy: "here she comes, weeping for the death of her nurse Lychorida: are you resolved to obey me?" Leoline, fearing to disobey her, replied, "I am resolved." And so, in that one short sentence, was the matchless Marina doomed to an untimely death. She now approached, with a basket of flowers in her hand, which, she said, she would daily strew over the grave of good Lychorida. The purple violet and the marigold should as a carpet hang upon her grave, while summer days did last. "Alas, for me!" she said, "poor unhappy maid, born in a tempest, when my mother died. This world to me is like a lasting storm, hurrying me from my friends." "How now, Marina," said the dissembling Dionysia, "do you weep alone? How does it chance my daughter is not with you? Do not sorrow for Lychorida, you have a nurse in me. Your beauty is quite changed with this unprofitable woe. Come, give me your flowers, the sea-air will spoil them; and walk with Leoline: the air is fine, and will enliven you. Come, Leoline, take her by the arm, and walk with her." "No, madam," said Marina, "I pray you let me not deprive you of your servant"; for Leoline was one of Dionysia's attendants.

"Come, come," said this artful woman, who wished for a pretense to leave her alone with Leoline, "I love the prince, your father, and I love you. We every day expect your father here; and when he comes, and finds you so changed by grief from the paragon of beauty we reported you, he will think we have taken no care of you. Go, I pray you, walk, and be chearful once again. Be careful of that excellent complexion, which stole the hearts of old and young." Marina, being thus importuned, said, "Well, I will go, but yet I have no desire to it." As Dionysia walked away, she said to Leoline, "*Remember what I have said!*"—shocking words, for their meaning was that he should remember to kill Marina.

Marina looked toward the sea, her birthplace, and said, "Is the wind westerly that blows?" "Southwest," replied Leoline. "When I was born the wind was north," said she: and then the storm and tempest, and all her father's sorrows, and her mother's death, came full into her mind; and she said, "My father, as Lychorida told me, did never fear, but cried, *Courage, good seamen*, to the sailors, galling his princely hands with the ropes, and, clasping to the mast, he endured a sea that almost split the deck." "When was this?" said Leoline. "When I was born," replied Marina; "never were waves nor wind more violent." And then she described the storm, the action of the sailors, the boatswain's whistle, and the loud call of the master, "Which," said she, "trebled the confusion of the ship." Lychorida had so often recounted to Marina the story of her hapless birth, that these things seemed ever present to her imagination. But here Leoline interrupted her with desiring her to say her prayers. "What mean you?" said Marina, who began to fear, she knew not why. "If you require a little space for prayer, I grant it," said Leoline; "but be not tedious; the gods are quick of ear, and I am sworn to do my work in haste." "Will you kill me?" said Marina; "alas! why?" "To satisfy my lady," replied Leoline. "Why would she have me killed?" said Marina; "now, as I can remember, I never hurt her in all my life. I never spake bad word, nor did any ill turn to any living creature. Believe me now, I never killed a mouse, nor hurt a fly. I trod upon a worm once against my will, but I wept for it. How have I offended?" The murderer replied, "My commission is not to reason on the deed, but to do it." And he was just going to kill her, when certain pirates happened to land at that very moment, who seeing Marina, bore her off as a prize to their ship.

The pirate who had made Marina his prize carried her to Metaline, and sold her for a slave, where, though in that humble condition, Marina soon became known throughout the whole city of Metaline for her beauty and her virtues; and the person to whom she was sold became rich by the money she earned for him. She taught music, dancing, and fine needlework, and the money she got by her scholars she gave to her master and mistress; and the fame of her learning and her great industry came to the knowledge of Lysimachus, a young nobleman who was the governor of Metaline, and Lysimachus went himself to the house where Marina dwelt, to see this paragon of excellence, whom all the city praised so highly.

Her conversation delighted Lysimachus beyond measure, for though he had heard much of this admired maiden, he did not expect to find her so sensible a lady, so virtuous, and so good, as he perceived Marina to be; and he left her, saying he hoped she would persevere in her industrious and virtuous course, and that if ever she heard from him again it should be for her good. Lysimachus thought Marina such a miracle for sense, fine breeding, and excellent qualities, as well as for beauty and all outward graces, that he wished to marry her, and notwithstanding her humble situation, he hoped to find that her birth was noble; but ever when they asked her parentage, she would sit still and weep.

Meantime, at Tharsus, Leoline, fearing the anger of Dionysia, told her he had killed Marina; and that wicked woman gave out that she was dead, and made a pretended funeral for her, and erected a stately monument; and shortly after Pericles, accompanied by his loyal minister Hellicanus, made a voyage from Tyre to Tharsus, on purpose to see his daughter, intending to take her home with him; and, he never having beheld her since he left her an infant in the care of Cleon and his wife, how did this good prince rejoice at the thoughts of seeing this dear child of his buried queen! but when they told him Marina was dead, and shewed the monument they had erected for her, great was the misery this most wretched father endured, and not being able to bear the sight of that country where his last hope and only memory of his dear Thaisa was entombed, he took ship and hastily departed from Tharsus. From the day he entered the ship a dull and heavy melancholy seized him. He never spoke, and seemed totally insensible to everything around him.

Sailing from Tharsus to Tyre, the ship in its course passed by Metaline, where Marina dwelt; the governor of which place, Lysimachus, observing this royal vessel from the shore, and desirous of knowing who was on board, went in a barge to the side of the ship, to satisfy his curiosity. Hellicanus received him very courteously, and told him that the ship came from Tyre, and that they were conducting thither Pericles their prince: "A man, sir," said Hellicanus, "who has not spoken to any one these three months, nor taken any sustenance, but just to prolong his grief; it would be tedious to repeat the whole ground of his distemper, but the main springs from the loss of a beloved daughter and a wife." Lysimachus begged to see this afflicted prince, and when he beheld Pericles he saw he had been once a goodly person, and he said to him, "Sir king, all hail, the gods preserve you, hail, royal sir!" But in vain Lysimachus spoke to him. Pericles made no answer, nor did he appear to perceive any stranger approached. And then Lysimachus bethought him of the peerless maid Marina, that haply with her sweet tongue she might win some answer from the silent prince: and with the consent of Hellicanus he sent for Marina, and when she entered the ship in which her own father sat motionless with grief, they welcomed her on board as if they had known she was their princess; and they cried, "She is a gallant lady." Lysimachus was well pleased to hear their commendations, and he said, "She is such an one, that were I well assured she came of noble birth, I would wish no better choice, and think me rarely blest in a wife." And then he addressed her in courtly terms, as if the lowly-seeming maid had been the high-born lady he wished to find her, calling her *Fair and beautiful Marina*, telling her a great prince on board that ship had fallen into a sad and mournful silence; and, as if Marina had the power of conferring health and felicity, he begged she would undertake to cure the royal stranger of his melancholy. "Sir," said Marina, "I will use my utmost skill in his recovery, provided none but I and my maid be suffered to come near him."

She, who at Metaline had so carefully concealed her birth, ashamed to tell that one of royal ancestry was now a slave, first began to speak to Pericles of the wayward changes in her own fate, telling him from what a high estate herself had fallen. As if she had known it was her royal father she stood before, all the words she spoke were of her own sorrows; but her reason for so doing was, that she knew nothing more wins the attention of the unfortunate than the recital of some sad calamity to match their own. The sound of her sweet voice aroused the drooping prince; he lifted up his eyes, which had been so long fixed and motionless; and Marina, who was the perfect image of her mother, presented to his amazed sight the features of his beloved queen. The long-silent prince was once more heard to speak. "My dearest wife," said the awakened Pericles, "was like this maid, and such a one might my daughter have been. My queen's square brows, her stature to an inch, as wand-like straight, as silver-voiced, her eyes as jewel-

like. Where do you live, young maid? Report your parentage. I think you said you had been tossed from wrong to
injury, and that you thought your griefs would equal mine,
if both were opened." "Some such thing I said," replied
Marina, "and said no more than what my thoughts did warrant
me as likely." "Tell me your story, "answered Pericles; "if
I find you have known the thousandth part of my endurance,
you have borne your sorrows like a man, and I have suffered
like a girl; yet you do look like Patience gazing on kings'
graves, and smiling Extremity out of act. How lost you your
name, my most kind virgin? Recount your story, I beseech
you. Come, sit by me." How was Pericles surprised when
she said her name was *Marina*, for he knew it was no usual
name, but had been invented by himself for his own child to
signify *sea-born:* "O, I am mocked," said he, "and you are
sent hither by some incensed god to make the world laugh
at me." "Patience, good sir," said Marina, "or I must cease
here." "Nay," said Pericles, "I will be patient; you little
know how you do startle me to call yourself Marina." "The
name," she replied, "was given me by one that had some
power, my father, and a king." "How, a king's daughter!"
said Pericles, "and called Marina! But are you flesh and
blood? Are you no fairy? Speak on! where were you born?
and wherefore called Marina?" She replied, "I was called
Marina, because I was born at sea. My mother was the
daughter of a king; she died the minute I was born, as my good
nurse Lychorida has often told me weeping. The king my
father left me at Tharsus, till the cruel wife of Cleon sought

to murder me. A crew of pirates came and rescued me, and brought me here to Metaline. But, good sir, why do you weep? It may be, you think me an impostor. But indeed, sir, I am the daughter to king Pericles, if good king Pericles be living." Then Pericles, terrified as it seemed at his own sudden joy, and doubtful if this could be real, loudly called for his attendants, who rejoiced at the sound of their beloved king's voice; and he said to Hellicanus, "O Hellicanus, strike me, give me a gash, put me to present pain, lest this great sea of joys rushing upon me, overbear the shores of my mortality. O, come hither, thou that was born at sea, buried at Tharsus, and found at sea again. O Hellicans, down on your knees, thank the holy gods. This is Marina. Now blessings on thee, my child! Give me fresh garments, mine own Hellicanus! She is not dead at Tharsus, as she should have been by the savage Dionysia. She shall tell you all, when you shall kneel to her, and call her your very princess. Who is this?" (observing Lysimachus for the first time). "Sir," said Hellicanus, "it is the governor of Metaline, who, hearing of your melancholy, came to see you." "I embrace you, sir," said Pericles. "Give me my robes! I am well with beholding—O Heaven bless my girl! But hark! what music is that?" for now, either sent by some kind god, or by his own delighted fancy deceived, he seemed to hear soft music. "My lord, I hear none," replied Hellicanus. "None," said Pericles; "why it is the music of the spheres." As there was no music to be heard, Lysimachus concluded that the sudden joy had unsettled the prince's understanding; and he said, "It is not good to cross him; let him have his way"; and then they told him they heard the music; and he now complaining of a drowsy slumber coming over him, Lysimachus persuaded him to rest on a couch, and placing a pillow under his head, he, quite overpowered with excess of joy, sunk into a sound sleep, and Marina watched in silence by the couch of her sleeping parent.

While he slept, Pericles dreamed a dream which made him resolve to go to Ephesus. His dream was, that Diana, the goddess of the Ephesians, appeared to him, and commanded him to go to her temple at Ephesus, and there before her altar to declare the story of his life and misfortunes; and by her silver bow she swore that if he performed her injunction, he should meet with some rare felicity. When he awoke, being miraculously refreshed, he told his dream, and that his resolution was to obey the bidding of the goddess.

Then Lysimachus invited Pericles to come on shore, and refresh himself with such entertainment as he should find at Metaline, which courteous offer Pericles accepting, agreed to tarry with him for the space of a day or two. During which time we may well suppose what feastings, what rejoicings, what costly shews and entertainments the governor made in Metaline, to greet the royal father of his dead Marina, whom in her obscure fortunes he had so respected. Nor did Pericles frown upon Lysimachus's suit, when he understood how he had honoured his child in the days of her low estate, and that Marina shewed herself not averse to his proposals; only he made it a condition, before he gave his consent, that they should visit with him the shrine of the Ephesian Diana: to whose temple they shortly after all three undertook a voyage; and, the goddess herself filling their sails with prosperous winds, after a few weeks they arrived in safety at Ephesus.

There was standing near the altar of the goddess, when Pericles with his train entered the temple, the good Cerimon (now grown very aged) who had restored Thaisa, the wife of Pericles, to life; and Thaisa, now a priestess of the temple, was standing before the altar; and though the many years he had passed in sorrow for her loss had much altered Pericles, Thaisa thought she knew her husband's features, and when he approached the altar and began to speak, she remembered his voice, and listened to his words with wonder and a joyful amazement. And these were the words that Pericles spoke before the altar: "Hail, Diana! to perform thy just commands, I here confess myself the prince of Tyre, who, frightened from my country, at Pentapolis wedded the fair Thaisa: she died at sea in childbed, but brought forth a maid-child called Marina. She at Tharsus was nursed with Dionysia, who at fourteen years thought to kill her, but her better stars brought her to Metaline, by whose shores as I sailed, her good fortunes brought this maid on board, where by her most clear remembrance she made herself known to be my daughter."

Thaisa, unable to bear the transports which his words had raised in her, cried out, "You are, you are, O royal Pericles" —and fainted. "What means this woman?" said Pericles: "she dies; help, gentlemen!" "Sir," said Cerimon, "if you have told Diana's altar true, this is your wife." "Reverend gentleman, no"; said Pericles: "I threw her overboard with these very arms." Cerimon then recounted how, early one tempestuous morning, this lady was thrown upon the Ephesian shore: how, opening the coffin, he found therein rich jewels, and a paper; how, happily, he recovered her, and placed her here in Diana's temple. And now, Thaisa being restored from her swoon, said, "O my lord, are you not Pericles? Like him you speak, like him you are. Did you not name a tempest, a birth and a death?" He, astonished, said, "The voice of dead Thaisa!" "That Thaisa am I," she replied, "supposed dead and drowned." "O true Diana!" exclaimed Pericles, in a passion of devout astonishment. "And now," said Thaisa, "I know you better. Such a ring as I see on your finger did the king my father give you, when we with tears parted from him at Pentapolis." "Enough, you gods!" cried Pericles, "your present kindness makes my past miseries sport. O come, Thaisa, be buried a second time within these arms."

And Marina said, "My heart leaps to be gone into my mother's bosom." Then did Pericles shew his daughter to her mother, saying, "Look who kneels here, flesh of thy flesh, thy burthen at sea, and called Marina, because she was yielded there." "Blest and my own!" said Thaisa: and while she hung in rapturous joy over her child, Pericles knelt before the altar, saying, "Pure Diana, bless thee for thy vision. For this, I will offer oblations nightly to thee." And then and there did Pericles, with the consent of Thaisa, solemnly affiance their daughter, the virtuous Marina, to the well-deserving Lysimachus in marriage.

Thus have we seen in Pericles, his queen, and daughter, a famous example of virtue assailed by calamity (through the sufferance of Heaven, to teach patience and constancy to men), under the same guidance becoming finally successful, and triumphing over chance and change. In Hellicanus we have beheld a notable pattern of truth, of faith and loyalty, who, when he might have succeeded to a throne, chose rather to recall the rightful owner to his possession, than to become great by another's wrong. In the worthy Cerimon, who restored Thaisa to life, we are instructed how goodness directed by knowledge, in bestowing benefits upon mankind, approaches to the nature of the gods. It only remains to be told that Dionysia, the wicked wife of Cleon, met with an end proportionable to her deserts; the inhabitants of Tharsus, when her cruel attempt upon Marina was known, rising in a body to revenge the daughter of their benefactor, and, setting fire to the palace of Cleon, burned both him and her, and their whole household: the gods seeming well pleased, that so foul a murder, though but intentional, and never carried into act, should be punished in a way befitting its enormity.

THESE·PICTVRES
AND·DECORATIONS·HAVE·BEEN·DESIGNED·WITH
MVCH·JOY·IN·THE·MAKING·IN·THE·HOPE·THAT
THERE·MAY·BE·SOME·WHO·WILL·FOLLOW·WITH
A·LIKE·PLEASVRE·AND·AMVSEMENT·SVCH·PLAY
OF·FANCY·AS·THEREIN·THE·ILLVMINATOR·MAY·HAVE
DISPLAYED—OR·HALF·CONCEALED—IN·AN·ENDEAVOVR
TO·LINK·TOGETHER·THE·GOLDEN·AGE·OF·ELIZABETH
TVDOR·THE·TIME·OF·CHARLES·LAMB·AND·THIS·PRESENT
YEAR·OF·OVR·LORD·MCMXXII·WHEN·ELIZABETH·ELLIOTT
HVMBLY·PRESENTS·HER·CONTRIBVTIONS·TO·THESE
TALES

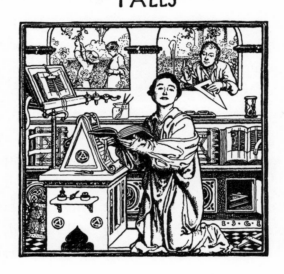

Date Due

Oct. 8, 2014			